PILLARS OF THE ESTABLISHMENT

There was initially no reply. So I rang again—
three times in fact. Then a gruff and slightly
irritable voice called out to me from behind the
net-curtained window, 'Oh come on in, damn you!
It can't be someone that I know, or you'd have
come in without waiting to be asked.' I found the
door to be unlocked, so I entered in the manner
now invited.

The lady who was seated in the armchair with
her back to me was either wearing a green wig or
had hair that was dyed that colour. It was in a
frizzy Afro style. The colour contrasted forcibly,
without in any way clashing, with the scarlet-on-
white floral dressing gown she was wearing. There
was the remains of a bottle of Gordon's gin on the
small table beside her, an empty glass in her hand
and no sign of any indian tonic or cordial. She
appeared to have forgotten already that someone
had been invited to enter, until I reminded her of
my presence with an apologetic, 'Good morning,
Lady Froome.'

Alexander Thynn is Viscount Weymouth of Longleat,
heir to the Marquess of Bath.
His other novels are *The Carry-Cot* (1972) and
The King is Dead (1976).

Pillars
of the
Establishment

Alexander Thynn

Hamlyn Paperbacks

PILLARS OF THE ESTABLISHMENT
ISBN 0 600 20483 9

First published in Great Britain 1980
by Hutchinson & Co. Ltd
Hamlyn Paperbacks edition 1982
Copyright © 1980 by Alexander Thynn

Although Nanny Marks was a real person, the anecdotes
and characters described in this novel are fictional.

The lyrics and music reproduced on pages 5 and 6
are from 'I play the host', produced by Pye Golden
Guinea records, courtesy of Des O'Connor,
words and music © Alexander Thynn 1974.

Hamlyn Paperbacks are published by
The Hamlyn Publishing Group Ltd,
Astronaut House,
Feltham, Middlesex, England

Reproduced, printed and bound in Great Britain by
Hazell Watson & Viney Ltd, Aylesbury, Bucks

Contents

Nanny Marks (1969)

*With this song I dedicate my novel
to the memory of Grace Marks (1886—1971)*

When the world was but a cradle, Nanny Marks,
when our jelly faces called within the dark,
  it was you that made us happy –
  shook the rattle, pinned the nappy.
It was you we really cared for, Nanny Marks.

When as minuscule employers, Nanny Marks,
you paraded us, well-mannered, in the park.
  There is much to be forgiven,
  (and yet – so is there to heaven,)
so we'll laugh, and bless you lightly, Nanny Marks.

When our minds had started ticking, Nanny Marks,
when our intellects ignited from a spark
　　which had come from out of nowhere,
　　urging 'Turn about, and go there!' –
you were puzzled and bewildered, Nanny Marks.

When our schools were left behind us, Nanny Marks,
when as fishes, we were striving to be sharks,
　　you were sad, and you were lonely –
　　we had talk for others only.
Did we hurt you, and bereave you, Nanny Marks?

When as targets of the gossips, Nanny Marks,
you would never entertain their false remarks.
　　You were lasting, you were loyal,
　　and beside us in that turmoil.
These are debts we should have honoured, Nanny Marks.

Now the days are growing shorter, Nanny Marks,
now you're waiting to be taken on that Ark,
　　now your eyes are dimmed with blindness,
　　do we show you any kindness?
Are we negligent and cruel, Nanny Marks?

How ungenerous is living, Nanny Marks,
while your ageing has been pitiless and stark.
　　It may seem that we ignore you,
　　but of this I can assure you –
that we never shall forget you, Nanny Marks:
no, we never shall forget you, Nanny Marks.

Tillot Family Tree

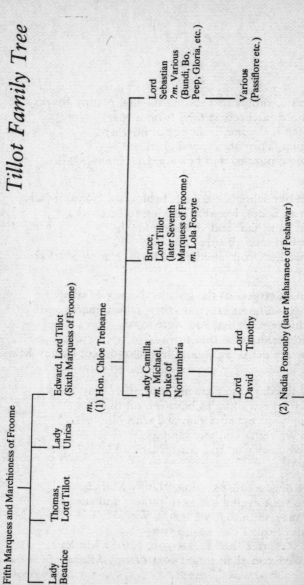

Introduction:
Sources and Forces

Author's narrative

No doubt you read in your papers recently how the contents of Luptree Court were put up for auction by Sotheby's, fetching more than £6 million. There was indignation, you will recall, in that so many revered works of art and pieces of exquisite antique furniture were thus removed from Britain; and even greater indignation in that most of the proceeds were promptly donated by the seventh Marquess of Froome to the Vatican, and to various branches of the Catholic church within this country. As to what remains of Luptree Court, it is now a hotel, fully modernized, and with a staff that is fast forgetting the former connection of the house with the Tillot family.

My name is Mr Neil Fairfield, junior partner in the firm of Carson and Fairfield. My concern in these events arose after I had been acquainted with the contents of a curious letter from a Mr Ron Tillot, addressed quite simply to: 'The House of Lords, London, England'. His own address was somewhere in Hobart, Tasmania.

Letter from Mr Ron Tillot to the House of Lords (1978)

Your Lordships,

Yesterday I was approached by some people who write for the papers and I see today that it is splashed across their front pages. They say that some day soon I'm going to join up with all you lot, sitting in the House of Lords and ruling the Old Country. Well, I've never been over to see the Old Country, so I don't know whether this is a good thing or a bad thing.

I suppose you'll be surprised that I'm writing to you like this. And you'll see from all these press clippings that I'm only a dustman down here in Hobart. But I've made a success of it. I now have my own fleet of garbage disposal trucks. And I'm sending along to you, with this letter, a bank draft for £1000, so that you can hire someone to do the job properly for me. They can tell me all about the Tillot family. I want to be in a position where I can make up my own mind whether I should sell up my business down under and join up with you in the House of Lords, whenever that seat becomes vacant. And these people from the newspapers were telling me that I wouldn't have to wait for very long.

I hope I've said enough to put you all in the picture. So I'll now say goodbye to your Lordships, for the time being in any case, although I hope to be hearing from you in due course.

I am, yours faithfully,
        (Mr) Ron Tillot

Author's narrative

As I have certain friendly acquaintances within the House of Lords, Mr Tillot's letter was forwarded to me, with an inquiry whether I might be interested in taking his brief. In response I wrote to Mr Tillot, offering my services, yet warning him that the research he demanded would exceed the sum presented in his bank draft. He replied affably that, if I could produce the information he wanted, he'd 'splash out all the dollars' I might require. Hence my acceptance of his brief.

I embarked upon this inquiry with the misgiving that I might eventually find myself as the legal representative of someone who was in litigation with the Vatican. It struck me that the Catholic church might prove to be a formidable, if not unscrupulous adversary, if it ever came to litigation concerning the rightful ownership of the Tillot family's heritage.

My special interest in attending the auction at Luptree Court was to acquire all documents relating to the recent generation of the Tillot family. In the event, this was made easy for me in that all such items had been thrown into a single lot: a collection of private letters, and such material, which had been collected and stored over the years in the muniments room, up on the top landing of Luptree Court. Most of the tale I have to tell will be drawn from this material.

For example, Edward Tillot, the sixth Marquess of Froome, comes vividly to life in the transcript of a long interview he gave to Mr Simon Manasseh, the American journalist. This was an interview given in 1970, when Lord Froome's prosecution was pending concerning the sale of narcotics.

The transcript was accompanied by a letter from Mr Manasseh requesting Lord Froome to notify him concerning any changes or omissions that he would prefer to see in the text. When this interview finally appeared in print, considerable changes and omissions had indeed been made, and some of the sixth Marquess's more extreme remarks had been muted. But I shall be sticking to the original transcript in my own text.

This was, of course, the very last interview that was ever given by the sixth Marquess. He died in Parkhurst prison hospital, after serving only six months of his two-year sentence; the cause of death being pneumonia, after participation in a demonstration protesting against prison conditions. The demonstration gave rise to new regulations about the use of hoses by warders in quelling prison riots.

Throughout his life, the sixth Marquess had been a magpie collector of all and sundry. Nothing that was sent to him he threw away. Most of the correspondence he kept has little relevance to the task I have now set myself. But I have made considerable use of the letters he received from the Hon. Chloe Trehearne, who became his first wife. There are two batches of her letters which I have incorporated into my text. The first covers her courtship and marriage to Lord Froome. The second consists of the letters that she wrote to her daughter, Camilla, the Duchess of Northumbria, during the period subsequent to the break-up of her marriage.

I conceived a great liking for the Hon. Chloe Trehearne, which persuaded me to use this lady of misfortune as the starting point in my quest to piece together an understanding of the Tillot family. For I had in mind that I should try and avail myself of the other end of the correspondence which was already in my possession.

For this reason, I traced her to a small ground-floor flat in Amsterdam. There was initially no reply. So I rang again — three times in fact. Then a gruff and slightly irritable voice called out to me from behind the net-curtained window, 'Oh come on in, damn you! It can't be someone that I know, or you'd have come in without waiting to be asked.' I found the door to be unlocked, so I entered in the manner now invited.

The lady who was seated in the armchair with her back to me was either wearing a green wig or had hair that was dyed that colour. It was in a frizzy Afro style. The colour contrasted forcibly, without in any way clashing, with the scarlet-on-white floral dressing gown she was wearing. There was the remains of a bottle of Gordon's gin on the small table beside her, an empty glass in her hand and no sign of any indian tonic or cordial. She appeared to have forgotten already that someone had been invited to enter, until I reminded her of my presence with an apologetic, 'Good morning, Lady Froome.'

There was a slight wince of irritation as her face moved half sideways, to cast a fractional glance in my direction — making me aware just how much of an intrusion my presence really was. Then, seeming to remember that some display of manners might be expected of her in this situation, she mumbled, 'Why do you have to be so bloody formal? Sit yourself down for God's sake.' And this I did.

I then held an interview of sorts with her — it consisted mainly of a monologue of my own, while Lady Froome lay back in the armchair with her expression vacant. Once she came to life briefly, to reach for the bottle of gin and fill her glass half full again.

I informed her in detail about this report on the Tillot family that I had been briefed to compile, and said that it appeared she had been the great letter writer in the family. Yet she didn't seem to understand any of this. From the manner in which a small flutter of a smile just occasionally lighted her expression, which was weary rather than sad, it struck me that she must be thinking of other matters. Much of her former reputation as a beauty still remained within those tired features. But she had given up trying to preserve it. Then she surprised me by saying that I could have them, before I'd actually asked for them in quite so many words. So I inquired cautiously what she meant.

'The letters. You can have them,' she said. 'That's what you want, isn't it? You can take them away and read them. You can burn them or do what you like with them. They were a waste of all my time and energy. Look what I got from it. Nothing! Not even some of the broken pieces! I don't belong to the Tillot family any more.'

I rose to my feet in the hope that they were now to be delivered into my hands. It seemed for a while that she had forgotten about my request, or even about my presence for that matter. I had to coax her with some gentle reminders. She then looked up with a start, and said, rather too fiercely for my liking, 'Over there, in the loo! Go into the loo and sit on it. And you'll find there's a box right beside you, with whatever remains of the letters I received from the Tillot family. Read as much as you want and then use them. That's what I do. I supply you with no other paper in this flat. It's all those letters are good for now, in any case. Do unto others as they did unto you!'

Having retrieved the box, I remarked with a certain disappointment that it only contained a mere handful of letters. She replied, 'What the hell do you expect? I haven't been saving up to go to the loo until the moment you arrived. Consider yourself lucky that there are any left at all.' And, after pausing for reflection, I realized that I was indeed lucky. For it would have taken less than a month to have disposed of the small testimony which now remained within my hands. If but a few letters out of this small pile have been of any use to me in my text, it is still better than having arrived too late to find any letters at all.

With apologies for my intrusion, and thanks for her cooperation, I took my leave of Chloe, the Marchioness of Froome.

With regard to the three children of the sixth Marquess's first marriage, my hopes had been centred upon my interview with the eldest, Camilla, the Duchess of Northumbria. For in some ways she represented a new perspective on the Tillot family, in her friendship with royalty and her general association with a more typically county set within the general spectrum of British society. But my hopes were to be largely frustrated.

She granted me an interview readily enough. So I journeyed up to Northwold Abbey by train, and went to see her at the appointed hour of twelve. I was ushered into the grandiose drawing room by a traditional butler, impeccably dressed, to discover the Duchess striking an ungainly, nervous posture in front of the fireplace. Her arm was extended in a rigidly obtuse angle, offering me her hand for a shake. She was a lady of forty-nine, as the records show, and it immediately struck me that she had both character and class: an inner knowledge that she could get away with extravagancies because the society she knew revolved around her, rather than she around the rest of society.

When I turned to probe into the real subject of my interest – the way the royal family behaved and how they viewed the peculiarities of the Duchess's relations – I rapidly discovered that I had overstepped the mark. She said, 'You must be joking! Do you think I'm going to reveal that kind of information?'

I tried to explain to her that I was only endeavouring to fulfil my brief: a task which required me to depict the Tillot family's social scene as broadly as it could be painted. And, if that field even remotely included the royal family, it would be regarded as most unprofessional of me to omit any account of their behaviour from my text. The Duchess emitted a short burst of laughter (of the sort which poked fun at the incongruity of finding herself involved in such a discussion). Then she said, 'Try your luck somewhere else, Mr Fairfax.' I reminded her that my name was in fact Mr Fairfield, but this was effectively the point at which my interview was terminated.

The eldest son of the sixth Marquess is Bruce Tillot, the seventh Marquess of Froome. But there was no possibility of my ever obtaining a meeting with him, let alone an interview, for he had not been seen by any of his family and former friends since he had taken holy orders and entered a monastery. In fact there are rumours that he has even renounced his title, so it could be a mistake to regard him as the seventh Marquess; though, on consultation with the directors of both Debrett's and Burke's Peerage, I find that they *do* regard him as such, since no official notification of a renunciation has ever emanated from behind those monastery walls.

Amongst the papers up in the muniments room at Luptree Court, however, was a personal manuscript in the seventh Marquess's handwriting. This handwriting matures over a long period of years and the entries are all scrupulously dated.

In it, the Marquess ponderously clarifies his own ideas on the drift of the life he finds himself to be living. On the first page, in characteristic style, even if the writing is clearly that of a juvenile, were the words 'WHY I THINK WHAT I THINK' (in capital letters thus, and underlined). Excerpts from it will be included in my text.

Another member of the family who was unavailable for interview was the sixth Marquess's second son, Lord Sebastian Tillot. He is resident abroad nowadays and made no attempt to answer any of my appeals for information, which I sent to the only address I could find for him.

One of the reasons I had for writing was to inform him that I was now in possession of a box of tape cassettes, which were clearly intended for his ownership. They had been made by the old lady who had served as a nanny to the Tillot children, ever since she first took up that appointment in 1931.

The tape cassettes were of the greatest interest to me, in that they furnished a skeletal framework of events, which incorporated all the family quarrels referred to in the testimonies of others. I might indeed have found it surprising that an old lady should have gone to all this trouble to set down on tape her thoughts concerning the trivial episodes which animated her existence. But the explanation was supplied in the batch of letters that I managed to retrieve from Lady Froome's water closet in Amsterdam.

Letter from Lord Sebastian Tillot, to Chloe, Marchioness of Froome (1954)

Mum darling,

I've just been round to see old Nan, and I'm recovering from it over a double vodka. You know how she goes on and on with endless reminiscences from all our lives, constructed especially to make us appear more significant than we ever really were – as if she regards us as the very pillars upon which the grand edifice of the Establishment rests. It is ridiculously flattering, as we all know. At the same time it wouldn't be right to discourage her, because this is just about all that is left for her to do nowadays. Well, I think I've finally hit upon the perfect solution. I went out and bought a small tape recorder for her, which I've just been round to deliver. I've even given her the first lesson in what use to make of it. But she's not being very quick to catch on as yet.

My idea is that she must have the material in all those reminiscences for anyone to ghost-write her autobiography. I might like to do it myself, if she'll let me. Once she has mastered all those buttons, she ought just to start reminiscing in the way she always does. It's best if she doesn't think in terms of it being one of us who might be listening. Far better if it's some imaginary reporter, who had written to ask her for an interview.

Anyway, I'll keep you informed on whether she is making satisfactory headway with the task. Let us hope it will keep her happy, if nothing else.

    Much love,
        Sebastian

Author's narrative

Nanny Marks had persevered with this task and had in fact completed it by the time her eyesight failed in 1970. She was then transferred to the old people's home in Froome where she finally died in 1971. She is buried nearby, in the cemetery at Corsley.

On listening to the tapes I soon came to perceive that there was a great underlying interest in all that Nanny Marks had to say – largely because she was the one neutral observer, who stood at the side of the Tillot family while all the feuding took place. And the Tillot family, eccentric though they may have been, furnish us with a microcosm of much that was going on in Britain over this period. Something that could be described as the fall and rise of the British Establishment. That is to say, part of it was in total collapse and disarray; yet strains of it were emerging triumphant to fight another day, with as little sense of any imposed compromise as ever they had displayed beforehand.

This then was the narrative which I saw as my skeletal framework for the task I was now setting myself: the present-ation for a Hobart dustman, of the Tillot family's recent history.

There were other testimonies more extensive than I have yet revealed. For, now that my report was beginning to take shape, I interviewed additional members of the Tillot family and their entourage. All of these characters will be introduced in my own narrative in due course and they will tell their own tale. The reader may form the opinion that I have been tempt-ed to do more than what was required of me in my lawyer's brief. Yet it will be revealed that I had other plans in mind for my material.

The list of my sources also represents the forces that the Tillot family were able to throw into the field against me, if you should wish to regard me as their adversary; though I myself would prefer to be presented as their objective social historian.

1

A Humble Start

1886–1920

Author's Narrative

The backgrounds of the sixth Lord Froome and Nanny Marks were in total contrast. There was also an age difference between them of nineteen years. It was a question of being born before or after the death of Queen Victoria. But they were both members of large families and grew up within a mile of each other.

I shall permit Nanny Marks, the elder of the two, to speak first about her childhood. I must urge you to listen to her testimony as if you were a visitor to her Beatrix Potter cottage (as she liked to call it). You perceive before you, in an armchair on the other side of the fireplace, a frail old lady with greying hair. She is talking to you constantly with barely a space furnished for interruption. Yet she interrupts herself frequently with little outbursts of laughter, as if somewhere the pathos of life's charade has been registered in her mind.

The Nanny Marks tapes

I had a very humble start in life. You see, my father was one of the charcoal burners on the Luptree estate. He worked for the old Lord Froome – I mean the fifth Marquess. And for *his* father, too, for that matter, although that was before my day. I never got to know my father very well. He was only at home with us of a Sunday, and that isn't long enough to get a proper memory of someone, even if he is your father.

I remember coming home one day leading an old tramp by the hand and telling everyone that I was bringing my Dad home for his tea. His face was all grubby, you see. It may have been this that made me think he was my father. But you should have heard my mother! She was furious with me. She felt I'd been putting her to shame, leading an old tramp through the village, and telling everyone that I was bringing my Dad home to tea!

We were quite a large family. The eldest was Bess. Then came me. Then my brother Jack. And the two youngest were Meg and Lottie. But Bess was a bit simple in some ways. So I was often regarded as the eldest.

I think I had the push to go out and do whatever had to be done. I remember the first time my mother took us down to the seaside. I could see the people swimming and it looked to me as if they were all wading out until the water came up to their necks. So I thought I was supposed to do the same. It was all very well until a wave came along; and then I found that I couldn't touch the bottom any more. And I felt I was drowning. I don't know how I got back to the shore. No one was watching me. But I must have been rescued, I suppose. I'm alive today, and that's all that really matters.

It was about this time that my father died. I must have been ten years old, I suppose. It was a terrible blow to the family. There weren't all those social welfare schemes in those days. When the father died, there was no one to bring home the pay packet. And that meant the workhouse. We all lived in fear of the workhouse. And a horrible place it was – in Froome, just below the cloth factory; although nowadays they call it an old people's home. I never went inside, but we'd all heard tales enough to know that we didn't want to go there. It would have been such a disgrace to have been brought up in the workhouse.

My mother was a hardworking woman, and we all did what was needed of us to make things run smoothly for her. Any little job was better than none, even if it was only a question of running errands. But I was the one who helped her with the main household duties. My mother couldn't cope with the task single-handed. So I learnt all about taking care of children, you see; what with Lottie being a mere baby at the time.

These were hard days – not only for us, but for everyone. Those nasty Boers had come out in revolt and were trying to break up the Empire. We knew that the war wouldn't be a long one, and it wasn't. But it was very tiresome while it lasted.

Mind you, things began to get better after a little while. It was Lady Froome who came to our rescue. She was a really good lady. So was Lord Froome himself, of course, but Lady Froome was something very particular. She had a presence about her, a dignity. What she wanted done must be done at once. Yet everyone knew it would be all for the best. She had suffered her share of afflictions. There was something wrong with her back and she spent most of her time in a wheelchair. She could walk, but only for short distances with the assistance of a couple of sticks. She was religious too. Christian Science is what they call it today. She wouldn't have anything to do with doctors – not for herself I mean, although I dare say she called one whenever her children were ill.

We had the greatest respect for Lord and Lady Froome down in the village – for the entire family, in fact. They were people who dedicated themselves to public service. But they did it in a quiet sort of way, without expecting to get anything out of it. Not like some of these millionaires of whom we hear tell who are only for doing good when there are people to notice them. But that wasn't like the old Lord Froome, or Lady Froome either. They were always civil to people, no matter what class of person they might be. They were gentle, not in the least conceited or arrogant. They knew just where help was needed, and did all they could to give it.

That was why Lord Froome was asked by King Edward VII to be Lord Lieutenant of both Somerset and Wiltshire, while he was still a comparatively young man. Everything in these counties revolved around him. Everyone loved him for being such a kind, unassuming gentleman. And we in the village held him in a very special esteem, because he was so close to us in every kind of way. Provided us with our livelihood, whether it was in the form of work up at the big house or on the estate, where my father had been employed. And all the cottages belonged to Lord Froome, as did the woodlands and farmlands for miles around.

My own family would have ended up in the workhouse, that's for sure, if it hadn't been for Lady Froome. She used to come round visiting the sick; and, when my mother's health was failing, she always included our family on the list. It might only be a basket of food, but I can assure you that it was still very welcome. We needed whatever help we could get. And I think Lady Froome took a rather special interest in myself, noticing how I had to nurse all the little ones whenever my mother was feeling poorly. I remember her saying that I'd make somebody a good wife. But I never did, you see.

Lady Froome had a large family, just like my own mother. But in this case there were two daughters and two sons. Lady Beatrice and Lord Tillot were the two eldest, being somewhere around my own age. Then came Lady Ulrica. And the youngest of all was Lord Edward, as he was then called.

Oh, he was a fine little boy, was Lord Edward. I can remember seeing him dressed up in a sailor's suit, as was the fashion then. He couldn't have been older than four. But there was a groom leading him round the grounds, as he sat up on a pony looking every inch the little Lord. You can't look like that unless you're born that way. I knew right away that he'd grow up into as fine an aristocrat as the Tillot family ever produced, although we had no idea at the time that he would eventually inherit the title.

The Sixth Marquess of Froome, the first extract from an interview by Mr Simon Manasseh

Q: Do you regard yours as having been a happy childhood?
A: Most certainly I do. But it was a completely different world then. Everything was so orderly. Or it seemed to us children that it was.
Q: Did you feel affection for your parents?

A: Oh yes. Or I did for my mother. We children were her life — perhaps because she was confined to a wheelchair for part of the time. But she was a remarkable woman. She saw visions of what was going to happen in the future. A bit of a medium in some ways too. In a house like Luptree Court that really meant something. She could tell you all about the family ghosts, almost as if they were personal friends. It's not that I go in for any of that kind of stuff myself. But she had some power in her which other women don't have. We all felt that. She was a truly remarkable woman.

Q What were your feelings towards your father?

A: Well, it has to be different with a man, I suppose. My two elder sisters worshipped him. But he never really managed to endear himself to either of his sons. I had an elder brother, Thomas, who was killed in the First World War, as you probably know. But I'm not sure if it's important that fathers should be liked by their sons. To be respected is what is necessary. And I certainly respected him. But he could be a bit gruff at times. He expected me to keep my distance. With my sisters, Beatrice and Ulrica, it was different of course. Daughters were just decorative in those days. You had to get them suitably married. Then you didn't have to worry about them any more.

The Nanny Marks Tapes

I was only just in my twenties when my mother died, and her death brought us even closer to the big house. The Tillot family never let people down. This is what I'd always been told, and I found it to be true. Lady Froome personally came to me and suggested that my sister Bess take up a position as laundry maid at Luptree. As my brother Jack had already started work in the forestry, there were now two pay packets to help make ends meet. In fact, Lady Froome was generous to us in a thousand little ways. But I haven't the time to go into all that at the present moment.

When Bess went up there to work, we became more involved in all that was going on at Luptree Court. Not that I'd ever been prepared to work as a laundry maid, personally. I wasn't cut out for that kind of thing. My hands are too soft. You can look at them now. When my mother used to examine them, she said they were the hands of real gentlefolk. And she was right, you know. Yet Bess wasn't quite the same as I was. Not in many ways, I suppose.

It wasn't any old person from the village who was allowed to set foot in Luptree. Mr Beyfus, the house steward, was most particular about these things. But I was always invited to the dances in the servants' hall. Not that I used to attend very often, mind you. I was kept far too busy for anything like that. Yet there was one a week, and I managed to get down there once in a while.

Oh, you'll never believe it, but these dances actually led to me getting engaged. It was to the third footman, the one whose duties were mainly assigned to the nursery. His name was Rodney, I remember. He was tremendously popular with all of Bessie's friends: the nursery maids and the kitchen maids, for example. I'm not sure why I admired him — whether it was for himself or for the prospects he made available to me. You see I'd never really spoken to Lady Froome's children at that time. Yet Rodney was often entrusted to take them for a ride in the pony cart. And, if they were passing through the village, he would sometimes suggest that they call in for a pot of tea and a slice of gingerbread — that had been my mother's great speciality, and I continued to make it for the family after she'd gone.

I found them such interesting people, the Tillot family. Even when they were young, they were interesting. I was greatly impressed by their good manners and their graciousness. I suppose this blinded me to the faults in the man who brought them close to me. I mean Rodney. It was their fine qualities which concealed his coarseness from my eyes.

Mind you, it was a proper engagement. He gave me a fine gold ring to wear. Look! I've still got it here on my finger. You may think me awfully silly to go on wearing it after all this time. But I never liked the idea of people thinking of me as an old maid.

Not that there was anything dirty in our relationship. Whatever happened could take place in front of everyone. There were none of those under-the-stairs, behind-the-doors goings-on. And, when I finally broke off the engagement, I had Mrs Pilcher, the housekeeper, as my witness.

In fact, it was Mrs Pilcher who had the sad duty of opening my eyes to what Rodney was really like. I'm not saying that it was all his fault. There was a stillroom maid who had been told off by Mrs Pilcher for behaving in a forward manner towards one of the grooms. The maid then turned her attentions to Rodney. And he wasn't a very *strong* person you see – strong in character, I mean. Well, it came to Mrs Pilcher's knowledge that the stillroom maid had got herself into trouble, as they call it. And the maid confessed that it was either Rodney, or the groom.

There were strict rules at Luptree Court. That was the way Lady Froome wanted the house to be run. And it wasn't as if Rodney didn't know what to expect if he broke them. But the first I knew about all this was when Mrs Pilcher sent one of the housemaids to ask me to accompany her back to Luptree Court. And then Mrs Pilcher explained to me that Rodney was a bad man and that I should break off the engagement. Then Rodney was sent for, and I did this in the presence of Mrs Pilcher.

Later the same day, Mr Beyfus was informed of the situation. Rodney, the groom and the stillroom maid were all dismissed from the household immediately. Lady Froome didn't like things of that kind happening at Luptree.

Author's narrative

Neither Nanny Marks in her tapes, nor the sixth Marquess of Froome in Mr Manasseh's interview, dwell at any great length upon their early lives. But it is clear that all those who lived at Luptree Court had a sumptuous style of living, a style which was never quite to be matched subsequently. This was the

Edwardian era. Both Mr Beyfus and Mrs Pilcher were waited on below stairs, in proud imitation of the standards that were set above. Yet Miss Marks stresses at one point that a nanny was never considered to be one of the household staff. 'She is more like a member of the family. She would get waited on all right, but in her own quarters, up in the nursery with the children.'

The First World War did not destroy this style of living, but it rattled the foundations upon which anticipations for permanence had been based. It could thereafter be questioned whether the British Empire would last for ever. It could be questioned indeed whether capitalism had the best solutions to offer the human race. But, to someone like Miss Marks, the essential impact of those war years was one of bereavement.

The Nanny Marks tapes

There's hardly a family around these parts that doesn't have its name on the village war memorial. And of course there's Lord Tillot at the very head of the list. Poor Lady Froome was laid up for more than a month afterwards. She used to have dreams. And, the night he was killed, she had a dream about him lying there in the trenches. She retired to bed immediately. And, when the news about Lord Tillot came through, the whole village felt as if they'd lost one of their own family.

We were not without losses ourselves. My own brother Jack was another that was killed. Or rather he went missing and was presumed dead. I often thought about him lying out there cold and unburied, until someone picked him up and placed him in an unmarked grave. With Lord Tillot it was different – which is fortunate in some ways. Our Jack wasn't as important as Lord Tillot, you see.

It was lucky that Lord Edward was still at school when the war ended. That kept him out of harm's way. And, of course, he now took over his brother's title and became Lord Tillot. I really don't know what would have happened if both of them had been obliged to go to war. Death was such a common event, as if God was no respecter of persons.

Meg and Lottie were fully grown by now. Meg had been walking out with a sergeant from New Zealand, who had been convalescing from a war wound in the hospital at Froome. He wanted Meg to marry him, and go back to New Zealand with him. I've always had the greatest respect for people from New Zealand. They're a better class of people than Australians. It's not as if they were descended from convicts or anything. They're just about as English as foreigners can be. And the Maoris aren't exactly black men.

Mrs Pilcher advised Meg to seize this opportunity to emigrate, to get a new start in life. I think she felt we'd had more than our share of troubles in life so far. And it was generally good advice she gave. So Meg set sail for New Zealand and she's never been back here since.

The Sixth Marquess of Froome, interviewed by Mr Simon Manesseh

Q: What effect did the First World War have on your style of living?

A: It transformed it completely. Well, it did in my case. I became the heir to Luptree after my brother Thomas was killed: so I was suddenly regarded as being a Very Important Person. It really means something at that age, you know. You begin to think you might be the cat's whiskers. No one had ever encouraged me to think that way before.

Q: Was this of any assistance to you in your relationship with your father?

A: Not really. It just meant that he expected rather more of me than he was ever likely to get. But that was his problem, rather than mine.

Q: In what way didn't you live up to his expectations? Could you give some examples?

A: Oh, I don't know. Well, I didn't read all those books in our famous library, for example. And I didn't take any interest in local politics. Not when I was a boy, or even as a teenager. I used to spend half my time up in the woods with Fred Thatcher who was one of the gamekeepers. He had his cottage up there in High Wood. I felt far more at home out ferreting with Fred than I ever did making polite conversation when our local Conservative MP came to lunch. It was my father who first arranged for me to go rabbiting with Fred. But there came a time when he regretted it. It was the way of life that I liked, up there in Fred's cottage; and Mrs Thatcher was such a homely woman. There was none of the formality I had to face at Luptree Court. I'm a real countryman at heart. You could say that about me.

Q: Did school make a favourable impression on you?

A: Not in the least. I always wanted to be back home in the woods, which I loved. School was an interference. I went there because I had to. But I wasn't any good at it, once I got there.

Q: Meaning?

A: Well, I wasn't too bright, if that's what you're getting at. I failed to get into Eton, despite a letter to the headmaster from my father, in which he tried to put over the point that you don't fail sons of Marquesses, especially those who will eventually become Marquesses themselves. But I was accepted into Harrow all right, without even having to sit for the exam. All that democratic stuff hadn't caught up with them in those days.

Q: But did you enjoy yourself while you were there?

A: Good heavens, no! I was always made to feel that it carried some kind of a stigma, because I hadn't managed to pass into Eton. All the sons of my father's friends had gone to Eton. And there I was as some kind of an outcast. An Harrovian! They covered up as best they could, however. They told everybody that I had been sent to Harrow because it was on a hill, and I had a weak chest. They said it would be better for me than all those fogs on the Thames.

2

Going Up in the World

1920–31

Author's narrative

It was Mrs Pilcher who helped Nanny Marks find her first
post as nanny. This was with the household of Colonel and
Mrs Bagshot, at Pitchford Abbas, near Salisbury. The colonel
was an occasional guest at Luptree shooting parties. Miss
Marks found herself in charge of a baby called Sarah. 'Such a
sweet little girl. I've never seen the likes of her fluffy golden
hair.' And she remained at Pitchford until a governess
intruded upon the scene – an appointment which she viewed
with the gravest suspicion.

The Nanny Marks tapes

If the truth were known, this governess was a most unsuitable
woman to take charge of any child. She had a wooden leg,
although she pretended it was only arthritis. I knew she was
lying. One day I trod on her toe, and she didn't even realize
that I had touched her.

She came to us when Sarah was eight, and we both took
care of her for a while. But this governess wasn't nimble
enough on her toes to contend with a little handful like Sarah.
There was one occasion they went up to London to see the
Victoria and Albert Museum. They were on a tram together.
Of course, when it stopped, Sarah jumped off in the twinkle
of an eye. But the tram moved off again while the governess

was still limbering up to get her wooden leg into a position where she could climb down. You don't leave children in the care of people like that, do you?

But Mrs Bagshot saw things differently. She seemed to think there was a whole sequence that every child must go through. First with a nanny, then with a governess, and finally with school. She explained to me in the kindest possible way that Sarah was growing up and wouldn't be needing me any more. She had waited to do this until she'd found some post for me to go to. But it's impossible to hear that you're not wanted any more without feeling wounded somewhere deep down inside.

I suppose it made me feel for a while that being a nanny is a thankless task. You give yourself to the full for a number of years. Then some nasty old governess arrives and you're told to move on. But you don't stop loving the child you raised from the cradle. You may have been a real mother to that child, but you've still got no say in the matter when the parents tell you that it's time to go.

Then comes all the heartache. The child doesn't remember you for as long as you might wish. I would send little Sarah a present at Christmas and on her birthday. And she would send me a letter or a card in reply. But, after a bit, she forgot about these things. I suppose it didn't seem important to her. She probably never realized that I would have liked to be remembered. It isn't nice to feel forgotten, not when you've loved somebody as much as I'd loved Sarah.

The Sixth Marquess of Froome, interviewed by Mr Simon Manasseh

Q: Did you make any lasting friends from school?
A: Not from Harrow. That all came later, at Oxford. There I met up with the stream with which I had been expected to mingle from the very start. People like Buffy Yeovil. The Earl of Yeovil, that is. They welcomed me into the fold as if I was some prodigal that had gone astray. And

yes indeed, those are friends who have lasted me a lifetime.

Q: Were you doing any better in your studies at this period in your life?

A: No. As I told you before, I'm not very bright. I didn't even sit for my final exams. The whole Tillot family has never been very bright, if it comes to that. Or not since the very early days, when we were still going up in the world. But we've plodded on for centuries, doing what people expected us to do; and doing it none too badly, it might be fair to add. So people grew accustomed to us ruling the roost from Luptree Court. On the whole, they even liked it that way.

Q: Would you regard yours as a democratic family?

A: If you mean did we believe in the system which kept us up there at the top, I suppose the answer is yes. But, if you're asking me whether we regarded the people we employed as being our equals, I don't suppose I could give you quite the same answer. Things have changed a lot since those days.

Q: How was your own relationship with the people your father employed?

A: Good. But it was a very strict hierarchy. My parents were at the top of it, of course. And we children came next. In fact we were treated like little gods. We didn't have to lift a finger if we didn't want to. The steward, the butler and the housekeeper had life made pretty easy for them too. It's the poor little blighters way down there at the bottom that I now feel sorry for. The pantry boys and the scullery maids. They couldn't have had a moment to themselves. Fetch this, or stir that! And a good tug of the ear if they were slow about it. Life for them must have been unbearable at times.

Q: You've described how the gamekeeper was a special friend. Did you have any special enemies?

A: Not any *real* enemies. But I didn't see eye to eye with some of them. The chauffeur, for example. He used to carry tales to my father. Yet he would continue to greet me with the same sickly smile each morning. I couldn't stand the man.

Q: Is there any particular such tale that comes to mind?

A: Well, yes there is. I bought myself a motorbike just before I left Harrow. I knew that I'd never be allowed to ride one if I asked my parents for their permission. So I kept it a secret, hidden out of everyone's sight down at the buildings yard. Nobody need have known anything about it at all. Yet Plumley went and told my father about it. So the motorbike had to go. If there was any way of doing it, that man would make trouble for me.

Q: Did your parents display an excessive regard for your safety?

A: Yes, they did. Perhaps it's because my elder brother had been killed in the war. From the age of ten, I was their sole chance of an heir to Luptree, because it was then too late for them to have any other sons. And they were always worrying about my weak chest. Thought I might die from tuberculosis, I suppose. Anyway, they kept me wrapped in cotton wool, as the saying goes. I was never allowed to do anything at all that they regarded as risky. All I wanted was to get out and be allowed to behave like other young men. But they wouldn't let me out of their sight.

Q: At what age did you finally emerge as your own master?

A: It wasn't really until after I left Oxford. I told my parents that I wanted to marry Chloe. And they didn't much like the sound of that. They regarded her as being too wild. So my mother came up with the idea that I ought to be allowed to see a bit of the world, to travel around America for a while. Then, if I still felt like marrying Chloe on my return, they would withdraw their objections. So I took off for what was originally intended to be a whole year to the States. That was the first occasion that I'd ever really been my own master.

Q: What did you do with yourself in that year?

A: I spent most of the time as a ranch hand in Texas. Not doing very much, mind you. I never even learnt how to use a lasso. But that was an age when everyone thought that being a cowboy was so glamorous. All those silent films from Hollywood, I suppose. I was thrilled to the whiskers just to think of myself as a cowboy.

Selected letters from the Hon. Chloe Trehearne's correspondence with Lord Tillot

Dear Lord Tillot,

It was a pleasure meeting you at the Ansleys' dance, although I thought the seating arrangements at dinner could have been improved. Poor Mr Barber on my left was only interested in golf as a subject of conversation, and I came perilously close to offering my services to him as a caddy; whereas Lord Harptree, on my right, gives me the impression that he expects every girl he sits next to to be his immediate conquest. And I generally prefer to think that I am being treated as something special. But I could see that Lucy Proudfoot had your own attention fully occupied. So I hardly think you felt cause to complain about the seating plan.

I enjoyed the dance, in any case. And I hope that you will keep your promise to invite me down to Oxford when some of your friends are next giving a party. I liked Lord Yeovil, incidentally. He laughs at everything, and he makes me want to laugh at it as well.

I'll see you again soon perhaps. In any case, you now have my address. So I hope that I shall be hearing from you.

I am, yours sincerely,
Chloe Trehearne

Edward darling,

I never realized that I was going to enjoy punting. I positively adore it, provided that I am always allowed to wind up the gramophone, rather than having to do any of that frightful work with a pole. Buffy did look funny, clinging to it as our punt drifted away. If the photograph comes out, do please send me a copy. But I was shaking the boat with laughter so much that I hardly think it will.

What we did, and what you said, are all very important to me. Please don't make a joke about it with Buffy and all your other friends. I'd positively hate to think you were doing that. I'd like to think that everything we do together is strictly personal, as if it were all taking place within a magic garden of our own creation.

Write and tell me that you love me. You realize, I hope, that it would be terrible if I had to take all these things for granted.

I send you all my love. (My liking for Richard Cavendish really doesn't count.)

Chloe

Darling Chloe,

I think you already know that I love you without the need to be asking such questions. In fact, for the first time in my life, I am discovering that all those slushy novelists may not have been talking quite so much bilge as I used to think when the masters at Harrow read out bits from books that are supposed to be famous. But you'll have to teach me more about kissing. I was brought up to think that mouths and spit were meant for eating and digesting one's food. I'm sure my father and mother never dreamt of using them in the way that you do. But it could be that I shall learn how to enjoy it, when practice has made perfect. The other things seemed to come rather more easily. I think it's possible that those parts of the body were made for that purpose.

Very much love,
Edward

PS   It would be safest to burn this letter. In fact, burn all my letters. I don't want them being used against me in any breach of promise case.

Edward Tillot,

I am not amused! I might even have said that *we* are not amused, if only I didn't have this terrible suspicion that *you* might be. But, in all seriousness Edward, you shouldn't write such things to me in a letter. I do not go suing my admirers for any breaches of promise. It is far more usual that they are promising me things which I *ought* to sue them about without even waiting for such promises to be broken. But the fact remains that I don't.

I'll make this point, too. I intend to keep each letter that you ever write to me – possibly embalmed, but certainly not incinerated. On the other hand, I shall probably never write to you again, in which case you will not have the opportunity to do as much to any more of my own letters.

I am yours, quite sincerely,
Chloe Trehearne

Edward my darling,

I think that it's positively wicked of Lord Froome to suggest that you go to America for a year, though I suspect that the idea may have originated with Lady Froome. Don't you think, my sweetie? You know that she didn't really approve of me after that weekend I spent at Luptree Court. I can't imagine why not. I insisted that Buffy chaperone us everywhere so that nobody could start getting unfavourable impressions of me. But I could see those cool, assessing eyes glinting up at me, so I felt most horribly wicked even though I had done nothing. Or nothing until I spilt the sugar bowl at breakfast on my last morning. And I suppose it would have been better if I had then apologized instead of laughing. But you do see that it was funny, in a way, because I had been trying so hard to be on my best behaviour.

You know, seriously, I am not in the least happy about this idea. All American girls are most terribly fast, even if they only look good because of all the powder and things that they wear. I feel sure that they will make you forget me. In fact, it would be silly if I were just to sit here pining for your company, knowing all the while that you are having such a good time over there on the other side of the Atlantic. Jimmy Harptree actually laughed when I told him my sad news yesterday evening. He said he knew that the Froomes would never accept me as their daughter-in-law – or not as the wife of their one and only son. He said that, if I really wanted to marry a Lord, I ought to pick on a family with a liberal tradition, instead of such dyed-in-the-wool Tories as the Tillots.

I became very angry with him indeed. The idea that I might be chasing after a Lord! I think he was really trying to flirt with me, don't you? But the thought of him even kissing me, with that horrible moustache, makes me shudder inside.

If only I knew for *certain* that you were going to wait for me during this year in America, my loneliness would be so much easier to bear. How can I be sure that you will still like me when you return? I was thinking last night, after Jimmy had dropped me back home in Eaton Square, that it would really be terribly funny if we could get married secretly *before* you set sail for America. It would be a sort of joke on them, if you see what I mean. Seeing how they always try to arrange everything in life for you. Well, this would be just one occasion when you had managed to arrange things for yourself, without their knowing anything about it at all. We could announce it to them later, whenever you felt the time was right. They would hardly be likely to make any fuss, if they realized we had been married for months, or even years. We could tell them about it on our silver wedding, if you like!

I don't suppose they've fixed everything up for your departure quite yet. Why not come up to London in the meantime? The staff at Grosvenor Square have so very little to do. And you could tell Lady Froome that you needed to buy suitable clothes, even if they won't be exactly the same as what they all wear in Texas. In any case, I must see you before you set sail. I feel there is so much that we could do, in order to *know* that nobody will be able to separate us ever again. But these things are better whispered into your ear, while you take me in your arms, than set down in a letter. Arrange to come up to London just as quickly as you can. I shall be waiting for you.

Your little pekinese sends you all her love,
Chloe

Darling Pekey,

I wish I could write such lively letters as you. They have been arriving so regularly that Mr and Mrs Ford obviously suspect that I am not quite such an eligible bachelor as they originally supposed. I know that their son is beginning to have his doubts on this subject. He is rarely at home because he is training for the army at West Point. But he was so friendly when we were first introduced — hoping for an invitation to Luptree Court, no doubt. But, after he had noticed all your letters arriving, he hardly bothered to speak to me any more. But they continue to push their fat, spotty daughter into my company in the hopes that, out of sheer boredom, I might propose to her. I won't, I can assure you of this. There won't even be a shotgun wedding, with me ending up as a bigamist.

In any case, I'm not bored. I seem to be riding a horse from dawn to dusk and I'm constantly being told which is the right or wrong end of a cow. I smile at every male visitor who comes to lunch, just in case he happens to be a Hollywood film director. But I hardly think Mrs Ford would allow me to meet any such person, in case he introduced me to those wild film stars, and then my attention might stray from her daughter.

I would like to be back in England with you, of course. Or, better still, I wish they would let you come out here and join me as my wife. But I realize that we've got to hang on to our little secret. I have stated in one of the letters I have written home to my mother that my intention is as firm as ever it was to marry you on my return, and asked whether they would consider reducing the period of exile to six months. But there has been no mention of this subject, as yet, in any of the letters I have received from her.

I love you, kiss you, and do everything to you,
    Edward

My darling (most darling) Edward,

I am head over heels in happiness. I take back any reproachful word that I might ever have uttered against your parents, now that they say you may return. They must surely accept our marriage, if they are saying that you can come home. Or haven't you actually told them about it yet? Oh, don't worry, my sweetie, if you haven't. Don't pout! I can't bear it when you pout. My Pouty-powkie. But I love the look on your face when your tight-lipped grin comes back again.

I'll tell you what. If you want that we keep it a secret, we'll do it that way. I see that it might be most terribly embarrassing for you to have to tell them about it now. Let's pretend that we've behaved exactly as they wished: that we obediently separated and that we now wait patiently for their permission to kiss in front of the altar. I'll be dressed in white, or course, although I won't object if you insist on wearing a scarlet buttonhole. But I'd prefer to do everything just as Lord and Lady Froome might wish. I want them to regard me as the perfect daughter-in-law.

> I am so faithful to you, it is unbearable,
> Chloe

The Nanny Marks tapes

. . . I was then put in charge of a little boy and girl called Benny and Jenny. Yet I never grew to love them like my Sarah. I hope you don't think I'm awful to say such a thing. But it could never be quite the same.

I think it was a mistake really that I agreed to take this post. I suppose it was just the way things worked out at that time. You seldom went to an agency in those days, or not if you could help it. If you were any good at being a nanny, you just got handed down between friends of the family.

But that was my mistake. I ought to have realized that Mr and Mrs Morgan weren't really to be regarded as *friends* of Colonel and Mrs Bagshot. A business associate isn't quite the same thing. Mr Morgan was very wealthy of course, and he lived in a nice house up in Manchester. But you can't make a silk purse out of a sow's ear, that's what I always say.

Mrs Morgan may have been all right. She was an American lady and never understood our ways. But it was Mr Morgan that made me feel ill at ease. You see he wasn't really what I'd call a gentleman. He was what people describe as a self-made man, having got all his money in the war from munitions. Mind you, he wasn't dishonest or anything. But he didn't have that little something that we'd call good breeding. He was over-friendly with the servants, for example.

It's not that I'm a snob, though I often wonder if it really matters if I am. In my view a snob is someone rather distinguished, someone who has distinguished views. If I'm a snob, then I'm proud of it. But Mr and Mrs Morgan wouldn't have understood these matters.

They soon began to talk about sending Benny to school. And I knew it wouldn't be very long before they would get in a governess for Jenny. In any case, that's what the parlour maid said to me one afternoon, when she brought up the nursery tea. She had such a malicious tongue, you see. I felt as if life was repeating itself. But this time I was determined that no one was going to push me around. If I had to leave, then I wanted it to be with dignity, in a manner of my own choosing.

The Sixth Marquess of Froome, interviewed by
Mr Simon Manasseh

Q: When you returned home, were there any further objections raised to the idea of your marrying Chloe Trehearne?

A: No. We went straight ahead with the marriage as planned. But it was a farce really, because we were married already. Chloe got me to take her to a registry office before I set sail for America. Yet, now that my parents had officially withdrawn their objections, we couldn't very well tell them that we'd jumped the gun. So we had to get married for the second time. And this time we were given the full works. It was the high society wedding they all expected of us.

Q: A year later, your wife gave birth to a daughter. In a

family like the Tillots, was this regarded as a disappointment?

A: Well, it was to my parents, I dare say. And Chloe was upset too. But I was delighted. You see, my mother had always been so damn certain it was going to be a boy. She once said to me, 'It's going to be a boy, because Chloe has a stronger personality than you, Edward. A baby's sex is the opposite to that of the parent who is dominant at the time of its being conceived.' I dare say she may have been right in saying that Chloe was the stronger personality at this particular time. But the point is that my mother was always so cocksure about her predictions – as if she had a private telephone line to God. So, when it turned out to be a daughter, I was *delighted!*

Q: How would you describe your occupation at that period in your life?

A: Occupation? Well, I'm not sure that it would be really true to say that I had one. If someone had shoved one of those forms in front of me which expected me to put something against such a question, I'd always been told that the right answer was 'Gentleman'. Or you could put 'Gentleman of leisure', if you wanted to go the whole hog. But it doesn't mean to say that I was sitting back doing nothing. I'd done my bit in breaking the General Strike, for example. And that was while I was still an Oxford undergraduate.

Q: What did you do?

A: I drove a bus. Buffy Yeovil and I both volunteered. And we did all right. I mean, we didn't kill any of the passengers. I drove and he sold the tickets. Nobody really minded if we got things wrong, so long as they got to their destinations all right. The important thing was to show all these Socialists where they had to get off. (Oh! Perhaps that was funnier than I meant it to be.) But it was true. It was a matter of calling their bluff. If we hadn't resisted them, we'd be a Communist country by now.

Q: What about your occupation during the early years of your marriage?

A: Still nothing that I could really call a job. Or I did have a *kind* of job. I was appointed to serve on the Council of the Duchy of Cornwall, as an adviser to the Prince of Wales. I liked the man. I always admired him right from the start. But it seems that he didn't like me. Anyway he asked for my resignation, which is the same thing as giving me the sack. But, in any case, this had never taken up much of my time. We had plenty to do just participating in the social whirl. Nobody even expected me to have a job in those days.

Selected letters from Lady Tillot's correspondence with Lord Tillot

My darling Powkie,

Just think of it! This is my first letter to you since we have been officially acknowledged by the world as husband and wife. But it doesn't stop me from protesting at the way you rush off to whatever places our royal family calls you to, just to attend the meeting of some silly Council that doesn't seem to do anything in any case. I feel lonely. Don't you realize that? I might be pregnant too, although it's only two days late as yet. I *want* your company, and I *need* your company.

Besides that, your parents do frighten me a bit when I'm living here alone with them, without you here to stick up for me when they think I am behaving badly. I promise you that I don't. It's merely that they seem to think I do. I'm not what they call decorous, though my misbehaviour only takes the form of giggling when I shouldn't and all that kind of thing.

I do see the point of their argument that we should continue living with them at Luptree for a few years; while I accustom myself to the Tillot way of life, as they call it. But I regard it as penal servitude when I am here alone with them. Still having to address them as Lord and Lady Froome shows just how little they truly regard me as an integrated member of your family. As you know, I am always far happier when we take off on a spree somewhere. Come back quickly, so that we can do just that.

> With all my love, from your oh so loving,
> Pekey

Edward darling,

(I am still going to call you my darling, even though you have done this terrible thing.) I continued crying for a full hour after you left the hospital, with our little baby Camilla howling there beside me in her cot. I took her in my arms and tried to explain to her just how awful you had been. But I only managed to infect her with my own sense of helplessness. So we sobbed in concert until we both fell asleep.

Can't you understand how heartbroken I am to know that you did this? I think I would have minded less if it had been with some girl that you met at a party. But with a tart that you and Buffy picked up in the street – that really hurts! Was it too long for you to wait until I am released from this bloody maternity hospital? I think I would have preferred it if you had said nothing about it to me at all. But I suppose you were feeling bad about it inside. So the confession came tumbling out of you, along with that huge armful of flowers.

Once I had reasoned it all out with myself, I felt it must be a punishment from God because I had been so angry that Camilla was a girl. But I know how you always pretend not to believe in God, just to spite your parents. So I won't say any more about that.

But I hope you do understand why I felt so miserable about its being a girl. I had been banking on it being the Tillot family's son and heir, for then surely your parents would have learnt to accept me. But there was Camilla, which meant nine months of looking ugly for nothing. I don't mean that I won't love her, but it was just the disappointment, you see. Yet I now feel that I have been well and truly punished for having such horrible thoughts.

In any case, I have done all my crying by now, so my eyes are dry once again. I want desperately to get that episode right behind us, so we can finally put it out of our minds. That is why I am sending this letter round to you by special messenger. I want you to come round here to the hospital as soon as you have read it. I want you to make love to me here in this hospital bed. We can lock the door, although I wouldn't really care if someone did walk in and see us. By doing this, we can wash away your memory of that dreadful tart. But it must be at once, today, before that horrid memory gets ingrained any further in your mind.

Come to me immediately, I am waiting for you. I am still, and always will be, the one and only person who loves you truly.

Chloe

Darling Edward,

We have a problem I think. You know how much I adore Nanny Smith, but even she is now talking about the need to retire. Do you think it's time that we made the matter official? You could give her a nice pension, perhaps even a cottage on the estate at Luptree, if Lord Froome will agree to that.

She complains of pains in the chest. I've been having a nightmare of a time, virtually doing all of Nanny's work myself, because she claims to be feeling 'so poorly'. And I find myself worrying about the future as well. If it's really true that I am pregnant again, I would never feel safe to allow her to carry the new baby in her arms. Suppose she had a heart attack and fell down the stairs! But I do understand how the situation is a difficult one to handle.

However my own situation is an equally difficult one. There is Camilla's safety to think about as well. But I daren't suggest to Lady Froome that she put someone else to the task of giving Camilla her meals, because I know very well that she regards this enforced maternalism as being good for me. She did criticize me the other day about the number of times that you and I take off for London. So there I sit, trying to convince them that I am motherly, while Camilla waves her spoon and fork in the air as if they were Union Jacks, spilling the food everywhere.

I had a serious talk with Lady Froome this morning about

finding a replacement for Nanny Smith. There must surely be someone in the village who will want to take the post. She has promised to have a word with Mrs Pilcher on the subject. I only hope they won't be long about it or I'll go stark raving mad — trying to behave as a motherly mother, which life never intended me to be.

Do you know, I actually look forward to the next election, after which (with any luck) you will be an MP. This will furnish us with the perfect pretext for setting up our own household in London, with only occasional visits down here to Luptree Court. I did what they expected of me. Yet, now that it's done, I want to start living again, with you especially, but also with all our friends.

All my love,
Chloe

The Nanny Marks tapes

I had always been in touch with all that had been going on at Luptree Court. My sister Bess was still working there for one thing. And I generally went back to the village for my holidays. So there wasn't much that took place that I didn't hear about sooner or later.

Well, I learnt on one of my visits home that Nanny Smith was retiring. And this came right when I was feeling that I could stand the Morgan household no longer. I decided that I would write to Lady Froome personally, asking her to put in a good word for me with Lady Tillot, whom I had not yet had the pleasure of meeting. And she must have done this for me, because I received a letter soon afterwards from Lady Tillot, saying I could go up to their house in Jermyn Street for an interview.

I shall be eternally grateful to Lady Froome for that last act of kindness. I always feel that it's such a pity that I never got the opportunity to thank her for it. She had been ailing for some time it seems and she didn't survive the winter. But I was glad to feel that she must have known before she died that I was coming to look after her grandchild.

I shall always remember the interview at the house in Jermyn Street. This was the first time that I'd ever seen Lady Tillot. As for Lord Tillot himself, I hadn't set eyes upon him since he was a mere schoolboy. But he still struck me as being so very young. I remember that he was sitting on a table in the drawing room, dangling his legs over the side. All the questions came from Lady Tillot. Her strong personality was apparent as soon as you'd entered the room. There was a beauty and confidence in everything she did – in the decoration of the room, for example. Everything in soft, whitish colours. What people call good taste.

Many years later, I asked Lady Tillot what it was that made her decide to let me bring up her children. And she answered, 'It's very rare, Nanny darling, to find someone who is entirely selfless. You just sat there talking about your sisters and about the other children you'd brought up. There was never a word about your own difficulties. It didn't take me five minutes to make up my mind!' That's the kind of woman Lady Tillot was, you see.

I can tell you one thing. When Lady Tillot wrote to tell me that I was being offered the post, I felt it to be the proudest day in my life. You meet all kind of nannies in my profession. And I'm not saying there aren't some very fine posts to be obtained in the homes of the gentry. But there's no doubt that there's something special about the aristocracy. To be taking care of *their* children is a matter of class. Your standing in the sight of other nannies goes right up. And, in this particular case, what with all the Tillot family's connections, it meant that I had come up very far indeed. Apart from looking after the children of royalty, I could not have had a better position. But, seeing that Luptree had always been my home, I couldn't have wished to go any higher anyway, even if I had had the chance.

I felt sad of course for little Benny and Jenny. But I couldn't persuade myself that they were really going to miss me, not now that other plans were being made for them. And I was able to make it quite clear to everyone that I was going *up* in the world, that I'd been invited to work for the aristocracy.

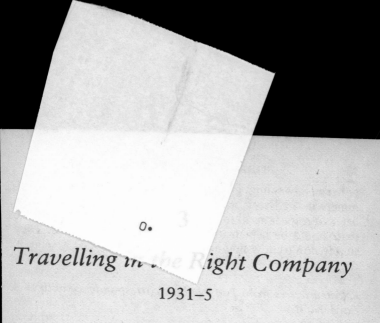

o. 3

Travelling in the Right Company
1931–5

Author's narrative

When Miss Marks took up her post as nanny to Lady Tillot's
three-year-old daughter, Camilla, an election campaign was
already in progress: the one which kept Mr Ramsay Macdonald in power, at the head of a predominantly Conservative National government. Lord Tillot was the Conservative
candidate for Froome, and it was a foregone conclusion that
he would retain the seat for his party.

The Nanny Marks tapes

We all had to go and stay at Luptree to assist Lord Tillot in
the campaign. I had only recently taken charge of my new
little girl, Camilla, who was just three at the time. But I could
see already that she was a determined little soul. I had to lead
her round the meeting hall carrying a placard which said,
'Vote for Daddy'. And such an expression of importance on
her face! It was as if she knew we had to drive those Socialists
from the Houses of Parliament.

The election campaign must have been an awful strain on
poor Lady Tillot. She was with child again, and this time it
was going to be Bruce. But she didn't shirk her duties as the
wife of a candidate. Accompanied Lord Tillot everywhere,
she did. And I can picture her now, ringed by a circle of

policemen, smiling graciously at a crowd of those nasty miners in Radstock, who were shouting horrible things at her. No respect at all for the fact she was a lady. People like that should be kept from the streets at election time. They simply don't know how to behave.

Selected letters from Lady Tillot's correspondence with Lord Tillot

Edward darling,

Nanny Marks is going to be all right, I think. She irritates me at times, going on and on drearily about some point she thinks I haven't registered properly. Occasionally I find that I am snapping at her impatiently, sometimes even rudely. I told her she was a wet fish yesterday, because she was going on so about it being time for Camilla to take her halibut liver oil. And she looked so pained in her expression that I wanted to tell her she was even worse things. But I managed to check myself.

Camilla is beginning to get quite excited at the prospect of having a little brother or sister. I have told her that it pops out of my tummy, without specifying where. I have noticed how her eye fixes on my navel. So I assume that this may go down in her memory as the hole from which babies emerge.

Was Max being serious the other night about our joining him on his yacht in the Caribbean for part of the summer? It might be deliriously fun-making, don't you think? Don't let him forget about it. It would help me to recover my figure after the birth of the baby.

I love you,
Chloe

Edward darling,

I feel so terrible, starting the holiday while you are still imprisoned in that horrible House of Commons. But we are all looking forward to the day when you are going to arrive. Max says that he will hold a fancy-dress party for us that same evening. It will be the reunion of the young lovers, as he calls it. He is adorable, and so generous too.

It is a real luxury yacht that he owns. And it's so nice never being tied to any one place for long. We are all getting tired of the Bahamas, so we'll probably move towards Trinidad within a day or two. But you needn't worry. We'll be at Kingston, Jamaica, the day you arrive.

The other guests are simply divine. There is a fantastically eccentric American millionairess called Mimi O'Toole, who has taken a great liking to me. I don't know if it's really for myself, or for the splendour of your father's title.

She is a widow. I am told by Max that she was a waitress at the time she met Mr O'Toole, and that he died from a heart attack during the honeymoon. Apparently New York high society pointedly declined all her invitations when she first came into her money. So she may be hoping to acquire respectability through her British friends. She realizes that we appreciate generosity more than her fellow countrymen do, or that we have a greater need for it, it might be more true to say. But she's tremendously funny, in any case.

She is also deliciously vain. I heard her telling Errol Fosdyke, the Hollywood film star, who happened to be sitting next to her at dinner, that her breasts had once been regarded as the pride of Paris; that they were as round and as rosy as apples. It set me wondering whether she had ever been something rather more than a mere waitress. But, whatever she may have been, she manages to carry it off superbly.

On the evening Max invited her to throw her own dinner party on board his yacht, we all found little presents wrapped up inside the napkins. For the men it was a gold cigarette case, and for the women it was a brooch with real jewels. I suspect that mine was rather better than the others, in rubies and emeralds. So we must keep her as a friend, don't you think Powkie darling?

Another of her oddities is that she wears a red wig, while managing to suppose that everyone believes it to be her real hair. Jimmy Harptree dared me to push her into the swimming pool the other day, just to see if the wig floated to the surface without her. But I refused outright, on the grounds that it might cost me many jewelled brooches at her future dinner parties.

I am counting off the days until you are here with us on the yacht.

> With all my love,
> Chloe

My darling,

Please can't we forget about that episode? You must admit that Errol is a glamorous figure, who can just about pick up his ladyfriends where he pleases. But I promise you that it wasn't like that with me at all. And, even when it happened, it meant nothing to me emotionally. It really didn't. It was just that I felt flattered, I suppose. For days on end he had been paying no attention whatsoever to any of those fabulously beautiful women who kept coming on board the yacht. And you were so long in coming out to join me. (I'm not blaming you; I realize that you were delayed, without meaning to be.) But it was something which happened – just like that. We sort of clicked together – for one evening only, mind you. It's not right that you should still be holding it against me. You ought to remember that there has been more than one occasion, now, that I could be holding against you.

Do write to me this time, and tell me that I'm forgiven. I hate having to confront you with all your aggressive talk about these things. If only you could get into the habit of writing letters, I'd understand so much more clearly how you feel.

> Your large, but tiny,
> Pekey

My darling,

It begins to look as if we made an excellent choice in appointing the new governess. The most important thing is that she gets on well with everybody, even with Nanny, although I had some doubts about this during the first week. You should have been here to see Nanny's demeanour when I first introduced them to one another. Miss Dawson was being overtly friendly, watching Nanny closely at the same time, so as to comprehend (I imagine) what manner of opposition the household might contain. But Nanny herself refused to look at her and addressed all her remarks to me, as if I was an interpreter or something. And everything she did say was pointedly about the children's health, or other matters that she assumed would be beyond the specialized knowledge of Miss Dawson.

But, within a few days, the miracle happened. I'm not quite sure what went on behind the scenes, but I suspect that Miss Dawson took the initiative by suggesting that she be invited upstairs to a nursery tea; and I am assuming that she did everything to encourage Nanny to feel that up there was her domain, and that she herself was a mere guest. But, whatever happened, it has worked wonders. Let us hope that this alliance will last, because I too find Miss Dawson a most likeable person, and far prettier than I'd ever expected a governess to be.

> Much love,
> Chloe

The Nanny Marks tapes

When Camilla was approaching her seventh birthday, Lady Tillot decided that it was time for her to have lessons. From my experience of these matters in the past, I was none too happy at this suggestion. But there was nothing I could do about it.

Yet I was worrying about nothing. Miss Dawson turned out to be a most unusual kind of governess. She was quite young and attractive, in a simple sort of way, if you see what I mean. Not dressy, or anything like that, but open and friendly. And, unlike other governesses that I've known, she used to come up to the nursery sometimes to have a cup of tea with us. Mind you, she only came in for a couple of hours each day. So we didn't see very much of her at that time, although we did later, of course.

Bruce was still too young to have lessons with Miss Dawson. His father was more concerned that he should be taught to be a trifle bolder, a trifle less afraid of everything. I think that Bruce was the only little boy I've known who was frightened by cartoon films. And I suppose they *can* be quite frightening if you stop to think about them. I remember one when Mickey Mouse was being chased down the gang-plank by a horrible old pirate with a peg leg. All the other children were screaming with laughter because the pirate kept on falling down. Yet Bruce was crying so loud that I had to take him home from the party.

It may have been because of this that Lord Tillot decided that Bruce must go down to Mr McPherson's gym and join the children's boxing classes. I always felt that three and a half was too young for a child to be taught how to box. But his father insisted that it was good for him. Not that anyone was really allowed to get a bashing, mind you. The instructor was very gentle. 'One to the point, and one to the mark!' That was what it was called. Isn't it awful that I know so much about boxing?

The real trouble was to find some other little boy of the same age who wouldn't be too big to be matched against Bruce. But eventually they managed to find one. And it was quite a little contest they arranged. Lined them up opposite each other, and then pushed them forward with the instructions, 'One to the point, and one to the mark.' But I don't think Bruce realized that the other little boy had been given the same instructions. He was taken by surprise, as it were. And the next thing we knew was that Bruce was lying on the ground – not hurt, but bewildered. Of course the audience found the whole thing terribly funny. But Bruce never wanted to go back there again.

Mind you, there were lots of things that Bruce *liked* doing. London was a lovely place for seeing things. And it wasn't as if Lord Tillot had to go to Parliament *every* day. Usually he could arrange with someone on the other side that both of them should be absent if there was an important vote. That way, nobody really minded if he took the day off.

I remember him taking us all to the pantomime one afternoon. And Uncle Buffy came with us. Uncle Buffy wasn't a *real* uncle of course. He was the Earl of Yeovil and had been Lord Tillot's best friend at Oxford. He was always coming round to have lunch at Jermyn Street.

Well, we were late in arriving at this pantomime. And, when we came in, there was a man on the stage dressed up as a hippopotamus. It looked so much like Uncle Buffy that he got down on all fours, and kept exclaiming, 'I'm a hippo! I'm a hippo!' This was in the kind of voice that the hippopotamus was using. But some of the people in the audience became very angry with us. They were shouting things like, 'Keep quiet!' Ever so rude they were! But of course we didn't have to pay any attention to them. They were a very ordinary sort of people.

I suppose that the things Bruce liked best of all were the conjurors. In London, the children's parties were quite frequent. He was always impressed by the way that a real live rabbit could be produced out of a hat. Thought it was proper magic, you see. And he loved anything to do with magic.

Camilla was always very good with Bruce. She took care of him at these parties, leading him by the hand to get the best seats for the Punch and Judy show, or seeing that he didn't forget to take his presents back home with him. Bruce worshipped her because she was like a little mother to him. And it was like that really. Three and a half years is quite a difference in age when you're a child.

Of course, the grandest of all the parties we ever attended was at Buckingham Palace. And Lord Tillot's children were singled out for rather special attention. This was Queen Mary's doing. As soon as all the children had filed into the state drawing room, bowing and curtseying as they'd been told, Queen Mary came over and took little Bruce by the hand. Not that he ever realized who it was. It was just the kind old lady who had been standing by the door, as far as he was concerned. But she made a special point, in front of all the other children, of helping him to choose his present. And it didn't pass unnoticed by all the other nannies at the party.

A little while later, Camilla too was singled out for royal attention. They were forming a special troop of Brownies at the Palace, for the benefit of Princess Elizabeth and Princess Margaret Rose. It was an honour to be invited to join this troop. And, of course, Camilla was one of the first to be asked. She became very friendly with the two Princesses — which was an advantage to her later in life.

Then such a sad thing happened. King George V died and the whole nation went into mourning. He was more than a King to most people. We really felt as if he'd become a member of our family. Particularly a family like ours, for we really were quite close to him. Bruce insisted that I hang above his cot a calendar with his picture on it. And he always referred to him as 'our gracious King' because that's the way we sang about him in the national anthem.

But his death meant there was a new King on the throne. Another King Edward. And we all thought he'd make an excellent monarch. He was someone with a mind of his own, someone who might restore to the throne some of the power that had been taken away by all those grasping politicians.

I don't mean that Lord Tillot was grasping. He wasn't. In fact, he wasn't cut out for a political career. I think, if the truth were known, he'd say that he simply didn't enjoy public speaking.

There was a second general election coming up, with Mr Baldwin taking the Conservatives to another victory. People knew that they were safe with Mr Baldwin, and they wanted his government to continue. (Mr MacDonald was never really the Prime Minister, you see.) In any case, Lord Tillot decided that he'd served long enough as an MP, so he didn't stand.

The Sixth Marquess of Froome, interviewed by Mr Simon Manasseh

Q: You became a Member of Parliament. But you only remained one for a brief period of time. As a way of life, didn't it appeal to you?

A: Good Lord no! Politics has always bored me stiff. Or it does when you're obliged to listen to the kind of drivel that our own politicians speak. I only stood for Parliament because it was what my father wanted me to do. Each generation of the Tillot family has sat as a Conservative for Froome at some time in his life. It's been going on like that for donkey's years. So I just had to do what everyone was expecting of me. I hated it, every minute of it. I was even sick on the night before I made my one and only speech in Parliament. The very idea of having to stand up and start speaking drivel was enough to give me butterflies in the stomach.

Q: Did you make any lasting friends from the House of Commons?

A: No. I simply wasn't in their class. And I don't mean that snobbishly. I was an amateur and they were professionals. And they sort of knew it, I suppose. But they were perfectly friendly with me, even the Socialists, if it comes to that.

Q: Were you well acquainted with any names of national standing?

A: Oh yes, I'm sure there were some. Let me think. Well, Stafford Cripps, for example. But he was never really one of Them. He was one of Us who had gone democratic. The sort of person that I imagine you're talking about is Nye Bevan. Oh, he was friendly with me all right. He used to write articles for Max Beaverbrook sometimes. And Max was a great admirer of Chloe. I can remember going into Max's office to find Nye Bevan sitting in a plush chair, with his feet up there on the desk and a drink in one hand – just like any of Max's millionaire friends. He waved a hand in my direction as I arrived. 'Hello, Edward,' he said, as if he really knew me. The fact that we might even then have thought of each other as vermin didn't seem to make any difference. In the House of Commons, we all had to be common. It wasn't the way of life at all that I had been used to at Luptree Court. By the time the next election came around, I knew that I'd had enough of it. The Froome Conservative Association had to find themselves another candidate.

The Nanny Marks Tapes

Lord Tillot didn't really have his heart in politics. The social life could be very tiring, you see. Lady Tillot probably felt more at home in society. I mean, more attracted to the idea of going out every evening to some party. There weren't many weeks that passed without some picture of her appearing in the glossy magazines. It was only the *Tatler* and the *Sketch* in those days, so there was no difficulty in keeping up with their movements. Lord and Lady Tillot were regarded by everyone as being two of the leading lights in Mayfair society.

Yet there were times when I felt as if the life they were leading might have been a trifle *too* hectic. I can remember waking up one night when they'd just arrived home from a party to celebrate the Grand National. They'd been at some hotel smashing up the glasses, the chandeliers, everything in fact. And it wasn't just them. The whole party had gone mad, it seems, without any of them caring two pins about the cost. It was all charged down to the winner, in any case.

But the sight that met my eyes was appalling. Lady Tillot had sprained her ankle while leaping over the banisters; and the guests had torn strips from a napkin to bandage it up for her. As for Lord Tillot, he'd cut his arm when he threw a champagne bottle through a window. But this hadn't been bandaged at all. They were sitting down there in the drawing room shrieking with laughter about the whole business. It was a noise fit to wake the dead. And it gave me such a fright, I can tell you. I could never understand how the children managed to sleep through these things.

But in some ways I think this kind of life may have been rather more to Lady Tillot's liking. Lord Tillot had perhaps a stronger love of the country, a greater need to get away from cities and things. Anyway, that was the decision he took. Early in the New Year, he announced to us that the Jermyn Street household was to be greatly reduced. They were to keep the house open, but only as a base for brief visits to London.

Our new home was to be Caldicott Manor, which was only a few miles from Luptree. It was very convenient that the previous owner went to live in the Bahamas around this time. So Lord Tillot made it known that he might be prepared to buy it. And his offer was accepted.

The Sixth Marquess of Froome, interviewed by
Mr Simon Manasseh

Q: After leaving politics, you reverted to doing nothing?
A: Yes sir, if you like to put it that way, I reverted to doing nothing. But I prefer to think of it as a time of settling down with my family, if you would really like to know.
Q: Your marriage at that time was regarded by most people as being a spectacular success. Is that the way you regarded it yourself?
A: Chloe and I were happy together. Happier than all the other marriages we saw going on around us. And that is saying something, let me tell you. For this was a time when the world itself appeared to be happy.
Q: Did the effects of the economic depression in the thirties ever hit your family personally?
A: Oh, if you're talking about that sort of thing . . . well . . . no, I don't suppose they did. I remember that we grumbled like hell because of having to tighten our belts a little. But it was a happy, sparkling world – despite all that.

4

A Calm Before the Storm

1935–8

The Tillot family's occupation of Caldicott Manor opened up a new period in their lives. It was a pleasantly spacious Georgian house, set in a large garden with herbaceous borders and neatly mown lawns. There was a large pond out in front, shrouded on one side by beech trees, and on the other side by a springtime spread of daffodils nestling under the cherry blossom. This furnished the setting for an elegant country life, sustained by the household staff who had accompanied them from Jermyn Street.

There was a butler, chauffeur, groom, cook, housekeeper, footman, housemaid, scullery maid and nursery maid. And then there was Lady Tillot's personal maid, the governess, and Nanny Marks herself.

Mr Walter Davis, formerly the butler at Caldicott Manor, has now invested his life's savings in the tenancy of a pub, The Hop and Grape, about a mile from Froome on the other side from Luptree. I approached Mr Davis there – he was usually addressed as Mr Davis, rather than as Walter, in these surroundings – and found him communicative on the subject of his former employer's household; he almost lectured me, making dapper hand movements, and displaying a confidence that suggested he knew what he was talking about.

He said, 'We had a great respect for Lord Tillot in those days. The whole household did. He was someone who expected things to be in apple-pie order. He liked things to be

erfect. And we knew precisely where we stood that way.
he white gloves for serving at table, for example. It was no
ood thinking you could get away with it if one of them
arried a stain, or if a button was undone. He had the eye of a
awk for such detail. And he didn't wait till after dinner to
ell you about it. He'd point to what was wrong, there in
ront of all the guests, sending you out to get it put right.
nd, if it happened once too often, well that meant you were
or the high jump. Out on your ear. And possibly without a
eference to go with you. Oh yes, you had to be on your toes
t Caldicott.'

I asked Mr Davis if he thought it right that such etiquette
hould be so rigidly observed.

He said, 'Depends what you mean by right, now doesn't it?
et's put it this way. If you were to go to dinner at Buckingham Palace, what would you expect to find? Even now, in
hese post-war years, you'd find things just like they were in
he days before the war at Caldicott. It was the way that both
oyalty and the gentry behaved. You expected it of them. And
you respected them for it. Of course, that way of life has gone
to the dogs since then. They may be able to keep it up at
Buckingham Palace. But we all know what has become of
Luptree Court.'

I asked Mr Davis if he had noticed whether the same kind
of atmosphere had prevailed in other households of a similar
standing when he had accompanied Lord Tillot as his valet
and loader upon shooting-party weekends and the like.

He said, 'A household took its tone from the person at the
top, whether it be Lord Thingummajig or Mr Snooks. He set
the style, and the rest followed. That's why Lord Tillot
insisted on everything being just perfect.'

'Oh, I can remember some weird households, if you want
to know about that. On one of the very first occasions I
accompanied Lord Tillot to another house, I can remember
their butler standing up after dinner in the servants' hall and
looking from one to the other of us young men and saying,
"Well who is it going to be? Who is coming to sleep with me
tonight?" I thought he might be joking at the time. But he
wasn't, you know. It was like that in those days. You just

took life as you found it in the house where you happened to be.'

The Sixth Marquess of Froome, interviewed by
Mr Simon Manasseh

Q: If your heart was never in public life, couldn't your father have enabled you to take a more personal interest in the running of the Luptree estate?

A: Oh yes, he could have done that. But he wouldn't. He didn't take any interest in it himself. Left it all in the hands of a ridiculous ex-army officer called Major Codrington, who knew all along that I'd sack him just as soon as I got the opportunity to do so, with the result that we were never particularly cordial to one another. But he had to display a minimum of respect towards me, because that's how things were at Luptree.

Q: How do you account for your father's not regarding you as a suitable manager for the Luptree estate?

A: He never trusted me. That was the sad thing in our relationship. He had absolute confidence in anyone who stuck by the rules: calling him M'Lord in every other remark or touching the forelock, if they were that low down the scale. But, if you tried to go your own way, as I did, he didn't feel that he could trust you. Or he wasn't prepared to take *me* on trust, until I had passed a whole variety of little tests, to see if I was yet doing things the way he would like them to be done. He allowed me to run the home farm, for example, but not the estate.

Q: Did you make a success of it?

A: Of the home farm? Well, no. Mind you, there was a lot that was wrong with it already. My father hadn't been concerned to modernize things. It was continuing to do things the way they had always been done which concerned him. Nothing had to change. So, when I came along, I thought it was time to blow a few cobwebs out of the system. I wanted to see it modernized.

Pigs were in fashion, for bacon; but they were all trying

out new breeds. So I thought the right thing to do was to build an up-to-date piggery. Well, I did this. I brought in an excellent architect, who had designed an orangery for my friend Buffy Yeovil. And it went up within six months, on a tract of waste land that hadn't been any use to the farmer beforehand.

But would you believe it? Within two years, there wasn't a pig in the place. The farmer was pig-headed. That's what he was! He said the piggery was exposed to the wind, or something, that the piglets kept dying. But the truth of the matter is that he was just too lazy to get up in the morning and walk that extra mile to go and feed them.

Q: Was this the reason why your father was so hesitant to continue with the process of handing over the estate to you in his lifetime?

A: Well, it was more a question of his having to decide the right moment for breaking the family entail. I'd always been on at him about it. Get it over and done with was what I thought. They only used to tie things up that way because they hated one another. But that was more than a century ago. We simply didn't need to keep paying all these lawyers to make life difficult for us. If only he'd have let me run things my way, it would have saved us a lot of problems in the end. I can tell you that, for sure!

Q: Did you feel as if you'd failed in farming?

A: I'd never even been interested in farming. Forestry, that's my pigeon. And Luptree Court, of course. My father never appreciated that Luptree meant more to me than anything else in my life. And, if you ask me, he was just trying to punish me because I'd chucked in that job as an MP, to make me feel I'd been irresponsible or something of the sort. Not that I felt like that at all. I just sat back and enjoyed myself.

Author's narrative

I managed to obtain an interview with Lady Beatrice

Cholmondely, elder daughter of the fifth Marquess of Froome. Lady Ulrica Howard, incidentally, declined an interview, with the phrase (which I quote from her letter), 'No one but a busybody would be wanting to write anything about my family, and I can assure you that I have no time for busybodies.' In the same post I received Lady Beatrice's letter agreeing to an interview.

Having emerged from this ordeal, which entailed a long drive down to Lady Beatrice's thatched former vicarage in Dorset, I formed the opinion that the two sisters had consulted by telephone about the advisability of an interview with me. More than this, I suspected that Lady Beatrice's acceptance was for no better reason than that the younger sister was intending to decline: a sense of rivalry about who was the stronger representative of the Tillot's family's ancient traditions being something which characterized their relationship no doubt.

Lady Beatrice was a strikingly handsome lady, with fiercely aquiline features. She was then in her eighties – almost an exact contemporary of Nanny Marks. She remained sitting when I entered, making a gracious apology about the current state of her sciatica. There was a walking stick leaning against one side of her armchair, which struck me at the start of our interview as looking rather more like a weapon in reserve than any ambulatory support. Yet I gradually discovered that, provided I was content to conduct my interview in the manner she thought seemly, she responded with a certain restrained cordiality.

'So what is it that you would like to know?' she inquired imperiously.

I explained to her that my principal sources of information to date had been the tapes left by Nanny Marks and Lord Froome's interview with Mr Manasseh. From these I had formed the impression that the relationship between Lady Beatrice's father and brother might have been frictional. I asked her if she might be in a position to explain why it had developed that way.

She said, 'They never used to understand one another. They were entirely different sorts of people.'

I ventured to ask what she meant.

She continued, 'There was always some little part of Edward that remained insensitive to the way that other people feel and behave. We used to refer to it as his cold streak. If you happened to strike it, you were liable to be taken by surprise. The truth of the matter is that he used to shock my father – simply by the absence of what my father regarded as common humanity.'

I inquired whether she had any particular examples in mind.

She said, 'It's not my habit to go telling tales out of school. And in any case, the incidents were all trivial enough in themselves. But there was all that *killing* when he was a boy. Always out with the keepers, wanting to be thrashing the life out of harmless little creatures. My father was a much more gentle kind of man. He didn't see the sense in it.'

The Nanny Marks tapes

Lord and Lady Tillot didn't spend all of their time with us at Caldicott. They could still go up to London whenever they felt like it. But they were nearly all at home for the weekends, when a lot of guests would arrive. All important names that one read about in the *Tatler* came down to Caldicott at one time or another.

There were such a lot of interesting things for them to do on these weekends. It depended on the season of course. But if there wasn't racing, or tennis, then it might be fox hunting, pheasant shooting or hare coursing.

Lord Tillot wasn't very fond of fox hunting. I think the real reason was that he didn't enjoy riding; not like Lady Tillot did, at any rate. Oh, she looked such a fine horsewoman, dressed up in her long black skirt, with hunting veil and bowler. She always rode side-saddle in those days.

Shooting was more in Lord Tillot's line. Camilla used to accompany him everywhere. And in the mornings she was sometimes allowed to walk with the beaters. But not after lunch, of course. The shooting became a bit wild after lunch, you see. I remember several occasions when a beater complained of being shot. But the head keeper kept them firmly in hand. He always reminded them that they were *paid* to be shot at. So there was nothing they could rightly complain about.

There was a lot else besides hunting and shooting before the war at Caldicott – the race meetings, for example. They were such *lively* occasions. There was one in particular that I remember. It was at Wincanton, I think. Lord Tillot and Uncle Buffy had hired a coach and pair, so that they could see the races better from on top of it. And I suppose they may have been having a few drinks, or so. But they suddenly decided that the race meeting needed livening up. So they took the cart horses out from between the shafts and started racing each other round the course. If they hadn't been Lord Tillot and Lord Yeovil, I expect the police would have stopped it. As it was, the whole crowd was cheering them. Oh, they loved to see the aristocracy enjoying themselves.

The Sixth Marquess of Froome, interviewed by Mr Simon Manasseh

Q: I believe that you were once regarded as one of the finest shots in the land. Did you regard yourself as what is described as a huntin'-shootin'-fishin' gentleman?

A: Not really. I enjoyed shooting all right. And I'm flattered if anyone has told you that I was as good a shot as all that. But then, going to a shooting school from time to time was all part of the expected upbringing. And there were regular weekend shooting parties at Luptree which my father did like me to run. I was not the official host, which was the role he kept for himself, but it was up to me to see everything ran smoothly. As for all those other sports, I wasn't really interested. Chloe was good at riding, mind you; so she enjoyed going hunting. But I only went along with her very rarely myself. As I saw it, the whole point of fox hunting was to get lost in the company of some lady you found attractive, so that you could spend the afternoon sharing a hayloft with her. But, whenever I looked around the assembled company at the meet, it struck me that all the women were far too horsey for my taste. I didn't want to share any hayloft with them. I preferred to stay at home.

No, I don't think it's right to say that I was a huntin'-shootin'-fishin' man. The fishing hardly came into it, as far as I was concerned. But there was the coursing, I suppose. Yes, you could be right, sir, to say that sporting activities took up a large portion of our time.

Q: Does it upset you when you read, nowadays, that coursing is one of those sports against which people protest on the grounds that it's cruel?

A: Cruel? Well the whole of life is cruel if it comes to that. What about the hawk who tears a little bird to pieces? Even cats for that matter. (Do you happen to own a nice little pussy cat?) I'm not trying to argue that man is any better than the rest of God's creatures. It's just that he finds himself standing there, way up on top of the dung-hill. So he can afford to push all the other species around. I believe that Darwin was right. My mother always used to say that he was un-Godly. But, even if he was un-Godly, he was still right, that man. He gave us the biggest stride forward the world has seen since — who shall I say? — Jesus Christ. Might is right. You can stand on your head, but there's no getting round it.

The Nanny Marks tapes

Oh, it certainly was a gay life we were all leading down at Caldicott. But it was on a smaller scale than things once had been up at Luptree, of course, in the days gone by. And there was one thing I missed: not meeting all those London nannies for a chat, except when we were invited over to some place for tea. But there were other things to make up for it, like the dogs and the ponies. There were about six dogs of all different shapes and sizes. Not any mongrels, mind you. All of them had a pedigree.

It was quite a young household, in comparison with many.

Particularly as far as the men were concerned. Lord Tillot preferred them to be younger than himself. I think he distrusted older men — didn't feel he had the right kind of authority with them. The butler was so young that we were all expected to call him by his Christian name, which was Walter. He was such a dignified young man, even in those days.

Walter used to accompany Lord Tillot everywhere, and this included the Wessex Yeomanry's summer camp. He went as Lord Tillot's batman, you see. I don't think they used to take their soldiering very seriously in those days. It was more to have a good time than anything else. All the riding events and competitions of other kinds! People were expected to do sporting activities in those days.

Letter from Lady Tillot to Lord Tillot

Darling,

You'd better hurry back from your Yeomanry camp just as quickly as you possibly can. For Mimi O'Toole has been mortally offended by our dear little Bruce.

You know how proud she is of being his godmother. She imagines that he holds her in equal regard and that some kind of special relationship exists between the two of them. Yesterday we both went upstairs to have tea in the nursery. And Bruce was throwing a tantrum because he wanted to play with the trowel that Mimi had given Camilla. He had been given the most superb yacht, but was refusing even to look at it. So Mimi took him up in her arms and started talking some ridiculous baby language to him. But Bruce (still screaming his head off) suddenly grabbed hold of her hair and started pulling. I can now confirm that she does wear a wig. I caught a glimpse of something slightly grey underneath. I doubt if Mimi will ever forgive our little treasure for this exposure, even though I rapidly turned my back and pretended not to see.

> All my love,
> Chloe

The Nanny Marks tapes

How you were allowed to behave rather depended on which position you held. There was Miss O'Hara, for example, who was Lady Tillot's personal maid. Now she was really quite lady-like, you know. But she had a strong temperament. For most of the time she was quiet and well spoken. But there were occasions when Lady Tillot herself could be a trifle quick tempered. She would say things she didn't really mean and perhaps fling a cushion at Miss O'Hara. Well, Miss O'Hara wouldn't stand for anything like that. If things were thrown at her, she would promptly throw them back. And Lady Tillot would accept this kind of behaviour, because she realized that she ought not to have started throwing things in the first place.

Walter's best friend was the chauffeur. We called him Mr Perkins, although I don't suppose he was really any older than Walter. Yet he was someone that we never got very close to. When he was driving the car, it was always the back of his head that we saw. Or, if we were going for a walk near the garage, it was only the soles of his feet that were visible, sticking out from under the Bentley. He loved that car better than any human being in the world. With anything mechanical, he was in his element.

Now, let me see, there was Mrs Potts, who was the housekeeper at that time. Such a treacherous woman, I always thought. You should have heard the way she ladled out love to the children whenever Lady Tillot was around. But as soon as her back was turned . . . well, that was a different story. 'Damn brats' is what she called them, when talking to one of her housemaids. She didn't mean me to hear, of course. But she had one of those voices which went rasping all over the house.

Not all the staff were English. It was generally the cooks who were foreign. There was one I remember called Mrs Hoffmann, who came all the way from Vienna. And she could be very difficult if you happened to get on the wrong side of her. But I was always careful not to.

I find that people from the continent are more emotional

than we English. And the one thing that raised her to the highest emotion was her admiration for Adolf Hitler. She hung a photograph of him on the wall of the kitchen, and she would tell the scullery maid of all the wonderful things he was doing for the Germans.

Mind you, it wasn't quite so odd to talk like that in those days. I heard many of Lord Tillot's friends speak well of Hitler. There was a time when he seemed the only person who could get things done. Not like that horrible man they had in Italy. Mussolini was all talk and nothing else. And he made such faces whenever he made speeches. You can't be any good as a politician if you look like a bullfrog.

Yet what they did to themselves on the continent all seemed a long way off. We had too much to occupy our attention at home. King Edward was having such trouble with Mr Baldwin. They wouldn't let him marry Mrs Simpson. I dare say that Mrs Simpson wasn't quite the most suitable lady that the King could have chosen. But he had a right to decide these things for himself. You can't have a King taking orders from his Prime Minister. It wouldn't be right.

It was during the autumn that little Sebastian was born. We were all so glad that it was another boy.

The Sixth Marquess of Froome, interviewed by Mr Simon Manasseh

Q: Were you happy that your third child was a boy?
A: Oh yes. It was only while my mother was alive that I hoped to have daughters. Sons were what I needed to provide plenty of heirs to Luptree. You can't bank on any future if there's only one, you know. They're apt to get run over or something. It's best to play safe. I'd have had four or five, if Chloe had been up to it.

The Nanny Marks tapes

I think Bruce may have been a little bit jealous of the new baby. You see, up to this time he'd been the only boy. Yet, now there were two of them, he may have felt that people weren't so concerned about him.

I had to scold him severely when I found he'd been putting nettles in Sebastian's pram. The poor little mite was crumpled up in one corner, crying pathetically when his bare little toes reached out and touched a nettle. Not that Bruce really meant any harm. I don't think he realized that he was causing his brother such pain.

But of course the things I remember best about this period were the Christmas parties at Luptree. Christmas was a lovely time in the years before the war. The whole family was reunited for the space of about two weeks, with Lord Froome presiding over the gathering.

Lord Tillot's two sisters would come without fail. Lady Beatrice and Lady Ulrica both had large families of their own. They had made suitable marriages, you understand. But that was years ago. And they had children of all ages by now.

There was quite a problem in the attitude of the other two nannies. The truth of the matter is that they were jealous of my position in the household. Seeing that I was the nanny to Lord Tillot's children, I had a superior standing. And they didn't like this at all. They didn't seem to understand that the heir to Luptree, and everyone connected with him, must rank as more important than the rest. Nanny Wiggins, who looked after Lady Beatrice's children, tried to argue that position should depend on age, instead of rank, which wouldn't have suited Lord Tillot at all, since he was the youngest in the family. But nobody ever listened to Nanny Wiggins, except for Nanny Birket. And of course, she had a biased view in these matters.

As for the children, Bruce minded terribly that Camilla should have older friends. I suppose it made him feel left out. But in a manner of speaking he was apt to bring it on himself. He had difficulty in keeping up with things.

All the stories that Camilla had ever told him Bruce was inclined to treat as fact. For example, he believed her when she'd told him that she was a fairy. It was an innocent enough little fib, and I'm sure she meant no harm by it. Titania's handmaiden was the way she had described herself. It was

supposed to be a secret between the two of them. But I heard
Bruce telling all his older cousins that his sister was a fairy. So
the secret came out. And Camilla was standing there as red as
a beetroot. We didn't hear so much about Titania's handmaiden after that.

*The Sixth Marquess of Froome, interviewed by
Mr Simon Manasseh*

Q: Was there any special relationship between yourself and
   your children, in these years before the war?
A: Well, they were too young for the most part. Sebastian
   was still a baby. You could hardly expect me to have
   developed a special relationship with a mere baby. But I
   was trying. I always used to think that, one day, I'd be a
   family man. That is to say, I saw a picture of myself in my
   years of retirement surrounded by my grandchildren at
   Christmas time, and with them all standing to sing 'For
   he's a jolly good fellow' for my benefit. just like we all
   did to my own father, during the Christmas parties at
   Luptree Court.

Author's narrative

I asked Mr Davis about the degree of cordiality in the relationship between different members of the Caldicott household staff.

He said, 'Oh, it was much like everywhere else. I mean
there were people you liked and people you didn't like so
much. You just picked your particular friends and left the
others alone. You didn't have to see so much of anyone you
found awkward. They had their job to do and you had yours.

'I had my own special mucker, as we called it in the army.
You know, special friend. Gordon Perkins. He was the chauffeur at Caldicott. We used to clear off whenever we got the
chance to have a drink with the lads up at the Froome Arms.
That's where I became a dab hand at darts, and where I got

my liking for pubs too. But Gordon had to be more careful about the drinking, in case it showed up in the way he drove Lord Tillot's Bentley next morning.'

The Nanny Marks tapes

I think I was happiest of all when Lord Tillot took us away for our summer holidays. I was able to feel we were a family together, with all the others left behind.

We went to some lovely places: the Norfolk Broads, for example. I'll always remember that holiday on the *Werry*. The *Werry* was the name of the ship, you see. More of a barge, I suppose you'd call it. But it was perfectly comfortable.

Such a nice man, the skipper. Did all manner of little things to making himself friendly with the children. I remember watching him sticking pennies into the mud beside a canal. Then he organized a treasure hunt for Bruce's benefit. Kept turning up pennies from under the soles of his feet. Said this was the way he'd become rich. And, after he'd clambered back on board, for the next quarter of an hour Bruce remained searching the river bank for more pennies. He was full of perseverance. Always was, you know.

Lord Tillot was the real captain. He decided whether we visit one place or another, and the skipper took us there. We were such a united family in those days. And it was lovely to get away from the rest of the world, even from the rest of the Caldicott household.

In some ways I like to think of that holiday on the Norfolk Broads as the most tranquil moment in my entire life. I'd come to know that I *belonged* to the Tillot family, in the way that I could never belong to anyone else. They had taken me in, and accepted me, even though I'd never really been one of their kind. Not originally, I mean. And it made me feel good to know how they wanted me.

5

The Thunder Begins to Roll

1938–9

The Nanny Marks tapes

Another summer we crossed over to the continent. Rented a house down on the beach at Arcachon, near Bordeaux. That's where the French wine comes from. I found it extremely interesting to visit France, to see the way that foreign people behave in their own surroundings. They're really not at all like Englishmen. I was always polite to them, but there was a lot they didn't quite understand. Not quite as civilized as we are in this country.

This was the summer of the Munich crisis, when things were looking very black in the world. Suddenly everyone thought we were going to be plunged into war, all within a matter of days. Lord Tillot decided there was no time to be lost. We packed our things and drove like mad to get back to the other side of the Channel before the submarines began shooting torpedoes at everyone. But it turned out to be a false alarm on this occasion. Hitler wasn't quite ready for war. And we certainly weren't.

Anyway, Mrs Hoffmann, who used to admire Hitler so much, went hurrying back to Austria. I'd seen her kissing his photograph, you know, and it wasn't very nice when she sometimes did it in front of the children. We found ourselves with a strange Czech lady as cook. Miss Kronenberg was her name. She was absolutely terrified by the way things were going in the world. Thought that the Germans would lock her up and exterminate her, if they came to England. Anyone who went down to the kitchen had to listen to her explaining that the shape of her head was Aryan, not Jewish. We all used to agree with her just to humour her. But, as Lord Tillot one day remarked, the Jews always give themselves away by the number of times they deny being Jewish.

The Sixth Marquess of Froome, interviewed by
Mr Simon Manasseh

Q: Was it a happy household during those years just prior to the war?

A: You mean the servants? Well, they had their good days and their bad. Take the nanny, for example. You wouldn't expect that she'd get on with the governess. They're bound to be as different as chalk and cheese. The one is an educated woman. Not like us, I dare say, but she's supposed to have learnt a thing to two while she was still at school. Yet the other is a simple country woman, with a love for children.

Mind you, it's not the ideal formula – all this wish for motherhood, coupled with a fear of sex. That's what it comes to, if you get down to it. Well, you can't expect two people so different to start playing ball together. But it did happen, just once, at Caldicott. We employed a governess called Miss Dawson at one time, who did play games with the nanny. But that must have been the exception which proves the rule.

Q: If they got on so well together, why did the relationship end?

A: I suppose you could say that Chloe and I put an end to it. But there were other things that weren't quite right, you see. The governess wasn't the best choice, in some respects. She wasn't enough of a disciplinarian.

Letter from Lady Tillot to Lord Tillot

Darling,

I fear we have a problem, which I'm leaving for you to

sort out as you think best. I don't really know if I ought to take the matter seriously. You'll be the best judge of that. But your sisters evidently do.

It was the evening after you drove up to London. Ulrica suddenly cornered me in the saloon and told me loftily that she wanted a word with me *in private*. You can imagine just how ominous she made that phrase sound: as if she were about to indict me on a charge of adultery, and to have me stoned by the assembled company of Tillots here at Luptree Court.

Well, I followed her in silence to the red library, feeling (and looking I imagine) very much the guilty schoolgirl. Then, after we had both sat down, she leant a little forward in my direction and said, 'It's Miss Dawson.' I almost started laughing, but restrained myself. I just couldn't for the life of me think what she could have done to upset Ulrica.

It transpires that Miss Dawson has regularly been accompanying Lord Froome on his afternoon walks. I felt like asking what the harm might be in that. Your father is an elderly man now and, even if there did happen to be some glimmer of romance in the situation, I hardly think it would lead to any babies being born. I simply can't get a picture in my head of your father making love to anyone at all, or not since your mother died. Yet Ulrica makes it sound as if Miss Dawson is dragging him down in any old patch of long grass, with intent to defraud us all of our rightful shares of the Tillot family inheritance. This kind of talk makes me feel so awful — as if we're a lot of vultures sitting round the Christmas table at Luptree, waiting for your poor father to die, and hoping he does it before making a fool of himself.

Edward, my darling, what are we going to do? I am writing all this in a letter so that you can deliberate. Beatrice later gave Ulrica her full backing, commenting that it is better to be safe than sorry. But Miss Dawson is such a pleasant woman; she gets on well with everybody. And the children love her. I now feel almost ashamed when I am in her company: as if I've got some dreadful dagger concealed in my handbag, while I make polite and friendly conversation to her. If you decide that she ought to go, we'd better do it quickly. I cannot stand the hypocrisy of my present position towards her.

All my love,
Chloe

Author's narrative

I dared to suggest to Lady Beatrice that her father might not have enjoyed being a widower as much as she imagined. 'Nonsense,' she replied. He wasn't frivolous. He was of a serious disposition. Suppose there had been a belated brood of the Tillot family to contend with. Think of all the legal suits that might have arisen after my father's death. For once, Edward acted sensibly in sending that young woman away. A stitch in time saves nine, as I was always taught to believe.'

The Nanny Marks tapes

The departure of Miss Dawson was a great loss to the household, especially in the light of who took the post of governess after she had gone.

Miss Prendaghast was such an *ugly* woman. Everything about her was ugly. It was something that welled up from deep down inside her, until it had seeped into all her thoughts. If I described a stunted old penguin to you, it might give you some idea of what she looked like. Only penguins don't wear pince-nez.

Miss Prendaghast's whole idea in life was how she could climb to the top of the tree. but she wasn't doing very well for herself: slipping down to a mere Marquess, after being governess to the children of the Princess Royal! We never stopped hearing about the Princess Royal and her family. Anyone would think she received a life-long pension from them. If you ask me, I expect they were very glad to see the back of her.

I can remember the occasion when she was first introduced to me. Lady Tillot had invited us both to come and have tea with her in the drawing room. And, when the telephone rang, it turned out to be the Princess Royal asking to speak to Miss Prendaghast. Anyone could see from the expression on her face that she was being told off about something; and Lady

Tillot was having difficulty not laughing. You see, there was something ridiculous about Miss Prendaghast – I mean in the way she kept bobbing into a curtsey. She was doing it just for my benefit, you know; just to impress me with the fact that it was the Princess Royal who was telephoning her.

She was a real grasper, that woman! Grasp, grasp, grasp, that's all she did. And those who opposed her had to be trodden under. Well, I had no intention of stepping aside for an old bag like Miss Prendaghast! And she jolly soon found this out!

Things came to a head when she went to Lady Tillot and suggested that she be allowed to handle the servants' pay. I don't suppose Lady Tillot gave the matter two seconds' thought. She never liked the chores that were connected with running a household, and it must have seemed a heaven-sent opportunity to hand them over to someone else. What she didn't realize was that Miss Prendaghast would let it go to her head. Not only did she take it upon herself to pay the servants, but she also seemed to think she was going to pay *me*.

I had to take a very firm line with her. I said, 'Oh no, Miss Prendaghast, I am not one of the servants, and I will *not* be paid by anyone except Lady Tillot herself. I am a friend of the family and, as such, Lady Tillot sees fit to employ me. But I am *not* employed by you, Miss Prendaghast, and I shall not receive money from your hands.'

You should have seen how furious she could become. It was in front of everyone that I said this, so I humbled her, you see. And she didn't like it one bit. Told me that I was trying to put on airs. But there was nothing she could do about it. And in future I always received my pay direct from Lady Tillot's hand.

Oh, she was such a mean creature! Her way of trying to hit back at me was to forbid Camilla and Bruce to come anywhere near the nursery. She persuaded Lady Tillot that they should move into bedrooms downstairs. And, since they now had their meals with their mother and father, I had little opportunity to talk with them at any time whatsoever. If I saw them alone for a second, I would run over and give them a kiss. Then I'd make my escape before the old dragon returned.

One day when I met Miss Prendaghast on the stairs, I told her just what I thought of her. I said she was trying to steal the children away from me one by one, until I had none left at all. And do you know what she replied? She said, 'Yes, Nanny, that's quite right. I'm going to steal them all away from you. Even that little baby you've got there in your arms. One day I'm going to have him from you. And he'll be working in the schoolroom with *me.*'

I said, 'Oh no, you will not, Miss Prendaghast! You will get Sebastian over my dead body! He's not going to fall into hands such as yours!' And I went straight upstairs again and locked myself in the nursery. That's what things had come to when Miss Prendaghast was around.

It was the strain of her being in the household that was responsible for Sebastian falling sick. And my goodness he was ill! In fact, there was one moment when everyone thought he was going to die. It was some kind of mastoid trouble and it affected both ears. This was before they invented antibiotics, so it was a serious matter in those days. We were all so worried, although Lord Tillot declared that one out of two sons was a loss he could afford. But he was still very anxious about little Sebastian. It was only his manner of speaking, you see. But all's well that ends well, as I always say. They operated on both his ears and Sebastian began to recover.

When we got back to Caldicott, Miss Prendaghast had become even worse than before. My absence had given her the chance to find her feet in the household. She thought she was going to push me around, you see. Came right out on the warpath as soon as I'd set foot in the household.

You'll laugh when I tell you this story! It's all so silly. But Miss Prendaghast had got it into her head that I'd been hiding in the nursery a pair of Camilla's pink knickers. She was taking out an inventory on all the underclothes that the children possessed. As if it mattered! Well, she came to the conclusion that a pair of pink knickers was missing. She probably had lost them herself, yet she decided that I must be hiding them in the nursery.

Up she came – thump, thump, thump with her short stubby high-heeled shoes – and started hammering on the nursery door.

'What is it you want, Miss Prendaghast?' I inquired.

'I want Camilla's pink knickers,' she replied.

'I haven't got them,' I told her, holding the door firmly so that it was only an inch ajar.

'Let me come in, let me come in,' she shouted.

'No, Miss Prendaghast,' said I, 'you are not going to come into my nursery. I haven't got your pink knickers, so there is no reason why I should let you into my nursery.'

Oh, you should have heard how angry she became.

'What have you done with them?' she screamed.

'I've swallowed them, Miss Prendaghast,' said I, 'that's what I've done. I've swallowed them.' Forgive me for laughing, but she never knew when to take me seriously, you see. But it was all I could do to hold the door against her weight.

'I *will* come in, I *will* come in!' she was shouting. And she was now pushing against the door with all her might.

At that moment I stepped back sharply, and pulled the door open as I went, saying, 'All right then, come in, Miss Prendaghast!' And she lurched through the door and fell flat on her face.

I didn't wait for her to get up. I just withdrew into the night nursery through the other door. And, by the time she was finally on her feet again, I'd picked up Sebastian from his cot and disappeared into the garden with him. These were the only tactics you could adopt with a woman like Miss Prendaghast. You had to outwit her by cunning.

Letter from Lady Tillot to Lord Tillot

Darling,

Miss Prendaghast is unbearable. With all this terrible talk of war which keeps floating round, I find myself wondering which will be the most terrible: the war itself, or having to share Miss P's undiluted company while you are away.

It has certainly been a terrible experience putting up with
er while you and Walter have been away at the Yeomanry
amp. I get the feeling that she is trying to show me that she
an replace both of you as the substitute man-about-the-
ouse; she has become ingratiatingly competent in all man-
er of unforeseen ways, with assumptions of new authority
o accompany it, of course.

I could bear all that, I think. But there is something faintly
inister about her as well. She pries. The other day I was
playing Head, Body and Tail with the children. Camilla
started hers with a face that looked very much like a carica-
ure of Miss Prendaghast: by which I mean that she gave her
emale head a huge hooked nose, hair in a bun, and a most
disagreeable expression. After she had folded this over, Bruce
added to it by drawing a body of a gorilla; and I finished it off
with the feet of a duck. But then it was handed back to
Camilla to write a name underneath it, and I don't know if
she did this on purpose (because we must remember that she
had drawn the original head) but she entitled it 'Miss Prendaghast'.

All three of us had a good laugh about this, because it
seemed such an accurate portrait of her. And, when the children went upstairs to bed, I threw all the used pieces of paper
into the wastepaper basket. Who could have dreamt that
Miss P would go and examine such litter? And she must have
done so before eight o'clock in the morning, because that is
when June would be expected to come and tidy up the drawing room.

It almost took my breath away when Miss P hobbled up to
me next morning with this particular scrap of paper in her
hand. Smiling fiercely, with intermittent sniffs, she said, 'I
couldn't help noticing this drawing lying here on the floor
when I came to have a look at the newspaper headlines this
morning.'

Don't believe a word of that, incidentally. I even took the
trouble to inquire from June, later on, if she might have left
any pieces of paper lying on the floor. But she hadn't. In fact,
she was quite offended that I should have asked.

Miss P chose to take the line that it was Camilla alone who

had done the drawing. She must have realized that it was a joint effort, and that I was guilty too. But of course, Camilla may have been intending that the head she had drawn should eventually be labelled 'Miss Prendaghast'. So there may have been some minimal grounds for her feeling offended.

I tried to talk her out of it, yet it was plain that I had met with no success. So what I finally had to do was to get the children together, so that we could play another round of Head, Body and Tail that same evening; I had explained to them that Miss P was upset and that we needed to put matters right.

My scheme was to get Camilla to draw a toothy, snub-nosed caricature of myself, to which I added the body of a hippopotamus, with Bruce appending four boots to the stubs. And Camilla dutifully labelled the figure 'Mummy'. So I then had the humiliating experience of having to show this drawing to Miss P next morning, in evidence that it was all harmless fun.

How she relished it! She kept flourishing the piece of paper under her nose, with comments like, 'It's not very flattering, is it? And not very accurate to portray you with such protruding teeth.' I suddenly felt my elbow waggling, as it does whenever I'm getting into a bait. I had to keep a hold of myself, with such even remarks as, 'Well, there you see, Miss Prendaghast. I'm sure that Camilla meant no harm when she drew you looking like. . . .' I almost said, 'the harridan that you really are'. But I substituted the phrase 'such a fierce lady' instead. And Miss P hobbled out of the drawing room, simpering softly, still clutching to her bosom this drawing of me which I myself had devised.

I really can't take much more of this woman. I'm on the lookout for a pretext to get rid of her. But I'm glad you agree that the children can both go to school in January. I may be able to last out until then. I hope so, because I funk giving Miss P the sack. I feel that she might end up by making me feel that it was she who had sacked me.

> All my love,
> Chloe

The Nanny Marks tapes

The trouble with Miss Prendaghast was that she simply didn't know when to give up. She was that kind of woman, you see. So I eventually went to Lady Tillot and tried to explain the situation as I saw it to be. Camilla was now twelve and Bruce was eight. It was silly for them to have a governess at that age. They would do far better if they went straight to boarding school. I could then take care of them in the holidays. And, since little Sebastian wasn't yet two years old, the services of Miss Prendaghast were altogether unnecessary.

Lady Tillot said that she would discuss the matter with her husband and a decision would be taken later. Yet, in the meantime, Miss Prendaghast had been talking to Lord Tillot, trying to persuade him that nannies are a hindrance to education. It was most untrue, I told him, when word of this came to my ear. I could read and write just as well as Miss Prendaghast. If the children needed instruction in these matters, then I was quite prepared to give it myself: if he didn't want to send them to school, that is.

I really don't know what decision Lord and Lady Tillot would have come to if Miss Prendaghast hadn't blotted her own copybook. You see, Lady Tillot was in the habit of leaving her desk unlocked. And I'd written a note to her complaining about some offensive remark that Miss Prendaghast had made to me in front of the servants. Well, she gave herself away. She couldn't have known anything about my complaint if she hadn't gone snooping through the papers on Lady Tillot's desk. And, when she saw that note, she couldn't resist taking up the subject with Lady Tillot. And that was her downfall. The decision was taken that Camilla and Bruce should be sent to boarding schools, and Miss Prendaghast must look for a job elsewhere.

It wasn't just Miss Prendaghast: a whole period of our lives was coming to an end, although we didn't fully realize this at the time. That autumn war was declared.

Author's narrative

I inquired from Mr Walter Davis how he had viewed the coming of war.

He said, 'It was shattering. It was the end to a whole style of living. Kaput! It just put paid to everything. Life had been running along so smoothly. Then suddenly we heard it announced on the radio that we were at war again. We'd done some training, even prior to the war, with the Wessex Yeomanry. So that's where our call-up papers detailed us to go: Lord Tillot as a squadron leader, and me as his batman. Not the kind of life I would have chosen for myself. But there it is. War is war.'

6

To Survive the Deluge

1939–43

The Sixth Marquess of Froome, interviewed by
Mr Simon Manasseh

Q: Did you regard the declaration of war as the end of an
   era?

A: Well, not at the time, I dare say. But that's the way of
   things. The world just goes jogging along until a war
   arrives. Then it's all fizz, bang, wallop, and things really
   start to happen. It's like in a game of backgammon,
   when you throw doubles. The whole board gets moving.
   The atom bomb gets invented, or whatever. In peacetime,
   our scientists get bogged down in trivialities: trying to
   invent sewing machines which sew faster. When a war
   comes along, you've got to get moving, or you're going to
   be the one that goes under. But you don't think of it as
   the end of an era when it happens. You just keep bound-
   ing ahead, without giving any thought to what you're
   doing.

The Nanny Marks tapes

At the start, I don't suppose it was very different from
peacetime, except that Lord Tillot had gone off to join his
Yeomanry regiment. They were among the first to be called
up. But he was able to spend plenty of time with the family
because we moved into a billet at Taunton, which was near to
the camp where he was stationed.

Then the news came through that the Wessex Yeomanry was to set sail for a secret destination. And Lady Tillot was so worried that they might be going to invade Germany. She kept saying that horses weren't supposed to be much good nowadays. Not against tanks and things. Yet it was horses that the Yeomanry had to use, so all we could do was to hope for the best. It was a tearful farewell: the Tillots had always been regarded as one of the happiest couples in Mayfair society. But we all believed that Lord Tillot would be back again within six months. So we didn't get downhearted.

Of course, Lord Tillot wasn't the only one to get called up. All the men in the household had to go. In fact, there was a reduction in the size of the household all round. no more housemaids and kitchen maids. Mrs Potts and Miss Kronenberg had to manage everything on their own. Even the stables had been emptied, with Lord Tillot taking two of the best horses abroad with him and the others being sold.

It didn't take us very long to work out where the Wessex Yeomanry had been posted. There were hints in some of his letters, so that you could guess. I remember Lady Tillot reading out a piece about them practising cavalry charges in an orange grove, and how Lord Tillot was the only one to skewer an orange on the end of his sword. And there were other bits about the veiled women smelling rather like their camels. He was in the Middle East, you see. In Palestine to start with, and then later moved down into Egypt, once the Yeomanry had been provided with tanks.

Excerpts from Lady Tillot's correspondence with Lord Tillot

(I shall in future confine myself to excerpts from these letters. They all begin with the word 'Darling' and end with the phrase 'With all my love, Chloe')

I miss you enormously, and I'm tremendously worried in case they have thrown you into battle. I'm sure I wasn't intended to be a war widow. God would never do such a wicked thing to me.

You'll think me terribly silly, I know, but I've made a pact with Him. It was Mimi O'Toole's idea. She came to stay the weekend before last and we both got sentimental in reminiscing about you. We were actually blubbing in each other's arms. Then next morning she said all would come out all right in the end, if only we had the strength to put our trust in God. But she thinks one has got to give something in order to receive something, and she reminded me that we have done far too little to see that the children are brought up as Christians. Mimi thinks that taking them to church at Christmas and Easter isn't sufficient. So she has just sent me a most beautifully illustrated book on the life of Jesus, with the suggestion that I read a chapter each evening to Camilla and Bruce before they go to bed. Then she feels sure that God will do favours for me.

I have started reading to them, so the pact ought to be in operation by now, although Bruce takes to the idea of having to listen to all these Jesus stories rather better than Camilla. I had to ask her not to keep looking at the clock last night. But I don't think God will blame me for such behaviour, when it certainly wasn't encouraged by me. In any case, He must know that my love for you is its own amulet. Wear me round your neck and keep me constantly enclosed within your heart, to make doubly sure that you will be returning to me safe and sound.

There is a lot going on to keep our minds preoccupied, which is a blessing in disguise, because it does at least save me from these constant worries about the way the war is going here in Europe, and whether you are safe out there, of course.

The Nanny Marks tapes

There were times when it seemed as if we had more to be anxious about living here in England. And it was poor Miss Kronenberg who was the most worried of all. After we read about the Germans using paratroops to capture Holland, she kept seeing them all over the place. Every time she looked out of the window at a passing plane, she would rush off to convince someone that she'd seen a parachutist jump from it.

One day Lady Tillot received a visit from a police officer, who came to warn her that Miss Kronenberg was using the telephone to report enemy landings about twice a week. He suggested we keep an eye on her. Didn't want the whole countryside thrown into a panic just because some mad old Czech woman saw parachutists in every cloud.

And then, when things really began to go badly for our side (there was Dunkirk, and all that business), she became too much for the authorities. They eventually sent a doctor who persuaded her to go into a hospital for a rest. I think you'd call it a nervous breakdown. And Mrs Potts took on the cooking instead of the housework.

In point of fact, the mental homes were quite useful employment agencies in those days. You see, they could release people to private service who weren't considered suitable for training in the armed forces. Yet the people they offered us weren't exactly what we wanted.

There was a Mr Gulliver who came to us as butler, and he seemed a most respectable person at first. But he overdid everything. For example, Lady Tillot didn't like the way he insisted on tugging down the hem of her skirt before she sat down in the dining-room chair. She didn't mind him pulling the chair back for her, but tugging at her skirt made her feel nervous.

One day Bruce was playing with a magnifying glass and got the rays of the sun to burn Mr Gulliver's hand. Then suddenly the gentlemanly side of his nature vanished into thin air. I could hear Mr Gulliver bellowing from up in the nursery. And, when I looked out of the window, I could see him chasing poor Bruce with a stick. It gave me the scare of my life, although I expect it taught Bruce to be more considerate in future. Naturally, Lady Tillot couldn't have goings-on like this in the household. Mr Gulliver was sent away. And we managed without a butler after that.

Excerpts from Lady Tillot's correspondence with Lord Tillot

A terrible soberness has descended upon everyone since Dunkirk. The thought of the Germans so close to us, waiting for the right opportunity to spring over the Channel, is strangely unreal. But it gives me that shiver up the spine that you feel when you believe in ghosts, even though you haven't actually seen one. I think we all feel a bit like that, bracing ourselves for an imminent confrontation, and doing our utmost to reassure one another that we are at ease and competent to cope. But, in my heart, I dread that I am not, that I shall be the first to disgrace myself, in a panic of self-preservation and mindless submission to the enemy, once I am really put to the test.

My greatest worry is that I took the wrong decision in not sending the children to America for the duration of the war. Mimi implored me to let her take them back with her. I have now missed the opportunity since the Atlantic crossing would probably be a greater risk to their lives than their presence in rural England during any invasion by the Germans. Anyway, that is what Mr Thompson seems to think.

Incidentally, he is coping wonderfully with all the responsibilities you have heaped upon his shoulders. So you don't have to worry about us, my darling. Whatever happens, we'll get through all right. Somehow it is almost fun, learning to pretend that we are brave. It's the general act nowadays, in which we all have a part to play.

I find the domestic problems such a headache. I never really appreciated before how much they can get on your nerves if it is really you that has to contend with them. But, of course, Mr Thompson is a great help. He marches into the drawing room and almost bows in greeting, displaying symptoms of embarrassment on the occasions when he discovers me in the process of entertaining some officer. It catches him in such uncharacteristic uncertainty as to how he should behave.

Author's narrative

Mr Thompson had been the estate agent at Luptree ever since Lord Tillot had finally persuaded Major Codrington that it was time for him to retire – an event which has been omitted from my text. The appointment of the new agent had been made, shortly before the outbreak of war, by Lord Tillot himself, rather than by Lord Froome. Mr Thompson had in fact been the political agent for the Froome Conservative party during the years when Lord Tillot had been serving as their Member of Parliament. So they had a relationship of some years' standing, and mutual respect even prior to these years. It is indeed evident that Mr Thompson had been entrusted with all the routine matters of household, as well as estate management, while Lord Tillot himself was fighting with the Eighth Army in North Africa and Italy.

I had no difficulty in tracing Mr Thompson for an interview. Since his retirement a few years after the war, he had married (for the second time) to a genteel young widow from the Wessex county set, who was perhaps the perfect complement to such a self-made gentleman.

Mr Thompson himself exuded an air of jaunty self-confidence. He had, after all, infiltrated the fringes of the British Establishment, completely as a result of his own endeavours. He was dressed (permanently, I imagine) in jodhpurs, a yellow waistcoat, and a sports jacket with a distinctively chequered pattern: to all appearances thoroughly at ease with this latter-day role of local squire, lording it over a small country house with its handful of acres, all of which he had acquired along with his marriage.

It was shortly after midday when I called. But there was a notable absence of any refreshment being offered. It struck me that Mr Thompson was pleased that I had come to interview him, because it enabled him to savour with a stranger some of his former prestigious connections. At the same time he encouraged me to appreciate that this was a business meeting of sorts, where I was the suppliant for knowledge about people that he, and not I, possessed.

His manner of speech was slow, with a cultivated nasal

drawl, while pausing frequently on the interjected syllable of 'ah' – sometimes in the selection of sufficiently elaborate words, in which his vocabulary abounded. I noted how he usually referred to Lord Tillot as Ed-ward: pronounced distinctly thus, in two separate halves. But, just occasionally, he would revert to the appellation of His Lordship, with a fraction of a glance in my direction, as if it was intended that I myself (in the absence of any close acquaintance with his former employer) would do well to adhere to such formalities.

While Mr Thompson discussed the early years of his employment at Luptree, I noted that he evidently regarded himself as the intellect behind most of Lord Tillot's plans to modernize the estate.

He said, 'When Ed-ward came up with an idea, he would turn to me and ask how it could be done. But, in those early years, we were constrained, of course, because his father, the Marquess, was still alive and officially in control. There were innumerable frustrations to be overcome in our daily experience.'

It took me some while to move the conversation forwards to my most important question. But I did finally get round to inquiring about the tribulations of the war years.

He said, 'They were severe times, but not without their elements of humanity. When his Lordship departed for the Middle East in defence of his country, he left me with specific instructions to see that no harm befell those that he had left behind. He had so to speak entrusted his family to my care. So I felt myself beholden to Ed-ward to lessen the severity of their hardships for the duration of the war.'

The Nanny Marks tapes

Food was quite a problem, of course. Not that we had too bad a time of it. There were always plenty of rabbits on the estate. And Lady Tillot had made some good friends among the farmers from her hunting days. We ate quite reasonably at Caldicott. But I realized I wasn't expected to know exactly where things came from. We had to survive, you understand, so it was best not to ask any questions.

In any case, the feeding of Camilla and Bruce was really a problem for their schools. Both of these were very fashionable places. In the case of Camilla, it was to Mrs de Crespigny, in Hampshire. Lady Yeovil had sent her daughter there. And so had Princess Claudia of Rumania. It certainly wasn't like any of those places we see caricatured in cartoons by Ronald Searle, where the girls all wear pig-tails and go round waving hockey sticks. At Mrs de Crespigny's, they were allowed to use a little lipstick when their parents came down to see them. Not too much, of course. Just enough to look elegant. And there were no school uniforms. Lessons weren't regarded as the most important side of education, you see. For a girl, it's social elegance that counts.

Now with a boy, it's different. Bruce had to be taught something or he wouldn't have got anywhere in the world. He didn't want to become too clever, I dare say. That's for children who need to climb up from a lowly station in life. If you're up there already, you don't need to be clever. And there are schools which understand these things. They teach them enough to get on, without pushing them.

That was the kind of place that Bruce had gone to: a school called Ashdale, which is near Ascot. The headmaster used to captain Middlesex at cricket: as a gentleman rather than a player, you understand. A large number of peers had sent their boys to Ashdale. And most of them went on to Eton. We could rest assured that Bruce was in safe hands.

When it came to the holidays, we were all together once again – just like old times. I know it's awful for me to say such things, but those first few years of the war were really quite fun in a way. It wasn't all hardship. The fighting was very distant for most of the time and there was nothing to make us worry very much, now that the likelihood of an invasion had been left behind. Even the air raids on Bristol or Southampton left little more than a red glow on the horizon, as far as we were concerned.

Of course, there were *some* occasions when we got a bit worried. I remember once when Lady Tillot was driving us all round Bath in the blackout. We were trying to get back home and she'd taken a wrong turning. Then suddenly the air-raid siren went and I became agitated — not so much for myself as for the children. It was my first experience of these things. I kept telling Lady Tillot which turnings I thought she ought to be taking, and I'm afraid I must have been irritating her. She suddenly jammed on the brakes, called me a silly old goose, and then hit me over the head with a newspaper. This was the only occasion that Lady Tillot ever lost her temper with me.

The news was sometimes sad, of course. Such a lot of people we'd known were getting killed around this time. Friends of Lady Tillot's, who'd been to stay at one time or another. Killed in action or just reported missing. And my sister, Bess: on her very first visit up to London, she missed the train back home again. Then a bomb landed on the waiting room at Paddington Station, and she was one of the fatalities. She always did make a muddle of things.

Yet nobody ever bothered to drop a bomb near Luptree. Or, on the only occasion they did so, the entire family slept through the air raid. We learnt next morning that poor old Farmer Ridgeway had caught it. A direct hit on his hay barn. But that was his fault. He'd been sitting outside mending a puncture by the light of an oil lamp. But his death served a purpose, I suppose. We were all much more careful about the blackout precautions in future.

In a way, the war brought everyone closer. I'm speaking about Lady Tillot in particular. The household was so much smaller, now that we all had to muck in together, as it was called. I felt that she'd become a real friend in those days.

Every Tuesday evening, we used to drive down to the village hall at Luptree, to attend the Women's Institute. Lady Tillot was president of course. It was a really good laugh we had sometimes: all the funny games that would be thought up by Lady Tillot for us to play. Oh, she had such a wonderful imagination! Never short of an idea. She could persuade anyone to do anything just for the fun of it.

Yes, they were lively days. And the Sharpshooters were stationed at Froome. Such a jolly crowd of people they were. And real gentlemen besides. They were in and out of Caldicott like nobody's business. Long parties late into the night, with the gramophone at full blast.

And that awful Mrs Potts – you should have seen the way she carried on. It wasn't as if anyone had invited *her* as a guest. But, as soon as she heard the sound of that gramophone, she would deck herself out in whatever fancy dress she could find and go prancing into the drawing room as if she was some kind of a cabaret turn. I'm afraid that Lady Tillot used to encourage her in these things. Yet I'm sure she wouldn't have done if she'd heard the way that Mrs Potts used to talk about her when her back was turned. I'm sure that half the stories that were circulating round the village must have originated with Mrs Potts.

Mind you, I'm not saying that Lady Tillot was doing anything she ought not to have been doing. It was only right that these officers should have been entertained. Gaiety is important when there's a prospect of life coming to an end just around the corner. It may be true that one or two of the officers were rather *particular* friends of Lady Tillot. But from the kind of things I've heard people saying, you would have thought that *anyone* was made welcome. Lady Tillot wasn't a bit like that. It was all so different during the war years, you see. Families had been split up through no fault of their own. And a woman needs company. It's no good pretending to be a nun.

Excerpts from Lady Tillot's correspondence with Lord Tillot

The Sharpshooters are a welcome addition to the Froome camp – the previous lot were all so dreary. With Jimmy Harptree being their colonel, I have found myself right at the centre of their social life. Freddy Galveston and Billy Minehead both asked me to send you their greetings, and they congratulate you on being out of quarantine for rabies. Those injections must have been awful.

You neglected to mention in your letter what happened to the poor little dog. I hope it didn't have to be shot. After all, you say that you took a swish at it with your baton; and dogs don't like that sort of treatment. But please be careful darling. It would be so humiliating to have to tell everyone that you were killed in the war – by a dog with rabies.

You must forgive me darling, for being a bit slow in answering your last letter. Yes, of course I'm missing you. This war creates such chaos in our lives that at times I really don't know whether I'm coming or going. And life at Caldicott can be quite hectic, especially when I have to give dinner parties, which is expected of me. The officers stationed here at Froome often feel jittery at the prospect of all that is to come. Nobody knows when or where they'll be called up to the front line. If they've got to do the fighting, my friends feel that it is up to the rest of us to keep them in a cheery mood – which is all that I am doing, I promise you.

You remember Conrad, our Muscovy duck? He always used to be such a placid creature. Well, he has now become the life and soul of my dinner parties. His timing is perfect. He waits until the port is being handed round for the second time. Then he starts tapping with his beak on the dining-room window until someone opens it to let him in; whereupon he waddles round the table, accepting (or demanding I should say) pieces of bread sopped in port. It doesn't take long before his sense of balance goes astray. Then pandemonium breaks loose at the moment we all try to persuade him that it is time he made his exit.

The other evening I was simply in hysterics. There was Conrad flapping lopsidedly around the dining-room table, pursued by two captains, a major and a brigadier, all on their knees striving to bring him down with rugger tackles. But they only succeeded in bringing down the candelabrum, which promptly shattered into smithereens. (Oh, it's all right – I'm sure it can be repaired.) Conrad was having one whale of a time, however. And, once we were all tangled up in a heap of bodies under the table, he made straight for the open window of his own accord, in what might almost count as a dignified exit.

The other star of the show is Potty. Everyone seems to call Mrs Potts 'Potty' nowadays. And she delights in it, emitting one of her coarse Cockney cackles every time she is addressed that way. Something I never realized about her before the war is that she is an atrocious old flirt. Like Conrad, she times her entries to perfection, waiting in the wings until a suitable atmosphere of rowdiness has built up in the drawing room. Then in she dashes doing a Knees-Up-Mother-Brown kind of dance, having decked herself out in the smartest items of military uniform from the pile that has been deposited on the hall table. And of course all the men rush up to kiss her for the delicious food she has cooked – which, incidentally, really is delicious, in the simple English tradition. Now that I have acquired a taste for it, I find myself wondering why we always went to the trouble of finding continental cooks, in the days before the war.

The Sixth Marquess of Froome, interviewed by Mr Simon Manasseh

Q: What experience did the war bring you?

A: If you mean sexual experience, the answer is none whatsoever. But perhaps that isn't what you're getting at. Well, the war was an unpleasant experience. I wasn't accustomed to being separated from my family. I even felt sentimental about them. I remember sitting in my tent, somewhere way out there in the desert, and gazing at a photograph of Camilla and Bruce making a sandcastle at Arcachon. And it suddenly occurred to me that I might never see them again, that I'd end up like one of those dehydrated mummies that people occasionally stumble upon by accident, when digging for something else. No sir, you're barking up the wrong tree on that one. The war was no joy ride by my book, I can assure you.

The Nanny Marks tapes

It sounded as if Lord Tillot was enjoying himself, in his own sort of way. He was a major now, and they'd given him the

Military Cross for his part in the battle of El Alamein. Shot up a battery of German artillery. He always did enjoy shooting, but this must have been a lot more exciting than pheasants.

When Lady Tillot read out bits from his letters, they were always quite cheerful. Yet it did sound as if he was missing the social life in London. He didn't like the Arabs, you see. And he was growing tired of being in the company of soldiers all this time.

I suppose that the Sharpshooter officer that Lady Tillot knew best of all was Lord Minehead. He always tried to make life more interesting by offering a bet on whatever we were doing. 'Go on, Nanny,' I remember him saying, 'drink another glassful of this wine, and I'll bet you a pound to a penny you'll be sick!' But he was a nice man really.

Lady Tillot became so worried about him when he got wounded. And it was all such a silly mistake. Not in the front line, or anything. They were merely up in Fife in Scotland, learning how to parachute-jump at night. But Lord Minehead managed to get a bit separated from the others and called in at a farm to see if he could borrow a bicycle. The only trouble was that the farmer thought that he might have other intentions: feared it might be a real German parachutist that he'd found hiding under the stairs. So he pulled the trigger of his shotgun – by mistake really. Anyway, that is what the police told us.

Lady Tillot was beside herself with worry, took a train to Scotland so that she could visit him in hospital every day. And the day he was allowed to come back to Wessex – well, that was the biggest party of them all. Ended up by setting the drawing room on fire – accidentally of course. The police were ringing up to tell us that our blackout needed attention!

Lady Tillot once asked me if I felt we were leading too gay a life at Caldicott. But I didn't think so in the slightest, and I told her as much. It couldn't have been very awful what Lady Tillot was doing. It didn't make the slightest difference to her relationship with the old Lord Froome, for example. She used to take the children over quite often to have lunch with him.

Excerpts from Lady Tillot's correspondence with Lord Tillot

Thank God you're alive. When I read in my papers how the Wessex Yeomanry had just gone into battle at El Alamein, I waited for days in fear that I was going to receive one of those dreadful telegrams. Somehow I was really expecting this to happen. I felt that God would be punishing me for all the terrible things I have ever done, by inflicting me with a sense of having your life on my conscience. But I feel so silly about it in retrospect, and so relieved.

In addition to all that, I am so immensely proud of you. And I shall be keeping my fingers crossed that the powers that be take up your colonel's recommendation. I always think that the Military Cross is just about the prettiest of all the medals that a man can wear; I especially like the colours on the ribbon. I shall buy myself a dress to match your gallantry.

It must be admitted that there is much gaiety in this war, but so much sadness as well. Without the gaiety, I think we'd all break down. There are too many people whom one has just got to know (to like and to admire) who then get themselves killed, sometimes on the very first occasion that they go into action. It can all be so cruel. Sometimes they get killed in a terrible mistake – just by accidents on the shooting range, and things like that. I find myself wondering how life can be so unsparing of men who really mean something – not only to myself, but to the world at large.

Don't be cross with me darling, but I fear there has been a little bit of a fire here in the drawing room at Caldicott. It is nothing bad, and Mr Thompson has already arranged for everything to be put right. Nobody is quite sure how it started, but we think that somebody must have left a cigarette somewhere they shouldn't have.

In point of fact it was all slightly hilarious in a strange sort of way. Smoke was billowing everywhere. Percy Fanshawe and Billy Minehead were terribly brave, putting wet towels over their faces and going inside to rescue some of the records. They managed to save two, and you'll never believe what they were. Percy came out with 'Red Hot Momma', while Billy found that his was entitled 'I'm Playing With Fire'!

Author's narrative

Through Mr Walter Davis, I discovered the address to which Mrs Potts had moved after retiring from domestic service. It was a small council flat in West Ham, which she was sharing with her younger sister. I counted three cats, a couple of goldfish and a canary in the entourage of these small but sprightly elderly ladies; the cats were so evidently well fed that their remaining appetites would have been unlikely to endanger the lives of the other pets.

I explained the purpose of my visit.

'Listen to this, Maudie,' she called out to her sister, who was in their kitchenette. 'We've got a young gentleman called in to see us. He wants to hear all about the shinannygins that went on down at Caldicott during the war. Better bring him a cup of tea and make him comfortable. Sit down there, love, by the electric fire. Don't sit on Ernest, or he may scratch you. Come here, my pet! Come and sit on your Auntie Flo's lap and make way for the gentleman. He doesn't like gentlemen, you know. He always thinks they're going to do awful things to him. He was doctored when he was a kitten. That was before he was given to me. But he's never trusted a gentleman since they went and did that to him.

'Now what was I saying, dear?' Mrs Potts's query was purely rhetorical. Then she launched into her tale, without the need for any further prompting. 'Oh, they were lovely gentlemen who came to stay at Caldicott Manor during the war. And we gave them a lovely time of it too. Myself and Lady Tillot. We were a right pair. It was up to me to tart up all the stuff they put into their stomachs. And . . . well, the rest was up to her.'

She followed this with what Lady Tillot had referred to as her coarse laugh. I noted that this was part of the presentation in any of her tales, coupled with chummy glances in the direction of her audience – just to check that any maliciousness she might have to offer was being duly appreciated. Perhaps the expression on my face was more disapproving than I intended to be observed. For she hastened to add, 'Oh, I thought the world of Lady Tillot. There was such a lovely warmth about her. They all found that about her. . . . Well, many of them did,' she added, reverting to an almost malicious tone of voice.

'Did you have any special favourites among the officers who came to Caldicott?' I probed.

'Oh, they were lovely,' said Mrs Potts. 'All of them were lovely. And very generous too. They didn't think twice about dipping their hands into their pockets and bringing out something for you to remember them by. I'm only talking about tips, mind you! There were some who'd enter into the spirit of things. Dress up in all Lady Tillot's finery, if you gave them half a chance. Or they'd go hunting foxes over the sofas – only the foxes weren't foxes, of course. They would be those blue-blooded Mayfair girls all tarted up for a weekend in the country. Fun and games with no strings attached. Lady Tillot knew dozens of them. It didn't take long to run any of those foxes to earth. And they'd all lost their brushes by next morning. But that's what they came for, in the first place.

'There was Captain Minehead – that's Lord Minehead of course. Now he was a fine gentleman, and very special to Lady Tillot. She wouldn't have him playing fox hunting with any of them fancy ladies she brought down from London. Not that he'd want to in any case, because Lady Tillot was more than a handful for anyone in those days. Not that he was bashful, mind you. I remember the day they were all picnicking down beside the pond at Caldicott. I had to lend him my bathing dress, because the ladies had borrowed all the ones belonging to Lady Tillot. Anyway, he was wearing it when he dived into the pond. But he wasn't the same shape as I am. So it all billowed out with air, making him look like a punctured barrage balloon that's come down on water. That's the way Lady Tillot described him! So he took the thing off while he was stood there in the water, and flung it up on the bank. Then he came out himself, as bold as

rass, pretending to be one of those men that look like goats
n posh paintings. But it was only Lady Tillot that he chased
f course. Wasn't interested in those other bits of fluff.'

Excerpt from Lady Tillot's correspondence with Lord Tillot

'm enormously glad that we chose Mrs de Crespigny's as the
school for Camilla, despite your father's insistence that we
ought to move her to the Bristol Academy for Young Ladies,
now that it has been transferred to Luptree. He may write to
you to try and persuade you to make the change. He seems to
think that she would be able to bicycle there daily from Caldicott and that the company would be good for both of us.
But I do hope you see, darling, that this wouldn't be good for
Camilla. I mean she has settled in so nicely at Mrs de Crespigny's. It would be so silly to uproot her at this stage. And
Mrs Tuffnel, the headmistress of the Academy for Young
Ladies, is positively masculine in her manner of regimenting
others.

I feel sure that Camilla is benefitting from the experience of
a boarding school. But please don't misunderstand me. I
really do love it when she is back here at home with me in the
holidays. She is growing up so fast. She has started to have
the curse and treats the subject with a sense of mystical
achievement. Almost because of this, I suspect, she seeks out
my company in preference to that of Bruce nowadays; while
he takes refuge behind schoolboy vanities, insisting that
everything other than his own occupations and interests is
'girlish' or 'boring'. Camilla declares that he is going through
'an awkward age'.

Author's narrative

Lady Beatrice spoke about the war years at Luptree. I had
started by inquiring about her feelings with regard to the
occupation by the Bristol Academy for Young Ladies of the
home in which she had been brought up.

She pursed her lips for a moment before saying, 'Well, it might have been a situation far worse than that, I can assure you. There was talk at one time of it being used as a Borstal reformatory school, because it so happened that their own premises down in Southampton were desperately required by the Admiralty. But my father put a stop to that, of course.

'No, I was in favour of Luptree Court being used by the Bristol Academy for Young Ladies, mainly because it was what my father wanted.'

Lady Beatrice paused for a moment, an expression of disapproval forming on her face. Then she said, 'Chloe ought to have allowed Camilla to attend that school. My father was greatly offended. He took it as a personal slight from her. But then she was like that. She was always insensitive in these matters. Too much of a tearaway by nature. On the go all the time. The razzle-dazzle side of life. My brother ought never to have married her.'

I inquired cautiously whether any criticism of Lady Tillot's marital conduct were being implied.

She replied, 'Well, of course we all knew that there were goings-on down at Caldicott. Stories filtered back to us from God knows where, and from London too. But it wouldn't have been right for any of us to have troubled my brother with such matters. Not while he was up at the front, with so many worries of his own.'

The Nanny Marks tapes

Caldicott had been given over, in part, to the war effort. Ever since the Blitz had started in London, a large number of children from the East End had to be found accommodation in the West Country. And Lady Tillot agreed to house one of these families. Of course, it was a great mistake really. Children from the East End of London simply didn't know how to behave when it came to living in a fine house like Caldicott. Not that they were given any of the best apartments, mind you. The cellars were turned over to them. (They had been emptied of wine during all those parties for the Sharpshooters.)

Mrs Trumper was what I would call a simple kind of person. She was content to wash the stairs in exchange for her free lodging. But her three daughters were a real menace. They didn't speak properly for one thing. I was always very careful to see they didn't play with any of *our* children.

The real trouble was that they were inclined to take liberties. They had the use of the back door, but this didn't entitle them to overrun the entire garden. Sometimes I would catch them at it, see them taking a short cut across the garden to reach Caldicott Lane. Oh, it made me so angry! I used to open the nursery window and give them a piece of my mind.

Coming from the East End, you see, they didn't really understand about society. They hadn't been brought up to appreciate that some people are at the top and others are at the bottom. They were cheeky. That's what I'd call it. They used to titter in the bushes whenever one of our children was taking a walk down the lane.

Now that Bruce was a schoolboy, he wouldn't stand for that. The Trumpers were 'oiks' – that's what he called them. He said there were plenty of oiks even in a town like Ascot, and none of his school friends ever stood any nonsense from *them*. Pelted them with conkers if they caused any trouble. And the Trumpers didn't even have a town to belong to. So you couldn't expect him to feel very kindly towards them.

Mind you, I'm not saying that he behaved rightly in doing what he did. There are limits, I'll admit. I don't think he ought to have placed a dead rat in their ventilator shaft. But I do see why he did it.

Oh, he got into such awful trouble about that! And it was all because the Trumpers called in the health inspector. There was no need for this, of course. It could have been sorted out between ourselves. Yet public inspectors are supposed to view the world from a public angle, so they came to ask some questions about what had happened. Not that they were unreasonable or anything. Lady Tillot explained that there had been a misunderstanding as to which was the ventilator and which was the rubbish bin. But we had to give Bruce a little telling off in private.

His action did serve one good purpose. The Trumpers

decided to go back home to London. The danger from bombing wasn't quite so great now. Anyway, they seemed to prefer it to living at Caldicott.

Excerpts from Lady Tillot's correspondence with Lord Tillot

I find myself so utterly bewildered by all these problems of class distinction. It's odd to think that we ever thought of ourselves as 'distinct', now that we are all striving so hard to be at one with the rest of the country. It's the only way of getting the war effort together, I suppose. Between you and me, darling, we *were* brought up to imagine that the world ran on rather different lines. Yet it would seem that nobody ever informed the Trumpers that this was so.

As you can well imagine, Nanny takes it upon herself to champion our cause. She regards Caldicott as a house under siege, where the enemy has actually managed to gain a foothold in our basement flat. Mentally, she has drawn up a whole series of frontier lines, which she regularly patrols, fully determined that no more of *our* territory will fall into their hands.

Part of the problem is that she has so little else to be doing with herself during the daylight hours, now that Sebastian is attending the infants' class at the Lord Froome grammar school. I hope we are doing the right thing in sending him to this place. But the truth of the matter is that I already find it hard work keeping the household together, *without* having to cope with the additional intrusion of some old harridan of a governess. Life is simpler this way. And it is necessary to keep parts of one's life simple, when everything else is so hectic.

I feel so very sad about Percy Fanshawe's death. He was far too young to get killed. And it wasn't even in action. He was here in London, on a week's leave. And we all went out on the town to celebrate. There were the usual air-raid warnings, of course, but we're getting so accustomed to that kind of thing. We just went on dancing, with the lights out and the glasses shuddering at each distant explosion. Then, suddenly, it was right on top of us. I hardly remember what happened, because I didn't really see or hear anything. All I remember is spluttering for breath, in a night-club where many of the tables and chairs were splintered, with the whole room filled with an acrid dust. And somewhere beneath it all was Percy. None of us really knew about it until the word spread round next morning. It had seemed at the time as if we all had far more important things to think about than to check if those who had arrived with us were still alive and well.

The Nanny Marks tapes

Some of the air raids developed into really exciting parties. What was so nice about them was that you never knew when they were going to happen. You might be somewhere on the other side of London, having a quiet drink with a couple of friends, when the air-raid siren would go. And you didn't want to go out on the streets after that. There were many occasions when Lady Tillot had to telephone through to say that she'd been trapped in the house of some friend. But we didn't need to worry. We knew that she'd be enjoying herself. And she always turned up safe and sound the following morning.

I remember one occasion when she'd taken myself and the children along with her. It was a party to celebrate somebody's wedding. A friend of Lady Tillot's from pre-war days. He was home on leave and had just been introduced to one of the ladies at the Windmill Theatre. All kinds of different people met each other then. And they'd decided on the spur of the moment to get married. You had to do things on the spur of the moment or nothing would get done at all.

Well, it began as a wedding celebration, and then the air raid started. So the party went on until the early hours of the morning, with all kinds of extraordinary things happening. People were so reckless in those days. They didn't like to think about the air raid I suppose, so they took pills to make them feel better. But there were two kinds of pills. Some of them were to calm you down, and some of them were to pep you up. It didn't really matter which you took. In either case, you didn't bother any more about the air raid.

There was a lovely Russian gentleman at this party. Not a Communist, mind you. He'd been fighting against them when he was last in Russia. But he invented a beautiful game where all the grown-ups had to contribute a couple of pills. And these were placed into a hat. A couple of saccharine tablets was all I could contribute myself. Then we had to pick out a couple of 'sweeties', as he called them, while keeping our eyes shut. I felt so odd afterwards, as if everything had taken on velvety edges. But I certainly wasn't worried about the air raid any longer, although Lady Tillot assured me that I'd swallowed nothing worse than a pill for bad breath and a pill to make my kidneys work better.

Mind you, these air-raid encounters didn't always lead to such happy experiences. I remember Lady Tillot coming home one morning to tell me that she'd been cooped up all night in an air-raid shelter with my former employer, Mr Morgan. His wife had gone home to America when the war broke out, taking the two children with her; while he himself had moved south, from Manchester to London. They'd even made him a magistrate, which only goes to show how things had changed. Lady Tillot didn't like him at all, and I felt so ashamed that she now knew what he was like. But I explained how I'd only gone to that household because I'd been urged to do so by Colonel and Mrs Bagshot.

The awful thing is that he kept pestering Lady Tillot for months afterwards, sending her boxes of chocolates. Said he had no use for them himself, but he didn't like to waste what was due to him on his ration card. And Lady Tillot didn't like to discourage him, for she knew how the children enjoyed the chocolates. A real nuisance he became, calling at the house personally. And he tried to be ever so pally with me on the occasions we bumped into each other. I really don't know why.

I don't suppose that Lady Tillot would have borne his company for five minutes, if it hadn't been for the fact that the Sharpshooters were now posted to Scotland to finish their training. So there'd been a gap in her social life until she took up with the Americans.

By this time, the whole world we were living in seemed to have become topsy-turvy. It was no longer the right time to pause and think about what was happening to us. People came and people went. But the important thing was that Caldicott, and Luptree of course, remained waiting for the return of good sense. We had survived the deluge, and that was the main thing.

Excerpts from Lady Tillot's correspondence with Lord Tillot

Life down in the village is no longer what it was, ever since the Yanks arrived. I can't say that I admire the blemish to the park made by their conglomeration of hospital huts, but they are certainly infusing us all with new expectations from life. I notice this in particular because the younger women at my Women's Institute gatherings are increasingly noticeable as absentees. And gossip is rife in the village about young Miss So-and-So or This-and-That being seen down in Froome on the arm of some GI, with her face 'all painted up like a hussy'. Do you think they used to say such things about me, darling, in the years before the war? Somehow I don't think they did. It's just that their own daughters are doing it now, which strikes them as being so terrible.

Fred Thatcher's daughter, Valerie, was the centre of one such rumpus. Apparently she turned up at the Froome Arms with a convalescent sergeant in the marines, who displayed his largesse in buying drinks for every pretty girl who happened to be present in the pub, until the local yokels would stand for it no more. A fight broke out and young Valerie is now regarded at Luptree's scarlet woman.

They are really rather charming, some of these Americans, and I see quite a lot of them now that Mr Thompson has rented out the shooting to them. They meet each Saturday. But they're nothing like the shooting parties we held before the war. With so many of the guns being army doctors and surgeons, the conversation tends to have a medical ring about it, with talk about a pheasant coming so low that they got a squint at its tonsils, or that the one that got away would need its fallopian tubes repaired before next nesting season.

It does seem a most curious coincidence that Colonel Ford, who is in charge of this hospital, is the son of that Texan Mr Ford, in whose house you were staying when your father was trying to keep us from marrying. I'm afraid he doesn't have such pleasant memories about you as you might hope. He keeps hinting that you took advantage of his sister, and that this was regarded locally as an invasion of Texan territory by the British Empire. He goes on to laugh about it, because he sees what is now taking place as the settling of old scores. I suppose he's talking about life down in the village, darling.

I find that I am worrying about you, just because they seem to be holding you in reserve. I keep on asking myself what terrible future battle they may be preparing for you. The campaign in Italy sounds to be so slow in comparison with the way you all swept across the desert in pursuit of Rommel. I keep imagining that, in desperation, the Allies may take some frightening gamble, and that yours will be one of the lives with which they'll be playing. So take care of yourself, both for my sake and for that of the children.

Sometimes I feel so guilty that we are not having a more miserable time of it, back here on the Home Front. I feel as if I'm building up to some terrible period of retribution against myself, when it will be my turn to suffer, instead of yours. And you do realize, darling, that it would make me suffer most hideously if you did get yourself killed? I promise you that with all my heart.

The Sixth Marquess of Froome, interviewed by Mr Simon Manasseh

Q: Did you ever feel worried that, by the time you returned home, the family scene that you once had known might have disintegrated?

A: Not fully, I didn't. Maybe I wasn't quite astute enough. But I got a bit of a presentiment in the change of tone in some of the letters Chloe sent to me. The later ones, that is to say. They weren't quite the same as they were at the start. I had a shrewd suspicion, by the start of the Italian campaign, that something fishy might be going on.

Author's narrative

Mr Walter Davis spoke of his own relationship with Lord Tillot, while he was serving as his batman in the Wessex Yeomanry during the North African campaign.

'It was a rum situation, I can tell you that. I'd had the world of respect for Lord and Lady Tillot ever since I'd gone to work for them at Caldicott. But army life is different, as you probably know. Some of my muckers didn't care two hoots about aristocracy and all that. Some of them didn't even come from Wessex. They'd been drafted in from London or the Midlands, because they had the right skills in mechanics or whatever. And you should have heard their comments about those of us who weren't prepared to stick up for our rights against any of those bleeding officers, as they were called – only the words they used were often a lot worse than that.

'I suppose it got me down in the end. I didn't want to give them the impression that I was some kind of servile creep, running to fetch His Lordship's map, or His Lordship's shaving water, at a mere clap of his hands. And he tried to be as strict as ever, you know. Seemed to think that the war made no difference in the way we ought to relate to one another.

'The truth is that I got a bit stroppy with him at times. Answered him back. Told him one or two of the comments that had come to my ears from the rank and file: that he was going to be the regiment's first casualty when we finally went into battle, for example. But it wouldn't be from an enemy bullet. It would be a bullet from behind, fired by one of his own men. Oh, he didn't like that one, I can tell you.'

Mr Davis paused here to chuckle softly, partly in amusement at his own nerve, and partly in affection for his former employer, whom he had thus so grossly offended. 'Well, it was the kind of situation which couldn't last,' he continued. 'A few days after that particular row, Lord Tillot called me into his tent and told me that he was returning me to other duties in the squadron. It was all quite friendly, mind you. He didn't throw the book at me for inciting a mutiny or anything like that. But we'd had enough of one another for the time being, and we both knew it.

'Mind you, that wasn't the last I saw of him. But I was soon transferred to another squadron; so, after that, it was only rarely that I clapped eyes on him. He had a reputation for being too much of a text-book soldier: fine on the parade ground, but never knowing quite enough about the men who served under him. I mean, not enough to command their loyalties in battle.

'But he did well enough when it came to El Alamein. And in Italy too. All of his tank crew copped it at Anzio, though Lord Tillot managed to scramble out alive. Wounded, but alive. And that was the last I heard of him for the remainder of the war, because he left the Yeomanry shortly after that.

'The day I quarrelled with him must have been my lucky day. I'd have been in that tank with him, serving as his gunner if I'd remained with him as batman. Poor old Nobby Carter got the job after me. But poor old Nobby is lying out there in the military cemetery at Anzio, whereas I'm here drinking with you at The Hop and Grape. And that's all the difference in the world.'

7

A Crack of the Whip

1943–5

The Nanny Marks tapes

I think it was Bruce more than anyone else who got upset when the news came through that Lord Tillot had been wounded at Anzio. He had gone into battle at the head of his squadron, where the tank had been blown up from under him. Got a piece of shrapnel in the chest which, mercifully, put him into office duties for the rest of the war. Saved him from having to take any part in D-Day or the campaign in France.

But the whole idea of his father being so near to death moved Bruce deeply. He seemed to think it was because none of us had been attending church during these past few years. (I've never been much of a churchgoer myself.) After this had happened there was no stopping him. Every Sunday, for five Sundays running, we had to traipse down to the village church and pray that his father might be saved. The poor vicar was so surprised to see us there, looked at us as if we were ghosts. But it may have done the trick, because Lord Tillot recovered from his wounds.

Of course, there was great excitement at Luptree when the boat brought him home. It was what they had all been waiting for. And Lady Tillot was very happy as well, although it had been a bit unexpected, if you see what I mean.

I'm afraid that Sebastian's first reaction, when Lord Tillot came up to see him, was to dive beneath the bedclothes. He could hardly remember his father, you see. And he wouldn't come out again, no matter how hard we coaxed him.

Lord Tillot's homecoming was quite a milestone in our lives at Caldicott Manor. We were over the top, and the rest of the way was all downhill. Yet, from another point of view, everything had been terribly mixed up during his absence. And it was now that we began to realize how difficult things had become.

I think he may have been upset at the way everything at Caldicott had become slack while he'd been away. Nothing in particular, but everything. There was Mr Hodges, for example. In the days before the war, he'd been expected to do little more than to come in twice a week and clean the silver. But, with all the rest of the staff called up for active service, he'd been required to take on some additional duties: seeding the garden and keeping the Bentley in working order. But he hadn't taken much trouble about these things. And some kind of a row was inevitable, once Lord Tillot had come home.

Yet, if the full story is to be told, I'm afraid the situation was more complicated than that. You see, Mr Hodges had been excused from military service because he had a collapsed lung. But, in some ways, he'd taken advantage of this illness. I mean, it wasn't exactly right that he should have gone round the village, accompanying the wives of all the people who had gone up to the front. I suppose, in a way, you might call it treacherous.

I think Lord Tillot may have disapproved of some of the things that had been going on. So he decided to give Mr Hodges the sack. And there was some bad feeling locally. They said that Lord Tillot was just trying to get a bad taste out of his own mouth. But this was a cruel thing to say. Lord Tillot was upset that the herbaceous border had turned into a chicken run. And he found a nest of mice in the Bentley's upholstery, which made him feel that Mr Hodges had been neglecting his duties. Lord Tillot liked things to be perfect, you see.

Yet I think it's just possible there may have been the smallest grain of truth in what they were saying down in the village. You see, things had been coming to a head between

Lord and Lady Tillot.

One of the first things to happen was that another of those boxes of chocolates arrived from Mr Morgan. And Lord Tillot wanted to know why he was sending them. Lady Tillot asked me to confirm that she was fed up with Mr Morgan's attentions and would like it greatly if he could be persuaded to leave her in peace.

Unfortunately, Mr Morgan happened to telephone at this moment. I suppose he wanted to inquire if his chocolates had arrived safely. But it was Lord Tillot who happened to answer the phone, and he was in rather a bad mood. I think he said something about Mr Morgan being a nasty common little man, and that he ought to keep his sticky little fingers for sticky little women. And then he rang off.

That was the last we heard of Mr Morgan, but then a more serious incident occurred – although it was rather funny in some ways. You see, there'd been an officer at the American Hospital called Major Giovanni. He was a rather stout gentleman who was generally smoking a cigar. But the rest of the officers used to joke about the way he regarded himself as some kind of a Don Juan.

Well, this Major Giovanni had been to the house on several occasions. Not at the usual times, and not in the usual manner. I think he liked to play games with Lady Tillot, hiding in the bushes and calling up to her bedroom window. I would have minded my own business if I hadn't heard someone calling 'Baby!' one night. I thought it might be something about Sebastian. But I looked outside and saw Major Giovanni by the light of the full moon, waving packets of nylons in the air, as if he were flourishing a pack of cards.

Well, Major Giovanni had been sent home to the States on leave and had only just got back, so he didn't know anything about Lord Tillot's return from Italy. And I think the others may have neglected to tell him anything, because they rather enjoyed playing practical jokes on one another.

Anyway, a few nights after his leave had ended, he turned up at Caldicott, long after midnight. And there was a poem he would sometimes recite, because it seemed to make Lady Tillot laugh. You know the one. It begins, 'The Owl and the

Pussycat went to sea, in a beautiful pea-green boat.' Only, when he recited it, he filled it out with a whole lot of miaowing and tu-whit-tu-whooing, to make it sound more funny, I suppose.

What he didn't know was that on this occasion Lord Tillot was going to open the door, to inquire what he wanted. I couldn't help feeling sorry for the poor gentleman. He must have felt so foolish under the circumstances. And he couldn't very well offer Lord Tillot the nylons which were bulging from his pockets. I could hear him stammering something about getting lost in the dark – or about his cat getting lost. And that's the last time he appeared at Caldicott.

Mind you, I felt sorry for Lord Tillot too. He might easily have got the wrong impression about the kind of things that had been going on at Caldicott. And I know he was upset at the way in which his wine cellar had been drunk dry by a whole lot of Sharpshooters whom he'd never met – or whom he was now having to meet for the first time.

I'm afraid that Sebastian came out with one or two remarks that might have been better left unsaid. Not that he understood what he was saying, poor little fellow. He was just trying to be funny, I suppose. But he kept on making remarks about 'Mummy's new boyfriends', even after Lady Tillot had tried to explain that such remarks were liable to make his father unhappy.

Excerpt from Lady Tillot's correspondence with Lord Tillot

My very dearest Edward,

I avoid writing 'darling' because I fear that, in your present mood, you would accuse me of insincerity, unjustified though such an accusation would be. But I feel the need to write this letter to you (and I wish it to be a tender communication), now that all the anguish of your homecoming is safely behind us.

I swear to you that I never intended, at any time, that you should be hurt. I never planned that these things should happen. They merely stand in evidence of what *does* happen.

when two such loving hearts (as indeed we were) become separated by the aberrant misfortunes of our generation.

I still love you, my Powkie, as much as ever I did before. Surely it's not necessary for us to keep reminding ourselves of all the silly little things which took place at Caldicott while you were away. They didn't mean anything. Or hardly any of them did. Well Billy Minehead meant a little to me, perhaps. But I promise that I'll never see him again, if you would feel happier that way.

The Nanny Marks tapes

It seemed to be very difficult, now that Lord Tillot had come home, to recover any of the family feeling that had existed before the war. Lord and Lady Tillot had learnt by now to steer their own courses in life. The togetherness had disappeared.

I think they had both changed. Lord Tillot certainly had. Before the war, I'd always felt that the person who really took the decisions was Lady Tillot. But now things were different. You could feel that Lord Tillot had decided to crack the whip, as it were. He became very firm about everything. Wasn't prepared to stand any nonsense.

This went for the children as well. He kept saying that discipline had gone to pot while he was away. Not that he blamed me for this, so much as Lady Tillot. Yet it wasn't really fair for him to say such things. We'd certainly been doing our best.

It was the two boys that he tried to take in hand. But that didn't prevent Bruce from being delighted to have his father back home again. He had developed a new kind of hero worship for him while he was away, especially after he'd been awarded the Military Cross. And, now that his father was back home with us, Bruce wanted to hear about all his war adventures down to the last detail. Oh, he was really quite bloodthirsty. Lord Tillot was totally unable to satisfy his curiosity. He had to invent stories about hand-to-hand fighting in order to keep him contented.

With Sebastian, the whole situation was rather more tricky. He remained curiously detached. I suppose he'd grown accustomed to the idea of not having a father. Never really wanted one now that Lord Tillot had returned. And he could be very wilful when he chose.

I remember one occasion when we all had to stay in some hotel in York, to attend the wedding of one of Lady Ulrica's girls. Sebastian was supposed to be a page. But he decided at the last moment that he didn't like the clothes that had been laid out for him. Locked himself in a bathroom and refused to come out, for love or money. There was nothing that could persuade him any different. So we had to call in the hotel carpenter. But, by this time, Sebastian had decided to unlock the door; so, when the carpenter arrived, we found him sitting there as good as gold, looking out of the window and counting the pigeons. It made us appear so silly, as if we'd made a mistake about his locking the door in the first place.

Sebastian got into such trouble at the reception. He must have gone round sipping wine from other people's glasses when I wasn't keeping my eye on him. And Lady Beatrice observed what he was up to. But, when she tried to tell him off, he did nothing but giggle. Sent home in disgrace, he was. But then he hadn't wanted to go to the wedding in the first place.

Mind you, he had his brighter days when things went right for him. In fact, he became quite famous all of a sudden. Got his name in the papers. And all because of something he didn't mean to happen.

It was the fault of Mrs Potts really. She should have been minding her own business in the kitchen, instead of trying to win over little Sebastian. You see, Lord Tillot had just bought a new dinghy for the pond at Caldicott. And he'd been teaching Sebastian how to row in it. But Sebastian had been told that he couldn't use it when he was alone. So he invited Mrs Potts to get in the boat with him. But just as she was stepping down into it, Sebastian started to row. And the silly woman fell in!

It would have been all right if she could swim. But she couldn't. And Sebastian hadn't learnt to swim either. But he did the right thing. He wound the chain of the boat round her waist and went to find the gardener. Got to her just in time, they did. She was almost dead from cold and she'd lost her false teeth at the bottom of the pond. But it was all loving endearments when the reporters rang up. She told them she'd bless little Sebastian until her dying day. Saved her life, that's what he'd done. And they made a big splash of it in the papers.

Bruce didn't like this, you know. I'm afraid he was jealous. He seemed to think that Sebastian ought to be punished for dropping Mrs Potts into the water. Instead of that, he was receiving fan mail from a lot of old ladies who regarded him as some kind of hero.

The truth is that Lord Tillot had a greater admiration for Sebastian at that time. He liked the little rebel in him. 'Obstinate little brat, gutty as hell!' was his way of describing him. Bruce was too earnest in his desire to be perfect. And perhaps this made him a trifle arrogant. 'He needs taking down a peg or two,' I used to hear his father say.

It was Lady Tillot who was Bruce's champion. I think she sensed that his father was being a trifle hard on him. And she may have felt that her own situation was similar in certain ways.

Author's narrative

During my interview with Lady Beatrice, I inquired whether her brother had displayed any signs of distress on his return from Italy.

She replied, 'Not noticeably. He probably realized then that his marriage wasn't going to last. But he tried to make a go of it, tried to pretend that none of those episodes had ever taken place. But if they happened, they happened. And that's all there was to be said about it.

'I think that Edward was far more upset about the children's behaviour. He'd always been strict with them, in the years before the war, hoping that they would grow up to be well mannered and polite. But they'd run wild in his absence.

And that was Chloe's fault. You can't teach children to grow up with any sense of decorum, if you don't practise some sense of decorum yourself. But, if it comes to that, the Trehearne blood has always been a bit wild. Edward should have perceived that, right from the start. Chloe could never have made anyone a good wife, nor a good mother. A leopard never changes its spots.

'That little Sebastian: he was a Trehearne if ever there was one. I could have predicted even then that he would come to no good. They sometimes ask in my newspaper where all this delinquency of the younger generation started. Well, I can answer that one. It started with children like Sebastian. I don't know where he learnt his practices. But he wouldn't have had far to look, if it was a question of needing some example to follow.'

I inquired whether she had any particular instances of Sebastian's delinquent behaviour in mind.

She replied, 'I could give you a whole list if I'd a mind to. Many of them petty enough in their own way, like frightening the living daylights out of old Mrs Marsh while she was strolling down Caldicott Lane. He thought he was Tarzan or something. Dropped out of a tree on her and threatened to chop off her head with a wooden sword. She went to see the village constable about that one. But Nanny Marks managed to persuade everyone that it was a harmless piece of fun.

'Where I really took objection was at his sexual precocity. There were occasions when I felt embarrassed at having to admit that he was my nephew. At weddings, for example, when children are supposed to be on their best behaviour. It wasn't as if he'd yet gone to school, so the responsibility for his upbringing must be laid well and truly at Chloe's doorstep.

'I've never been so embarrassed in my entire life as when a very good friend of mine, who shall remain nameless, came up to me at this wedding with a complaint that my nephew had been *showing things* to her little girl. In my day women weren't *shown things* until they were married. And a lot less trouble they got into that way, too.'

*

inquired of Mrs Potts whether she had any particular affection for the Tillot children.

She replied, 'They were bleedin' little perishers for the most part. Not a bit like their mother, of course. Or not when it came to gaiety. None of her go-out-and-amuse-yourself spirit.

'Camilla would spend most of her time in what had once been the school room. She read books or played the gramophone, and all that kind of thing. But she never once came into the kitchen to give me a hand with the cooking. They'd been brought up to think that they were above all that sort of thing. Not by Lady Tillot, but by Nanny Marks. Oh, she was a right snob, that Nanny. And it brushed off on them. Not that they could help it, the poor little dears.

'That Bruce: now he was the worst. Had that toffee-nosed look about him that made it seem as if he was doing you a favour to reply to your "Good morning". I can remember when he was still quite small, and I asked him what he was going to be when he grew up. You'll never guess what he replied. He said, "I'm going to be the Marquess of Froome." Served me right for asking such a silly question, as if the likes of him were going to tell me that he'd like to be an engine driver!

'Oh, I'd a soft spot for young Sebastian, I'll have to admit. But then he saved my life. Mind you, he wouldn't have needed to, if he hadn't dropped me into the pond in the first place. But I'll give him his due. He was a plucky little youngster, even if a mite too cheeky at times. I took some lip from him that I wouldn't have taken from any of the others. And, when I found that someone had been getting up at night to scoff whatever remained of the household's meat ration for that week, I'd let him get away with it – even if he did have the nerve to suggest that it was my poor cats who had done it. They'd have been bloody circus cats by then, if they were opening fridges and the like.

Excerpt from the personal manuscript of the
Hon. Bruce Tillot

Now that I am a prefect, it is time for me to understand why I am so highly regarded. On the other hand, I have always been highly regarded. So there may be nothing unusual for me to understand.

The Tillot family has always been held in high regard. I say 'always' because it must in any case have been for a very long time. Sir John Tillot was the first to become a Knight. This was because he was very clever at finding monasteries which King Henry VIII could dissolve. But he also took some of the money for himself. It was Sir John Tillot who built Luptree Court. But he only did this after Henry VIII had died. If he had built it any earlier, he would have had his head chopped off, because one wasn't allowed to be any wealthier than the King.

Many of my ancestors who were descended from Sir John Tillot have also been politicians. Some of them were quite important. Sir Thomas Tillot wasn't really a good politician, because he was hoping Monmouth would be made King when Charles II died. But Charles II didn't like that, because he thought it would be fairer if his brother James became King instead of Monmouth. This is because Monmouth's mother hadn't married him.

To make sure that James would become King, Charles arranged for someone to murder Sir Thomas Tillot when he was driving away from St James's Palace in his coach. Of course, he didn't admit to doing this because the people would have been very angry. He hanged somebody else for it instead. But the rest of the Tillot family decided not to be angry because Charles II agreed to bury Sir Thomas in Westminster Abbey, which was a great honour. And they were turned into Lords, because they didn't make any fuss about the murder.

After that, they were always good politicians and did what the Kings wanted them to do. So they were turned into Marquesses, instead of just being Lords. The Kings used to drop in to shoot pheasants, whenever they happened to be passing by. It was all very friendly. So the Marquesses were turned into Cabinet Ministers, which is rather like being a prefect, I imagine, although it's more important, because it's not just at school.

I intend to be a Cabinet Minister when I grow up. I doubt if I'll become Prime Minister because the Tillot family has never produced any Prime Ministers. But I think I'll be a good Cabinet Minister, because I'll always do what the King wants me to do, which will be the same as God wants me to do.

What is wrong with the world today is that we are forgetting to think about God. When I become a Cabinet Minister, I'll try to change all that. God is more important than me. God is more important than all of us. Yet, because the Tillot family is more important than most other families, I must do my duty in getting people to see and do what is right.

Excerpts from Lady Tillot's correspondence with Lord Tillot

Bruce really is extraordinary. He seems to have been bitten by the religious bug. His letters to me sometimes contain hymns, written by himself, with instructions how they should be sung. The verse below is to be sung to the tune of 'There is a green hill far away'.

> I love this world of good and ill,
> Though evil through it stray,
> But God will make it good, He will,
> If all of us will pray.

I tried it out this morning, tra-la-ing away in my bath. I got into such fits of laughter that my bottom slipped on the soap, and I went under the water. I'm sure it was God punishing me for my irreverence.

Listen darling: Billy has written to me to say that he is due for a spell of leave back in England. And he has asked me most pointedly if he could come down to Caldicott, just to get accustomed to the idea that you have me, whereas he does not.

You know that he doesn't mean all that much to me any more. And we both know that you have your other ladies, just as much as I (occasionally) have my other men. So wouldn't it be sensible to get this little bit of the past into better perspective? Of course, I'll understand if you say no, but I can't help feeling that the right decision will be to say yes.

The Nanny Marks tapes

I'm afraid there was the most terrible trouble when Lord Minehead came home on leave from the campaign in Normandy. Perhaps it was a mistake on the part of Lady Tillot to invite him down to Caldicott Manor for the weekend.

Lord Tillot and Lord Minehead were playing backgammon, and the amount they were playing for had risen rather too high. But Lord Minehead said he'd accept Lady Tillot instead of the sum of money that would otherwise have been down on the table. So they continued with the game on that basis: though, if the truth were known, I think that Lord Tillot had agreed to it purely in fun.

Everything might have been all right if Lord Minehead had not won. But I'm afraid he *did* win. And then there was the most terrible scene. Lord Tillot seemed to think they'd only been discussing the right to accompany Lady Tillot for one particular evening; whereas Lord Minehead insisted that it was for as long as he pleased. They became dreadfully angry, calling each other such awful names that Lady Tillot sent the children upstairs to the nursery.

It was so embarrassing for everyone, you know. Lord Minehead packed his things immediately and phoned for a taxi to drive him to the station. He said he would wait there until Lady Tillot joined him. But she was the one person they hadn't consulted during their quarrel. And it turned out that she didn't really want to leave with Lord Minehead after all. So the taxi driver had to go back to the station, and deliver him a letter from Lady Tillot.

The Sixth Marquess of Froome, interviewed by Mr Simon Manasseh

Q: Did you hold Lord Minehead responsible for the collapse of your marriage to Chloe Trehearne?

A: Our marriage was a casualty of the war, like many another. But Minehead had something to do with it of course, even if Chloe did have other fish to fry. But you may be right in supposing that I resented Minehead's behaviour, more than that of any of the others.

Q: In what way?

A: He was no gentleman. I can't help it if he happened to be a Lord. He was no gentleman.

Q: You are referring, perhaps, to the manner he conducted a game of backgammon with you?

A: Well yes, if you insist in sticking your nose into such private matters. Any gentleman would know when a game has become a farce. If you're really gambling, you don't go betting your wife as part of the stake. Or, if you do, you accept that there isn't a real game in process. You're sharing a joke. And a gentleman knows how to share a joke, whereas the *hoi polloi* do not. I discovered that particular evening that Minehead was just one of *them*.

Excerpt from Lady Tillot's correspondence with Lord Tillot

What can I say? It is all so utterly absurd, and so unlike Billy to take such action. I fear you must have offended his pride, even before this terrible game had started, by telling him that it was *common* to carry a comb in his pocket. Don't you feel that another set of values is creeping up on us nowadays? And surely it must be preferable if people like Billy take the plunge by doing these things? I know that you always look impeccable, but the day may come when you *want* to whip out a comb and tidy your hair, in private of course. But it will be that much easier for you to *decide* to have that comb in your pocket, if men like Billy are facing up to the problem already.

I doubt if Billy really intends to go through with his threat to get you thrown out of White's Club, because it would make him look so silly, for one thing. And it would hardly be sufficient compensation for him to know that it would be making you look pretty silly too. If I were you, I'd just ignore the whole business. These things blow over as a rule.

The Nanny Marks tapes

Lord Minehead managed to get Lord Tillot banned from White's Club for failing to pay his gambling debts. Or they asked him to resign, which amounted to the same thing. There was no mention of Lady Tillot, mind you. Yet the money involved was quite considerable, I believe. And it upset Lord Tillot enormously. Before the war, he'd spent a great deal of his time at White's Club: drinking, or playing backgammon with his friends. But he had to give up all this now that Lord Minehead had become so unreasonable. And it meant that he didn't see so much of his former friends.

Excerpt from Lady Tillot's correspondence with Lord Tillot

No Edward, I must protest. You are being most unfair. I *didn't* advise you to do nothing about it whatsoever. I merely suggested that you ought to put the matter to the back of your mind, for the sake of your own sanity, as much as for any other reason. I suppose you do realize that you strike many people as being utterly irrational in most of your behaviour. I say this for your own good. I'm really not trying to defend myself, because I simply don't think that I have done anything which *needs* to be defended.

The Nanny Marks tapes

This episode was the last nail in the coffin as far as Lord Tillot's marriage was concerned. Things had been going from bad to worse, ever since his return from Italy. And now he seemed to be blaming Lady Tillot for the way his name had been dragged in the mud over these backgammon debts. Some of their rows were a distress to hear. It was best for both of them, really, when Lady Tillot decided to move into the house in Jermyn Street. She seldom came down to Caldicott again.

This was tragic for the children. Of course, they used to go and stay with their mother whenever they went up to London. But this wasn't as frequently as they might have liked. And it was Bruce who was getting really isolated. He had always been so dependent on Camilla in the past. Yet now she was acquiring friends of her own age and had little time for her younger brothers.

I don't know, there were moments when I felt that we were all animals in a circus. We'd been going round doing a general act for everyone, when suddenly the ringmaster had arrived and everything had changed. At the crack of his whip, we'd separated out into individual acts. I think I was the only one who remained trying to keep in an act with everyone else. If I hadn't been there, I don't know what would have held us all together.

Excerpt from Lady Tillot's correspondence with Lord Tillot

Of course I am capable of living apart from you, if that is what you really want – though I wish you weren't so hypocritical as to pretend that it's because of my affair with Billy. That died a natural death more than two years ago.

I know what's really the matter with you. You're in the clutches of all those tarts, who allow you to think that you're a martyr at my hands. Well, good luck to you! If that's what you *want* to think, then nobody is standing in your way. -

8

A Weasel at the Door

1945–8

Author's narrative

The post-war era began with Mr Attlee's Socialist government. Mr Churchill's appeal to the electorate 'to help him finish the job' had been ignored. Conservatives took what comfort was available in blaming the new government for the inevitable austerity.

According to Nanny Marks, you could see the government were up to no good just by looking at them: 'There was Sir Stafford Cripps, who was always grimacing as if he'd sucked a lemon. And, as for Mr Attlee himself, his picture reminded me of those children's books in which the villain is a weasel. If I'd seen him coming down the road, I'd have picked up my children in a jiffy and scurried back to my rabbit hole.'

It was also the period when the pound was first devalued, when the Empire began to crumble with the loss of India, and when Mr Nye Bevan described the British upper classes as being little better than vermin.

The Sixth Marquess of Froome, interviewed by Mr Simon Manasseh

Q: Did your experience of the war change you in any way?
A: You mean, did it change the way I thought about life? Well, I suppose it did. For one thing, I learnt respect for the Germans. I didn't have it at the start. I thought they

were a load of old Krauts who took life far too seriously
and all that kind of thing. But the more we'd battered
away at them, the more they'd dug themselves in and
battered us back. And they were methodical about it too.
Far more so than our own boys, who were always
grumbling and grousing. The Germans had come to do a
job, and then they got on with it.

I never had any active service after I was wounded at
Anzio. But, in the closing stages of the war, I was sent to
act as a liaison officer between the British and American
forces, to sort out some of the administrative problems.
Well, I was talking with an American colonel in the mess
one morning, and I'll never forget his words. He said,
'Take a look around you. Look at their farms. Do you see
any of the filth that you'd find back home? I can tell you
this, Major. We're in the process of destroying one of the
finest races that ever lived on this earth.'

I saw quite a lot of this colonel during the weeks which
followed. And quite a few of his remarks lodged somewhere deep in the back of my mind. I would argue like
hell with him, at the time – just as much as all the rest of
us did. We called him a Kraut-lover, a Fascist, and all the
rest. But he stuck to his guns, and there was a lot of truth
in all that he said. I got to thinking about it afterwards.

Q: Are you trying to tell me that, during the closing weeks of
the war, you were actually converted to Fascism?

A: Well, that would be putting it too strongly. But I became
interested in these matters. I read *Mein Kampf* – in English of course. And blow me down if I didn't discover
that I rather admired Adolf Hitler.

Q: What was it precisely that you found yourself able to
admire in him?

A: His sheer guts, I suppose. After all, he took on the whole
damn world in a war, and came within an inch of winning it.

Q: Do you defend his methods?

A: Oh, he was ruthless, I'll admit that. But it takes guts to be
ruthless. Who else would have dared to send millions of
Jews to the gas chambers?

Q: Are you now arguing in defence of his anti-Semitism?

A: Well, between you, me and the bedpost, none of us has ever greatly admired the Jews. They've got in everyone's way, since time immemorial. But nobody dared do anything about it. Or not until Hitler came along.

Q: Would it trouble you greatly to know that I am one hundred per cent Jewish, despite the fact that I am an American citizen?

A: You? No, come off it! You're kidding me. No, well I see you're not. But don't get me wrong. I've known some delightful Jews. Our cook was Jewish, just before the war. She cooked really splendidly. I signed some papers that would help her get into Israel.

Q: Apart from the anti-Semitism, were there other parts of Hitler's philosophy which you admired?

A: No, it wasn't the anti-Semitism. It was the efficiency. The drive. All that getting down to brass tacks on how to set the world moving again. And, believe me, when I came back from the war, my whole household was in a mess. It needed a strong arm to sort things out properly. I dare say it's true that I learnt something from Hitler: but, as a philosopher, far more than as a politician.

Q: Are you saying that you endorse Fascism as a philosophy?

A: It isn't too bad a philosophy. At that time, it was the only answer that anyone had thought up to Communism. If it was going to be a Communist world, or a Fascist world, then I knew which side I wanted to support. Certainly not the side of the proletariat. I can assure you of that.

Q: Did you see Communism as an imminent threat to post-war Britain?

A: They'd voted in a Socialist government. And not for the first time, damn it. We had to watch our step, or we'd have landed up in the soup. All those demobilized soldiers no longer thought like any of the old-timers. The hedgecutters on the Luptree Estate, for example. Once I found a couple of them just sitting there, bone idle. But, when I shouted at them, they answered me back. Asked me how I expected them to get on with their work, when I supplied them with leather gloves which were full of holes. This made my blood boil. I told them that, since they'd put in a government which was taking all my money away from me, then they'd have to put up with the gloves I could afford to buy them. They could lump it and like it – or collect their cards, and clear off.

The Nanny Marks tapes

Some people knew how to read the signs and decided to leave England while the going was good. My youngest sister Lottie, for example. She and her husband had been corresponding with Meg, who had gone to settle in New Zealand long ago. And now they decided to follow her. They had a couple of grown-up children, and the whole family wanted to make a new start of it in Meg's home town.

I was sad in a way. What with Bess and Jack being dead, it meant that I was the only one to remain in England. But then my situation was different. I couldn't think of leaving my children, you see.

Another person emigrated from England around this time. Oh, you'll never guess! It was Miss Kronenberg, the mad old Czech woman who was our cook during the early part of the war. She wrote to Lord Tillot asking for a character reference. Wanted him to sign something to say she'd been a practising Jew during the time she was at Caldicott Manor. She was going to Israel, you see. Lord Tillot signed everything she asked. Said that, if they wanted her, they could have her; and that it was probably a Jewish plot to drive out the Arabs!

But then, if some were leaving, just a few of the old staff were coming back. Walter and Mr Perkins, for example. Walter had been such an unpretentious young man before the war, but he'd now become what you might call an old soldier. Thought he knew all the answers to everything. And I'm afraid Lord Tillot encouraged him in this. There was a feeling that they were two old comrades returning arm in arm from the wars to sort out everything that had been happening at home. That was the spirit of these days, you see. Only it wasn't too nice to feel that we were things they had to get sorted out.

Author's narrative

I inquired of Mr Walter Davis if he had found it easy to apply to Lord Tillot to have his old job back at the end of the war, since they had been getting on so badly in North Africa.

He said, 'I regarded it as my right, to tell the truth. We weren't going to have any of that unemployment which followed on from the First World War. There'd have been a revolution if they'd tried that one on us. We knew our rights and we asked for them. Not that I'm saying it wasn't embarrassing.

'What I did was to write to my old pal Gordon Perkins, who'd been the chauffeur at Caldicott until he joined up in the Service Corps. Then we wrote a joint letter to Lord Tillot, asking if we could come over for a talk about getting our jobs back. And, as it turned out, all ran smoothly.

He took each one of us aside to have a word in our ears. The gist of what he said to me was that it would be best to let bygones be bygones and start afresh, or rather from the point where we'd left off when the war started. But, of course, it could never be quite like that. War is bound to change things. It makes people see each other in a different light. When they are thrown together like that and have to react under a different kind of situation. It was impossible to see them, afterwards, as what you'd supposed them to be before.

'Not that it made all that much difference in most ways. But I wasn't going to touch my forelock any longer. For one thing, as you see, I'd grown a bit thin up on top. I didn't have much of a forelock to touch. But I didn't jump to answer that bell quite so fast as I might once have done. And he didn't expect me to either.'

The Nanny Marks tapes

Lord Tillot felt that something had to be done to get the Tillot family back on its feet again. Since he reasoned that the main trouble was that discipline had been slack, he told Walter there must be a taste of army life at Caldicott.

Then Walter would strut round the house puffing his chest out like a little bantam cock. Snapping out orders which he expected Bruce and Sebastian to obey. It was terrible really that he was allowed to carry on like that. Not at all how servants used to behave in the old days. But times were different.

Sebastian didn't seem to mind the new discipline so much as Bruce. Sebastian just treated it as an excuse for a little horse-play; he pretended he wasn't going to do as he'd been told, and then Walter would get hold of him and wrestle him to the ground. It was all one big game as far as Sebastian was concerned.

Bruce felt more sensitive on the issue. I suppose he remembered how things had been different before the war. He withdrew from everyone, tried to keep himself aloof. But Walter wasn't going to let him escape just like that. He started jeering at him, telling him that his father thought him gutless. And I think this may have wounded Bruce deeply, because he always cared so much about the way Lord Tillot thought about him.

Then one day I came round a corner in the garden to find Walter bullying Bruce most terribly. He had him down on the lawn and was twisting his foot so it was somewhere way up in the middle of his back. And Bruce was crying out that he'd do whatever Walter wanted of him.

Oh, I was so furious! Walter just stood there with a sullen expression on his face, saying that he had to run this house as Lord Tillot wanted it to be run. I told him he could get *me* down on the ground and twist *my* foot if he liked. But I wasn't going to stand by and watch him do such things to Bruce.

Author's narrative

I asked Mr Davis what he thought of Lord Tillot's children.

'I was under instructions from Lord Tillot to put a little character into them. There'd been too much women's influence in their lives, from Nanny Marks and the like. He feared they might become namby-pamby and molly-coddled. "Treat 'em rough, and they'll grow up tall and strong." That was Lord Tillot's motto. It was the same with the trees in his forests. He didn't have any patience with them, if they couldn't show that they were fit to survive.

'Bruce was the trouble. He'd been around for a little too long before the war came and changed everything. He'd got all that hoity-toity stuff into his head and it wouldn't come out. He'd keep looking at you with a faintly supercilious air, as if he were accusing you of not keeping to your station in life; though he knew full well that he was on his own now in any of that kind of talk. He was the one that was truly isolated from the family, quite as much as Lady Tillot, I dare say. Yet, while he was living in our midst, we had to roll him in the mud a bit, just to make him see that he wasn't any different from the rest of us.'

The Nanny Marks tapes

Camilla had now left Mrs de Crespigny's school and had gone up to RADA. That's the place in London where all the most promising young actresses are taken on for their training. She was very keen on the idea at this time. And Mrs de Crespigny had *insisted* that she try for a place. She had the right kind of personality to get what she wanted out of life. And, if that was what she wanted, Lord Tillot felt it might be best not to interfere.

Bruce was at Eton now, while Sebastian had gone up to Ashdale. It's a pity that the two boys never quite overlapped at school. It might have assisted them to develop a closer friendship. But five years is a big gap. And they never quite bridged it.

It was sad for me that *all* of the children were now living away from home for three-quarters of the year. And there was less for me to do, of course. But I was one of the family, so there was no question of my going. Lord Tillot put me in this nice little cottage in Caldicott Lane and I've lived here ever since. There has always been plenty to keep me occupied. Lord Tillot would send over bundles of sheets or whatever needed mending. I like it here immensely. There's not many people have a Beatrix Potter cottage to live in, and I regard myself as lucky.

But Lord Tillot had his troubles, of course. I think he was upset at the way his marriage had gone wrong. And his irritation was apt to be worked out on the children.

It was Bruce in particular who managed to upset his father. 'The boy's got no gumption!' he said. And it was true in a way. Bruce was inclined to sit round the house doing nothing particular at all. He preferred his visits up to London, when he would stay with Lady Tillot. But they were only brief visits, and they left him a trifle moody.

His school work was suffering into the bargain. At any rate his first few reports from Eton were far from satisfactory. But Lord Tillot wasn't greatly worried about this. The way he looked at it was that Bruce had already shown that he could get good marks for his work. So this was just a bad patch and he was sure to recover.

There was more cause to be worried about Sebastian's reports from Ashdale. He'd never accustomed himself to any strenuous school work, and it didn't look as if he was going to take to it. Lord Tillot felt, even at this stage, that we were going to have trouble from him. 'The boy simply doesn't try.' I remember him saying. 'He could do twice as well as Bruce, if only he'd try.' But it was no use thinking that Sebastian was likely to pay much attention to those sort of remarks. He never did.

It wasn't that he didn't *like* his father. It was far more that he didn't *know* him very well. During the holidays, I'm sure that he spent far more time down here in the cottage with me than up at Caldicott. I was the person he really trusted, you see.

I remember one day he brought me over a lovely big cucumber as a present. It was wrong of me really to have accepted it. I ought to have known that he'd brought it over without his father's consent. But I certainly didn't foresee the fuss that all this would cause.

Mr Standish, the gardener, had been saving this cucumber for the horticultural show at Froome. And it seems that he was left without a suitable entry, now that it had disappeared. So he took his complaint to Lord Tillot, who made some inquiries. He questioned Bruce and Sebastian separately, and both of them denied any knowledge of it. Yet, when Bruce came to me and said something about the cucumber, I knew precisely what had happened and said so.

It wasn't that Sebastian had meant to *steal* the cucumber. I think he supposed that Lord Tillot would *want* me to have it. Yet, because he was a bit frightened of his father, he found himself saying the wrong thing. And then he found it difficult to correct himself. But I was hoping my explanation would put things right for him.

Unfortunately Lord Tillot didn't see things quite in the same light. He insisted that Sebastian had *lied* to him, and had stuck to his lie in spite of continual questioning. He remarked to me that Sebastian had a criminal character and that he'd come to no good if he went on like this. Lord Tillot was always one for taking judgements to extremes.

The only really warm relationship that he kept up in these days was with Camilla. He'd never been quite so harsh with her as he had with the two boys. I think he felt from the start that a daughter was a mother's concern, but the boys had to grow up in the manner that *he* wanted.

Author's narrative

Mrs Potts had a tale to contribute concerning this period of the family fortunes. It related to Camilla's burgeoning interest in the other sex. Or, to be more accurate, it related to the interest which the other sex was beginning to invest in the Hon. Camilla Tillot.

'No, she didn't have no boyfriends,' said Mrs Potts. 'Not
eal boyfriends. But there were those that would have liked it.
Mr Thompson's son was one of them. Gareth Thompson. We
never saw much of him, because he was brought up by Mr
Thompson's first wife, after they divorced. But there was the
odd occasion when he'd turn up.

'Anyway, this Gareth was a grown man by now. And he
was brought along to Caldicott Manor one night for dinner.
Not that it was intended. But Lord Tillot couldn't turn round
to Mr Thompson and say that he was no longer invited – just
because he had dropped in to say hello.

'There were several other guests, so he was lost in the
crowd. But not to us, he wasn't. Every time that Walter came
out with the dishes, I'd ask for the latest. How was Gareth
getting on with Camilla? (Because he'd been sat next to her.)
Had he managed to get his hand up her skirts? So Walter
started paying them some special attention.

'They'd gone through the subject of rugger. But that didn't
lead to much. Then he came back to say they were talking
about pigs. And Camilla was beginning to look all flirty with
her eyes. It was just a game with her. She wanted to see how it
worked. He was telling her that pigs made good pets. So
Camilla tells him that there's nothing she wants more in this
world than a pet pig! And for the next half-hour they just
gazed into each other's eyes, talking about pigs being nicer
than dogs, and dogs being nicer than cats, and cats being
nicer than canaries or goldfish. When Walter came in with
the final instalment (picked up at the keyhole no doubt), I felt
like dishing them up with pigswill instead of pudding.

'What took us all by surprise was Gareth turning up on the
doorstep a couple of mornings later with a present for
Camilla: the most beautiful little piglet I've ever seen, all pink
and black in little blotches. He said he'd been to ever such
trouble to find it for her. Pigs were still on the ration you
know.

'There were some red faces now, I can tell you. Camilla
made Nanny go down to say she was still having her bath.
So Lord Tillot had to go out and accept the gift. Then, after
he'd got rid of Gareth, he wanted Camilla to explain why

we'd got landed with a piglet and what we were going to do with it. And Camilla was trying to pretend that there must have been a misunderstanding – though she wasn't very good at pretending. So finally she blurts out that she'd told him that she wanted it as a pet, but she'd only been joking. So that settled it. Lord Tillot told Walter to take it away, and I was asked to cook roast piglet for the next batch of guests. Not that I ate any. I'm no cannibal!'

Excerpt from the personal manuscript of Bruce, Lord Tillot (This was written in his second year at Eton, shortly after the death of his grandfather.)

I am beginning to get used to Eton, although I still don't enjoy the fagging and the beatings-up. I see that it may be good for my character, however, provided that I keep at it long enough. When I first came here, I was disappointed to find myself so unimportant once again. It wasn't nearly such fun as being a prefect at Ashdale. But, when my tutor saw that I wasn't enjoying myself, and that I wasn't mixing with others very well, he helped me a lot by explaining that it is always more interesting to be a small fish in a big bowl, than to be a big fish in a small bowl.

I do understand what he meant. Eton is a very big bowl for any fish to be in, and I feel privileged to belong here. Provided that I work hard, I may become a big fish even in this bowl. Eventually, perhaps, I may even be elected to Pop, if I can become popular enough with the other boys. But it would be silly for me to become too ambitious at this stage of my career at Eton.

Now that I am a Lord, I think this will help me to become popular. Not that I am at all glad that Grandpa is dead. It was far too expensive. Yet, despite the fact that the other boys make jokes about my now being a Lord, I think they secretly think that it's something rather important for a person to be. So their jokes are quite friendly really.

Eton is the school where most of the really important people send their sons. Even some of the Socialists in the government today came from Eton. And, in any case, it is the Conservatives who really govern Britain, because we happen to be a country that doesn't like changing very fast. And the leaders of the Conservative Party nearly all came from Eton. So it is important for me to do well here at Eton, and to make plenty of friends, because these are the people who are going to really matter in my life.

I doubt if the Socialists will manage to last for very long in government. Nobody here seems to think that they will. They always make a mess of things and they are making a mess of things right now. My tutor says that it is perhaps quite a good thing that they were elected into office at the end of the war, because any government was bound to make a mess of things under the circumstances. So it is far better that the Socialists are making this mess, instead of it being us. This way, it will be much easier for the Conservatives to remain in power once the country has settled down into its normal behaviour.

The Sixth Marquess of Froome, interviewed by Mr Simon Manasseh

Q: What was the aspect of this Socialist Britain which you disliked the most?

A: The taxation, to put it in a nutshell. They didn't allow you to be sick any more. And the death duties were the worst part of it all.

Q: This was the period in which your father died. Was there never any real possibility of avoiding such crippling death duties as then had to be paid?

A: Yes, of course there *might* have been, if only my father hadn't clung on to everything for so long. He'd been about to hand things over to me just before the war. But, with me out there on the battle front, the lawyers argued there was a greater chance of it being me who kicked the bucket rather than him. So, when he finally got round to signing the necessary documents towards the very end of the war, it was too damn late. The Socialists went and passed that act to say that all such gifts would be fully taxed unless they were made five years before death; and my father only managed to survive for three of them. But we've all got to go some time. I suppose you could say that's life.

The Nanny Marks tapes

Lord Froome's death was terrible news for the Tillot family. But he was over eighty and his heart wasn't as good as it once had been. The real problem was having to pay all those death duties.

It's all such a silly story, if the truth is to be told. Lord Tillot had never got on very well with Lord Froome's chauffeur, Mr Plumley. I don't think he'd ever really forgiven him for that business about the motorbike. In any case, Lord Tillot was apt to display too little consideration for Mr Plumley's feelings.

Lord Tillot had always been someone who detested untidiness; and Mr Plumley kept a small kitchen garden in the corner of the park near the stables. It wasn't an offensive kitchen garden, except that it ought never to have been situated so close to a beautiful house like Luptree Court. I suppose that Lord Froome must have given his permission for it during the war, when kitchen gardens were indispensible. But the situation was different now. And, since the whole estate had by this time been handed over, Lord Tillot decided it was time for a general tidy-up. And that's when the kitchen garden was ploughed into the ground.

I'm afraid Mr Plumley took it very ill. You see, nobody had warned him about Lord Tillot's intentions. And his strawberry patch was just coming into fruit. But he wasn't even given a chance to pick them.

That evening, he went to see Lord Froome. Of course, nobody knows exactly what was said, but I believe Lord Froome telephoned Lady Beatrice that evening, and expressed some of his indignation about Lord Tillot. Anyway, that was the talk in the family at the funeral; because that night, Lord Froome had a stroke and died. So Lord Tillot had to pay the most crippling death duties.

Such a shame really when you come to think of it. A house like Luptree needed all the funds it could get. But now the whole blinking lot – you'll excuse my language – had fallen into the greedy hands of those Socialists.

This is when Lord Tillot became Lord Froome, of course. Not that he ever sat in the House of Lords; because he wasn't interested in politics any longer. And Lady Tillot became Lady Froome for that matter, although I never think of her that way, since she was always Lady Tillot to me during the period when I knew her so well.

Author's narrative

I inquired of Lady Beatrice Cholmondeley whether she felt the death of her father as a severe blow.

She replied, 'Of course, I did. So did everybody for that matter. He had set the tone for the life of the entire village. There had been such dignity about it. And everyone knew precisely where they stood. It was a tragedy that he couldn't have been left in peace for a little while longer.'

I queried her use of the phrase 'left in peace'.

She said, 'Well, it could hardly be said that my brother left him in peace. As soon as the estate had been handed over to him, he launched out upon a whole programme of innovations. Totally unnecessary innovations. Sending men to pull down all the outside lavatories in the village – hardly even waiting for the sheds to be vacated. And what did people want with any of these flush lavatories inside their houses? Half the tenants regarded them as new-fangled and refused to use them: only they had to in the end, because there wasn't anywhere else to go.

'The thing which had really infuriated my father was the way Edward had this mania for getting everything clean. Chopping down undergrowth or dredging the lakes at Luptree. My father had always cultivated the natural look in things. He'd let things grow wild because it was more beautiful that way. But, no sooner was the ink dry on the documents transferring the estate ownership into Edward's hands, then along he comes with his mechanical saws, his bulldozers and his dredgers, causing havoc all round, and doing it with a vengeance just to make my father feel that he'd let things rot.

'I shall never forgive Edward for his thoughtlessness, if it wasn't his spite. In any case, he got his just desserts. He finally drove my father into an apoplexy and he died that night. Mind you, he was a diabetic, so he probably hadn't got long to live in any case. But he might have been able to hold out until those death duties were no longer due.'

The Nanny Marks tapes

Many people of lesser personality would have thrown in the sponge after paying all those death duties. but not Lord Froome (as we now called him). It's something that good breeding does for you. If you have it, you can get on in life. And you can carry the rest with you. If you haven't, you just throw in the sponge when disaster strikes.

Naturally, Lord Froome had a lot of thinking to do. There wasn't enough money left to support a house like Luptree Court – not after death duties had been paid. So he decided to open it to the public. Not in the manner that other noblemen used to do before the war, just in a casual manner once or twice a week. There was a really big opening with a great fanfare of publicity. And it worked. People came flocking in for miles around. They all wanted to see what the inside of Luptree Court was like – and were quite prepared to pay for it.

But there were those in the village who felt that Lord Froome had been going against the tradition of the place by making use of cheap publicity. And the pony rides were another thing they frowned on. They seemed to think it was the thin end of the wedge, and that very soon there'd be roundabouts and everything else. And of course, they weren't far wrong!

The way Lord Froome felt about it was that he liked to see people enjoying themselves, especially when they were making him a handsome profit. Oh, I think he dealt marvellously with the situation. All those horrible Socialists trying to suck the life-blood from his veins. But they didn't even manage to get him down. If you're that kind of person, you survive. He could teach them a lesson or two.

*The Sixth Marquess of Froome, interviewed by
Mr Simon Manasseh*

Q: Were there any aspects of the post-war world to which you took a liking?

A: Good Lord yes! I'm a post-war person. It was only after the war that I really managed to do anything at all. And that wasn't until after my father had died.

Q: I imagine that you are now speaking of the time when you threw open Luptree Court to the general public. What induced you to take such a step?

A: It was largely the force of necessity. There were all these death duties on my father to pay. But in an odd sort of way, this turned out to be the great turning point in my life. It was such a challenge. You see, Luptree Court has always been in my blood. It was unthinkable that I should let it fall into the hands of all those Socialists. My family had built the place, lived in the place. And now they expected me to give it up – just like that. Well, I wasn't going to do this without a damn good fight. And it succeeded. I made a big publicity splash of the opening. And it turned out that this was precisely what the public wanted to do with their weekends. They came flooding in to pay their half-crowns. So it wasn't any longer necessary to think in terms of selling the place. I'd managed to prove that it could pay for its own upkeep.

Q: Did you enjoy the new image you then acquired as a showman?

A: Well, parts of it, of course I did. Seeing that everyone is looking up to you as if you're the cat's whiskers. And knowing for once that I'd *earned* this respect. I enjoyed that, I dare say. Yet basically I'm a very shy person. I don't like being out there in front, in a position where everyone starts looking at me. I need to push myself to the front, feeling nervous that everyone is going to start booing when I get there.

Q: But the experience enabled you to overcome such timidity?

A: In part, sir. But only in part.

Author's narrative

I move now to the last piece of Mr Thompson's evidence. I inquired of him how he regarded the new order, now that Lord Tillot had become the sixth Marquess of Froome.

He replied, 'I had always been in the habit of working hand-in-glove with Ed-ward. We had known that he would eventually be running the estate, indeed the house too. So it is not as if we were caught without a plan of action in mind, once the opportunity had presented itself.'

I asked him whether he personally had been responsible for formulating this plan of action.

He replied, 'It would be incorrect for me to take credit for it entirely. In every plan of action, there needs to be that little red or green light which signifies whether the machinery should stop or go. I think it would be reasonable for me to claim that the mathematics within the machine's computerized mechanisms were perhaps of my own calculation. But that little green light which flashed go-go-go was entirely of Ed-ward's inspiration.'

I asked the reason for his sudden retirement, right on the brink of Luptree Court's momentous opening to the public. There may have been a hinted suggestion in my query that he himself had been less in favour of the revealed plan of action than he was now prepared to admit.

'My dear sir,' he replied, 'there comes a time in everybody's life when the wear and tear of flesh and bone becomes apparent – to oneself, if not to others. But there was also a reason of inestimable importance to myself, in that I had recently persuaded the good lady who is now my wife to accept the prospect of marriage with me.'

I inquired about the appointment of his successor.

'Ah . . . you mean Bonniface,' he replied. 'Mr Bonniface was a personal friend of mine. In fact I introduced him to Lord Tillot – it must have been several years before the war. He was one of our local barristers. He had done some most remarkable work for us. So, when His Lordship had been appraised of my intentions to retire, I ventured to suggest that he give due consideration to the possibility of appointing Bonniface in my place.'

I asked Lady Beatrice Cholmondeley about the change in local atmosphere, once the new Marquess had thrown open Luptree Court to the general public.

Lady Beatrice replied, 'Well, it disgusted the rest of us of course, just as much as it would have disgusted my father. The idea of dignity isn't compatible with tourism. All those horrible half-eaten ice-cream cones, and little Johnny relieving himself much too publicly against the yew-tree hedge. It was a departure from a whole way of life. I may have got used to it by now, because I'm bound to appreciate that the world has indeed changed. But, in those days, it was different. And I didn't like the idea that it had to be Edward who was actually pioneering these activities.'

9

Recovering the Birthright
1948–52

The Nanny Marks Tapes

I think this was a period of recovery all round. It was as if society was trying to get back into the old way of doing things, and shrug off the war as if it had never happened. Or, in the case of the children, life was only just starting, so they could make what they wanted of it. There were opportunities for everybody, in spite of the way the Socialists had been trying to keep us all down. It just needed a little more time for us to get into the swing of things.

Camilla, for example: she wasn't quite happy about her life at RADA. We all knew she could become a wonderful actress, if she wanted to. But that was the question. *Did* she really want to?

I think it was very sensible of her to appreciate so young that some professions are not quite suitable. They're controlled by the wrong sort of people. And acting is one of them. Of course, it may have been very different in the past. There was a time, I believe, when you could move up into court circles that way – like Nell Gwynne, for example. But nowadays there was less scope.

Camilla realized how the other students didn't have the same understanding of life that she herself had. You couldn't expect them to. They hadn't been brought up that way. It was all theatrics, as Camilla used to call it. They used to take themselves too seriously, as if they believed acting to be the only thing they had to do in life. But this wasn't the way Camilla viewed things at all. She knew perfectly well that there were more important things. So she didn't allow herself to get involved in the same way that some of the others did.

Yet Camilla had always been sensible — far more so than either of the boys. She realized what was good for her and what was not, so, when Lord Froome began talking about coming-out balls and all that sort of thing, she soon gave up the idea of becoming an actress. There was no *future* in that sort of business, if you know what I mean.

Letter from Chloe, Marchioness of Froome,
to Lady Camilla Tillot

Camilla my darling,

How silly of you to think that I could possibly mind your telephoning me. And what made it all the more delightful was your appearing later to have lunch with me. Only I do apologize for the fare. Salads are what I eat nearly all the time nowadays. Someone told me a few months back that I was actually getting fat. I'm not going to take that kind of remark lying down. So I'm back in training again. And, watch out, because I'll soon be as beautiful as you are and ready to compete with all comers (even if they are daughters).

You asked me about RADA. No, I don't think you are necessarily taking the wrong decision. When you are either starting or leaving a profession, careful thought is indeed necessary. I understand your reasons for wanting to be an actress. But I also understand what your teachers say about acting being a dedication. Finally, if you have doubts in yourself, I feel sure that these do not relate to your talent (which has already been displayed), but they may well relate to some inner knowledge of your own capacity to put this goal above all others in your life.

Always come round to see me, *any time* you feel like it. I have missed you so much. But I was nervous of getting in touch with you first, in case you no longer wished to see me. After all, Bruce did continue to pay me the occasional visit.

But I'm happy that we *now* see no barrier between us. I look forward immensely to your next visit.

> All my love,
> Mummy

The Nanny Marks tapes

Camilla was the most enormous success as a debutante. During the three years that she attended those parties in London, she received fifty-seven proposals. Three of them from Dukes, and a couple from foreign Princes besides. All the papers wrote such lovely things about her. Not many people are called the debutante of the year for two years running. And she really was beautiful. Not flashy like one used to see in those American magazines. She wore very little make-up. A lovely round face with the most perfect complexion. The kind of face that you learn to appreciate if you come from the right sort of background.

Camilla was never untrustworthy. Girls knew how to behave themselves in those days. They went out to night-clubs just as often as the girls do now. But they knew where to draw a line. I'm not saying that there mightn't have been a romantic moment now and then. But that's a different matter to the kind of things we read in the papers of today. Camilla never went too far.

It helped having the right friends. In those days, if you attended the London season, it was possible to get taken up by the right sort of people. Camilla's boyfriends were mostly from the Brigade of Guards (the officers, of course). Very interesting kind of people, especially when it came to the Household Cavalry.

Most important from Camilla's point of view was that she'd become an intimate friend of the royal family. She'd remained in touch with Princess Margaret, even while she was at Mrs de Crespigny's: because her best friend there had been a godchild of the Queen. Yet, with all her new friends in London society, they were now back on good terms again. And it was very interesting for Camilla when she got invited

Balmoral and places. It made us all appreciate that she'd done the right thing in abandoning all that acting business.

Excerpts from Chloe, Marchioness of Froome's correspondence with Lady Camilla Tillot

What a lovely idea! Yes, of course I'd like to come to your coming-out ball, provided that Daddy won't mind. But I think you ought to check very carefully with him about this before we actually decide that I am going to attend. Perhaps I ought to mention that Daddy and I are not really on very good terms just at present. I'm sure that it won't last like this for very long. But I would hate for you to tell all your friends that I'd be coming to your ball, only to find that Daddy didn't really approve of the idea. Please let me know what he says.

I really am most tremendously excited. It seems years since I last went to a ball. I feel almost as if I were a teenager once again: tossing over in my mind such problems as what I shall wear and whom I am liable to meet. This last question does trouble me a little. There are so many people I used to know that I simply don't see nowadays. Maybe they simply won't recognize me. Maybe they simply won't *want* to recognize me. I am filled with the most terrible jitters, but I promise to be there. And I'll comply with all the instructions that your father requires: doing a little Cinderella act in reverse. I'll arrive in rags one minute before midnight, and then – at the strike of twelve – you'll hardly recognize me!

I did so enjoy myself, darling, more than I can remember in a long time. Most of it was just knowing that I was your mother again. But also, just a tiny bit, that I was your rival!

Goodness, I was a success! Wasn't I? Did you see the way two young men had a barging match to be the one to dance 'Do Ye Ken John Peel' with me? In the end I told them that they'd better pull me like a wishbone, though I wasn't promising to grant any of their wishes.

*

I'm so sorry darling if you felt that I misbehaved. I'm also sorry that one of your friends should have expressed his disapproval of the blue rinse in my hair. It came out a bit stronger than I intended, though I can assure you that it has not been dyed.

It is sometimes difficult for parents to get these things into perspective – just as much as I imagine it must be difficult for the children. I think you're mistaken, however, in imagining that anything which I did is liable to blot your marital prospects. It was evident to everyone at that ball that there was no one on the entire dance floor who radiated such positive appeal as you – not only to the young men, but to those of my generation too. An old beau of mine came up to remark that I'd produced the finest rose in this post-war garden. And goodness I was proud of you, my darling, especially when I come to think that just a little bit of you is like myself.

The Nanny Marks tapes

Bruce was doing quite well at his work, passing his School Certificate with a whole lot of distinctions and credits. We never expected that of him. 'Shows what a wonderful school Eton must be.' That's what Camilla said.

And it's perfectly true. Eton *is* a very wonderful school. It's the top of the tops, as they say on the wireless. There are all kinds of schools, but Eton is one in itself. Not only does it take you away from home so that it can get its hands on you; but, when it's got you there, it pumps personality into you. Nobody leaves Eton without being turned into somebody more individual than they were when they started. That's why they all grow up into Prime Ministers.

Being there made such a difference to Bruce. He began by being such a serious boy. His father always said that he didn't have any humour. And I see what he meant. But Eton managed to shake him out of himself.

Perhaps it's the way they have of giving all the boys separate rooms as studies. He was able to think about himself so much that he saw he oughtn't to be like that any more. And

obody gets molly-coddled at Eton. They're quite rough with
heir boys, you know. Nobody minds because that's the Eto-
ian method of turning People into Somebodies.

What Bruce was best at was rowing. He did very well in the
umping fours and was given a cap for it. When he came
ome for the holidays, I could tell that he was happy. He used
o sing the Eton boating song to me. Such a lovely song. I
vonder they don't play it more on the wireless. Let me see,
ow does it go?

> We'll swing, swing together,
> Steady from stroke to bow;
> And nothing in life shall sever
> The chains that be round us now.

uch fine words I always think. And it's exactly what Eton is
ll about. The boys there learn to realize that they're a team.
They're the people from the top drawer: the Establishment,
or whatever else you like to call it. And they learn how to get
on with each other, to assist each other in the battle for
survival. That's what I call true loyalty. And loyalty is so
mportant in this world.

It's such a shame that Sebastian never took to school in
quite the same way as Bruce had done. Ashdale was a *good*
school, if you didn't need pushing. But they weren't quite so
good with the boys who didn't *want* to work. And the trouble with Sebastian was that he was deliberately idle. He
seemed to enjoy getting himself into trouble.

Mind you, he was always quite cheerful about his troubles.
He was never somebody to let misfortune get him down. In
fact, there were times when I felt he was a little too pleased
with himself. This took the form of a certain cockiness, especially in the company of girls.

In those days young boys didn't really have girlfriends. But
Sebastian was a little before his time, I sometimes thought.
One summer, Lord Froome took the two boys down to
Cornwall for their holidays. And I went too – just like in the
old days, except that Lady Tillot wasn't there.

We were staying in a hotel, which was also some kind of a
farm. And there was a young girl called Milly, who was the

daughter of the place. Well, she wasn't what I would call a *nice* young girl. She was a little bit older than Sebastian and she seemed to have picked up one or two nasty ways. It wasn't that they were doing anything very terrible, I don't suppose. But she had an underhand way of going about things. A sort of hide-away-in-the-corner slyness if you see what I mean. There were times when I might come round the edge of some rocks and she would quickly move away from Sebastian, as if she had been doing things she didn't want me to see. Furtive: that's the word. Milly was furtive, and dirty-minded.

I always discouraged the children from doing anything dirty. And, like the others, I had brought up Sebastian to be a clean boy. But I'm afraid that Milly gave him some bad habits which he never really forgot. Mind you, I've no objection if children make a joke of things we don't talk about in public. That's only natural. But I don't like it when it starts to affect their behaviour.

I'm afraid Lord Froome didn't really help me in correcting this fault in Sebastian. I think he was amused at what he described as the boy's precocity. 'Sebastian has got sex appeal,' I remember him telling me. 'You either have it or you don't. And Sebastian has it.'

Excerpts from Chloe, Marchioness of Froome's correspondence with Lady Camilla Tillot

Yes, it is true that Daddy and I don't see eye to eye on many issues nowadays. I wouldn't fret yourself too greatly about it, if I were you. It is something which is happening all around us. If we started to get troubled by it, there'd be no end to anyone's miseries.

It is far too early yet to speak in terms of divorce. Naturally the subject does get mentioned. And we do discuss this matter with our particular friends, which we (both of us) do have. But divorce is something very final and not necessarily the right solution. It is impossible for me to say more on the subject now, because I always find it a little bit difficult to know precisely what your father might have to say on the subject; which could of course be very different from what I have to say myself.

No darling, I simply cannot agree with you. Divorced parents are no longer a reason for being refused entry to the royal enclosure at Ascot. In fact, I don't think it ever was. I think you had to be divorced yourself to get barred. And I suspect that they don't even apply this rule any too strictly nowadays.

Try to see it this way, darling. I really do have my own life to lead – just as much as you, or anyone else does, for that matter. Even if we do go ahead with our plans for a divorce, it won't make any difference to the way we've been living our separate lives over these past few years. All of you children have learnt already to contend with life, without my presence. How can you argue that an official recognition of our separateness will now make any difference to you?

I do ask you to try and understand everything during these months that are ahead of us. I get so confused about everything that I could hardly blame anyone else for getting confused about it too. There *are* some terrible things being said and I'd be happier if you prepare yourself for them. Always try to see both sides of the story, and then I feel sure that both Daddy and myself will have no reason to complain.

The Nanny Marks tapes

I didn't have the heart to feel upset at Lord Froome's remarks. He was going through such a difficult period in his own life. He and Lady Tillot had finally decided to divorce. And the newspapers were printing such unpleasant stories about the two of them. Such untrue stories! They should never have been allowed to get away with it. I'm sure Lady Tillot had never behaved in the manner they suggested. It wasn't as if the people they tried to link her name with were even gentlemen. They made it sound as if she went out with someone different almost every night.

And poor Lord Froome! They said such awful things about his temper. I'm sure that, if he'd ever used a riding-crop on Lady Tillot, I'd have been the very first to know about it. It's envy really. That's what makes people do it. The papers should have been punished for printing such lies.

Lady Tillot was allowed to keep the house in Jermyn Street without paying any rent for it. And she was still able to see as much of the children as she desired. But living up in London the whole time put her at a distance from the rest of us. She used to write to me from time to time. Such nice letters: full of exciting stories about the odd theatrical people she'd been meeting. And I don't think it really matters if you mix with that sort of company once you've reached a mature age. I'm sure Lady Tillot knew how to make them keep the right distance.

I shall always believe that the divorce made Lord Froome secretly unhappy. It was as if he withdrew from us, and withdrew all his feeling of warmth for the children. I think he felt as if his family had let him down in some way. He didn't trust us any more.

The Sixth Marquess of Froome, interviewed by Mr Simon Manasseh

Q: Was the divorce a painful process for you?
A: Of course it was painful. Once the lawyers get your private life in their clutches, they make it sound as if anything might have happened.
Q: Did anything happen?
A: Of course it did. But what kind of a question is that? No I'm not going to answer that kind of rubbish. You car move on to your next question.

Excerpts from Chloe Marchioness of Froome's correspondence with Lady Camilla Tillot

No, your father is most unkind in suggesting such a thing. Something that you might not realize at the moment is tha people do need affection from others, in order to keep the harshness of the world at a distance. Some people can find this affection within their own domestic situation, waiting for them like a baby on the doorstep. All they have to do is to take it in. Others have to hunt for it. This doesn't turn them into bad people. It is simply a human situation which needs to be understood.

Now, look here, Camilla, there comes a point when I've got to tell you that you're going too far. It's all very well for you to keep on about *my* behaviour, but what about your father's, if it comes to that? I don't want to be dragged into a whole discussion of it, but there are other things which make a marriage break up, besides adultery (as you call it).

I think I must take the line that you are not yet quite grown up enough for me to tell you about these matters. For one thing, I don't want to damage your relationship with your father. Once people are married, it is quite usual that they fight. It is not the only thing they do. But it does happen. And, when it happens, both parties sometimes become thoroughly nasty. Normally we can manage to forget these things next morning. But, when a divorce is being battled out, it becomes necessary to dig up even the most sordid details.

Oh, it's positively awful. I agree with you, my darling. But who could possibly have foreseen that they'd go and write about it in this vein? It would have been far better if they'd printed *all* that had been said. That would have set these quotations within their true context. As it is, I could really cry. But, in any case, it's now all finished and done with. I am a divorced woman. And, to that extent, I am free.

The Nanny Marks tapes

Lord Froome had plenty of other things to occupy his mind. The public opening of Luptree had been such an enormous success that all the other stately homes had copied him, which meant that he had to keep thinking up new ideas in order to be one jump ahead of them. And I sometimes felt that he preferred these new activities to the idea of reviving his family life.

Mind you, he really did have some brilliant ideas. He'd seen how the British public could be persuaded to take an interest in their own history, if only it was fed to them with a few swings and roundabouts. (Oh yes, he had the whole lot at Luptree by now!) So he started thinking about doing it on a broader scale: how he could treat the whole West Country as if it were a treasure house, and arrange for people to visit the region from a central hotel at Luptree.

As was only to be expected, this idea of transforming the unused half of Luptree into a public hotel was enough to drive Lady Beatrice and Lady Ulrica wild. They wrote such angry letters to Lord Froome on the subject.

Author's narrative

Lady Beatrice had this to say to me: 'Over the course of time, it became sheer and utter vulgarity. I had predicted from the start how things would go. Yet, by the time they all began to listen to me, it was too late. The last time I took my poodle for a walk in the park he couldn't even find room to lift his leg, for fear of upsetting some courting couple.

'I wrote to my brother because I didn't want to discuss it with him personally; but somebody had to tell him quite bluntly that he'd taken things too far. Our ancestors were most surely turning in their graves, anticipating that they'd be next on the agenda for commercialization. Presented as mummies, no doubt.

'Edward's reply to me was by no means satisfactory. To express what he said rather more politely than he himself managed to do, he told me to mind my own business. Well, if it isn't *my* business, then I should like someone to tell me just whose business it is!

'All those little cubicles with Mrs What's-her-name from the village dressed up as a gypsy, promising you some piece of

irresponsible misbehaviour before the year is out. My sister
Ulrica nearly lost one of her guests from a heart attack on the
last occasion she set foot in the park. The poor lady went
through a door marked WC in a perfectly *bona fide*
endeavour to spend an honest penny. But a few moments
later she rushed out screaming, her skirts billowing up round
her neck. These were wind cupboards, not water closets, it
was afterwards explained. But I'm surprised my brother
didn't get sued for assault for playing tricks like that on the
public.

'And all that business about inviting everyone to come and
stay with the Marquess. Crumpets and buttered toast, along
with an aristocratic handshake. And that's all they were ever
liable to get, I can assure you, because Edward never made
much sense after the first half-dozen drinks or so. And I'm
told that he really hit the bottle to summon up enough nerve
to get through those ordeals.

'That was the real problem with my brother. He was hitting the bottle far too frequently. It is my personal belief that
he took all these decisions to make a mess of Luptree while he
was under the influence. I'm afraid it is one of the failings in
my family. The Tillots are either teetotallers or tipplers.
They're never anything in between.'

I inquired of Mrs Potts how she had reacted to all the
innovations which were introduced to the Luptree estate after
the death of the fifth Marquess, especially without Lady Tillot on the scene, importing her very special spice to the manner in which life was to be lived.

She replied, 'Cor luvvaduck! I've needed to adapt myself to
all kinds of situations in my life. So I wouldn't be likely to fall
down on this one. Not bloody likely!

'No, I'll admit the changes didn't suit me always. There
wasn't the same life about the place. Not at Caldicott Manor,
I mean. But Walter and myself would get carted over to the
big house for all those special occasions, when Tom, Dick
and Harry from the other end of the world would come
hobnobbing with His Lordship.

'Oh, I didn't mind it. It was a lark. As long as somebody

was enjoying themselves, I was quite happy to have my own chuckle. But it wasn't the same as in the old days. Not the same as when Lady Tillot was around.

'Sometimes I'd shove Walter aside and come in myself to serve the soufflé, or whatever it might have been, just to get a look at their faces, if the truth were told. But, when I looked at them, they just looked back at me. We were like animals on different sides of the bars. But who's to say which of us was in the zoo?

'I remember there was one occasion when I found lying outside a large hat of the sort that you see Americans wearing in some of those cartoons. And there were cameras and all those kind of gadgets too. So I called to Walter and told him to lend me one of His Lordship's cigars. (He kept them for all the tourists.) Then in I rushed doing one of the Knees-Up-Mother-Brown dances, wearing all these hats and things. I thought for a moment that it might be just like the old days, with Lady Tillot and her friends twirling me round their arms in a gay fandango. But after I'd done my big entry, I realized that it wasn't going to be like that at all. So I stopped, and they all started clapping as if I'd been the cabaret. I never tried that stunt again.

'Oh, I did miss Lady Tillot. There's a lot of terrible things that have been said about her since. But she did have life. And it's sad to live without life.'

The Sixth Marquess of Froome, interviewed by Mr Simon Manasseh

Q: When it came to opening a wing of Luptree Court as an expensive hotel for foreign tourists, did this impinge greatly on your own life style?

A: Impinge? We didn't pinch each other, if that's what you mean. No, I really mean that we got on fine together. It permitted me to meet people that would never have come my way under normal circumstances. People like you, for example.

Q: Would you have been prepared to put me up at the

strictly limited price I'd have been prepared to pay?

A: Do you mean that you'd have quibbled about the bill? Good Lord, sir, we couldn't have put up with that! The tourists who came to stay at Luptree Court were being given Privileged Service, with a capital P and a capital S. If you couldn't have afforded the bill, then you would have gone somewhere else.

Q: What did this Privileged Service entail?

A: You had me for one thing. I wasn't exactly the butler or the cook. We had Walter and Mrs Potts doing all that. And I didn't exactly sing or dance. But I told a funny anecdote or two, while sipping a glass of sherry with my guests. Anyway, *I* thought my anecdotes were funny. Perhaps you wouldn't. I really don't know. They became a bit repetitive, I'll have to confess. I grew lazy after learning which ones went down best.

Q: Can you truthfully tell me that you enjoyed these activities?

A: Truthfully? Well, if you insist on my being truthful, I suppose the answer is no. I'm too shy. But there was always the occasional delightful surprise. The elderly couple from some State I'd never heard of in your God-damn continent. And blow me down if they wouldn't turn up with a granddaughter who could have been Miss World! The trouble is that I'd usually fortified myself for these occasions with the odd drink beforehand. (The very idea of sipping sherry disgusts me. But it was cheaper than whisky, to give my guests. And more in line with what they expected to be given in a nobleman's palace, I might add!) Anyway, by the time I was making polite conversation to them all, if there happened to be a Miss World in their company, I was managing to see four of them. So I felt outnumbered and reverted to being shy.

Q: Did your guests ever regard you as being marriageable material for their daughters, or granddaughters? You were, after all, in the process of getting your divorce.

A: Good heavens, no! At least I don't think so. It wasn't part of our advertising campaign, if that's what you mean. *I* wasn't included on the menu!

Author's narrative

Mr Bonniface, formerly a local barrister, was at that time the new estate agent at Luptree. I had no difficulty in tracing his present whereabouts, for he had lived permanently, since his retirement, in an affluent farmhouse in the vicinity of Salisbury. He shared it with his wife (a lady of myopic good looks) and, on the particular date of my visit, with two rather noisy grandchildren.

Mr Bonniface himself was of portly build, with a pair of large spectacles thrust forwards on a reddened nose. The thumbs of his two hands tended to revert to a position where they were hinged in his waistcoat pockets. I also noted that he preferred to be standing rather than seated, which enabled him to *address* his visitors, rather than to converse with them.

He said, 'As you probably may have gathered, I received the appointment from Lord Froome shortly after he had inherited the marquesate. Those early years will always be the ones when I truly felt that I had a personal contribution to offer to the Luptree estate. I came from a different world from that of Lord Froome – a whole different milieu. But I brought to his organization something which he himself lacked: a knowledge of the British middle classes. I speak to you now as a professional representative of the British middle classes, and I always encouraged Lord Froome to view me in precisely the same light. I had to speak up to him and inform him just how *we* would react to some particular idea.

'The instalment of a restaurant and cafeteria is a case in point. Lord Froome wanted to construct the whole thing as a single unit, with everyone rubbing shoulders together at the till. I had to tell him that the British middle classes wouldn't stand for it. The man who's earned himself a respectable living in life has also earned himself the right to sit at a separate table, and preferably in a separate restaurant. It was detail of this sort that Lord Froome was apt to overlook. He preferred to lump the entire British public into one.'

During my conversation with Mr Walter Davis at The Hop and Grape, I had the good fortune to be present when Mr Gordon Perkins dropped in. Mr Davis remarked on his arrival and suggested that I put some of my questions to him. Perkins had risen higher in the Luptree hierarchy than Mr Davis had ever done. In fact, he was still employed in the organization at a managerial level.

Mr Perkins was short of stature and of a quiet disposition; he had nicotine stains around the fingers of his left hand. I found him alert, rather than nervous, and he became rapidly more conversational after a few drinks. I asked about his own involvement in the opening of Luptree Court to the public.

He said, 'It happened at a time when many chauffeurs were going on the dole. People couldn't afford that sort of a luxury any more. Or not unless they were in a big company or something. So Lord Froome persuaded me to try my hand at being one of the guides, with some of my old chauffeuring to do as well – just as much as was needed.

'I'd get some odd customers on many of those guided tours. You'd have thought they'd come to a place like Luptree to look at the architecture or the pictures. But there was always the odd birds who just wanted to hear something scandalous – whether it related to one of the family portraits or to somebody who was living today. They wanted to hear that somebody had done something he shouldn't have done and how it had all been hushed up.

'So eventually I had to get together with all the rest of the guides and invent these things. We thought up stories, then asked Lord Froome if he felt they sounded suitable. Oh, we didn't make anything too awful happen. But there had to be several villains in the family. It didn't really matter what they might have done, as long as it was just enough to whet the public's appetite – like being a member of the Hellfire Club, or something of the sort. There was a whole debate as to which ancestress we should select, from the entire stock of family portraits, as the one who used to dance naked on the lawns in front of all her domestic staff. And the one bishop in the family got landed with half a dozen illegitimate children, and a mistress who was an actress – so we could go on to claim that this was the origin of all those stories about actresses having something to tell bishops.

'I only really struck lucky when Lord Froome thought up

this Wessex gimmick. At the start we'd been relying too much on people driving down from London to see the beauties of Luptree Court. But what we needed was an idea to keep them there. Get them moving around the place a little, spending money wherever they went. And that's where I came into my own, because I was both guide and chauffeur. I had the right qualifications for Lord Froome to put me in charge of this side of the enterprise.

'I didn't know anything about Wessex when it all started. I came from the Midlands myself. Or from Mercia, if we're going to call these regions what they used to be called once upon a time. But there was sense in Lord Froome's using these names for the purposes of tourism. I mean Wessex really is different from anywhere else in England. It's the most rural, agricultural part of the country. It's certainly not like the industrial Midlands, where I come from. And it's not like London and all that metropolitan region, with those dormitory towns to north and to south of it. So Wessex is a wide territory, with an identity all of its own: all the way down west from London, until you come to Cornwall, I suppose; which is different again, because of its being purely Celtic.

'What Lord Froome set out to do was to make Luptree Court the tourist capital of Wessex: using it as the point from which to take tourists all over the region. And, if people didn't know what Wessex was when they started, they certainly did by the time they'd driven everywhere that I could take them to – and by the time they'd spent their last pound too, I should add. Lord Froome was quite a sharp businessman, in his own way. At any rate, he had the flair, even if he didn't have the solid financial know-how.'

The Sixth Marquess of Froome, interviewed by Mr Simon Manasseh

Q: Was the idea of Wessex a piece of gimmickry that you took from Thomas Hardy?

A: Not at all. In fact, the original Wessex of early Saxon times didn't even include Thomas Hardy's Dorset. No, I was trying to go to the very heart of the matter, to show people what the West Country is really all about. The story of King Alfred's struggle against the Danes, the Monmouth rebellion, and all that kind of thing. I don't know much about any of those things myself, but it creates interest if you employ people who do. There are plenty of good stories, and nobody really knows where they happened. Alfred burning the cakes, for example. I suppose it must have happened somewhere. Do you think it really happened somewhere? Anyway, it's good for business if people are allowed to think it happened right here. It only needs a little imagination on the part of the guides. Perkins, who used to be my chauffeur, he was rather good at it. Suggested that the little hamlet of Kings Bottom got its name that way – though it sounds a fatuous idea, if you ask me: as if King Alfred burnt those cakes by sitting on them or something. But the public believe anything they're told.

Q: Are you telling me that you set out to bamboozle the British public?

A: Bamboozle them? I don't think so. But there's plenty of cash in a good gimmick. I don't have any grandiose ideas about what Wessex really is. All I know is that we have this identity and that it relates to tourism, as much as it does to anything else. In fact tourism is the very life blood of the West Country. I was doing them all a service in promoting the name of Wessex.

The Nanny Marks tapes

Camilla was doing very well for herself. She'd been appointed a lady-in-waiting to Princess Margaret. It's a tremendous honour when things like that happen to you. They didn't *have* to choose her. But I know one thing. They couldn't have made a better choice. And it was such interesting work.

Nothing strenuous, of course. Things like carrying Princess Margaret's money. The royal family aren't allowed to do such things for themselves.

And they got on so well together. I think that Princess Margaret had always wanted to be an actress, if the truth were known. Secretly, of course. And Camilla had been very near to becoming one. So they arranged little sketches together and acted them for the amusement of the royal family. Camilla told me the Princess had real talent in that field. It's a pity so few people ever got the opportunity to see them.

I must say that I do think we're tremendously lucky, as a nation, to have such an interesting royal family. If you go to other countries, the Kings and Queens are such tiresome people. But *our* royal family consists of people we can really love. They're no different from the rest of us in many ways. But they have dignity. Real dignity.

Sebastian had gone to Eton by this time, although he never liked it from the start. Perhaps it would have been different if Bruce had still been there to look after him a little. But he wasn't. And Sebastian always found it difficult to adapt himself to any manner of discipline.

Yet Bruce was doing very well for himself. He'd chosen to go into the Household Cavalry to do his national service. Or it wasn't Bruce who decided this. It was really that Camilla had told her father that this would be best for him. The way she looked at it, a regiment was a man's chance to meet the right sort of people.

Author's narrative

I inquired of Mr Davis whether Bruce, Lord Tillot, had appeared to enjoy his military service.

Mr Davis emitted a short ripple of laughter. 'Bruce? Not ruddy likely! Those first few weeks he spent at the Guards' depot in Caterham made this stand out a mile. He'd have given up the ghost there and then, if he hadn't been allowed to come back home on leave every weekend: after the first month of his training, that is. Not that he particularly wanted to come home. I mean he wasn't getting on so well with his father, at that time. I had instructions to refuse all of his reverse charge telephone calls. ("The young blighter can learn to pay his own way in life," was the way Lord Froome put it!) And there wasn't anyone else for him to see, unless he went running over for a gossip with Nanny Marks.

'But I'll tell you the reason he came back home to Caldicott, once they were prepared to issue him with weekend passes. It was because I'd polish his boots for him. He'd just lie there on the sofa in the drawing room thumbing his way through the pin-up magazines he'd brought back home with him, while I slaved my guts out polishing those flippin' boots. They'd be mirror bright before he shoved them into the saddle bags of his motorbike and sped back to Caterham. Never a word of thanks. But he did tell me that it made life a lot easier for him. The shine would just about last until he came back home again the following weekend.

'If it hadn't been for those boots, he'd never have made it — becoming an officer, I mean. So he does have something to thank me for.'

Excerpt from the personal manuscript of Bruce, Lord Tillot

It has taken me quite a long time to get accustomed to being an officer in the Household Cavalry, which is strange in a way. Coming from Eton, I find so many of my former school-friends doing their national service alongside myself that I ought to be able to slip more naturally into the accepted spirit of things.

It's not even as if my friends are better officers than myself. They spend just as much of their time drinking as I do. But they somehow seem to *do* better, in the sense that they make fewer mistakes. I know that this is supposed to be an elite regiment, and that all of us were chosen to be here because we somehow fit into this pattern of being elite. I mustn't make such a terrible disgrace of myself as I did last autumn in my first manoeuvres with the regiment. My real trouble is that I try too hard. By worrying too much whether or not I am truly elite, I become the very opposite and start making mistakes. This time I shall stop worrying and perhaps I shall become a credit to my regiment.

The Nanny Marks tapes

It wasn't all that easy for Bruce, even after he'd received his commission. I'm afraid he wasn't accustomed to ordering people around, in the manner they expected in the army. He'd always been under the influence of one person or another, whether it was Camilla or his father. So this kind of situation was new to him.

There was such a chain of little things that went wrong. And his colonel became very angry with him. He had to do all the orderly officer's duties for a whole month on end. But then gradually things began to go right for him. The regiment was out in Germany at the time patrolling the border in armoured cars. And there were huge manoeuvres which lasted for several weeks in the summer.

Well, Bruce told me that he went on doing the same silly things that he'd always been doing, but the difference now was that they worked out right for him. He got lost in the middle of a forest, for example, and happened to come out at the headquarters of the opposite side. They seemed to think he'd done it on purpose, you see.

And there was another occasion when he'd had a little too much to drink. And his troop was sent out at night in front of the brigade's advance, so that only his troop would get shot up, instead of all the rest of them. But, when they opened fire on him in the middle of all that blackness, he just stood up in the turret of his armoured car and started shouting rude words. He intended them for his squadron leader rather than the enemy, he said. But the other side seemed to think this was the sound of a whole infantry regiment charging. So tanks and all the rest switched on their headlights, and made a run for it. All that was left for Bruce to do was to lead the regiment into the very heart of the enemy lines. And nobody seemed to know *what* was happening by the time morning dawned.

Oh, the colonel was so pleased with Bruce after that! It came at a good moment, you see. The regiment had been making itself a bit unpopular in Germany, because they'd been hunting the local cats. (They had brought out a pack of foxhounds with them.) There had been an awful occasion when Lord Yeovil's eldest son had struck one of the local farmers with his hunting crop. The army authorities were a little unreasonable about this when the complaint was lodged. Yet Bruce's success during these manoeuvres created a very different impression. The regiment received a telegram from a brigadier at headquarters congratulating them on their fine performance on the field of battle. Yes, Bruce was quite a little hero after that. He was even persuaded to sign on after his national service had ended.

Author's narrative

Mr Perkins was talking to me about the developments at Luptree. He said, 'I think it was my idea to build up a fleet of Rolls-Royces. Not brand new ones, and not quite so old as to be vintage models. But just old enough so we could pick them up at a reasonable price. And this gave our tours a special tone, which had the edge over our rivals. People liked to be seen getting in and out of these Rolls-Royces, painted up brightly in the family colours of gold and black, with the Tillot coat of arms on each side. They mightn't have given a second thought to the idea of going to visit the particular cathedral, stately home, or whatever it may have been on the route for that day. But the ride was something special. And I took them by all the little side roads, where they could get the best of the scenery. Thatched cottages beside lazy little streams. Not the sort of scenery you see when you stick to the main roads.

'Then other people used to chip in and help what we were doing: getting in on our act, if you like to think of it that way. The places we stopped to have lunch, for example. They were good little restaurants, tucked away in some village pub or other. They'd a right to be called gourmet restaurants in their own way. And, with the stream of customers that we'd be bringing them, they were soon putting special Wessex dishes on the menu. Inventing them for the most part, because nobody seemed to remember any longer what a Wessex dish really might be. But they got the barmaid all dolled up like a country damsel, with the barman in a yokel's smock too. It was just a game, as far as they were concerned. But there was good money in it. So they were willing to play.

'Well, once you start on one of these things, the idea begins to snowball of its own accord. The wing that had been given over to it at Luptree Court just wasn't big enough to hold all the tourists we were drawing. What we needed was a whole chain of little motels dotted all over Wessex. Well, not exactly motels. Country mansions really, which otherwise were going to rot because they were too cumbersome for a single family. This was Lord Froome's new idea. To take them over and do them up as motels. But, to do that, he needed unlimited capital. And that's where Sir Ben Jones entered the scheme. The perfect partnership was the way we saw it: seeing how Lord Froome owned Luptree and Sir Ben owned all those hotels in Bristol and Southampton.

'Lord Froome hit it off very well with Sir Ben in those early days. He'd pick the houses he wanted the organization to buy, and Sir Ben wasn't in the habit of asking too many questions. Very soon we had a whole network of them in the vicinity of cities as far apart as Plymouth, Gloucester, Oxford, Windsor and Winchester. And that just about covered the whole territory of the original Wessex. As managing director of the Wessex motels, it looked as if Lord Froome was all set to become a millionaire. And I don't mind admitting that I wasn't doing too badly myself.'

The Sixth Marquess of Froome, interviewed by Mr Simon Manasseh

Q: How did you come to team up with Sir Ben Jones?
A: It was chance really. I found myself sitting next door to

him one evening, at a charity dinner in Bristol. Both of us up on the top table, of course: as part of the spectacle which all the others were paying to come and see. And he was asking me about what I'd been getting up to at Luptree recently, and what kind of plans I had for development.

Well, I don't suppose I'd normally have spoken out about any such plans. But you know what a few drinks can do. And he'd been talking about splashing money all round the place. So I tried to outdo him by talking even bigger. Made it sound as if he only needed to splash a little of his cash in my direction, and I'd soon be making a fortune for both of us. And blow me down if he didn't take me at my word!

Q: I take it that you and Sir Ben took an instant liking to each other?

A: Well, yes and no is the answer to that one. You must remember that I had been well wined and dined on that occasion. And Sir Ben is accustomed to such occasions, and uses them to advance his business interests. He's all affability at one moment, while he darts in to fix things up the way he wants it to be. But that's the last you ever see of him. Once it's fixed, he never wants to see you again. It got me wondering, later, if I hadn't been a bit of a sucker somewhere along the line. I might have held out for better terms or something.

Q: What was your special line in big talk, which appealed to Sir Ben?

A: I suppose it was my idea of cashing in on the snob appeal in a place like Luptree Court, and linking this to what he was describing as an expansion of the leisure industries. I was arguing that, if people nowadays were going out for the day with money to spend in their pockets, then the right places where you could take it all away from them must be those with snob appeal.

People don't mind being robbed by a Lord. They even think it enhances their status. That's why so many con-men pretend to be Lords. The thing that people can't stand is to be robbed by their equals, or by their inferiors. That's why all those seaside holiday camps could never compete with me because at Luptree Court I had a public who literally wanted to be robbed. And Sir Ben appreciated that we might expand the business further afield.

The Nanny Marks tapes

You know, I really do have the most tremendous admiration for Lord Froome. I don't think the public ever appreciated what a *service* he'd done for them. I'm sure he deserved one of those honours we keep hearing about – far more than most other people, anyway.

Yes, everything was going splendidly for the Tillot family nowadays. For everybody, in fact. There was a feeling in the air that we'd all fully recovered from the effects of the war. The Establishment was still intact, and they'd recovered their birthright, if you see what I mean. Not only in the way they lived, but in politics as well.

At long last they'd succeeded in getting rid of Mr Attlee and his crowd. It was so wonderful to have Mr Churchill as our Prime Minister again, even if he was getting a bit elderly by this time. As a nation, we owed him such a tremendous debt. I felt happier about this now that people had voted him back into office.

10

Slipping into an Unmarked Grave

1952–4

The Nanny Marks tapes

In spite of all these exciting things that were going on in the world around me, there were moments when I couldn't help feeling a bit sad. I'd never really grown used to the idea that I'd been put into retirement. The children didn't come to see me quite so often as they once had done. 'You're forgetting your old Nan!' I used to tell them. But they weren't really, of course. It's just that they had so many other things to do. But I couldn't help wondering what was going to become of me if they did forget that I existed. It was as if things were beginning to come to an end.

It was about this time that Camilla got married. Mind you, it was a highly suitable match. You probably read about it at the time. She married the young Duke of Northumbria. But I call him Michael, of course. He's a cousin of the Queen. He always struck me as being by far the most interesting of the young men who moved in court circles. Most of us were delighted when she brought him down for us all to meet.

Michael was such an elegant young man. You could see it in the clothes that he wore. Everything was faultless. He had a reputation for this throughout London. But his real home was in the north. He lived at Northwold Abbey, which is one of the most lovely stately homes. It's famous for its grouse moors, as you probably know. The royal family goes with him for the opening of the grouse-shooting season.

I'm afraid Michael didn't quite see eye to eye with Lord Froome. They were different sorts of people really. Yet I think that what he really objected to was Michael's manner. It made Lord Froome feel so terribly awkward, what with Michael being a Duke and him only a Marquess. He said that sons-in-law should be respectful, no matter what their rank.

Most of the villagers went up for the wedding. But neither of Lord Froome's sisters, I'm afraid. They made their excuses. But the truth is that they hadn't forgiven him for turning Luptree into a hotel.

I can tell you we were all on our very best behaviour that day. None of the Tillot family put a foot wrong in fact. Not like William Walpole. I never really understood how they even came into each other's company. Willie Walpole had such a terrible reputation, as a ladies' man, if one troubled to read about these things in the Sunday papers. I would prefer not to believe anything they wrote about him: only it wasn't right that he should be getting up to all his tricks on this day, of all days – with one of Camilla's bridesmaids too. Without Willie Walpole, I don't suppose that the adoption societies would be in business. But none of these goings-on were noticeable at the time. Everything has to look just right when royalty are present.

The Sixth Marquess of Froome, interviewed by Mr Simon Manasseh

Q: Do you feel that your daughter was bettering herself in the right sort of way by marrying a Duke?

A: *Bettering* herself? I'm not sure I ever regarded it quite like that. I'm quite happy to be a mere Marquess, thank you! I'd have regarded it as an even better marriage if she'd managed to splice herself to some millionaire. One of these Greek ship owners, or someone like that. No matter what he looked like, just so long as he was as rich as Croesus.

Q: Could you explain that remark?

A: Well, aristocracy isn't what it was. Having the cash, that's what counts. If I went into a smart London restaurant nowadays, and someone like Onassis came in just after me, when there was only one table left to go, then he'd be given it. I can promise you that. It's no good being a mere Duke or Marquess. You've got to be one of the royal family at the very least, before you'd get priority over Onassis.

Excerpt from the personal manuscript of Bruce, Lord Tillot

I must register my sincere satisfaction that Camilla has made such a good marriage for herself. Marriage to the right person, for the right reasons, is so important in society, especially now, when our whole way of life is being reviewed critically by those who only envy all we stand for.

Michael will make Camilla an excellent husband. He has all the right connections in life to enhance the traditions which she herself inherited. I think they may be happy together as well. This is because they understand that they both belong to the same rank of human being. They perceive where each other's interests lie, and will take steps to protect them against the attacks of others.

I regard it as most important that I should make a good marriage. Naturally I have certain persons in mind, whom I regard as ideal. But sometimes they are too ideal, in that I don't really see myself getting into a position where I could advance our relationship towards any satisfactory conclusion.

Nevertheless, it *would* be ideal to establish permanent bonds between my family and those families which are even better respected than mine. I don't think I should permit myself to curtail my ambitions at this juncture. It is possible that I really have been brought up to succeed in life. I ought not to be too pessimistic in these matters.

The Nanny Marks tapes

I'm afraid the marriage was followed by a little bit of a distancing between Camilla and her father. But that may have been due to a misunderstanding. It was to do with the Coronation. The royal family had been rather slow at getting round to it. Yet, now that it had been arranged, Lord Froome was expected to attend at the Abbey. But he'd lost interest in all those sort of things, for his whole life nowadays was concerned with the expansion of Wessex Motels.

The trouble is that Camilla didn't see it that way. She felt it was a slight, I suppose, her being such a friend of the royal family. And she wrote a letter to her father which might have been expressed too bluntly. She made the mistake of thinking that he must still believe in the same things that he once believed in. But Lord Froome had moved into a different world since then.

Then, a few months later, the Lord Lieutenant of Wiltshire died, and someone had to be appointed to replace him. Now by all rights, if there's a Duke available, they appoint a Duke. And a Marquess is appointed before they stoop to an Earl. That's the way it goes, you see. But in this case they appointed the Earl of Warminster as Lord Lieutenant of Wiltshire, without even consulting Lord Froome about whether he would be prepared to take it on.

Now this offended Lord Froome. He had never particularly liked Lord Warminster. So he came to the conclusion that *somebody* was trying to give him a rebuke, because he had failed to attend the Coronation. Not that he really thought it was Camilla, mind you. But he supposed that she might have been consulted and agreed to the rebuke in principle.

Well, from Lord Froome's point of view, this kind of treatment was disrespectful, especially when it involved a daughter. Camilla's relationship with her father was never quite the same.

The Sixth Marquess of Froome, interviewed by
Mr Simon Manasseh

Q: It is rumoured that your own relationship with the royal
family is precarious. Would you care to comment upon
this?

A: Not particularly. I prefer to comment on things which are
important to me. My relationship with the royal family
simply isn't important to me. They've gone their way,
and I've gone mine. It's sufficient that I should be able to
offer them a gracious dip of my head forwards, whenever
I happen to bump into them, which isn't very often, I can
assure you.

The Nanny Marks tapes

Now let me see; about Bruce. I think he was going through
quite a happy period these days. He'd been able to play an
important part in the Coronation, riding at the head of his
troop as part of the royal escort. He looked so wonderful sat
up there on his horse. It must have taken his batman ages to
clean all that shining armour. The Household Cavalry have
such wonderful uniforms.

He'd been posted to Knightsbridge now, which was much
pleasanter for him. It enabled him to experience a bit of the
social life in London. He was a frequent escort of Princess
Alexandra at one time, you know. It came out in all the
papers and this gave him a certain standing in the public eye.
She was such a *nice* girl. It's such a pity that nothing came of
their friendship.

Excerpts from Chloe, Marchioness of Froome's
correspondence with the Duchess of Northumbria

It sounds to me as if some of the information you have been
given about my 1940 Club is mistaken. I promise you that
there isn't a donkey on the place, and every single one of the

ladies who entertains my customers is certainly older than her declared age (which, in my official employment register, gets put down as eighteen).

Don't you think it might be too much of a simplification about life to suppose that all is beauty and sunshine? Perhaps we wouldn't enjoy it quite so much if it were uniformly that way. I'm not saying that it's pleasant when we have to involve ourselves with things that are harsh and ugly. But life does contain those aspects, just as much as it contains the beauty and the sunshine.

The only sensible suggestion that I can really make is that you come and visit me here, so that you can see this place for yourself. Don't come at the peak of business hours. That would only embarrass you. But there isn't a great deal going on in the afternoons, not unless someone has rung up to make a special appointment. But, in any case, I'll keep one afternoon free for you. Just name the day, and I'll put out the welcome mat.

I'm so glad that you took a liking to Trixie. I find her a Godsend. In fact, she's a real daughter to me, though I don't say that in any way making a comparison between yourself and her. It's just that I've reached an age when I need a pair of younger shoulders beside me, on to whom I can unburden some of the fetch-and-carry problems of life. Trixie is good to me in that respect, and I treasure her for it.

I hope you noticed that there is nothing common or vulgar (as you once vaguely hinted) about the way I effect introductions within my establishment. If one of my clients had made an appointment to come and see me that afternoon, it would have been exactly the same as the scene which you yourself witnessed. In other words I would have offered him some tea or coffee, or a brandy perhaps. And, just as I did with you, we'd have sat there looking through my album of photo portraits – though I dare say the conversation about each individual girl might have been different. Then he might have suggested a meeting with one or another of them. And, a little while later, she'd have entered, just as Trixie did. You will no doubt remember that there was nothing lewd about her

attire. If I'd been having tea with the Archbishop of Canter-
bury, she could quite as easily have sat down beside us.

The Nanny Marks tapes

Now what is there for me to tell you about Sebastian? Well,
I'm afraid he'd run into some trouble. The headmaster had
decided that they didn't want him to remain at Eton any
more. The older boys were a little bit too *fond* of him it
seems.

I didn't know what to think about it at the time. But I've
since had a long talk on the subject with Lady Tillot. It's
really quite natural, you see, for older boys to be fond of the
younger boys. It's all part of the growing-up process. Then
they move on to other things, like older ladies for example,
before marrying and settling down with someone a little
younger than themselves. I think it goes to show how *attractive* Sebastian must have been. It wasn't just *one* of the older
boys who grew fond of him. There were *lots* of them. The
headmaster decided that there were rather too many. So
Sebastian was sent home to us.

Of course, Lord Froome did his utmost to explain to the
headmaster that it wasn't really correct to sack the son of a
Marquess. Yet the headmaster had a reputation for being
what they call 'pink'. That means he was a little bit sym-
pathetic to Socialism. So I'm afraid he didn't pay much attention to these arguments.

In any case, Sebastian was about sixteen years old now, so
it wasn't as if he had to attend school any longer. And what
decided Lord Froome to wash his hands of him was the fact
that he ran away to London to join his mother.

Excerpt from Chloe, Marchioness of Froome's correspondence with the Duchess of Northumbria

No, I refuse to accept that Sebastian learnt any of these practices from myself. There may be several occasions when I

have gone to bed with homosexuals. But I have never, even once, encouraged two men to have sex together – usually because I'd prefer that such men were fantasizing about going to bed with myself.

The latest batch of rumours that have come into my parlour is really quite extraordinary, darling. Many of my clients have younger brothers who are still at Eton. So there may be more than a grain of truth in what they say.

Apparently Sebastian was sacked for selling himself – to a whole list of people, as far as I can make out. He had this friendship with one of the older boys in his house, who arranged for the lustier members of Pop and sixth form to come and have a look at him stripped naked. This cost each of them 2s. 6d., and I'm not sure how much it cost them if anything further happened. But Sebastian made the mistake of keeping an account of who came in, and how much had been paid, probably because he didn't trust this friend of his. But the account book was discovered by the boys' maid, who took it to his dame, who took it to his tutor. And that's how Sebastian came to be sacked, among all those others. It sounds as if it will rank among one of Eton's greatest scandals!

You must see, darling, that it makes my own behaviour far more reasonable in the light of what really goes on in this world. And I promise you that I'll do my utmost to see that Sebastian gets launched upon a normal sex life just as quickly as I possibly can. I'm sure he'll have no difficulty in these matters. Several of my girls have already commented on his photograph in my bedroom. But I have no intention of pushing him in *their* direction. The Queen of Sheba herself (if available) will be in reserve for him, when he comes to stay with me!

The Nanny Marks tapes

I felt it was such a *pity* there had to be this rift between Sebastian and his father. His not coming down to Caldicott meant that I saw so *little* of him nowadays. It was so depressing that they were all moving away from me. I began to feel really bad about it at this time. There was no one at all with whom I could discuss what was happening to the children. I certainly didn't want to go down the road for a gossip over the garden fence with someone like old Mrs Marsh. That wouldn't have been proper. One must learn to be discreet if one has been sharing the confidence of a family like the Tillots. But it was sad that the children so rarely came to see me any more.

I'm afraid I wasn't taking very good care of myself over this period. I've always had a delicate build, so I don't have to eat very much. Yet perhaps I'd been eating even less than I ought to.

Then one day I woke up to find myself in Froome hospital. The milkman had noticed that there were several days' supply untouched on my doorstep. And he called the ambulance. But it was still quite a shock for me to find myself in hospital.

And, as I lay there, I kept on thinking to myself that one of the children would come to see me. Or perhaps even Lord Froome would have the time to get away from his business commitments. But I didn't really know if they'd even heard that I was ill. One of them might have noticed that my weekly letter hadn't arrived. Yet they received so many letters nowadays. It seemed possible that they might not miss mine at all.

I remember having such a strange dream while I lay there in hospital. I thought we were back on the *Werry* on the Norfolk Broads. But there were now two boats. Lord Froome was at the helm of one of them, and we were all urging him to go faster from inside. The other boat had such an awful shadowy figure at the helm: like those pictures of *Death* that you see in cartoons. And the boat was filled with such common, ordinary people. Yet it was gaining on us. And I felt so afraid.

Then suddenly I could feel someone's hand touching me. And a voice was saying, 'Nanny darling! It's me! I've come to see you!' And when I opened my eyes I saw Lady Tillot sitting there, holding my hand. But I didn't say anything because I thought it was all part of the dream. I just lay there looking up at her, but feeling as if she'd saved me. Then she laughed softly, saying, 'Dear old Nan: what's been happening to you?' And I began to wonder if it was really true. I couldn't make out if I was dreaming or not dreaming; or even whether I was alive or dead.

So I asked her, 'Where am I?'

She kissed my hand and said, 'You're in hospital. But everything's going to be all right. I've brought you some flowers, and a lampshade to go on this light by your bedside'. And I looked at her. And then I looked around me. And I realized that what she was telling me was true.

Excerpt from Chloe, Marchioness of Froome's correspondence with the Duchess of Northumbria

Have you heard that old Nan is in hospital at Froome? I went down there to visit her yesterday, and I'm afraid she's not making a great deal of sense. It could be that she's slipping. Do remember how kind and selfless she was to all of us. She would love it if you managed to send some flowers, or something. And perhaps you could let Daddy and the others know that she isn't very well. A word from them might make all the difference.

The Nanny Marks tapes

You know I really think that Lady Tillot saved my life on that occasion. Apparently the doctors had been in touch with her. She was the only member of the family they could find, I suppose. She said that I must come up to London as soon as I was well enough for a period of convalescence. And this was lovely for me because she still had Sebastian staying with her.

I found that the house in Jermyn Street was a lot different from when I'd last been there. Lady Tillot had converted the cellar into a night-club. And she was running it with the assistance of the lady who shared her flat. A lady called Trixie Cardew, who became quite famous later, as I expect you'll remember.

It was a most unusual sort of club in some ways; mostly for gentlemen, I noticed. But there wasn't any need for them to bring ladies with them because Lady Tillot and Miss Cardew provided such excellent entertainment on their own. They had persuaded various friends to come round and help keep the gentlemen amused.

And they used to play such games! It was quite like the old days in the Women's Institute. But I wasn't required to take part this time. Lady Tillot just sat me down at a table and gave me a glass of champagne, telling me to keep quiet and to watch.

I remember that Lady Tillot was dressed in a long flowing gown, covered in sequins, with a glorious array of brightly coloured ostrich plumes. She reminded me of some of our visits to the pantomime. Anyway, she stood up on the stage and stopped the band playing to say that it was time for everyone to play a game called 'Tired Businessmen'.

She then got all the gentlemen sitting on separate chairs in the middle of the dance floor. They had to relax completely, as if they'd just returned home from a hard day's work. Then Miss Cardew and some of the other ladies were sent to cheer them up. They would loosen their ties, and open their shirts for them. Then they would start massaging their troubles away. You could see that the gentlemen were enjoying themselves, because they had to be reminded so frequently that they were tired businessmen. They weren't allowed to become 'frisky', as Lady Tillot called it.

Most of them went upstairs afterwards so that the game could continue with the gentlemen lying down. You see, if they were really tired businessmen, they wouldn't want to remain all evening sitting upright in a chair. Lady Tillot came and explained all this to me while the game was still in progress. It was such an original way of running a night-club. But then Lady Tillot always was an original sort of person.

I never knew quite what to make of Miss Cardew. She was distinctly odd in some respects. I think she must have been frightfully sensitive to all manner of heat. Anyway she told me that clothes stifled her, so she was always taking them off. Not without some good reasons, mind you. I remember her spilling chocolate mousse down the front of her dress. And she took everything off so that she could clean herself properly. It was strange, I thought, that Lady Tillot had chosen such a lady as her business partner. But what it really shows is just how broadminded a person like Lady Tillot can be. It was as if she never even noticed these things. She could rise above it, you see.

Mind you, I wasn't the only person to feel embarrassed by Miss Cardew. I remember Sebastian being sent to fetch another bottle of champagne, and him returning to say that he couldn't fetch it, as Miss Cardew was sitting undressed in front of the refrigerator. But Lady Tillot merely snorted with laughter and told him to remove Miss Cardew to the nearest bed. But he never returned with that bottle of champagne. The poor lamb must have been frightened of her, you see.

Anyway, I was feeling a lot better for my stay in London. And Lady Tillot wrote to all the children, urging them to write to me more frequently, which they did, God bless their little hearts!

Excerpts from Chloe, Marchioness of Froome's correspondence with the Duchess of Norhtumbria

Talk about Lazarus! Nan seems to be as frisky as an old goat. She sits with all my young ladies, sipping champagne with them and remarking upon the gentlemanly appearance of some of my clients. The latter respond by standing amazed, uncertain whether Nan herself is really supposed to be present in such company.

Nobody need trouble themselves about Sebastian. It is now clearly established in the minds of all here that his sexual inclinations are perfectly normal. Far too normal, for the comfort of some of my girls. They've nicknamed him Salacious Seb. But I expect he'll manage to outgrow it through general exhaustion.

11

A Phoenix from the Ashes

1954–5

The Nanny Marks tapes

There were times when I felt as if I'd become a completely new person, when I'd been saved from that hospital. They tell a story about that bird the phoenix which gets all burnt up and then rises as something entirely new from its own ashes. Well, that's the way I felt. It was as if I'd become someone different altogether.

The word seemed to have got around that I was available to help people. You see, now that my own children had grown up, there was time spare for me to go to other families – when their own nanny was on holiday, for example. And the children would call me Grand-nan, so as not to confuse me with their own nannies.

Camilla was one of the first to invite me for a visit as Grand-nan. She had a little boy now, called David. This was to their London house, in Belgrave Square. She'd done it up so nicely. And I soon became accustomed to Michael's rather aloof way of addressing people.

I think the real thing about Michael was that he liked to keep himself to himself. Sometimes, when I would talk to him over the breakfast table, I got the impression that he preferred to read his newspaper. But serious-minded men are very often like that.

He was always very particular about his bathroom, I remember. I didn't realize this at first or I'd have been more careful. But one day he took me on a tour of all the bathrooms in the house and said, 'All of these, Nanny, are for you. You may have *one* of them, or *all* of them. But the one bathroom you *cannot* have is the one that I'm going to show you now, because that's the bathroom that I personally use!' He liked to keep himself to himself, you see.

Camilla was expecting another baby shortly. (This was to be Timmy.) It meant that she couldn't accompany Princess Margaret on as many functions as she would have liked to have done – which was probably fortunate, in a way, or they might have blamed her for allowing Princess Margaret to fall in with the wrong company. They ought to have been a little more careful, really, in their appointments to the royal household. If they'd stuck to Old Etonians, this kind of problem would never have occurred.

That's why I think that Bruce would have been such a sensible choice as aide-de-camp to the royal family. It was a post he would have dearly loved to hold. We were all discussing the matter when he came round for a drink one evening at Belgrave Square. He was a captain now, and I think what he really wanted was for Camilla to say a few words in the right person's ear so that his name might be considered favourably when the next appointment was to be made. There were rumours that the post would soon be vacant. But Camilla wasn't as encouraging as she might have been. And I think Bruce was a trifle offended.

It wasn't that they were *against* him, mind you. They went on discussing the matter after Bruce had left. But, from Michael's point of view, an aide-de-camp to the royal family needs to be quite a personality in his own right; and he didn't think Bruce had the right qualifications. 'Your brother is just a college boy, dressed up as a tin soldier,' was his way of putting it. And Camilla seemed to think it was a pity he'd been dropped by Princess Alexandra, since that wouldn't help his chances either.

I was really feeling a bit sorry for Bruce over this period. He took things terribly to heart when life wasn't going exactly right for him. And Camilla seemed to think he was going through some crisis in his emotional development. It involved his relationship with women, she said. I don't think Bruce had the same values as the rest of his army friends. He was very serious about meeting the right woman one day, and did not want to feel that he'd given himself recklessly to someone who was undeserving. But it's very difficult to maintain this way of thinking when you're in the army. That's what Camilla said. And she thought the subject had been tormenting him a lot recently.

According to Camilla, Bruce had had some terrible experience. She knew what it was, but preferred not to talk about it in detail. All she would say was that there were some low clubs in the West End, where women *give* themselves for money. And it seems that, one evening, when Bruce and his army friends had had a little too much to drink in the officers' mess, he was persuaded to accompany them to one of these places. And Bruce was horrified by what he saw going on there.

Excerpts from Chloe, Marchioness of Froome's correspondence with the Duchess of Northumbria

Let me assure you that I am just as troubled about the situation as you could ever be. It's not what Bruce may have seen which torments me. (Surely that must have been coming to him one of these days?) But I feel guilty that we all permitted him to grow up viewing life through these pearly-gate glasses. You're as guilty as I am, darling. You've got to understand that *we* were the models which he had in mind while formulating all these ideals about the purity of womanhood. How precisely this happened is a question that I'd prefer a psychiatrist to answer, because it leaves me floundering with a feeling that I may be getting out of my depth.

Buffy Yeovil was in here last night, and he gets the feedback about what goes on in the officers' mess at Knightsbridge Barracks from his son. The picture has now been clarified for me. You know the way all those boys refer to me as Ma T. Well, it seems that Bruce knew all their stories about Ma T. But it never clicked in his mind that Ma T was me. Hence this stupid practical joke they played upon him.

The Nanny Marks tapes

Camilla seemed to think that Bruce had suddenly turned against women. He regarded them as being impure, you see. I got the chance for some long talks with him during these weeks, because he used to come round to collect me, so I could accompany him to those open air meetings which were addressed by Billy Graham.

Oh, he took this movement terribly seriously, you know. He said there was a spiritual hunger in the younger generation, that it was time for everybody to rediscover the joys of Christ. It's silly of me. I oughtn't to be laughing. But he was so earnest about the matter, if you know what I mean.

I'm glad there was no one there to see me. We had to file up to the stand where Billy Graham had been preaching and display our conversion before the eyes of the world. I was really quite worried about Bruce. I was never quite certain whether Billy Graham was God, or the devil in disguise. And, with Bruce lingering to be near his master, I felt that I'd better keep my eye on him, because one never knew – the devil might try to take the hindmost, as the expression goes!

Excerpt from the personal manuscript of Bruce, Lord Tillot

Since there is nothing that I can truly trust in this world, the answer surely must lie elsewhere. *Somewhere* there must be a recipient of man's trust, since the alternative is too horrible to contemplate.

I am thrilled that Billy Graham is going to preach to us here in London. I would have preferred it, I dare say, if the word had been given by an Englishman, rather than an American. On the other hand, it could be argued that the Americans haven't yet had their share of being truly elite in this world. (I'm not sure that money ought to count.)

What I like about this man is his sincerity, and his determination to get back to the original message which Jesus was trying to teach to us: that God is love, and that, if we lack love in our lives, then the solution is to turn to Him. But, in this case of course, He is only appearing in the form of Billy Graham.

Excerpt from Chloe, Marchioness of Froome's correspondence with the Duchess of Northumbria

I think we ought to encourage Bruce in this new outburst of religiosity. It's not that I view Jesus Christ as a woman substitute (for men, that is), but I do feel that Bruce has needed *someone* to cling on to from the days of his childhood. If we smash it all up for him, he'll have nothing left at all. And we should remind ourselves that he always has been very faithful to Jesus Christ, in one way or another, even if he does have his lapses.

The Nanny Marks tapes

Later, Camilla wrote and told me that Bruce had turned away from religion, but that he'd been drinking far too much lately. And apparently there was some awful row when he got slightly tipsy at a party the Queen was giving at Windsor Castle. Princess Alexandra went over to tell him that this was not allowed. And Bruce very stupidly answered her back. Told her that he'd like to be rude to her, but that he couldn't because she was a Princess – which of course was very rude of him indeed. And he ought to have realized that the royal family would be offended.

Sebastian came to pay me a visit soon after this. He was staying at Caldicott in an attempt to make things up with his father. But it wasn't going too well for him. Lord Froome had always been one to insist on good table manners. And I'm afraid that Sebastian's table manners had become atrociously bad ever since he'd been staying with his mother. Things came to a head when he took a large mouthful of cauliflower cheese which turned out to be too hot for him. So he spat it out into his hand.

Apparently Lord Froome was simply furious with him.

Said that Sebastian wouldn't have dreamt of doing that kind of thing if the Duchess of Kent had been sitting at the table, so he wasn't going to permit it to happen, even when there was just himself. The trouble is that Sebastian couldn't take these rebukes as seriously as they were intended, which irritated his father still further.

Sebastian was very lucky in some ways. We found that he didn't have to do his national service because he was partly deaf in one ear. (That was the effect of his mastoid trouble when he was a child.) But he wasn't able to get on with his father, so he moved up to London again, living on a very small allowance that was provided for him by Lord Froome.

Excerpt from Chloe, Marchioness of Froome's correspondence with the Duchess of Northumbria

Sebastian can really be quite funny you know. He came back from delivering my birthday present for little David and described the scene as follows. He says that you're always highly nervous when he puts in an appearance at your house, as if you're convinced that he's going to burn cigarette holes in the curtains or leave rude messages for your guests to find tucked away behind the cushions on the sofa.

On this occasion, he claims that you did as always offer him a drink but, while you sat there with little David on your lap, you appeared to have forgotten about opening the parcel, so that appropriate words of thanks could be conveyed back to me. Instead, you were indulging in jerky conversation which jumped from one subject to another.

Then, very gradually, you began to undress little David. And it was only when you came to the point of presenting the naked little David to my parcel that you suddenly shook your head and proclaimed, 'I must be mad!' I'd love to know if this story has any truth in it.

The Nanny Marks tapes

I think that Sebastian may have found it difficult to make ends meet. That's why he went to work for the William Hickey column on the *Daily Express*. Of course, he didn't really like doing that kind of work. It can get you in the most awful trouble writing gossip about your friends. But there weren't many other jobs in London that would have suited him. It wasn't as if he'd left school with some degrees or anything.

One good thing was that it kept him busy. And he was acquiring quite a reputation for himself, so Camilla wrote and told me. People were careful not to be nasty to him, in case he decided to be nasty to them back.

But then he did something that he really shouldn't have done. I'm sure he didn't *mean* to cause all the embarrassment that it did. Yet he should have been more careful about what he said. I expect he was jostled into doing it by his editor.

You see he wrote a long article about the new wave of sex clubs throughout London. And it was very naughty of him to have included Lady Tillot's 1940 Club on the list. In fact he made out that the most terrible things were happening there. I was always having to tell the people in the village that it was just one of Sebastian's little jokes.

But I'm afraid his mother didn't see it like that. I received ever such an angry letter from her in which it was made quite clear that he had offended her. In fact she asked me to tell Sebastian that he could keep away from the 1940 Club for as long as she continued to employ a bouncer.

Sebastian got a great deal of money for that article. He must have done, because he bought me a television set for Christmas, in addition to this tape-recording machine which he gave me for my birthday, while he still didn't have very much money to spend. But things were easier for him now. He told me how he'd given up his job on the Hickey column. Said there wasn't any need for him to work any more. And he'd got his own flat now, somewhere just off the King's Road, which was the part of London he liked best of all.

But he kept well away from Caldicott Manor. He said he had only to sit in the same room with his father for five minutes and they'd start quarrelling. If it was necessary for him to come down for anything, he generally asked me to put him up here in the cottage.

Excerpt from Chloe, Marchioness of Froome's correspondence with the Duchess of Northumbria

Talk about a snake in the grass, I find I've actually been harbouring one in my bosom! Cleopatra beware: I now know their poison stings!

Do you remember Marilyn? (She was the tartiest of all my tarts.) I now hear that she went splits with Sebastian on cooking up that article. Sebastian could never possibly have done it all by himself. You can't milk acid from a nanny goat. (I wish the sexes were right for this analogy.) But Marilyn has been trying to get her own back on me, ever since Trixie fell through the two-way ceiling mirror on top of her performance with a couple of transvestite homosexuals. She accused me of receiving money for Buffy's supposed pleasure at the accident. Anyway, she no longer works for me. And I've put the word around that she has recurrent attacks of urethritis – which is true, incidentally.

Letter from Lord Sebastian Tillot to Chloe, Marchioness of Froome

Mum darling,

I do understand how you're probably not feeling particularly friendly with me at the present moment. But I still thought I should write you this letter, in the hope that it might put what I did in slightly clearer perspective.

I wasn't knocking you and the 1940 Club, so much as admiring it, presenting it to the general British public as the in place to go. You see, I really do believe this. London is just beginning to wake up. In a few years' time, people will hardly recognize this city. And it will all be due to the vitalizing efforts of a few great heroines like yourself.

I'm playing my own small part, as best I can. In my particular group of friends, we all take turns in supplying the premises for that night's party. The only trouble is that our various landlords are beginning to object, on account of both the noise and damage.

> Much love,
>   Sebastian

The Nanny Marks tapes

One thing that *was* going very well for Lord Froome was his private life. At long last he'd become interested in someone else's company. Miss Ponsonby was such a beautiful lady. Not only beautiful to look at, but beautiful to talk to as well. She'd worked in Paris as a mannequin for Dior – oh, it must have been for quite a number of years. Her face was so well known nowadays that she could spend as much leisure time in England as she pleased. We'd read in the papers that her only remaining ambition was to marry and settle down.

Lord Froome invited me up for tea one day when they were both there. And I could see how happy they were, sitting there in front of the television holding hands. It made me think what a pity it is that all of us can't be like that for ever.

The Sixth Marquess of Froome, interviewed by Mr Simon Manasseh

Q: Would you like to say anything about your first encounter with Miss Nadia Ponsonby?

A: Oh, certainly. There was this big charity gala being organized at Luptree Court, with a fashion show at which some of the top French designers were displaying. Mind you, I'm not in the least interested in fashion. But I told them they could put on the show, if they got Nadia Ponsonby to be one of the models.

  I didn't think for a minute that she'd say yes. She seemed such a distant figure, even though I was always

seeing her photographs in the glossy magazines. In fact, I
had one of them stuck up in my bathroom at the time.
Fully clothed, mind you. There's nothing indecent about
any of this. It's a photo that's still in my bathroom today,
if it comes to that! Anyway, as she agreed to be one of the
models, I had to stick to my part of the bargain, which was
to give them free use of Luptree Court for this fashion
show. It was too late for me to back out.

Well, I sat right through that fashion show. I had my
eyes riveted on Nadia practically the whole time, but she
never looked once in my direction. Then, when it all came
to an end, there were some children who came rushing up
to ask me for my autograph. I'm quite used to it. It's
always happening, to tell the truth. But on this occasion I
excused myself, for they'd just given me an idea.

I rushed over to where Nadia was standing and said,
'Excuse me, Miss Ponsonby, but could I possibly ask for
your autograph? I want it to go with the photograph I have
of you in my bathroom.'

She just laughed and said, 'Of course'. And this led to me
inviting them all back to Caldicott Manor to have a drink.
And well . . . a month or so later, I knew her intimately, as
you might say.

Author's narrative

It was with some difficulty that I managed to obtain an interview with the sixth Marquess's second wife. She had remarried since his death, to become the Maharanee of Peshawar;
and I discovered that she was not readily available for many
months. My letters were always answered by a secretary,
who fended me off with excuses (sounding plausible enough)
that the Maharanee was currently engaged in activities in
other parts of the globe.

My final tactic was to wait until I read in the *Evening
Standard* that she was currently staying at Claridges, with her
daughter Lady Buddleia Tillot (which is to say the sixth Marquess's fourth and youngest child). 'Buddy' was quoted as

saying that she had persuaded 'Mummy' to let her come back to England to see for herself what the punk rock scene was all about. Knowing how shy and secretive the Maharanee was by repute, I did not try for an appointment this time. I merely presented myself at the reception desk, and asked if I could see her. The reply came back that she wasn't up yet. But I countered this by passing a message back to say that I'd wait downstairs, being careful to take a seat where I could watch all three staircases and the lift simultaneously.

My tactics were successful. After a long wait of more than three hours, which brought us into the afternoon, I observed that the Maharanee was descending the front staircase, with Buddy on her arm, and casting furtive glances from behind huge sunglasses into the hall below; she was wondering no doubt which, if any, of the assembled visible males might be this intrusive Mr Fairfield. I think it was Lady Buddleia who identified me first, in terms of suspicion, for I noted how she gave a hurried whisper in her mother's ear; the latter froze momentarily against the wall halfway up the stairs. By then, however, I was already up and on my way to introduce myself; she accepted gracefully that I had her trapped, and invited me to join her for coffee at one of the tables. Lady Buddleia was rather less willing to accept my intrusion. A tall slender girl of twenty, with her hair bobbed short and streaked with both violet and silver. I also noted that she wore what looked like a small ruby on a pierced left nostril. But she clearly regarded me with impatience. I heard her whisper (none too softly) as we moved towards a table, 'Really Mummy! You always give in far too easily.'

The Maharanee turned to her immediately and said, 'Buddy, why don't you go off to Bond Street and pick up that camera you wanted? Then come back here to fetch me before going on to that exhibition. It won't take very long, will it?

Buddy hesitated a moment, deciding what line she was going to take. Then she turned to me and said, 'Why do you have to bother us? You're some kind of reporter, aren't you?

I corrected this assumption. So she added, 'Well, even if you're not, I don't like what you're doing. I wish you'd go away. Why don't you go and investigate something interesting

– like the way young people feel in this country?'

I suggested that I might very well like to do this, if she would assist me in this task. She snorted in reply, throwing her handsome face into the air, before adding, 'Go and do your own dirty work. I'm nobody's henchman.' Then she departed, leaving me to open my interview with the Maharanee in an atmosphere of mutual embarrassment.

I found the Maharanee's brand of shyness to be something very personal: she was childishly coy, and I could almost picture her sitting in the grass playing with daisy chains; but, at the same time, she exuded sex appeal, with a tantalizing promise of tomorrow's love. It was evident that she wanted to get this interview behind her, so she wouldn't have to be bothered by me again. And I saw that she was accustomed to getting her own way passively.

My questions to her were initially on the subject of her courtship by Lord Froome and the gist of her replies was as follows.

'Yes, indeed I found Edward attractive. There was something of the little boy in him. I mean, who else would have run up to ask for my autograph in such pompous surroundings? But there was also something of the knight in shining armour about him. I remember, on this particular occasion, the man who was accompanying me – he wasn't a special friend, well, not *really* – was certainly irritated at the way I was permitting Edward to flirt with me.

'This was when we were back at Caldicott Manor, having rather too many drinks, I suppose. This friend of mine suddenly threw his brandy all over me. And Edward was there, like a shot. "Leave my house instantly!" and that kind of remark. I thought there was going to be the most terrible fight. But my friend apparently thought better of it. He just departed. So there we were, Edward and I, left alone together – not completely, of course.'

I inquired about her emotional confusions concerning the Marquess and the Maharajah, at a time when she was evidently held in high esteem by both of them, and was also regarded as being available.

She replied, 'My relationship with Freckles, my present husband, hadn't really developed at this time. Or not to the extent that we were in love with one another. Edward was always someone very special to me from the start.'

The Nanny Marks tapes

Camilla never approved of what she called the unsavoury gossip columns, although she did read them of course. She didn't like it, for example, when they started writing things about Sebastian. I think she felt it was his fault really, that he did silly things just to attract public attention. Giving a pyjama party in the underground, for example. She didn't think that anyone in their right minds would want to attend a pyjama party in the underground. But that's what Sebastian did. Or that's what the newspapers *said* he did.

And ever such a lot of things were written about his flat in Chelsea and about his quarrels with the neighbours. LORD SEB LOVES HIS SQUALOR was one of the headlines. And there was a picture of him with a beatnik girl lying on a pile of rags in the middle of an empty floor. It was cheeky really, because none of us ever called him Seb.

What Camilla disapproved of was the way he must have invited the photographer into his flat. She felt he was asking for all the bad publicity he got. But I don't think Sebastian looked upon it in quite the same way. He told me once that he was emerging as a public figure, and it was all rather fun.

But it was difficult sometimes. There wasn't always the opportunity to explain to people that what had been written wasn't exactly true. And it was very easy for people to get the wrong impression, like Lord Froome did, on several occasions. He was really quite upset at Sebastian's behaviour and stopped the allowance he was giving him.

'The boy's going to the dogs!' he said when he came to call on me, one day. 'You used to spoil him, Nanny. That's the trouble.'

'Oh no,' I answered. 'I never used to spoil him. I just let him have his own way, because he was the kind of boy who *needed* his own way.'

But Lord Froome didn't see it like that. He said it was a case of sparing the rod, and spoiling the child.

But he didn't really mean it, you know. He was just upset. It was probably because there had been reports in the paper that Miss Ponsonby was going to marry the Maharajah of Peshawar. It wasn't true, mind you, like most things they write. But he was feeling unsettled, I suppose. And it was correct, I believe, that Miss Ponsonby had gone on holiday to India.

Lord Froome's favourite, at this time, was Bruce – of the sons, I mean. It was the reaction, perhaps, from thinking that he may have been too severe on him, and too soft with Sebastian. And he felt Bruce hadn't obtained his just rewards from life. He had done quite well at school. In any case, he'd always worked very hard. And he'd always done whatever his father had wanted him to do. And now he seemed to have got stuck with the army. I mean it was clear that he wasn't to become a general, or anything. So Lord Froome was concerned to help him in every possible way.

That was why he went to his lawyers and worked out a system for handing over the estate to Bruce at this early age. It was something they had been urging him to do, because the Tillot family would be unlikely to survive another batch of death duties like the last lot. Bruce was quite prepared to let his father keep half the capital for himself. As the lawyers pointed out, the main thing was to save himself from having to pay such enormous death duties.

Although he was still very much in control, Lord Froome was moving into retirement. Like myself, in a manner of speaking. There were quite a lot of similarities between Lord Froome and myself, now that I come to think about it. Retirement didn't alter the fact that we were both at the height of our powers and doing very well all round. He too was a phoenix, you see. Wessex was alive again. And the world was ours!

The Sixth Marquess of Froome, interviewed by Mr Simon Manasseh

Q: I believe it was around this period when you handed over the estate to your son. Am I to assume that you had great confidence in him?

A: I don't think anyone really had *confidence* in him. He wasn't the sort of person you had confidence in. But he wasn't doing anything particularly silly at this time. So I thought it was a risk worth taking. I thought that he'd be prepared to play ball with me. Let's put it like that.

Q: Was there any real necessity to hand the estate over to him at all?

A: Well, you know what all these lawyers are like. They're always trying to persuade you that you're liable to fall under a bus tomorrow morning. And after I'd seen how we'd been crippled by death duties when my father died, I was anxious that it didn't happen to the family a second time. I shall always hold it against my father that he couldn't bring himself to trust me sufficiently to hand over the estate. That cost us a fine packet, as you well know. And I wasn't going to have people saying that I'd shilly shallied in the same way; leaving the final decision until it was too late. I just told the lawyers to get it over and done with, to let both Bruce and myself take whatever might be coming to us, and to do away with all this silly business about a family entail.

Q: Am I to understand that Lord Sebastian was to get nothing at all out of this arrangement?

A: Why should he? He was the younger son. He didn't expect anything in any case, or nothing more than the paltry little sum which was guaranteed to him under his mother's wedding settlement. But I can see you don't understand the way we work in this country. It's a case of eldest son takes all. The family remains powerful that way. And the younger sons have to show a little gumption in life or they go under. It's a case of sink or swim. But it's been like that for donkey's years.

Q: I believe that Lord Sebastian's behaviour at this time was regarded in media circles as irresponsible. Do you feel that this British attitude of privilege according to primogeniture might in any way account for his behaviour?

A: You mean, did he feel left out, and behave stupidly as a result? Well, he might have done. It's difficult to know precisely what may be going on in another man's head. But I think you're confusing the matter by using all these long words. Some people do stupid things, just because they feel like doing them. And, if you ask me, he probably got a kick from it, because he knew I'd be reading all about it in my paper next morning. Turn over the bloody page, and there he'd be, large as life, blowing a raspberry at some press camera. But the raspberry was intended for myself in a strange way.

Author's narrative

I asked Mr Walter Davis how he received the transfer of power from Lord Froome to Lord Tillot.

He said, 'I think his father took pity on him. That's the only way I can account for his folly in handing it all over to him, lock, stock and barrel. Well, all but some of the cash, I dare say. But, if you've got a son that's as gormless as Bruce was, I expect you'd feel that you've got to do something about it. I mean you feel responsible for him, because you produced him. It's too late to think about throwing him back into the sea with all the other fishes.'

I inquired whether the transfer of the Luptree estate made any difference to the running of the Wessex Motels; my questions were addressed specifically to Mr Perkins.

He replied, 'No difference at all, or not while Bruce remained in the Household Cavalry. It was part of their gentlemen's agreement that he'd allow his father to go on running the show. So everything was going ahead at full steam.

'Lord Froome's big concern now was to launch what he named the Wessex League. He'd already built up the Wessex Motels. But that was more of a personal organization. He now tried to bring all the other local tourist industries into the same game: no longer in rivalry, but supporting each other in their matters of common interest.

'There were all the stately homes in Wessex for a start. Some really big ones, like Longleat, Wilton, Blenheim, Badminton, Beaulieu and Montacute – just for a start. And there were no end of lesser places. They were all asked to pay money to this new Wessex League, so that the "Bring a Tourist to Wessex" campaign could be launched. The places which refused to pay were merely excluded from all the joint publicity.

'Then it didn't take long for some of the county councils to wake up to the fact that they were missing out on good revenue by not taking up the Wessex League as their own concern, through the medium of their various tourist boards. If they hadn't woken up pretty sharply, the Wessex League would have put them out of business. You can't afford to be too parochial these days, even if the idea is the promotion of a region, rather than the country as a whole.

'I remember that Lord Froome was tickled pink at the way all these county councils suddenly came over to his cause. "Stick-in-the-muds" is what he called them as they sat there hedging their bets until they saw what leads there might be to follow. Well, it was Lord Froome who gave them the lead. And it amused him to see them all falling into line, as if they'd thought up the idea for themselves.

'I dare say people enjoyed having a good laugh at Lord Froome, and whatever they happened to be reading about him or his family in the papers. But what it all boiled down to in the end was that they were a lot better off than if he'd never been around. The hotels and restaurants were fully booked, and the shops had a better turnover. It didn't matter to them if they had to dress up in funny hats occasionally or find a group of young people who'd do a morris dance on the village green. People were becoming Wessex-conscious all of a sudden. And it was all in their common interest. They were just reminding themselves that they were together, in some strange sort of way.'

12

A Tilt at the Establishment

1955–9

The Nanny Marks tapes

There were some ways in which things weren't quite right with this world we had created. Not that it was *our* fault, although I think we were far too trusting in those days. We did everything to make life run smoothly for people, but they had no gratitude, although they managed to conceal the way they felt about us at first.

In the general election, for example, they were very careful not to come out in the open and vote Socialist. But it was a feeling they were harbouring up inside them. A nasty kind of poison that was waiting to come out: a desire to be spiteful, just when the moment suited them.

Mind you, there were some people who liked to pretend they were Socialists, just for the devilry of it. Like Sebastian, for example. Do you know that he came round to visit me, and brought with him a poster supporting Mr Gaitskell? And he wanted me to stick it up in my window. I'd have died of shame if any of the villagers had seen it there! Sebastian was only doing this to tease me, I know. But he was growing interested in politics. He said that half of his friends in Chelsea were Socialists. London must have changed a lot since the days when I knew it.

He told me that the big idea nowadays was to have a tilt at the Establishment. The Establishment had got society back into their control, so they had to be dislodged by fair means or foul. And the one thing they couldn't protect themselves against was humour. Sebastian wanted to poke fun at them in every possible way.

I told him that it was rather silly, really, seeing that he was a Lord. He was just hitting out at himself. But Sebastian liked to think that he was no longer part of the Establishment. He said he'd gone over to the other side.

As for Bruce, I'm afraid the Suez crisis upset him tremendously. He was all set to be shipped out to Egypt, when the fighting stopped. Yet, having been so near to fighting in a war, he found that his conscience was troubling him. It wasn't that he was against Mr Eden, or anything like that. He was as upset as any of us that the British Empire was slipping away from our grasp. But he kept on asking himself if anybody has the right to kill people. It wasn't as if he'd joined the army to kill people, you see.

Excerpt from the personal manuscript of Bruce, Lord Tillot

It alarms me that the world is turning back to violence once again. It is all very well for people like myself to expound to others the true message of Jesus Christ, but the seed is evidently falling upon barren land. It is the prophets of our material world who evidently have the ear of the people.

I am led to ask myself if I have not evaded one of the responsibilities which fall naturally upon the shoulders of someone born to my position in life. I am speaking here of materialistic example, in contrast to the spiritual path which I have hitherto been investigating. Perhaps I should strive to become more a part of this post-war world, and acquaint myself with the way that life now is really lived. Then perhaps I would have greater service to render unto God, from the sheer utility of my service unto man.

The Nanny Marks tapes

Now that Luptree and the Wessex Motels officially belonged to Bruce, his interests were wider than they had been. And

Lord Froome was urging him to resign his commission, to take a more active interest in the administrative side of Luptree, while still letting his father have the final say in everything, mind you. So that's what he decided to do.

Lord Froome had got it all working so nicely by now. He invited me into his office on one occasion. And there was a huge map of Wessex on the wall. I remember him tapping it with his ruler and saying, 'Come on, old Nan, tell me where you'd like to go. Stonehenge, Avebury and Glastonbury? The Cheddar Gorge and Shearwater? The New Forest? Or the Quantock Hills? Wherever you'd like to go, I'll fix up a free trip for you.'

Author's narrative

I inquired of Mr Perkins what differences in style were perceptible when Lord Tillot finally took up his duties as the managing director of the Wessex Motels.

He replied, 'I'll give him this. He certainly put his heart into it at the start. This was just after he'd left the Household Cavalry. He went rushing all over Wessex, meeting the managers of the various motels in the Luptree group. But he never really got the knack of putting himself over to them as a person. Others had to step in quickly, to keep the sound of music going on all round him.

The Nanny Marks tapes

Camilla and Michael were doing very well for themselves too. She'd given up her position as Mistress of the Robes now that there was talk of Princess Margaret marrying Mr Armstrong-Jones. Not that she disapproved of him, even if he was only a photographer. (One has got to remember that his stepfather was an Earl, and he did go to Eton.) The real problem was that David and Timmy were quite a handful for her at times, on Nanny's day off you understand.

But Camilla and Michael remained as intimate with the

royal family as they'd ever been before. Camilla told me *such* a funny story about Prince Philip, from the last time they'd been to stay. Apparently there were a whole lot of Highland cattle grazing on the outskirts of the grouse moor. And one of the bulls had run wild. Yet nobody knew about this at the time.

So there was Camilla ambling quietly along with Prince Philip at her side, when what should they see come charging down the track to meet them but a great big bull. Naturally, their first reaction was to dive into the heather. And there they remained for the next minute or so, scarcely daring to breathe.

Prince Philip nudged Camilla and suggested that they were perhaps being rather ridiculous. So out they came on to the track again. Yet, at this particular moment, the beaters happened to arrive on the scene. So what they saw was Camilla and Prince Philip climbing out of the heather with sheepish expressions on their faces.

Oh, I think Prince Philip is the most wonderful person. I love it when he stands up for himself. We need that kind of person in the royal family. If newspapermen squirt nasty things at you, then squirt them back! That's what Prince Philip does. I know there are people nowadays who'd like some kind of a stuffed scarecrow for a King. But they're not going to get that kind of thing while Prince Philip is around. He is always someone who knows when to take the initiative.

Michael and Prince Philip are very similar people in many ways. Both of them manage to keep abreast of the times. At this time, Michael was emerging as quite an expert on antique furniture. He'd been picking up odds and ends at various country sales, and then reselling them to foreign buyers in London. He'd made no end of a profit that way. Camilla told me one day that, if he went on like this, he'd soon be a millionaire.

It really surprised me sometimes how much Camilla had changed since the days when she was a little girl. She no longer had that unworldly magic quality she always used to display. She seemed very much *at home* in society nowadays. Yet this may have been what she really wanted in the first place. In any case, she seemed to have all the things she could possibly have wished for in their house in Belgrave Square.

And what next? Well Lady Tillot wrote and told me she was extending the area of the 1940 Club, so the clients could choose between the atmospheres of London and Berlin. Such a good idea, don't you think? She'd gone into partnership with a certain German gentleman called 'Fruity' who was the manager of some night-club in Hamburg. He was going to assist her in this venture.

Excerpt from Chloe, Marchioness of Froome's correspondence with the Duchess of Northumbria

It's such fun undertaking all this redecoration in my 1940 Club. The walls of the main night-club are now frescoed, as if it were London in the Blitz. We've even got the front end of a Spitfire, on whose wings the nightly cabaret is performed, and with the pianist sitting permanently in its cockpit. My ladies are all dressed in uniform. Anything from Waafs and Wrens to Red Cross nurses. They look surprisingly sexy in these outfits, possibly because the rest of London is veering to the other extreme of more flagrant, unsubtle display.

What you probably remember as 'the room at the back' has now taken on the atmosphere of a debauched Gestapo headquarters, with plenty of booze, and sluttishly dressed whores, in marked contrast to the ladies next door. This room is under the personal direction of Fruity, my partner from Hamburg. He encourages the men to don some Nazi hat or helmet, and then to stride back into the London Blitz room, where they are greeted with ribald cat-calls from my more British clientele. But, in reward for their efforts, they usually get taken prisoner by some of my ladies in uniform, who march them off to the room upstairs for a little private interrogation.

The Nanny Marks tapes

Trixie Cardew, with whom Lady Tillot used to be in partner-ship, was spending a little time in prison nowadays. There had been some most unfortunate business when Lord Yeovil had started paying calls at the night-club. He had been quite attentive to Miss Cardew, it seems. But one night she found him in the ladies' cloakroom discussing the cabaret with one of the girls who should have been up there on the stage. She was indignant at the delay. People were getting restless.

But it was wrong that she lost her temper with Lord Yeovil. There were some huge hat-pins in a pincushion on the ladies' dressing table. She took one of these and stuck it into him – somewhere rather low, I believe.

Anyway the jury decided there may have been things in her favour, because Miss Cardew had been led to believe that Lord Yeovil had been too affectionate with a whole succes-sion of the girls that evening. Of course, Lady Tillot was very upset about Uncle Buffy getting hurt like this. But I don't think she really minded about the departure of Miss Cardew. In her letter, she said it had done the world of good for the 1940 Club. The takings had trebled.

It was a time of prosperity all round. Mr Macmillan was a very *able* Prime Minister. He was quite right when he told the people that they'd never had it so good. And they ought to have been grateful to him. But they weren't, you know. You should have seen all those vicious cartoons that tried to poke fun at him in some of the papers. And on the television too. People were becoming cruel in their efforts to be witty about politics. Satirical programmes were all that people seemed to like.

I think it's true to say that I too was becoming a bit of a celebrity around this time. It was all part of a general concern about nannies being a dying race. And it's true in a way. Neither for love nor money can you find a good nanny now-adays. Or you need to be very lucky if you do. People just can't afford them. They take care of their own children. So there aren't the young girls who choose to make it their pro-fession any longer.

The *Queen* ran a lovely article about the most famous nannies from the days before the war. And they gave me the pride of place. Ever such a big photograph of me. And they sent a young lady down to interview me, to ask what I thought about the way the world was going.

Then television thought it might be a good idea to do much the same thing, only their questions were different. I remember them asking me if I'd found, in my experience, that parents were apt to interfere in the upbringing of their children. So I answered, 'Not at all! Lord and Lady Tillot never interfered in the slightest with what I did. In fact, I always found them exceedingly helpful in any task that I had to perform.'

Oh, and I must tell you about Mr Higginbottom. He ran a little antique shop near the market place in Froome. I'd been seeing him because Michael had asked me to tip him the wink if something rather special ever came into the shop. And Mr Higginbottom would sometimes drop in for a cup of tea and tell me about the latest bits of furniture he'd acquired.

Then one day he brought a bunch of flowers with him. And he talked to me about his grown-up children and how he'd been ever so lonely since becoming a widower. And I began to wonder where on earth this was all going to end.

He went on for several months like this. And, when I told the children about him, they would tease me so! Even Lord Froome dropped in one day to ask me if I'd seen anything of Mr Higginbottom lately. But I ask you, honestly, now how could I ever think of becoming Mrs Higginbottom? And I couldn't very well have asked him to change his name to something more dignified.

Lord Froome himself had finally remarried, which made everyone very happy. But there was still no sign of his getting back on good terms with his sisters. (And I'm afraid there never was to be.) Yet all the children came down for his wedding, although Michael said he couldn't be there because he had to deliver a valuable commode to Balmoral.

It was most unfair that the papers had to print this. There was so much else they could have mentioned: like the clothes Miss Ponsonby was wearing, or the wedding presents they

eceived. And no one was quite certain who had passed it on
o the papers in the first place.

I'm afraid there were some nasty tongues who said it was
Sebastian. They seemed to think that he still made a little
ortune on the side by ringing up the newspapers with bits of
gossip that happened to come his way. But I'm sure there was
no truth in what they were saying. Sebastian may have been
naughty, but he wasn't unkind.

Author's narrative

In my conversation with Lady Beatrice Cholmondeley, I
inquired how she and Lady Ulrica had taken to the idea of
Lord Froome's second marriage.

She replied, 'Edward was entitled to marry just so many
times as he pleased. My sister and I are sufficiently old-
fashioned to believe that a second marriage is the first sign of
intemperance. That is to say, unless the original spouse has
been honourably put in a box below ground.

'Oh, I had no objections to Miss Ponsonby: the Maharanee
of Bangladesh or whatever it is she calls herself now. To tell
the truth, I've never even met her. We live in different worlds.
I could never have pictured myself twirling around up there
on those fashion boards.'

I inquired whether her absence from the nuptial celebra-
tions might not have been construed by the rest of the family
as a mark of her disapproval of the marriage.

She said, 'In that case, my actions would have been construed wrongly. The truth of the matter is that my sister and I
were already too old for such goings-on, with all of our
second cousins once removed coming up to plant slobbery
kisses on a cheek which I wouldn't even have been extending.
And that horrible horde of little children, throwing caviar at
one another. Ulrica came and discussed the matter with me,
and we decided that everyone would be far happier if we just
stayed at home, sending a word of personal greetings
instead.'

The Nanny Marks tapes

Miss Ponsonby was so *good* for Lord Froome in those first years of their marriage. (But of course, from now on, she was addressed as Lady Froome, except when she was doing something for one of the fashion magazines. Then she appeared as Nadia Ponsonby, in the same manner as always.) She had such a homely side to her personality. I only wish she'd developed it more. And she could get anything she wanted out of Lord Froome, just by asking. That's why he sold Caldicott Manor and moved into Luptree Court. Or just into a wing of it, round at the back. It didn't interfere with the motel side of the business: not even with the stately home.

The Sixth Marquess of Froome, interviewed by
Mr Simon Manasseh

Q: Did the marriage improve, or impair, your relationship with your eldest son, Lord Tillot?
A: Well, Nadia made a big effort to win him over. She cooked all his favourite recipes for him, whenever he came to us for a meal. And she's a damn good cook, especially when she had someone like Mrs Potts to help her. For a while all seemed to be going fine. But it was an uphill task, and such an effort too. All these new dishes to try out. And you never really knew whether he was enjoying them, or just eating them. She once told me that it was like laying out sacrificial plates in front of a stone statue, sculpted so that it was looking up into the clouds. I can see what she meant.

Author's narrative

In my conversation with Nadia, the Maharanee of Peshawar, I asked about the initial period of her marriage to Lord Froome.

She said, 'Edward was a very sweet person, but also a very

hy person. I don't think anyone realized how much he had to
brace himself to do things in public. So what really brought
us together was the private side of life, the fact of cosily
sharing each other's company, entertaining a few of our
friends perhaps.'

This led me to inquire what form such entertainment was
liable to take.

'Oh, charades,' she said. 'We generally played charades. In
fact, I always have done, ever since I was a little girl. But it
took quite a while before Edward got the knack of doing
them properly. The first time I gave him something to do, I
remember it was, "A knight in shining armour". I thought it
would be so *easy* for him to perform, since this is precisely
what he always was in my eyes. But he got into such confusions trying to make them all grasp the difference between
day and night that he never even got to the shining armour
bit. They'd either given up or fallen asleep. I can't remember
which.

'It was that little incident which made Edward give me this
beautiful brooch you see I'm wearing.' (I observed that there
was indeed a small knight in shining armour, made from
silver and diamonds, pinned to her coat lapel.) 'Edward was
always so sweet and generous in his presents. 'I've never
known anyone like him, except Freckles of course.'

I asked how she had responded to the idea of finding herself with a ready-made family.

She said, 'Well, I suppose the numbers were a bit imposing.
But we all lived nicely distant from one another, for most of
the time. Of course there was Bruce, who was always rather
closer. And I suppose it could be said that we had difficulties
from time to time, but nothing that couldn't be cleared up
with a smile to two.'

I remained more persistent on this point, indicating that I
had indeed heard that the friction between her and Lord
Tillot had been considerable.

She said, 'Well you *could* say that of course. I always
found him very agreeable myself, but there were times when
he didn't *connect* very well. I mean he didn't pick up on what
was really happening.

'I was telling you about Edward giving me a knight in shining armour – which of course I treasure greatly. But, when Bruce saw me wearing this, he seemed to think that I *collected* knights in shining armour. Maybe I'd described things a bit wrongly to him. All I know is that, when Christmas arrived, he presented me with a whole set of knights in shining armour, from the toy department at Harrods. And nobody had quite the heart to explain to him that they would have needed to be given to me by Edward for it to have made any sense.'

The Maharanee was looking into my eyes with a softly melting look. But then, quite suddenly and unexpectedly, she burped. Instead of ignoring the event, or making some genteel gesture of dismissing it (either of which I might have anticipated), her face suddenly collapsed into an expression of comic deflation, as if burping had been a reversion to some metamorphic inner self who had suddenly exploded upon her more contrived graces of today. Yet, in the same instant, I perceived an appeal for sympathy and humour in her eyes, which probed to see if I could take this acquaintance with the Maharanee's former identity. And I understood immediately that her most cherished friends preferred her when she slipped a bit from all these airs and graces of an imposed throne, into something more ravishingly debauched and commoner than any manner in which she nowadays would normally permit herself to behave.

I think she might have argued that life is a continual round of charades. You take them on, and some of them actually become real in terms of the public image. And, by the time you get round to playing the self that you once were, it is just another of these charades; the only difference is that you treat it affectionately and with humour, like the funny friend from long ago, who just sometimes pops in to pay us all a visit.

The Nanny Marks tapes

I did feel a little sorry for Lady Tillot: now that there were two Lady Froomes, so to speak. But I can't believe she minded very greatly. Camilla told me she was rather fond of his Mr Fruity from Hamburg. Yet, Camilla didn't really seem to like Mr Fruity. He was rather a *young* man, you know.

She had gone round to visit her mother at the 1940 Club, and he had insisted on drinking champagne from one of her shoes, which she regarded as a mistake. 'It may have been all right for the forties,' she said, 'but it was rather bad taste for the late fifties.'

Excerpt from Chloe, Marchioness of Froome's correspondence with the Duchess of Northumbria

No, my darling, I don't think I ever really expected you to take a liking to Fruity. But you must appreciate that he does know a great deal about the business in which I happen to be. He is also extremely efficient. And, besides all that, I do need a man about the house, in more senses than one. If you lived the life that I do, you'd soon get fed up with the constant presence of too many womenfolk, I can assure you.

The Nanny Marks tapes

We now come to the time when Buddleia was born. Or that's the name that Lady Froome gave her, although everyone called her Buddy, for short. Camilla says that her father and stepmother chose the name because it was while sitting under a clump of buddleia that they first began to think about the birth of a little baby. Such a romantic story I always think.

Lord Froome had altered considerably from what he'd been like in the old days. I mean, he never used to pay much attention to Bruce or Sebastian when they were babies. Not to the extent of offering to change their nappies, or anything like that. Yet, with Buddy, it was completely different from the start. I think that was Lady Froome's influence. She didn't want to employ a nanny. But she needed a helping hand from her husband.

Author's narrative

The Maharanee of Peshawar spoke to me about her pleasure in becoming a mother.

She said, 'Of course, it was a pleasure. Find me the mother who wouldn't say just that! Yet Buddy was a very particular pleasure to me, because I imagined I might have neglected having a child for too long. She came as such a surprise to us all. Or not really as a surprise, because we had been planning it in a certain sort of way.'

I asked if she could be more specific concerning *what* sort of way.

She replied, 'Well, you know how there are all these old wives' recipes for having a baby?'

I confessed that I did not.

'Well, there are. I thought *everyone* knew that. But, in any case, Edward and I decided to try some of them out.

'The one we found the most effective was "the dance of the watersplash". It has to be beside a buddleia plant, which must be beside a waterfall. These things are so difficult to find. I really don't know where all these old wives managed to find them in the first place.

'Anyway, a very good friend of mine reminded me where one was to be found, and I persuaded Edward to come along to it with me. It was a very simple dance really, though Edward always did get terribly embarrassed about dancing. But it was all quite rapid. Mind you, there were a few other things that we had to do as well. But it was the magic that was important. Edward never did believe in magic. But I think that the birth of Buddy made him give a second thought to all these matters.'

The Sixth Marquess of Froome, interviewed by Mr Simon Manasseh

Q: The birth of your second daughter, Lady Buddleia, must have been a great joy to you both. Were you hoping for a daughter or a son?

A: Nadia would have been happy in either event, for this was her first child. But I must confess that I was very satisfied at the outcome. The truth is that, from my experience in these matters, I produce far better daughters than I do sons.

The Nanny Marks tapes

In some ways, Buddy's arrival marked the beginning of a terrible new conflict within the Tillot family. She wasn't six months old before Lord Froome was talking about setting up a new company named after her, which would work in partnership with Wessex Motels, but with an independent board of directors. And it was at this stage that Bruce's lawyers began to get anxious. They seemed to think that capital was being taken from the control of Wessex Motels and put into the hands of Buddleia Ltd. And they insisted that he must stand up for his rights.

Well, Bruce was never particularly good at standing up to his father. But his lawyers went on at him for so long that he agreed to have a try. I'm afraid he must have put the argument a trifle tactlessly, for it offended his father greatly. (I heard all this from Camilla.) But then Bruce got offended as well, because his father wrote him several rather severe letters. It wasn't the letters themselves that Bruce minded. It was the fact of their being typed out by Lord Froome's secretary. It made him feel as if he was being rebuked in public, rather than it being just a private word in his ear. And what made him angrier still was that he didn't yet employ a secretary of his own. So he was unable to answer his father's rebukes in a manner that was equally public.

I'm afraid that their quarrelling soon got quite out of hand. Bruce didn't want to receive any more letters from Lord Froome's secretary, so he called round in person to have a word with him. And, for the first time in his life, Bruce and his father were shouting at each other. And some very terrible things were said on either side.

Author's narrative

I asked Mr Bonniface, the estate agent at Luptree – who was after all in a better position than anyone else to perceive the professional intricacies of the dispute between Lord Froome and Lord Tillot – whether the quarrel had made life difficult for him.

He replied, 'Indeed, sir, you could say that again. I have always held the belief that it is impossible to serve two masters. And here was a case in point. I was being asked to do the impossible. And there was nothing within my professional experience which made me think I was the right man for their purposes.

'You see, it had all been so different at the start. Then there had been one master. And you must remember that I had been appointed by Lord Froome. So it was difficult for me to switch loyalties at the drop of a hat.

'When Lord Froome first made over everything to Lord Tillot, it was done very much in the spirit of taking me to one side with a wink and saying, "Now that's just to satisfy the lawyers. But you and I know better. I'm the boss as much as ever. And Bruce will do as he's told."

'Now I did have my severe reservations when I saw the line that Lord Froome was taking. I'd advised him from the start that it might be a more considered action to do this handover business in gradual instalments – just for everyone to get used to the idea. But that wasn't Lord Froome's way of doing things. It was all at once and damn the consequences, because he never really appreciated what the consequences might be.

'I'm afraid we did have certain problems in this matter. Lord Froome found it difficult to understand that he had never in effect *owned* Luptree Court. He was the tenant for life as they call it. In fact, he'd never owned anything quite in the way he imagined that he did: neither the house, nor the estate, nor the capital. They were always under the control of trustees, before it was that of Lord Tillot himself (which was the effective result of them breaking the family entail). It was much the same with the Wessex Motels, if it comes to that. For the bulk of the capital was the property of Sir Ben Jones, while Lord Froome at the start, and then Lord Tillot, had a life interest in its management.

'Now I never found it an easy task to convince Lord Froome that this was the right way of viewing things. He seemed to think that the law was a different game from family politics. I could only offer him my professional opinion in these matters. But he'd just wink and say that nobody would know any different if the two of us continued to play along together, in the manner that we'd always done beforehand.

'I felt obliged to remind him at one point that he was urging me to compound a felony. For there can be no doubt, in my professional opinion, that Lord Tillot was now entitled to be fully consulted on everything that went on at Luptree. But Lord Froome's attitude was that it was all too easy to pull the wool over his son's eyes, so he need never really come to hear about what was happening on the estate. And I regret to say that, in accordance with that policy, many an investment was made within the Luptree organization which might never otherwise have seen the light of day. But I'd like to stress this point, sir. At no time did I ever act in a manner that I did not regard as being in the best interests of the Luptree estate.

'But, as I've said before, it was an impossible situation, and there were some sticky moments for me when Lord Tillot demanded to know why he hadn't been informed about this, that and the other. It was all very well for me to reply that he'd better ask his father about these matters. He was within his rights to insist that I clarify the position for him myself. And there were certain points that I did indeed find it very difficult to clarify, notably with regard to the vagueness of the division between Wessex Motels and Buddleia Ltd; two separate companies, yet ones where the funds had been in the habit of flowing fairly freely across the lines of division.

'I put it to Lord Froome, "I'm an old dog now, and I want to retire while I'm still at peace with the entire world. I've done most that you ever asked me to, except that which I regarded as being illegal. It is time that you allowed me to fade out from the picture."

'Lord Froome was quite upset about this. He was worried

that Lord Tillot would now be able to appoint some agent who wouldn't understand the family situation in quite the same way that I'd been given to understand it. H₋ urged me to put off my retirement just long enough to give him a chance to persuade Lord Tillot to take a trip round the world or something. Then he'd be in a position to appoint my successor single-handed. But I excused myself from doing this last service for him because, in my professional opinion, it would have been unethical.

'I think that I did choose the right time to retire. If I'd remained a moment longer, I'd have been involved in all the feuding which ensued. I don't think Lord Froome was ever quite happy about Lord Tillot's choice of Colonel Penny as my successor. But I don't suppose that any of us expected him to be.'

The Sixth Marquess of Froome, interviewed by Mr Simon Manasseh

Q: How would you account for the quarrel between Lord Tillot and yourself?

A: He didn't stick by our gentlemen's agreement that I was to run the place. He suddenly got it into his head that he was going to do all this himself.

Q: Did you object to this?

A: Of course I objected. I wouldn't have dished him up with a stately home, a chain of motels and a tidy sum of capital in his bank, if I'd thought he was going to throw me out on the street next morning. It was all smiles before I signed those documents, but a very different story later.

Q: Are you suggesting that he cheated on you?

A: Of course I am. How else would you describe his behaviour?

Q: Mightn't Lord Tillot claim that you only ever did a deal with him that was in your mutual interest?

A: Mutual interest be damned. I was acting out of the kindness of my heart, to save him from paying death duties.

Luptree Court and all that was in it belonged to me. I didn't have to give it to him, you know. It seems madness now. But there you are. If you love a place sufficiently, you want to see it handed down intact to your successors. And it's a risk you have to take that they might turn round and spit in your eye, once they've got all they wanted out of you.

The Nanny Marks tapes

I suppose Bruce must have been hurt and angry. In any case, he decided to take a more personal control of everything. But Camilla felt that he was being horribly unfair. After all, it was Lord Froome who had built up Wessex Motels into what it had become. It wasn't just Luptree Court any more. It was a whole thriving business concern. And to take it away from him just because they'd been in disagreement about money seemed to her unnecessarily severe. In fact, it was disrespectful.

'There's a commandment on the subject,' I heard her telling him. 'Honour and succour your father and your mother!' And I suppose this was a point that must have slipped his mind.

Bruce didn't seem to see things that way at all. When he learnt that Lord Froome had been trying to sack him, he became absolutely furious. He said it was time that he cracked the whip for a change. And he did too. He wrote to his father saying that he and Lady Froome must pack their personal belongings and move out of Luptree Court. He said that the suite was required for the managing director of Wessex Motels.

Well, you can imagine how furious his father was at that. He wrote to Camilla saying that neither God nor the devil were going to get him to budge. But the awful thing is that he could have been obliged to if Bruce had insisted.

Author's narrative

I asked Lady Beatrice if she had any views upon the fearful spate of quarrelling which disrupted the relationship between Lord Froome and Lord Tillot.

She replied, 'My personal feeling is that Bruce had a duty to perform and was giving of his best. My only criticism is that Bruce's best was fairly low on the scale by other people's standards. But I wrote him a word of encouragement, that he must stand up to his father at all costs, and put a little sanity back into the workings of Luptree. It may have helped, you know. What Bruce was lacking was backbone. This always had to be supplied to him by others.'

Excerpts from Chloe, Marchioness of Froome's correspondence with the Duchess of Northumbria

Bruce does sound as if he's being a bit silly, if you ask me. As if it really matters who cracks the whip (as he calls it) in a concern like Luptree, where, in any case, it is his father that he is dealing with. But I couldn't very well do as you suggest in writing him a 'none of this nonsense' letter. I've never even had a Christmas card from him since that unplanned visit he paid to my club.

I do see your point that it might be difficult having your father and Nadia actually living in the same apartments, alongside your own family. He'd probably start teaching young David and Timmy to hold their knives and forks correctly, which wouldn't go down well with Michael. And I dare say that Nadia might keep suggesting the replacement of your lovely old damask with all her pretty little frills and things.

But don't you think there might be a possibility of letting him know that you could house him elsewhere in Northwold Abbey? It does appear to be sufficiently long and rambling for you to find such a corner. I feel that it might give him strength in his present negotiations with Bruce, just to know that he does have this alternative to abject surrender: the idea of a departure with dignity, while he looks for a place of his own. I know that your father wasn't very pleasant to me at the time of our divorce. But I always do remember the good sides of him, as well.

The Nanny Marks tapes

Camilla was ever so worried. She suggested to Michael that they ought to offer him a wing of Northwold Abbey. But Michael was only prepared to let him have the Dowager's Lodge. And it seems that Lord Froome was offended when this was put to him. He wrote Camilla an angry letter in which he said he wasn't going to be treated like a lot of bloody evacuees from the Blitz. Lord Froome uses strong language sometimes.

I'm afraid Camilla didn't like the tone of his letter at all. She felt wounded, I suppose. She'd only been trying to help her father. And she tried to explain to him, in a letter, that he was taking an unreasonable attitude, reminding him that everyone had their ups and downs in life, even the royal family. Yet the only reply she received was a postcard to say that one family was enough for everyone, and that, in her case, she'd better stick to royalty.

The Sixth Marquess of Froome, interviewed by Mr Simon Manasseh

Q: Did the rest of your family rally round to your support?
A: I didn't need anyone's assistance. I fight my own battles. And Bruce wouldn't have the gumption to remove a kitten from its basket. I just had to stand up to him. Told him that, if anyone was going to get me out of Luptree Court, then he'd have to do it with his own bare hands. And I assured him that I'd put up a damn good scrap into the bargain. So he never got round to doing anything at all.

The Nanny Marks tapes

It was awful really. Yet Camilla was still prepared to sort things out for Lord Froome. And she managed to persuade Bruce to let his father go on living at Luptree Court on the top floor, on condition that he never set foot on the motel side of the house, while he installed himself in the more sumptuous apartments, which they had formerly been occupying. So their difficulties were solved for the time being, except of course when they happened to meet on the stairs.

This was the first time that Bruce had set up house for himself. (Before that, he'd been sharing a flat with a friend in Knightsbridge.) So he wasn't really accustomed to the problems of running a domestic staff. I believe he tried to persuade Walter and Mrs Potts to leave Lord Froome's employment, and come down to the grander apartments he was living in. But they would have none of that. They wanted to stick by Lord Froome.

I always felt she would be the last person to stick by anyone who employed her. Anyway at this time Bruce employed a new couple. They weren't actually a couple if the truth be told. Or they were. But you see Bruce had always felt himself to be more at ease with his mother than with his father. Perhaps this may have influenced him. Anyway he made the unusual choice of taking into his service a lady called Miss Puddock as his cook, and a lady called Miss Pertwee as his butler. And of course I know that he was impressed that they were asking for very little in wages by modern standards.

Miss Puddock always told us that she had been the matron at a school for little boys. But, if you ask me, this was something she had imagined. Little boys don't *like* someone like Miss Puddock, even if she did regard herself as a lady. And her harelip would have been enough to frighten a scarecrow. Besides that, I'll never believe that Miss Pertwee had been one of the schoolmistresses, either. She didn't even speak properly, if you ask my opinion.

Some of the things they said about Bruce down in the village were awful. Old Mrs Marsh came to ask me one day if it was true that he only had one change of underclothes: because

that's what Miss Puddock had told everyone down at the
Froome Arms. The trouble was that Miss Puddock enjoyed a
glass of sherry and when she began to feel nicely comfortable
was liable to get a bit over-excited.

Author's narrative

Mr Perkins told me his own viewpoint on the family quarrel.
He said, 'It soured up the whole works. Nobody knew where
he stood any longer, whether he was a Lord Froome man or a
Lord Tillot man. Everyone was looking over his shoulder,
wondering who might stab him in the back because of some
remark he'd made or because his allegiances were wrong. It
wasn't at all healthy for the organization.'

   Mr Davis broke in at this point to say, 'It wasn't healthy
back at home, if it comes to that. I can tell you that I had had
quite enough of shifting households. Caldicott Manor up for
sale: so we all troop to Luptree Court and occupy some of the
finest apartments. Then in comes Bruce screaming, "Everybody out! Up you go to the top landing!" Well, that's fine
and dandy for once in a while. It makes a change, I dare say.
But you can't go making people jump through too many
hoops, or they'll want your guts for garters.'

Excerpt from Chloe, Marchioness of Froome's correspondence with the Duchess of Northumbria

Buffy came in last night. It is the first time he has been here
since his accident and all the girls were queueing up to discover if the surgeons had managed to save his genitals from
the state they were in when I last saw him. I can assure you
that they've done wonders. He ended up by giving a private
cabaret in the room upstairs, twiddling his cock like a lasso,
and asking who would like to be his heifer.

   The odd thing about those police investigations connected
with Buffy's accident is that I am now on most amicable
terms with all the detectives in this part of London. And it
really does help when you're in my line of business. There can
be such trouble otherwise.

The Nanny Marks tapes

Sebastian was having his difficulties too. He'd been getting into rather bad company of late. A gambling crowd. He was mixing with people with more money than was good for them. I asked him about it once and he assured me that he fleeced them of more than they ever got from him. Yet the fact remains that he was getting badly into debt.

Now there's some people it might be safe to cheat and some that it might not. And the trouble with Sebastian was that he was inclined to choose the wrong people. Well, it seems that he made several bets in quick succession, trying to cover up his losses, until it had reached an enormous figure that he couldn't possibly pay.

Excerpts from Chloe, Marchioness of Froome's correspondence with the Duchess of Northumbria

I have some rather disturbing news, which I think somebody ought to pass on to Sebastian. But, since I am no longer in the habit of communicating with him, I feel that this warning ought perhaps to come from you.

I think I told you how I was on very good terms with the police nowadays. Well, Detective-Sergeant Distemper called in to have a drink with me the other day and said he ought to warn me that my son is in trouble with the Soho underworld. For a moment I almost laughed at this pronouncement because I was thinking of Bruce (an idea which merely filled me with incredulity). But, on being given further details, I discovered that it was Sebastian and that he may indeed be in some considerable danger.

It does sound as if he's been most tremendously stupid in reselling a property for which he hadn't even paid to a friend of the notorious Mr Jack Spot; this was especially stupid because he'd just discovered how he himself had been taken for a ride and the house was full of dry rot. I dare say he *did* think he was on to a good business deal when he first committed himself to pay for it. But, if you find you've made a

fool of yourself in such matters, you don't try to get out of
your difficulties by slipping a sharp one to the friends of Jack
Spot.

Sebastian came to see me the other night, and I'm glad to say
that we went some distance towards repairing our injured
relationship. What does irritate me a bit is his pretence that
he's a Socialist now. It's all so silly, seeing the way that he
was brought up.

I'm afraid I had to refuse his request to let him lie low in
my club, until they take the heat off him. He had this ridiculous idea that nobody would pay much attention to him if he
were to dress up as one of my young ladies. 'Not on your
Nelly,' I had to tell him. I wasn't in all honesty so much
concerned about his safety, as I was about mine. The last
thing I want is Jack Spot nosing around in here to see if I'm
harbouring refugees from his justice. And what do you suppose someone like Buffy would say, if he went to test out his
new equipment, only to find that one of my young ladies was
a young man?

The Nanny Marks tapes

I know that Sebastian was very frightened by the whole situation. He would have telephoned his father about it if he
dared. But he wasn't quite sure any more how welcome he
might find himself.

Anyway, he came to me instead. In the middle of the night
and in the company of one of those young ladies that I'd once
had the pleasure of meeting when I was staying at Lady Tillot's 1940 Club. He said he could sleep on the sofa, if I could
put up the lady in my spare bed.

Then next morning he explained to me what was going on.
He said there was somebody called Mr Spot who had
threatened to slice off his nose and make a meat sandwich of
it. He'd also said that England wasn't quite big enough for
the two of them. Mr Spot's advice to Sebastian was that he
should emigrate to Australia. And that's what he'd decided to
do. Or rather, he'd chosen South America instead, just in case

some friend of Mr Spot might be waiting for him in Sydney. And he wanted to take his lady friend with him, it seems.

I had to go over to Luptree Court in the morning and persuade Bruce to buy them a couple of passages. He said he couldn't very well go over there himself, because he wasn't quite sure how much time Mr Spot had given him to emigrate. And he felt that Luptree was the obvious place for Mr Spot to watch.

You know there's one thing about Sebastian. He may have been rather bad in some ways, but he never did anything by halves. If he was going to be bad, then he really earned his money's worth! Now that's what I mean by being an interesting sort of person!

Mind you, it was rather a difficult task that he'd given me. The sum of money that he'd asked me to collect for them was by no means small. I could hardly have blamed Bruce if he'd turned me out of the door. In fact, he wasn't very pleased at all. He said, if Sebastian wanted to con him out of a few hundred quid, then he damn well ought to have the courage to come and say so. But I explained to him that Luptree Court was being watched by Mr Spot and that there was some hurry for him to get out of the country quickly.

So Bruce booked a passage for Sebastian on a boat that was going to the Caribbean and arranged for the ticket to be sent to me at my cottage. He said that he would pay for him to go as far as Cuba, but no further. He thought that a good dose of Castro's Socialism might purify Sebastian's politics for a lifetime. And he refused to provide a passage for the lady friend, which was very difficult for me to explain to both of them. I'm afraid that Sebastian's last words, when I saw them off on the train to London, was that his brother was a stingy something-or-other, which was all a bit unfair, seeing that Bruce had paid a good half of what he'd been asked to.

Excerpt from Chloe, Marchioness of Froome's correspondence with the Duchess of Northumbria

I must say that, for once, Bruce does seem to be displaying

some glimmerings of humour. I got a telephone call from Sebastian this morning (reverse charges of course) to say that he is being packed off to Cuba 'to broaden his outlook on the world', as Bruce apparently described it.

Sebastian's reason for telephoning wasn't so much to say goodbye, as to inquire if I was prepared to pay the fare for his intended companion for the voyage. This turns out to be none other than the ghastly Marilyn, who has evidently reappeared on his scene. He seemed to think he was doing me a favour, in offering me this chance to exile her from London. But I told him that I would hardly be doing either him or myself a service by enhancing Marilyn's chances of emerging as my daughter-in-law.

The Nanny Marks tapes

I know that Lord Froome did eventually get to hear about Sebastian's departure, and about the debts too. I met him when I was shopping in Froome one day, and he told me that he was becoming increasingly disenchanted with his two sons, and with Camilla too for that matter.

I really did think it was most unfair of him to take this attitude, and I told him so direct.

But Lord Froome just laughed. 'Good old Nan!' he said. 'Loyal to those bleeding brats as usual!'

I reminded him that he still had one bleeding brat (as he liked to call them), and that he'd better learn to take good care of her.

'Ah! Buddy's different,' he said. 'Never hand your children over to a nanny, and you learn to nanny them yourself!'

And I see what he meant. Now that he was no longer a managing director, Lord Froome had all the time in the world to devote himself to Buddy. And it struck me how he possessed many of the right qualities to become an excellent nanny.

13

The Flesh and the Devil

1959–64

Author's narrative

To find Colonel Penny, the estate agent at Luptree who had
succeeded Mr Bonniface, I had to drive up to Norfolk, where
he was currently employed as the agent on the Duke of
Anglia's estate.

I inquired how he viewed the situation he had discovered
on taking up his employment on the Luptree estate.

He said, 'Hardly one I'd have chosen, if I'd realized what it
was going to be all about. Not enough of the usual kind of
stuff that gets shoved to an estate agent to perform. I can
cope with all that all right. But this job needed a couple of
ambassadors; one representing Lord Froome and the other
representing Lord Tillot.

'In a funny sort of way, I was quite well qualified for the
job. I mean, before I was paid off by the army, I'd been one of
those odd-bod colonels attached to the diplomatic corps: the
Far East in my case. So, in some ways, it was just like slipping
back into the old routine, knowing that there were two forces
at war with one another. And mine was the duty to see that
neither of them ever really got a chance of coming to blows.'

I inquired whether it was Lord Froome or Lord Tillot who
had created most of his problems over this period.

He said, 'There was always this difficulty in my relationship with Lord Froome, in that it was Lord Tillot who had
appointed me. Well, it was Claude Pike, his solicitor, really.
But he was acting on behalf of Lord Tillot, who just signed

along the dotted line whenever he was requested to do so by one of our team.

'The trouble with Lord Froome was that he had broken loose from the team. He had become a maverick, as Claude once remarked. Less easy to manage, now that he was out there on his own. And of course, I was the poor scout who was always shoved out there in front of the troops, to discover if he was going to give battle that day. It affected our relationship, I'm afraid. Whenever he saw me coming, he had that look on his face as if to say, "Oo-er, what are you going to try and wheedle out of me this time?".'

The Sixth Marquess of Froome, interviewed by
Mr Simon Manasseh

Q: I understand that Lord Tillot often employed the services of others in giving battle with you. Did you bear special animosity against any of these in particular?

A: There was Colonel Penny of course. The trouble with Penny was that he was a gentleman, and I've always held that it's a mistake to employ a gentleman as your agent. Besides that, I could never stand the man. It's my private opinion that Bruce only appointed him because he knew I'd detest him. All that business about him being a colonel, when I'd left the army at the end of the war as a mere major. It was his own way of getting a dig at me.

Q: Were there any particular episodes which infuriated you?

A: It was his whole manner that I couldn't stand. He'd never leave a subject alone. If I said no to start with, it isn't likely that I'd be saying yes tomorrow. But he'd go on and on at me, day after day, treating it all as if it was some huge public schoolboy joke. The big wheeze that I was supposed to be sharing with him. And it got on my nerves. I snapped at him on more than one occasion.

But there was a *particular* episode which brought down the curtain on our relationship. The damn fool left a letter he'd written mixed up with a whole batch of others for me to sign. And this one properly cooked his goose. I don't know if he imagined I was some kind of a rubber stamp, putting my signature on all that he laid before me, regardless. But I always do take the trouble to read what I am being asked to sign. And, this letter was to our family solicitor, complaining how awkward I was being and suggesting that Pike himself come down to talk some sense into me.

Well, naturally, I blew my top. You'll probably say that it was the chance I was itching for, and you're damn right! So I told him that, as far as I was concerned, he could pack his bags and leave. But things weren't quite so simple as that, because Bruce didn't see that there was sufficient reason for sacking him.

Q: Were you able to resolve the relationship in any way at all?

A: I resolved it in my own way, I suppose. It meant that, if Penny wanted to get anything out of me, he couldn't come and see me himself. He had to send one of his underlings, like Midgeley, the estate foreman, with whom I always got on like a house on fire.

Mind you, I did sometimes get the opportunity to deal Penny a backhander. He'd had all this writing paper printed with his name on top, boasting about his degree in agriculture or whatever it was. And he'd also had printed as bold as brass that he was agent to the Marquess of Froome. (Poor little Bruce only got a secondary mention.)

Well, the odd occasion arose when someone who'd received a letter from Penny would reply to me direct, even though the subject matter was technically nothing to do with me. And it always gave me a special pleasure to write back to the person concerned, regretting that the colonel still saw fit to describe himself as my agent, when he knew perfectly well that I had sacked him long ago.

Author's narrative

I inquired of Colonel Penny if there had been any specially serious quarrel with Lord Froome.

He said, 'I'm afraid there was one most terrible incident. I'm an awful duffer sometimes, and I mislaid a letter that I'd written to Claude, telling him how Lord Froome wasn't what I'd call an ideal employer. And it turned up in the batch that I'd left on his desk for him to sign. I'll never know how it got there. That's the trouble when you're working on an estate where they're all fighting. You never know who might try to stick a knife in your back. But you can well imagine that Lord Froome himself wasn't any too pleased. So I had to keep my distance from him after that.

'But there wasn't any of that kind of problem with Lord Tillot. He didn't have to be told about everything. That could be left to our team, who would get down to brass tacks later in thrashing it all out. But, in one department or another, it all began to work efficiently, once I'd managed to chop loose the dead wood which had accumulated over the years.

'Oh, there were some silly moments. I hardly know whether to trouble you with them. You see Bruce had this bee in his bonnet that he was a bit of a decorator. He was going round the rooms at Luptree doing them according to his own taste, insisting on choosing all the wallpapers himself. Well, you and I know (I dare say) that this is a woman's task. But he had this idea that he had better artistic appreciation than all those experts that I could have brought in to advise him, if only he'd given me the chance.

'Anyway, you can imagine what indignation arose when Midgeley's men papered the drawing room so that the pattern was upside down. Bruce was hopping mad and insisted that it all had to be done again. I hardly dared tell him that it was all his own fault for not bringing in the professionals. He seemed to think he could dispense with them, you see.

'But I soon found the right way to tackle this one. I told Midgeley that the best way of getting on the right side of Lord Tillot was to butter him up. So we devised this plan where Midgeley would bring his camera and ask if he could take some photographs of the drawing room now that it was completed, pretending that he admired it as a piece of interior decoration. And Bruce was tickled pink. So were Midgeley and I, of course, knowing that there wasn't even a film in the camera. Oh, we had many a private giggle about that one!'

The Nanny Marks tapes

Bruce did get something in exchange for paying Sebastian's boat fare to Cuba: the use of his flat in Chelsea. He needed this because Miss Puddock and Miss Pertwee were getting on his nerves. He didn't feel comfortable down at Luptree. He could only endure it for the weekends.

They weren't really a suitable couple at all for Bruce. Miss Puddock had a touch of the devil, you know. Bruce told me she used to regard herself as bit of a lady, but I think she just liked putting on airs. And she could be really difficult at times. One of the worst occasions was when the Lord Froome Grammar School came over to Luptree Court to celebrate the founding of the school 250 years ago. Bruce wouldn't permit his father to officiate at the ceremony in any part of the house which he controlled, so the task of entertaining the governors fell to himself. A matter of cocktails while watching a display of fireworks from the window. The rest of the school was gathered on the lawn outside.

Bruce had invited me to attend the party. So I was able to see Miss Puddock close up for the first time. She came up to me, glass in hand, as if she were one of the invited guests, and said, 'And you must be Nanny, I suppose. Our paths don't happen to have crossed when you come to visit Lord Tillot. I am sometimes detained in the kitchen you see.' Well, I ask you!

And worse was yet to come. She completely gave up handing the drinks round, being content to see Miss Pertwee scurrying to all corners of the room, while she engaged the Bishop of Bath and Wells in conversation. I heard her telling him that she came from a medical family, whatever that might mean. and that she wouldn't now be in domestic service if it hadn't been for the ill-fated circumstance of her father's death.

Bruce eventually realized that she was drawing too much attention to herself. So he told her that she could go to bed. But not a bit of it! Miss Puddock now insisted that she had her duties to perform, and she wouldn't consider letting her poor companion do all the work. So Bruce called on Miss Pertwee to persuade her to depart. But she merely shook her head and said that this would be impossible.

It was quite an awkward situation all round. The fireworks had just begun. But none of the board of governors was watching them. Their attention was riveted on Miss Puddock. And Bruce had to do something about it now, or people might begin to feel that he had no control over the situation. So he put his head down and started pushing her towards the door. Then, as quick as you can say knife, Miss Puddock did the same, only in the other direction. They looked like a two-man rugger scrum. And Bruce, being the heavier, won!

If I'd been him, I'd have sent her packing without further ado. But he seemed to think that this would be doing her an injustice. He was always troubled by points like this. It was a question of his feeling that he ought to have made it clearer to Miss Puddock before the party started that the drink was strictly for his guests. So he just gave her a scolding instead which I hardly think could have served any good purpose, since Miss Puddock wasn't the kind of person who could ever think of herself as being in the wrong.

Anyway, I expect you now understand why Bruce felt it was necessary to get away from Luptree, for part of the week at least. Domestic staff were certainly not what they used to be in the old days. So it was more comfortable for him, in some ways, to take care of himself in a small flat up in Chelsea, and just to put in an appearance at Luptree Court at the weekends – to keep open his claim on the house.

Excerpt from Chloe, Marchioness of Froome's
correspondence with the Duchess of Northumbria

Surprise of surprises! Bruce rang the doorbell this afternoon and asked if I was at home. So we had coffee together. But first of all he had a little speech to make, which he performed standing by the window. He declared that there may have been a period recently when he had thought harshly of me but, on taking into due consideration all that was going on in this world, he had decided to offer me the hand of friendship – which I took.

He is using Sebastian's flat in Chelsea, it seems, and tries to avoid going home to Luptree Court as much as he can. This is because of the awful couple that are looking after him down there. Apparently Miss Puddock tries alternately to mother and scold him. In her mothering mood, she becomes all coy, telling him that he's a 'naughty boy', and must hand over his socks so that she can wash them; whereas, in her scolding mood, she tells him that his sheets are perpetually 'soiled'. Bruce looked at me earnestly and asked if it was perfectly normal for men to have 'nocturnal emissions' when they were devoid of women's company. I told him that I was no great authority on this subject, since none of my menfolk *were* devoid of women's company, or not while I was around.

Anyway, I persuaded him that it was time to have a good fling at life, before the various canals in his body got clogged up. He looked a trifle dubiously at me for this remark, and then said, 'Clogged up with what?' But I did manage to persuade him in the end that a philosophy of 'don't save it, rave it' might be in his best interests, in view of all the privations to which he has subjected himself in the past.

The Nanny Marks tapes

Bruce's use of Sebastian's flat made an enormous difference to his whole way of life. When he'd been in the Household Cavalry, he'd not been seeing London from such a different angle. Yet, in Chelsea, he met a different *type* of person.

On one of his visits down to Luptree Court he came over to have tea with me (although I always keep a bottle of sherry at hand for the children or Lord Froome). Anyway he told me that he was having a lovely time. What surprised me most was the number of attractive young women that he met. He was very anxious to talk to me on this subject. More than either of the other children, Bruce was the one who liked to listen to my advice, even if he didn't always abide by it. But it seems that these young women kept falling in his lap. He just picked up the telephone when it rang and there they were. They must have been friends of Sebastian, I suppose.

I warned Bruce that he ought to be very careful about these girls. He was a wealthy young man now, not to mention that he would one day be a Marquess. In fact I'm not sure if there was a more eligible young bachelor in the whole of London. These Chelsea girls would try to catch him if they could. And Bruce had always been such a clean boy. I told him that he ought to be on his guard.

But Chelsea is a very wicked place nowadays. It's full of the flesh and the devil, as they used to say. I used to wonder at times if Bruce wasn't allowing himself to be led astray. Quite often he would give a peep-peep-peep as he went driving past the window in his new Jaguar sports car. And I would look out to catch a glimpse of him. But it was always with a different girl. He used to bring them down to Luptree for the weekends, I believe.

Then he met Lola Forsyte. You know about her, I expect. In those days, the papers always described her as the deodorants dollybird – because everyone had seen her on their television screens advertising some particular brand of deodorant. She was very beautiful, I'll give her that. I liked her fuzzy red hair and the odd kind of clothes she wore. But I'm not sure if she was really very suitable for Bruce.

Excerpt from Chloe, Marchioness of Froome's correspondence with the Duchess of Northumbria

Have you heard about Bruce's new girlfriend, Lola Forsyte? I think she's even more glamorous than the last one. Not that he's ever brought her here. But I do still move in the circles of Lola and her kind, whether or not Bruce is aware of the fact. So I went up to have a conversation with her on the last encounter.

She knows precisely what she's up to, despite the limpidly faltering gaze which she casts around her, like a fisherman's net. She's one of those women who only have to enter a room and all the men suddenly become fidgety and inattentive to their conversational partners of the moment.

If she fancies Luptree Court (and I am informed that she does indeed), I suspect that we may soon be hearing wedding bells.

The Nanny Marks tapes

When Bruce brought Lola round to see me, I could tell from the start that he regarded her as someone rather more special than the others. And I realized she was trying to make a good impression on me when she arranged for a box of cosmetics to be delivered to my cottage immediately after her visit. Not that I have ever really used these things. Yet I know it was important to Bruce that I should *seem* to like her. So I did my best not to disappoint him.

But this Lola. Oh, I've heard some terrible stories about the way she used to go on up there in London. And I certainly wouldn't like to repeat them to you. I'm afraid she must have been leading Bruce an awful dance. But he'd always been a very patient person, once he knew the goal he was striving for. And that's the way it went, you see.

Excerpt from Chloe, Marchioness of Froome's correspondence with the Duchess of Northumbria

Of course, darling, I did realize that in all probability Lola has slept with half of London. But I hardly think it's the duty of either of us to inform Bruce of the matter. Even if he did tell you that he is only the third lover that she has ever had, I think it safest that you should ride along with his fantasies. It might be argued that fantasies play an important part in our lives. In any case, they are a buffer against reality. And, believe me, it's far more comfortable for most of us to possess this buffer than be without it. It doesn't mean that we won't open our eyes eventually to the state of life as it really is. But it furnishes a convenient time-lag, in which parts of us are already preparing for the ultimate shock.

The Nanny Marks tapes

One day when Bruce drove over to see me, he was smiling from ear to ear. I knew he had something important to tell me and I could guess what it was. What *did* surprise me was how few of the family came to the wedding ceremony, even if it was only a small one at Froome church. It made me feel as if the whole duty fell on my shoulders of speaking out when the parson said that bit about for ever holding our peace. But I kept my mouth shut, I can assure you. Bruce would never have forgiven me, you see.

Excerpt from Chloe, Marchioness of Froome's correspondence with the Duchess of Northumbria

Honestly, my love, it was quite unnecessary for you to decline Bruce's invitation to the wedding on my account. He did in fact drop in to see me beforehand and explained how Lola had experienced a 'protected' upbringing, so he was anxious (at this particular stage) to avoid complications in his own relationship with her by introducing her to his mother. I told him that I quite understood.

The Nanny Marks tapes

I knew from the start that Lola would never get on with Miss Puddock. It only needed one row and it didn't take many weeks before they'd had it.

Miss Puddock started out on the wrong foot by trying to insist that Lola should take her evening meal at 7.30, instead of at 8.00. Bruce had been willing to fit in with Miss Puddock's way of life before he met Lola. But he felt that Lola had a right to decide these matters for herself and he told Miss Puddock so.

The trouble with Miss Puddock was that she could never see things from another person's point of view. She had this feeling that people were getting at her and she didn't want to bend to their wishes. She suggested that, if Lola wanted her dinner any later than 7.30, then she ought to come out to the kitchen and do the washing up for herself. But this wasn't the way Lola had been brought up. So there was a bit of a row about all that, with Miss Puddock looking round for the right kind of ground where she could dig in her heels and stand up to Lola.

She was never very sensible in these matters, and the final row came because Lola had accused her of over-cooking things. Miss Puddock protested that no one had ever protested that she over-cooked things, and she flounced off in a huff.

I suppose she must have wanted to teach Lola a lesson. Anyway, that evening, they were having rabbit for dinner. And Lola always liked things to be served up in the old manner, using the silver serving dishes with their silver covers on top.

Well, Miss Puddock deposited the dish in front of Lola, then walked out of the dining room, without so much as a by-your-leave or thank you. When Lola lifted the lid, what did she find but a skinned raw rabbit, looking up at her from the dish with its two sightless eyes.

I can't imagine how Miss Puddock thought she was going to get away with it. Or perhaps she didn't. Perhaps she'd decided she was going to leave in any case, because that is precisely what happened – although the hour of her departure may have been a trifle more prompt than she'd been expecting.

After that, Bruce and Lola employed a Spanish couple, who suited their purposes rather better. But I never got to

know them very well. Whenever we met, I could never understand a word they were saying. They ought to teach English
to foreigners when they're still young. That way, they'd have
a better chance of learning it properly. But they were a nice
couple – always full of smiles. And Bruce told me he couldn't
now think why he'd tolerated Miss Puddock and Miss Pertwee for so long.

When I next saw Lord Froome, I asked him what he
thought about the whole business. But he wasn't particularly
interested. He said that, as far as he was concerned, Bruce
could marry whomsoever he pleased, and that he was damn
lucky to get someone as attractive as Lola. But then he was
still feeling bitter towards Bruce because there'd been another
flare-up.

It was all so silly really. I never could understand how these
things came to happen. But Lord Froome was putting in a
couple of new bathrooms up at the top of the house, and he'd
chosen roller-type holders for the lavatory paper. Yet, when
Bruce came to hear of these alterations (which were being
carried out by his own workmen from the buildings' yard), he
decided he would prefer it if there were letter-box-type
holders for the lavatory paper instead. The idea in his mind, I
think, was to have standard equipment throughout the entire
house.

But Lord Froome didn't take it that way. When he discovered that his roller-type holders had been replaced by
the letter-box variety, he summoned Mr Midgeley and
threatened to have him sacked. Then Bruce took an equally
firm line and said Mr Midgeley would be sacked if his own
letter-box holders were removed. So Mr Midgeley went back
to Lord Froome and asked him to think up some manner of
solution that would enable him to keep his job.

There was such talk down in the village about all this at the
time. Some people took one side and some people took the
other. There were those who said that, since Luptree Court
belonged to Bruce, he ought to be allowed to choose the
bathroom fittings. But most people felt that he was being
unreasonable. Since Lord Froome was the person actually
living up there on the top landing, they thought it was a bit

high-handed of Bruce to interfere. But a solution was found in the end, because Mr Midgeley suggested that he should instal both types of holder for the lavatory paper. And Lord Froome was satisfied with this, because he could see to it that the letter-box variety remained empty.

What Lord Froome wanted, I think, was to do up the top-passage suite so that it became a perfect dwelling place. He was always worried that he might lose Lady Froome. He had the idea that she might be drawn back to her career, and spend less and less of her time at Luptree Court.

I was able to ask Camilla what she thought of Bruce's marriage when I went for a short visit to her house in Belgrave Square. She seemed to think that it wouldn't last for very long. She had invited Bruce and Lola to come and stay at Northwold Abbey, and thought then that Lola might be a trifle too *experienced* a young woman for someone of Bruce's temperament.

I'm afraid it wasn't too happy a visit for several reasons. Michael's acquaintance Willie Walpole was there, and he always did like playing the peacock. I suppose it's true to say that he was a rather more colourful personality than Bruce had ever been. But Camilla agrees with me that it's not right for anyone to be over-friendly with the hostess's brother's wife. She thought it might be on that list of relationships that sometimes gets pinned up inside the church door, as things to avoid – if one can help it that is to say.

There'd been some other causes for ill-feeling too. Camilla had attacked Bruce on his treatment of their father, saying that he was guilty of gross ingratitude: taking the gift that would save him from having to pay death duties, and then spitting in Lord Froome's face, as it were.

No, I'm afraid it was an unfortunate visit all round. And, one morning, Bruce had simply packed his bags and departed, leaving Lola to follow later by train. And he never wrote Camilla a thank-you letter, which she regarded as most ill-mannered.

Excerpt from Chloe, Marchioness of Froome's correspondence with the Duchess of Northumbria

think you're being very sensible. What difference does it make if the piece of fluff that attracted Willie's attention that might just happened to be Lola? He is not strictly speaking our responsibility.

It's such a pity you had harsh words with Bruce on all these other subjects. Yet mightn't it be possible for you to write him a letter, presenting a different kind of interpretation to the night's events? Perhaps you could say that after dinner Willie offered Lola a ride in Michael's new motor boat, and that it ran out of fuel at the bottom of the lake. But you might slip up on this one, if Lola has already told Bruce some totally different kind of story.

The Nanny Marks tapes

This wasn't the end of Bruce's marriage, not by a long way. A great many troubles were still in store for him. But that was only after Sebastian had returned from South America.

He had been out there for more than one year, when someone wrote to him to say that Mr Spot had been sliced up by Mr Hill. So there was no particular danger if he returned to England. And he worked his passage home on a cargo boat.

It seems that he'd never gone to Cuba after all. He had left the ship at Jamaica, and then got a lift on a private plane to Colombia. Then he'd hitched his way south to Chile, and finally ended up in Brazil. He was full of the adventures he'd had, swimming with the piranhas in the jungle. I think he was inclined to exaggerate those stories for my benefit.

Excerpt from Chloe, Marchioness of Froome's correspondence with the Duchess of Northumbria

Have you seen Sebastian since his return? He's been round here on a couple of occasions. I found to my horror that he was adorned with a horribly scraggy beard, brown for the most part, but with a streak of white hairs from the point of his chin. He claims the white is growing from the spot where Bruce hit him with a hammer when he was three.

He explained the hirsute refinery in terms of its being the badge of a true Socialist. So I did my best to explain to him that it didn't read like that, back here in London. People were far more liable to think he was a sailor, or that he was concealing a weak chin. And, in any case, didn't he think it rather unfair for all male Socialists to be flaunting such badges, while their female comrades can do little to match them in such zeal?

I did ask him what had become of Marilyn, by the way. He said that she had actually flown out to join him, when he was in Paraguay, with an air ticket screwed out of some fire-arms dealer who believed he was going to cash in on the deal during his next trip to Chile. Sebastian claims that he quickly quarrelled with her again, and then traded her for a donkey with one of those mestizo Indians who run houses of an inferior nature to my own in the northern regions of the Argentine.

I never know when to believe his stories. All I can say is that I have since had it confirmed that Marilyn *did* fly out to South America and that she had not since returned.

The Nanny Marks tapes

The immediate difficulty was to get Sebastian doing something worthwhile for his living. He seemed to have taken against work while he'd been in South America. He'd fallen into the company of all those bearded Fidelistas. (I think they must have been the equivalent of our beatniks.) All he seemed to think of nowadays was how to build the new society, after destroying the old. In any case, it was all rather silly in some ways.

Bruce decided that the best policy was to take Sebastian on holiday in the Bahamas, where he might get the opportunity to sort him out a bit. And Lola was to accompany them, which was a big mistake in my opinion. You see, Lola was the kind of girl who lived on the sensation of the moment. I don't suppose she really *wanted* Sebastian any more than she wanted Bruce (or even Willie Walpole if it comes to that). Yet she enjoyed the atmosphere of rivalry she could create. And it was very easy for her to do this kind of thing, what with having the two of them at her beck and call, way out there in the middle of nowhere.

Mind you, I don't know exactly what took place. All I know is that they each returned from the holiday on a different date. And Bruce remarked to me that Sebastian was a good-for-nothing layabout, in every sense of the word.

I felt so sorry that things should have worked out like this. For Bruce had been acting from the goodness of his heart in taking Sebastian on holiday. So I urged him not to give up that easily. There was still every chance that Sebastian could be brought back to a sensible attitude, if only he were assisted to find his feet. I suggested that Bruce ought to give him a small allowance, or something that would just tide him over until he found a worthwhile job.

Well, Bruce did write to Sebastian. But what I didn't realize at the time was his intention to make the allowance *conditional* on Sebastian leaving Lola alone. If you ask me, he ought to have seen now that Lola was no good for either of them. Yet Bruce was never one to let go. He'd made up his mind that he was going to stick by Lola, and neither love nor money could persuade him otherwise.

Of course, from Sebastian's point of view, the arrangement was a satisfactory one. I don't suppose he cared two figs about seeing Lola. But he did need some manner of allowance, now that his father seemed to have washed his hands of him.

Excerpt from Chloe, Marchioness of Froome's correspondence with the Duchess of Northumbria

It really does seem as if Lola is a perfect little minx. I am told by our common friends that it was she, and not Bruce, who first conceived this idea of taking Sebastian with them, and that the possibilities of playing them off against each other were already clearly sketched out in her mind, right from the very start.

The Nanny Marks tapes

It was then that Sir Reginald Duckworth died. Sir Reginald had represented Froome in Parliament ever since Lord Tillot (as he then was) had been its member. So there now had to be a bye-election at Froome. And the local Conservative Association approached Bruce to find out if he was prepared to take up the family tradition.

I don't think Bruce had ever been really interested in politics up till this moment. Yet everything was running smoothly in his Wessex Motels; and, now that he was married, the idea of becoming a Member of Parliament rather appealed to him. It would improve his standing all round.

Yet, before I go on with that story, I must tell you about Sebastian's visit to Northwold Abbey. He wasn't exactly invited, I'm afraid. It seems that he was getting himself into debt once again. And he thought he might manage to persuade Michael to lend him something.

But I think Michael may have resented this occasional intrusion of Camilla's brothers. 'I married you for your money, and not for your relatives!' I once heard him say. (Some of his remarks to Camilla were meant to be teasing.) So, as soon as he'd gathered the impression that Sebastian's visit was to scrounge money, his attitude might have been off-hand. Anyway, he urged Sebastian to put forward the date of his departure because his room would be required for Lord Snowdon's dressing room. (It would soon be time for the royal family's annual weekend on the grouse moor, you see.)

The only trouble is that Sebastian didn't set out for London, as he was supposed to have done. He told me afterwards that he couldn't have done, even if he'd wanted to, since Michael didn't come up with the money for his train fare. So he hitched a lift to York, where some of those scruffy friends of his had pitched their caravans.

Well, I don't know whose idea it was, but one of them suggested that they ought to hold an anti-blood sports demonstration outside Northwold Abbey, to coincide with the royal visit. Just a small one, but none the less embarrassing for all that.

I don't know what you think about all these anti-blood sports people. But I know what I do! Sebastian was being led astray by their nonsense. It was this idea of the new society which attracted him to them. What he never understood was the destructiveness of their aims.

Sebastian was terribly naughty. He'd designed a poster, which he hung up afterwards on the wall of his flat in Chelsea. You remember those Cerebos Salt advertisements? Well, he'd drawn a picture of a small chick, wearing a crown like Prince Philip might have worn. And there was a caricature of Michael running after it, firing a blunderbuss. And the caption read, 'Would *you* like to be peppered on your tail?'

Well, it seems that they stood there, waving their placards, at the point where the shoot was due to assemble. And, when the royal family arrived, Sebastian started to saunter over towards them. There were people in plain clothes present whose duty it was to protect the Queen. And they rushed to form a barrier between her and Sebastian, as if they thought he intended to throw a bomb at her or something. But he didn't do anything of the kind. He suddenly changed his direction and walked up to Camilla, kissed her on the cheek and inquired whether he'd left his pyjamas under the pillow.

Of course, Camilla didn't know what to reply. She didn't really want to admit to anyone that this was her brother. But she had to explain it to the Queen, later, or there might have been some wrong impressions about the pyjamas under the pillow.

It was Willie Walpole who had the presence of mind to know how to act. He reached quickly forward and walloped Sebastian a good sound blow on his ear-hole. But Sebastian knew better than to hit him back. He merely lay down in the mud like a young puppy dog. And all his friends started chanting, 'No blood sports! No blood sports!' And next morning the story was carried in all the newspapers, with photographs of Sebastian lying there in the mud. One of the scruffy brigade just happened to have his camera at the ready, I suppose.

Excerpt from Chloe, Marchioness of Froome's correspondence with the Duchess of Northumbria

Yes, I do understand that it must be terribly embarrassing to have Sebastian giving offence to all these royals, when they are your house guests. But, if I were you darling, I'd treat the matter more light-heartedly. I'm sure the Queen is quite accustomed to people trying to be rude to her. But I expect she sets this against the far greater number of people that she sees trying to be nice to her. I suspect she may have far more problems with the ones who are trying to be nice to her than with the ones who are trying to be nasty, because the former manage to get closer to her, I imagine.

The Nanny Marks tapes

Surprisingly, Bruce took a rather different view of Sebastian's behaviour from the others. Of course, he couldn't afford to get officially involved in any public comment which might reflect on his loyalty to the Queen – not with the bye-election coming up. But I think he'd always been harbouring a private resentment at the way he'd suddenly been dropped from court circles. Besides, he wasn't feeling any more friendly towards Michael than towards Sebastian, if it comes to that. He told me privately that he thought Sebastian had displayed more spunk than he'd ever imagined he had in him. And he sent him a cheque for several hundred pounds on the strength of it.

This was a terrible mistake as far as Bruce was concerned. The trouble was that he didn't really understand just how different Sebastian had become, now that he was involved in politics. Sebastian's ideas had been pumped into him by the scruffy brigade. He was no longer himself.

He did the most terrible thing. The devil had really got into him by this time. He used the money Bruce had sent him to put down a deposit for his candidature as a Wessex Regionalist, at the bye-election for Froome. Now I ask you, was that a reasonable thing to do? But he did it.

The Tories were going through a difficult patch at this time. Perhaps you'll remember that people had been saying a few nasty things about the way certain Ministers had been over-friendly at times. But, if it comes to that, Lady Tillot was friendly with all these people as well. So they can't have been really bad.

Excerpt from Chloe, Marchioness of Froome's
correspondence with the Duchess of Northumbria

No, my love, this time you have no cause whatsoever to get worried. Whatever some of my ladies may have been doing to get their names in the papers, I can promise you that I have never slept with either of the gentlemen you mention. They have long been friends of mine. They have both been known to pay occasional visits to my club and they have both been known to have a drink at my table. But never have I spoken either to one, or to the other, at the same table. Nor have I ever had carnal knowledge of them in bed, either separately or together.

My personal view is that the press is (once again) trying to make a mountain out of a molehill. Whether you are a British Minister or a Russian diplomat, you still require to have a sex life. And what does it matter if the tastes of such a pair in sexual partners does just occasionally happen to coincide? If people go on like this, the poor men will be truly traumatized, and then neither of them will have any sex life whatsoever.

The Nanny Marks tapes

There's one thing I will say: it's not right to drag emotions into politics. It's what they do on the continent, I'm told. Yet I'm afraid that Sebastian was doing it at this bye-election, although not in the usual manner, I suppose.

He argued that the Establishment had to be overthrown at any cost. And he was prepared to stoop pretty low at times, to achieve it. Any promises he had made didn't seem to worry him at all. He was prepared to wade right in and give one to the point and one to the mark! And I'm afraid to say that Bruce was never quite ready for these things.

Sebastian chose the bye-election, of all times, to renew his attentions to Lola. She was an awful girl really. She appeared on the Regionalist platform, holding hands with Sebastian and talking about free love in politics, and all that kind of thing. I'm sure Sebastian didn't like the idea of being photographed by the press holding Lola's hand, but that's the way she worked, you see. She probably wanted to make Bruce jealous.

Author's narrative

In my conversation with Mr Walter Davis and Mr Gordon Perkins, I inquired about these disruptions within the Tillot family resulting from the Froome bye-election.

Mr Davis said, 'Well, it was bound to cause disruptions, now wasn't it? I mean, there was one brother taking up the call of duty, as he saw it. Then along comes the other brother and gives him the "up yours" sign, while running off with his wife. Well, I ask you, wouldn't that kind of thing cause havoc if it happened in *your* life?'

'It was certainly a talking point for the Froome voters,' said Mr Perkins. 'Yet, from the very start, I'd regarded it as being an interesting campaign. It gave us something to think about for a change, quite regardless of the fact that two of the candidates were brothers whom we all knew personally.'

I asked Mr Perkins to describe the issues, as he saw them. He said, 'Well, I wasn't so interested in what the Labour candidate had to say (although others were, of course). But the confrontation which gripped my own interest was this idea of Bruce asking us to vote for the way of life that we all knew so well, against Sebastian who was saying that it was time to get the world sorted out into a different kind of political perspective. No more big states, like America, Russia or China. Not even semi-big states like Britain, France or Germany. Instead of that, we should all be the size of something like Denmark. And that's where Wessex comes into its own. Not as an independent state, but as one of many little regional states who have all given up some portion of their sovereignty to the parliament which holds them all together. Though I must confess that Sebastian was never precisely clear on whether he thought of that parliament in terms of the United Kingdom, a United States of Europe, or even a United World.'

'He was talking about a parliament for Wessex itself, if you ask me,' broke in Mr Davis.

'That as well,' said Mr Perkins, 'even if he was calling it a Witan. But he was still talking about it within a wider federal structure. He described it as quasi-autonomy. And I must admit that it gave me plenty of food for thought. So did it to plenty of others I could name, as I discovered when I went down to the pub to discuss with my mates how the election was progressing. (I used to go to the Froome Arms in those days.) It's not that I was ever liable to vote for him, even if he hadn't withdrawn from the contest. But I admired him for thinking up such an original approach to politics, instead of just attacking Bruce by claiming to be a Communist or something.

'At the one meeting I attended which Sebastian was addressing, I remember his saying that here in Froome he was giving a push to a very small snowball, which would eventually roll on through Britain, until it came to Europe, and then on again until it rolled throughout the entire world. There was some laughter in the audience at the time. I may even have laughed myself. But I've got to admit that the remark wouldn't look quite so silly, here in 1978, as it did then.

'We hear a lot nowadays about Scotland and Wales gaining their autonomy. So why not Wessex too? And Mercia if it comes to that. Then there's Anglia. And up there in the north, I suppose it will be Northumbria and Lancastria. So by the time all this has happened there won't be very much left of England, except for a little patch around London, stretching down to Dover, I dare say.

'But I think that Sebastian would have claimed that even that little shrunken England was too large in terms of its population (I mean if all countries have got to be about the size of Denmark.) So they'd probably have to split up what remains of England along the banks of the Thames, though I haven't the foggiest what they'd call the southern bit, unless it's Sussex.

'The trouble was really that we had no way of knowing how serious Sebastian was being in his campaign. You never do know with him. But there were several occasions when I heard it said by one or another of the Froome voters that his ideas were ahead of their time. I'd go as far as saying so myself. And, in any case, he brought a little colour to the bye-election. Most other elections I quickly manage to forget.

'Mind you, he owed a lot to Lord Froome for these ideas; not so much for the political slant, but he could never have raised the idea of a quasi-autonomous regional state of Wessex if it weren't for the fact that Lord Froome had already been reminding people what Wessex was all about. It's no good for some politican to stand up and say, "We're all Wessexmen. So come and vote for Wessex!" People need to *feel* that they might be Wessexmen first.'

The Sixth Marquess of Froome, interviewed by
Mr Simon Manasseh

Q: Did you approve of the idea when Lord Tillot and Lord Sebastian turned to politics around this time?
A: In Bruce's case, we all did. It was part of the family tradition. Precisely what Sebastian was getting up to is a little more difficult to understand. What I like to think is

that the boy always did have a bit of respect for what his old Dad had done. Taking up this gimmick I'd used for getting tourism on the move in this region. At the bottom of his heart, I suspect that you'd find he admired me for it. So, when he gets this idea of upsetting Bruce by standing for Parliament against him, he takes up the same gimmick I used, in political form. But he managed to talk a lot of nonsense in the process.

Q: In what way did you find his ideas nonsensical?

A: I can't pretend to have studied exactly what he said. But the whole idea of recreating a separate state of Wessex is ridiculous. We don't want to go back to the way things were in the past. We've emerged from all that. We want to live in the present.

But what particularly irritated me was his way of proclaiming that Regionalism was the last hope of *democracy*. All that talk about one man one vote on an international scale! I think he was saying that all countries have to be divided up into units of the same size (in terms of their population) before world democracy can take root. But who wants it to take root? In fact who is really interested in democracy? We may *pretend* to be, for the sake of winning votes. But it's power which really counts. And we're not going to win any more power for Britain, if we split up into a whole series of regional states.

Q: Can you explain your considerable distaste for democracy?

A: Democracy never gets anywhere. There's too many people trying to take decisions at the same time. That's no way to run a business, and it's certainly no way to run a country. If you look at history, the only times people made a great spurt forwards is when they were under the control of one single man: a political giant, no matter what he preached. The wolfpack follows its leader. And democracy only works well when it is doing precisely that, with Churchill for example.

Q: If you were asked to assess the relative ranking of Churchill and Hitler, in which order would you place them?

A: There was a time at the end of the war when I'd definitely have put Hitler first, because I was trying to judge the two systems, in relation to what we ought to choose. I saw all the chances that Hitler had – in his freedom to take decisions, and to act – set against all the frustration that were put in Churchill's way, even to the extent of getting thrown out of office. So I did argue for a while that Hitler would go down in history as a greater man because, as I saw it then, Churchill's main claim to fame was that he was the man who defeated Hitler.

But, I wouldn't answer the same way any longer. I mean, quite a long period has elapsed since the end of the war. It's no longer a question of supposing that Churchill was the one to draw the lucky cards. We've got to admit that he had the foresight to back a winner, when he had even helped to train that winner; and he knew that it would go on winning during this whole period of history we've been living ever since. That's why I now think Churchill was the greater man. He *won*, and he's *still* winning. It's not to say that I admire democracy. But I appreciate you've got to make those kind of noises, if you want to win the game.

Q: Couldn't it be said that Lord Sebastian was making precisely those kind of noises in his presentation of Wessex Regionalism?

A: Well, it rather depends how far you're prepared to go, now doesn't it? I mean, if you become *too* democratic, then you might as well hand over the government of this country to the trades unions. And then we'd be in one hell of a mess. But I don't think Sebastian ever grasped that point. He went on talking about one man, one vote, without realizing just how many of these voters there really were, and just how irresponsible they can be when it comes to casting that vote.

Q: Are you branding your son as being someone who is himself politically irresponsible?

A: Oh, I didn't mean to go quite so far as to say that. No, if you really want to know what I think, it's what I've already told you. Sebastian was taking a leaf out of the book of his old Dad. He was catching on to my gimmick about Wessex, and using it for his own ends.

The Nanny Marks tapes

Bruce was most terribly angry with Sebastian. Felt that he'd been turned into a public laughing stock. And he asked me to do an errand for him. So I went round to see Sebastian at his political headquarters, in a camping site on the Froome disposal area, and I brought to him a letter which offered very suitable terms for him to stop all these antics.

Sebastian agreed to them immediately. In exchange for quite a substantial sum of money, he stood down in the bye-election. He told me that he didn't have a chance of winning, anyway; and he didn't care about losing his deposit, since he was now being given ample to cover it. And, as part of the bargain, he returned to London immediately, which made Lola realize that she had no one other than Bruce to turn to. So she returned to Luptree Court.

Yet, in spite of all this, those horrible Socialists managed to win the seat. It was dreadful really. And it was the first time in more than a hundred years. I think it was David Frost who was to blame. He was always sniping at poor Sir Alec on television, as if it was *his* fault that he had such a funny mouth.

Bruce was most upset, I can tell you. He said he wouldn't have gone into all this political business if he'd known he was going to be insulted. But he was even more upset when Sebastian wrote to me asking me to inform Bruce that both he and Lola ought to request a blood test urgently.

I wasn't quite sure why Bruce found this so offensive. But it seems that Sebastian had caught some strange disease while he was in South America. And it had taken quite a few months for it to develop. What Bruce resented, I think, was that Sebastian hadn't gone for his own blood test sooner, if he suspected that he might be carrying the disease. Yet now it was too late, for the test revealed that both Lola and Bruce had caught this infection too.

I don't really see why Bruce should have been so upset about *this* part of all that had been going on. Everybody catches something sometime, as I always say. But he *did* object to it strongly. He said that if he ever caught hold of Sebastian, he'd wring the little blighter's neck. Unfortunately he made the remark to some friend of Sebastian. And a few days later, it was reported to the press.

Excerpts from Chloe, Marchioness of Froome's correspondence with the Duchess of Northumbria

I always did believe in poetic justice, and here is the proof of it! Sebastian came round to see me and said that he was terribly worried because he suspected he might have syphilis; and that, if he had it, then he might have given it to Lola as well. I told him that the two of them had better come round the next morning, when the doctor who makes a regular check-up on my young ladies was due to pay us a visit. This is Dr James, whom I don't think you've met.

Well, he took blood tests and diagnosed syphilis in both cases. And he went on to ask for a list of possible contacts (or the people they'd each slept with over the past six months). Sebastian trotted out a short list of names and promised to communicate personally with them on the issue. But Lola became all coy, until she finally confessed that she didn't know all their names, though she thought that most of them lived somewhere near the King's Road.

Naturally, we were all a bit worried in case Bruce had got any of his purity contaminated (which wouldn't be poetic justice at all). But Lola assured us that there was little chance of this being the case, since Bruce had 'hardly ever' slept in the same bed with her since the big break-up.

But, who knows? 'Hardly ever', by Lola's standards, might mean fucking twice a night on the occasions they were together. Dr James advised that I ought to take it upon myself to advise Bruce to come and see me, next time that my girls are having their monthly check-up. That way we'll know for sure. He doesn't think it safe to rely upon the promises of the two culprits that they would put him fully in the picture, and I feel obliged to agree with Dr James about this.

It certainly wasn't an easy letter for me to write, so in the end I put it to him quite bluntly. I told him how Sebastian and Lola had availed themselves of the opportunities of my free medical service. So he'd do well to do the same – just in case he'd been unlucky.

It's terrible, I know, but Bruce has been most unlucky. Apart from having the genuine ailment, his psychosomatic fears that he was about to be diagnosed as a syphilitic have brought on all manner of side effects, which never afflicted either Sebastian or Lola. Dr James has advised him to take a long rest.

As for me, I shall have to discard my belief in poetic justice for ever. Life can be most cruel, and most unpoetic at times.

The Nanny Marks tapes

What couldn't have been foreseen was that Lord Froome was going to get interested in Lola. I don't suppose he'd have met her in the normal run of events, seeing that he wasn't really on social terms with Bruce. But Lola had once been on good terms with a gentleman who was influential at White's Club. In fact it was probably at Lola's suggestion that this gentleman had helped Lord Froome to be given his membership once again. It kept the club more aristocratic, if they could keep all the Dukes and Marquesses on their list. And there was no longer a problem about Lord Minehead. He'd never been heard of since he went to Sumatra. (Camilla says that he accepted a bet from Lord Yeovil that he couldn't spend an evening with the latest wife of the President, which she seemed to think was rather foolhardy of him).

But Lord Froome probably felt grateful to Lola for her efforts in these matters. So he may have invited her out to dinner a few times. And, what with Lady Froome being in Tokyo at the time . . . , Well, he was at a loose end, so to speak. But, as you can imagine, it did cause tremendous additional problems when Bruce got to hear that his father was also involved in this unhappy relationship.

In point of fact, he only got to hear of it several months later, when his doctor told him that Lord Froome appeared to be suffering from the same unusual infection as Lola and himself. But this was no reason to get jealous. He seemed to think that his father must have been doing a lot worse things than just taking his wife out to dinner, which I'm sure is all that ever happened.

Excerpts from Chloe, Marchioness of Froome's correspondence with the Duchess of Northumbria

The story gets curiouser and curiouser! I received the first communication from your father in many a year. He telephoned me, apologizing first (with great gallantry) for intruding upon my long-established privacy, but declared that he had something of a private and strictly personal nature that he wanted to discuss with me. I told him by all means to come round.

Well, to cut a long story short, I'd better tell you straight out that your father too has syphilis, and indirectly from the same source. He himself took far too long in coming to the point. He just sat there twiddling his thumbs, and saying that he had embarrassing admissions to make. So suddenly I had guessed it all. I just said to him, 'Now come along Edward. What you've come here to tell me is that Lola has given you the syph!' And he sat there staring at me amazed, and distinctly worried too, in that he imagined the word must have already reached me from others, when he was so convinced that he'd kept the secret to himself, (Nadia having spent the last four months in Tokyo).

I asked him why he hadn't gone to see his own doctor about it, to which he replied characteristically that he himself is so well known locally, that word would somehow have reached the papers. He felt that, by coming to me, I'd be able to put him in touch with some doctor who was accustomed to treating in confidence the more delicate ailments of celebrities. So, naturally, I put him on to Dr James.

The question which intrigued me personally was how he ever got the opportunity to sleep with Lola. But apparently it was quite simple. I dare say you've heard how your father does all these keep-fit exercises nowadays: jogging through the park and ending up with a cold plunge in the lake. Well, apparently Bruce didn't suspect that things might be heading in a dangerous direction, when Lola suddenly took it into her head to start swimming in the lake before breakfast – quite independently, as it were.

Edward quotes Lola as saying that Bruce did begin to question her, at one time, on whether they ever ran into each other, when she went out for these early morning swims. Apparently she just made a joke of it, saying that men of *his* age were incapable of getting an erection, let alone an orgasm, which of course is one of those subjects upon which all of you youngsters are apt to delude yourselves.

You must keep all this information in strict confidence, my darling. I realize that I oughtn't to be telling you these things. But there can't be very much harm in the exchange of views on family matters between mother and daughter. And we see each other so rarely nowadays that it has got to be done by letter.

find that I've done something absolutely terrible! When I sent Daddy to Dr James, I neglected to tell the latter that Bruce hadn't been told that his father had contracted syphilis. And Dr James, knowing that they had both contracted it from the same source, calmly assumed that all these matters were out in the open. So Bruce, when he went round for his next lot of injections, received a homily upon the dangers of sharing his wife with other men, even if it were only with such intimate friends as his father. And as he sat there glumly, without uttering a single word, the whole story (or enough of it) was soon spilt into his ears. By then, even Bruce couldn't fail to jump to the right conclusions.

He came round to see me immediately afterwards, to ask my advice as to what he should do, his line being that he couldn't very well divorce his father, since he already regarded him as being divorced. But he *could* divorce Lola, and he wanted my opinion as to whether such an act would be ethical. With the question put to me in precisely that form, I found it very difficult to answer him. So I advised him to sleep on the matter for a month at least. And, if he still feels like divorcing her when that period is up, then he ought to do as his heart dictates — though I advised him to leave your father out of the divorce citations, confining them to Sebastian and any others he might like to name. Bruce looked at me bleakly and replied that there hadn't been any such others.

The Sixth Marquess of Froome, interviewed by Mr Simon Manasseh

Q: Did you approve of Lord Tillot marrying Miss Lola Forsyte?

A: Well, she was a most attractive girl. I'll give her that. But she was too much for Bruce to handle. I could have told him that right from the start. But he wasn't interested in my opinion of course. He was apt to treat me as if I had one foot in the grave. But I pride myself that I managed to show him there was still a little life in the old dog yet.

Q: How do you mean?

A: Well, I showed him that he couldn't just ignore me. If he was going to pinch a few of my privileges, then I was darned well going to pinch a few of his. And he didn't like it, I can assure you. He wrote and told me that he'd rather have no father at all than a father who had no moral scruples. Pompous ass that he always was!

His letter rambled on for pages, trying to explain my turpitude (as he called it) in terms of disobedience of the ten commandments. I wrote back to say, first of all, that he himself was a fornicator, or had been until he lost the opportunity. Secondly, he was being silly to accuse me of incest, since I hadn't even bothered to marry his wife. (It simply wasn't necessary when she had always been so willing.) And thirdly, I commended him on his decision to have no father at all. That way, we could both agree that he was an utter bastard.

Q: Am I to conclude that this virtually put an end to all communication between the two of you?

A: More or less. There were always intermediaries when it was necessary. But I was glad to be able to wash my hands of him. To tell the truth, I was coming to the conclusion that having sons isn't a very profitable business. We could well afford to have most of them gelded in childhood, leaving just sufficient for the survival of the species. Daughters are a far more profitable concern. They repay you with a little affection. Or they do sometimes.

The Nanny Marks tapes

I'm afraid Bruce felt so bitterly towards his father that he started divorce proceedings immediately. I did try my best to put a little heart into him, to make him feel less face-to-face with all these misfortunes. I told him how all the little girls that I sometimes looked after inquired how Big Bruce was getting on. (There was a Little Bruce in one of the families, you see.) But it didn't seem to cheer him up in any way at all.

Excerpt from the personal manuscript of Bruce, Lord Tillot

I find it so difficult to discover a rewarding approach to life. I emerged from school believing that the solidarity of family ties, with all its avenues of approach to the established powers in our society, would be sufficient to carry me through life on a wave of success and achievement. But I rapidly discovered that it wasn't going to be as easy as all that.

In endeavouring to follow Christ, looking inwards to my conscience as the personal instigator of all that I should do, I was obliged to admit that my conscience was capable of making a fool out of me. It may have been partly in disillusionment that I turned to the opposite extreme, of pursuing Mammon instead of God. But the fact is that I'm not very good at pursuing Mammon.

It ought to have been easy enough for me to find my place within the Conservative party. Yet, in the event, I discovered that my own family, which everyone regarded as my greatest political asset, turned me into a public laughing stock, so that my hopes for a rewarding (if undistinguished) career at Westminster must for ever be abandoned.

My marriage is also collapsing in ruins. Somehow I didn't offer my heart to the right person. Perhaps there is something wrong with me which makes me incapable of offering my heart to the right person.

That is why, more and more, I find myself contemplating the possibility of a life where the decisions are taken out of my hands: to serve both God and man simultaneously, in the manner that others may choose for me. It is time that I investigated the way of life as it is practised within monastic orders. In the absence of other solutions, it could be that I might find one there.

14

The Cookie Begins to Crumble
1964–8

*Excerpts from Chloe, Marchioness of Froome's
correspondence with the Duchess of Northumbria*

I think it's all so stupid of Bruce to bring your father into the
divorce citations. He's already going to have enough trouble
from the press in citing Sebastian. Yet father and brother as
joint co-respondents will present them with a bonanza of
orgiastic analysis, which may take years for the public to
forget. Perhaps I ought to whisper the names of a few other
co-respondents in his ear, in the hope that it might divert his
wrath from his own kith and kin. What do you think?

What irks me more than anything else is the way Bruce
argues that he is doing all this not for himself, nor even to
expedite the divorce, but to protect the public from such
unscrupulous scoundrels (as he dubs them). I told him not to
be so bloody absurd! Does he think that your father and
brother are going to go lurking outside churches, to pounce
on virgin brides emerging fresh from their visit to the altar?
There are times when Bruce gets my goat. In fact, I can feel
my left elbow waggling viciously, as I sit here writing to you
about it.

I'm afraid we made the wrong move. It seems there's no
possibility of persuading him to drop your father and Sebastian from the citations. Yet he *is* proposing to cite the whole
damn list of names that we compiled for him, as additional
items that is to say. This divorce case promises to be even

more sensational than my own. If only there were royalties to be obtained on our family's contribution to the gutter press, we'd all be millionaires by now.

What Bruce neglects to perceive is that everyone will be hooting with laughter at him. And, because it doesn't concern their own lives in any way at all, the public will probably be more envious than censorious about your father's inconsiderate cruelty.

I sometimes feel that Bruce is evolving into one of life's true victims. Belatedly perhaps, I am tempted to query your father's much proclaimed maxim: 'Throw them in at the deep end, and they'll learn to swim fast enough.' I know that you yourself learnt to swim very well, and Sebastian is as resilient as a cork. Yet a philosophy as harsh as that may have its casualties after all.

This is too much! Bruce has written to tell me that he refuses to listen to any advice from a 'woman of Babylon'. If he's going to speak of his own mother like that, then I'm going to wash my hands of him. I have quite enough trouble contending with all the usual epithets, like trollop, strumpet, bawd and whore. And I refuse to have 'woman of Babylon' added to the list by my own son. (Ex, that is to say.)

Really Camilla, I am finding life just too cruel for words. I had imagined that I'd find your father grateful for all my efforts to persuade Bruce to drop the citation – despite the fact that they weren't successful. But I find on the contrary that he's even more furious with me than he is with Bruce. He says that it was only because I leaked the information about his having contracted syphilis that Bruce discovered about his swims with Lola, which makes *me* the guilty party by his standards.

Honestly darling, what can I say against such calumny? I swear before God that I never told a living soul about your father's ailment. (Except for you, or course, but that doesn't count, because you're my daughter.) I have tried to persuade Dr James to write to your father and explain that these declarations had to be made, in accordance with that Hippocratic oath that all doctors take. But he doesn't seem to think that the oath really covers this issue. He argues that doctors should be regarded as healers who must stand aside from the legal battles between their patients, which leaves me with no one at all to champion my cause and mitigate your father's anger against me.

Of *course* the gutter press were going to fasten upon such details. But that doesn't give your father any justification to say that I planned it this way, in revenge for all the things he accused me of doing in our own divorce case. I am simply not such a scheming woman. And the very idea that he can *think* these things has stuck in my gullet.

It's no use, I can't take it. When I said I could help him cure his ailment, it was a sad mistake. I ought to have insisted that he go to his National Health doctor and inflict upon him his paranoiac fear of press persecution. That way, I wouldn't have been slid down to square one in this horrible game of Snakes and Ladders. And I don't think he'd really have resented it, if I had declined my assistance. For we'd both have been able to rely upon the existing buffer of years spent without meeting one another, to effect a gracious and dignified exit on the brief reunion. As it is, I find that we're hating each other, with myself as the offended party once again.

The Nanny Marks tapes

Everything was going wrong these days. The general election had finally come round and Sir Alec had been defeated. And who was this Mr Wilson that we'd got in his place? Why, he couldn't even speak English properly. Sir Alec was a man you could trust. But not this Mr Wilson. His whole idea in politics was to level people down, not up.

And what was the society that these Socialists had brought with them? The nation had gone to pot, I tell you. Pot! Pot! You understand what I mean? Yes, ever such nasty things were beginning to happen. And all you could hear on the wireless was a lot of screaming girls, although somewhere in the middle of it a record of the Beatles might have been playing.

Lady Tillot was very sad at the way things were turning out. Not at all like the good old days in the war. I called in to see her one day when I was up in London and we shared a bottle of champagne, although sharing perhaps isn't quite the right word. I'm afraid Lady Tillot seemed to have been drinking rather heavily of late.

Then the German gentleman came into the room. And I didn't like the way he treated Lady Tillot. He was a tall, fair-haired young man with flashing white teeth and a nasty smile. He was holding her very roughly by the hair, while pretending that he was being affectionate. I was looking at Lady Tillot with concern.

But she smiled at me, and said, 'You worry too much, Nanny darling. It's not worth all the trouble. It's just how the cookie crumbles! It's bound to crumble in the end!'

Excerpt from Chloe, Marchioness of Froome's correspondence with the Duchess of Northumbria

I saw Sebastian the other night. He came to pay one of his rare visits to my place. So I asked him why he didn't put in more regular appearances. He would be doing his mother a good turn if he could persuade some of those trendy young friends of his to give the new haunts around the King's Road a rest and pay a visit to the old 1940 Club instead.

But he just laughed and said, 'This kind of entertainment isn't necessary any more. We take it where we find it. And it's free.'

The awful thing is that I believe he may be right. I've got a horrible feeling that my kind of establishment may belong to the past. I'll have to evolve with the times, if I'm going to remain in business at all; but it's so difficult to know what direction to take, in order to satisfy the carnal appetites of your modern generation.

Fruity argues that we ought to go way out by stimulating

the unfulfilled fantasies of young people, which would also serve to tantalize the palates of all our more jaded, but traditional, roués. But the territory is new to me, and I fear that the direction of such a club might pass over completely into Fruity's hands: a prospect that could be alarming.

The Nanny Marks tapes

Another person that I was worried about was Camilla. You see, Michael had lost a great deal of money ever since the Socialists had made such a mess of things. His investments were in the wrong things, she told me. It looked as if they would have to sell one of the grouse moors in order to pay what they owed in supertax.

Michael explained that they wouldn't any longer be able to afford to have me come and work for them when their own nanny was away.

'I'd willingly do it free,' I tried to explain to him.

But Michael shook his head. 'No Nanny, that wouldn't be fair. And besides, you're not as young as you used to be. You ought to be taking things easy at your time in life.'

That isn't the way that I see things. You're as young as you feel, is what I always say.

But I'm afraid age does have its disadvantages. It's a kind of restriction. I couldn't get out and see people quite as much as I formerly had done. Not even when it was someone who lived as close to me as Bruce.

I don't think he'd ever really recovered from the loss of Lola. He seemed to have turned his back on the world. The only person who could approach him nowadays was a gentleman from Downside. He'd become most interested in the Catholic faith, you see, and was taking some instruction.

I did see him once, when I was taking a walk through the woods. But I felt as if I was disturbing him. He was sitting there on a log, reading a book on the life of St Jerome. I tried to get him talking about things as they'd been before. Asked him if he was going to stand for Parliament again. But he simply wasn't interested in anything like that.

It was as if we'd all been playing musical chairs. And most of us had managed to find a seat when the music stopped. Yet Bruce was the one that got left out. And I thought the pain showed on his face a little.

Final excerpt from the personal manuscript of Bruce, Lord Tillot

I think I may be halfway along the path towards my solution for life. But of course it's not just *my* solution. It's the one that belongs to everybody, because it is the solution of the universal church of Christ. Or perhaps I ought to say the universal church of humanity, for there can only be one church, whether I adhere to the Catholic interpretation of its significance within this world or to that of any other faith.

In the doctrines of the Catholic church, I am finding a faith to which I can surrender myself. It's comprehensive. It's all there somewhere. All has been written down and formulated. The requirement for me is merely to accept, and to ask others to show me where to look.

I am afraid of seeking the right spot for my steps to land. I want to be part of a universal discipline, where I am carried along by life's great river, towards the ocean of perpetual unity: with God, with the universe, and with my fellow man – all rolled into one. The Totality may be the expression I need.

I am having increasing misgivings, however, about the advisability of making any further entries in this manuscript. Each time that I sit down to make such an entry, I am essentially withdrawing myself from this idea of a Totality, to which I should have surrendered. I am seeking to plot the map of my own Self, as distinct from that Totality. It cannot be healthy that I permit myself such a luxury. And, if this turns out to be the last of my entries, the explanation will lie in what I have just written.

The Nanny Marks tapes

Sebastian never came anywhere near Luptree nowadays. He wouldn't have been regarded as very welcome, I suppose, either by Bruce or by his father. Yet he did write to me from time to time, although he neglected to tell me that he was going to get married. It wasn't a marriage really. He called it an anti-marriage. I read all about it in the papers.

I'm not sure what it was that he thought he was up to. If you ask me, it was because all his friends were anti the war in Vietnam, anti-this or anti-that. They all had to be anti-something nowadays. So Sebastian must have decided that it was time for someone to have an anti-marriage.

Of course, you wouldn't get any English girls doing that kind of thing. Yet there were so many Jamaicans and Pakistanis coming into London at that time. There didn't seem to be any way of keeping them out.

Well, it seems that he was sharing his flat with some Pakistani girl. And they held this great party to celebrate what they described as an anti-marriage. People didn't really know quite what to make of it. '*Is* he married, or *isn't* he married?' was what his father wanted to know.

I think Lord Froome was worried, to tell the truth. Not that he was greatly interested in Sebastian's welfare any longer. But, if Bruce failed to produce a son, then the title would go to any son of Sebastian's. And it would hardly have been suitable if the heir to Luptree was *coloured*.

Excerpts from Chloe, Marchioness of Froome's correspondence with the Duchess of Northunbria

Sebastian and some of his friends have started paying regular visits to my club. So my innovations are perhaps a success. They are impressed with the private cabaret upstairs, where I've got two West Indian girls doing all manner of things. They assess what the fantasies of the evening's audience may be and play to excite them with orgasmic zest. Downstairs they have to keep the performance more restrained. But, in the room upstairs, they can really let themselves go.

Sebastian has a rather beautiful Pakistani girlfriend nowadays – called Bundi. She goes everywhere in a sari, from which her belly protrudes, with a piece of red glass (as I imagine it to be) placed provocatively in her navel.

I received an invitation to Sebastian's anti-marriage celebration, which I delightedly accepted. (So rarely do I get asked to these festive occasions!) I even took my two West Indian girls, Bo and Peep, to perform one of their milder cabarets to the assembled company. Bundi, who was more than a little inebriated by this time of the evening, had to be restrained from joining in with them. Sebastian was at pains to explain to her that she was supposed to be virginal on her wedding night.

The Nanny Marks tapes

But there's no doubt that Sebastian was still enjoying himself. I read in the papers how he'd taken on two more wifelets (as he called them). Not that he'd got rid of the first, mind you. And he was quoted as saying that there was still room for one more in his Chelsea flat. I'm afraid his choice in colour was getting darker, if anything. One of them came from Tobago, and the other from Granada (wherever these places may be).

Excerpt from Chloe, Marchioness of Froome's correspondence with the Duchess of Northumbria

Sebastian is an unmitigated shit! I use strong language, because that's the way I feel.

You know how I pinned all my hopes for the club's recovery on my two West Indian girls. Their cabaret was really exciting people. Telephone calls to inquire precisely when they'd be performing. My clientele increasing, instead of dropping, for the first time in several years.

Then Bo and Peep come in to tell me that they're leaving.

And the next thing I hear is that they're living with Sebastian and Bundi, in a *maison à quatre* as far as I can gather.

Naturally I went round to see him and demand exactly what was going on. It was all charming blandishments, as ever. Sit down, Mum. . . . Have a drink, Mum.' But I would have none of it. I asked him if he realized that he was putting me out of business by this piece of treachery. All he would say was, 'Cool it! Just cool it!' – as if I were his cook, or something.

Bo and Peep were hiding themselves in the kitchen with Bundi for most of the time. Ashamed to show their faces to me no doubt. But, when they did put in an appearance, I could see that Peep's belly was as big as a pumpkin. And I was in no mood to be nice to her either.

I said, 'That's what comes of leaving my club, where the pill gets fed to you as part of the menu!'

Then Sebastian had the cheek to reply, 'No Mum. The reason they left your club is that they actually wanted to have one up the spout, which is precisely where I have been able to be of some assistance to them!'

I wasn't going to stand there listening to any more of that. I just told him that I washed my hands of him completely, and that henceforward he could be *other* people's problem, but not mine. And all he did was to shrug his shoulders, saying that he didn't want any more 'aggro'.

I sometimes wonder where all these new words come from. Do you think they bring them in with them from the West Indies and Pakistan?

The Nanny Marks tapes

I felt sorry for Lord Froome, you know. His own marriage wasn't running quite as smoothly as we might wish for him. Lady Froome did love to travel round the world. And there was always someone that she'd known in days gone by who would suggest that she go and visit them. She found it difficult to resist the opportunity of a few months in the sun.

Yet Lord Froome always had Buddy. He adored Buddy,

you know. And what with Lady Froome spending more and more of her time abroad, he had to learn how to be both mother and father to her at the same time. The thing I liked was when he used to take her for her daily ride in the car. I used to sit at the end of the garden and wave to them as they passed.

Excerpts from Chloe, Marchioness of Froome's correspondence with the Duchess of Northumbria

I don't think you've met Detective-Sergeant Distemper. He's the policeman who was so charming at the time of Buffy's awful accident. But he has turned into an utter menace ever since he was transferred to the vice squad. It's not that he is any less friendly. He still drops in for his drink and a chat with the girls. But he now manages to make it quite plain to me that his favour has a price, and that he could make life very difficult for me if I didn't manage to see things his way. I suppose he's right, so I just do as he says. But his price keeps on going up.

Fruity is in real trouble, I'm afraid, and may have to slip back over to Hamburg while he still can. Not that I shall miss him greatly, even if he misses me. All this fantasizing has gone to his head and he was been trying of late to act out all his own fantasies on me; and I simply don't happen to share his taste in such matters.

The trouble arose because he fell out with Distemper. Fruity had insisted on doing all our transactions with him personally, and the moment arrived when Fruity declined to pay the price demanded, and threatened to report Distemper to his superiors. The next thing he knew was that he got roughed up by one of these Soho gangs, who had come to tell him that Distemper was a personal friend of theirs and that they didn't like any tuppenny crook from Hamburg upsetting him.

Well, I'm sure you can imagine just how much that made my elbow wobble. It wasn't Fruity so much that I minded about, but just the fact that these things can happen to us here in Britain. I thought that nowadays we were supposed to be above such corruption. And, once again, I find myself wondering if it didn't creep back to us from the colonies.

Anyway, I decided to take the bull by the horns and I stomped off to Scotland Yard, where they promised my complaint will receive their due attention. But nothing has happened since, apart from Fruity being given the shock of his life by some supposedly drunken driver, when he was crossing the road from the club to where his car had been parked. He seems to think that he's a marked man and doesn't want to wait around to discover if he's right.

Really darling, I don't quite understand your attitude. Surely you're not trying to tell me that I mustn't get involved with a prosecution of the police because that might ruin David's chances of marrying Princess Anne? I would have thought that such speculations are about a decade premature. But, in any case, don't your loyalties to myself override such considerations? Doesn't it occur to you that I am being subjected to the most intolerable humiliations in what I have come to realize is an over-centralized, authoritarian, bureaucratic, police state?

I shall not describe how much you offend me. I find that the pressures on me are becoming too great all round. This is no longer the kind of country to which I am prepared to grant the privilege of having me as one of its citizens. You need have no fear of me undermining your status with the Establishment. I have dropped all my pending prosecutions; and, as soon as I have got my business affairs in proper order, I shall be emigrating to Holland – to Amsterdam probably. My bank will forward any letters to me. Not that this need trouble you, since this letter is the last communication you will be receiving from me.

The Nanny Marks tapes

I got a letter from Lady Tillot to say she was leaving England for good. And she wanted me to come up to London and say goodbye. I went immediately.

I was glad to find that Mr Fruity had returned to Hamburg. Glad, because I don't think Lady Tillot regretted his going. She told me that the 1940 Club was losing money. She'd decided to close it down. But she wasn't too depressed about this, as she'd already acquired the premises for a new night-club in Amsterdam. 'Amsterdam is where the future lies, Nanny darling,' she declared.

She had such a lot of ideas for the new club, and we sat discussing them over a bottle of champagne. One always has to be on to something new, was the way she saw it. And the next thing on the list was going to be 'gay liberation'. That's what she called it. And I thought it a splendid idea. Lady Tillot was always tremendously gay and tremendously liberated. She was just the right person to launch such a movement.

Nothing at the 1940 Club was going to be of much use to her in Amsterdam. She said she was going to get rid of the lot – lock, stock and barrel. And she wanted me to take something as a memento of her. I chose the most lovely riding crop, which would remind me of the days at Caldicott Manor, although I don't think it was the one that she used at that time. It was rather different in some ways. All rubbery, with leather thongs. One that had been made abroad, I should imagine. I've given it pride of place on the first shelf of my what-not, over there in the corner.

It was such a sad occasion. Lady Tillot wanted to hear all the latest about Lord Froome and the children. They'd given up coming to see her, it seems. And then we started talking about old times: about Walter, and Mrs Potts and Mr Perkins. She only remembered the nice things about people. And, when she recalled the way she'd once hit me over the head with a newspaper, because I'd been too agitated during that air raid in Bath, she suddenly leant over to me and began to cry on my shoulder.

'It's all right,' I told her, 'you didn't hurt me in any way at all. I *liked* being hit on the head with a newspaper.'

And then she wanted me to sing with her. So she called in some of the young ladies who helped her to entertain the gentlemen who came to the club, and we sat round the table in a circle drinking champagne and singing songs like 'Auld Lang Syne' and the Eton boating song, until we had to break up the party because the first guests were arriving.

Now what else is there for me to tell you? Let me see. Well Camilla wrote and told me how David was enjoying it very much at Eton. I was ever so pleased that they'd chosen, after all, to send their boys to Eton. I'm glad to think that the tradition isn't going to die when all of us are gone. There are still going to be old Etonians, even then! It would be terrible for the people who came after if there was nothing left for them to look up to.

Sebastian would like to see the place transformed into what he calls a post-graduate college. But that would be terrible. There would be no more nice little boys with top hats walking round the streets. Oh, I'm so glad that Camilla's children have the chance to enjoy Eton as it always was.

It's sad, but I don't suppose Bruce will ever have any children now. He finally decided to withdraw from life completely. Took holy orders and joined the Benedictine Abbey at Downside. I didn't know what to think about it really. Of course, if he felt that this was the only way he could find any happiness in life, then I'd have no wish to dissuade him. But I couldn't help thinking that his life might have been very different, if only that dreadful Lola hadn't come along.

*The Sixth Marquess of Froome, interviewed by
Mr Simon Manasseh*

Q: How do you view the prospect of approaching the declining years of your life, without any of your male heirs having yet produced a legitimate son who could ultimately succeed to the marquesate?

A: It isn't much good worrying about it, as far as I can see.

With one of my sons all impotent and saintly, and the other a nigger-lover, it looks to me as if the marquesate is on the rocks, with the Tillot family transformed into a bunch of gollywogs.

Author's narrative

In my conversation with Colonel Penny, I asked him whether the situation had got better or worse over the period when he had been managing the Luptree estate.

'I can only say worse,' he replied with a grin. 'When I first arrived, it was at least possible to speak to my two employers. But in the end I was speaking to nobody.

'I'm not saying that Bruce became unfriendly. He was as charming as ever, on the occasions when I managed to corner him. But he'd departed from us, gone up there on a cloud, in personal conversation with the Almighty, as we sometimes used to say. I couldn't helping realizing that he wasn't much interested in anything I had to say.

'But this meant that my own position at Luptree was becoming impossible. My particular role in the organization was to appear to others as Lord Froome's and Lord Tillot's personal representative. That is the way that the team worked. I was the go-between. But, when people saw that I had no real messages to deliver from my employers, it undermined my authority.'

The Nanny Marks tapes

There were some tremendous complications when Bruce finally became a monk. He'd taken most of the Tillot family fortune into the abbey with him, except for the part which was now tied up with the Wessex Motels. And this mainly belonged to Sir Ben Jones, who had been Lord Froome's original backer. So Luptree fell under Sir Ben's direction and control, even if he chose to describe the Wessex Motels as a public company.

Lord Froome was simply furious. He said it was bad enough having given birth to some reincarnation of Jesus Christ, but having to request the permission of a public company to remove a letter-box-type lavatory-paper holder from the wall of his own bathroom was even worse. And, after he'd written a couple of rude letters to Sir Ben, he received a polite request to vacate his suite of rooms up on the top floor of Luptree. Things had come to a sorry state indeed.

Author's narrative

Colonel Penny had this to say about the increased influence of Sir Ben Jones: 'He'd always been someone who kept out of the picture, leaving us to go about our own business. But, when he came to hear that Bruce was departing this world to become a monk, he suddenly began taking an active interest in all that was going on, with a view to taking over the reins himself, no doubt.

'Well, I remember that, on one of those occasions when he came whizzing down to Luptree, I was on my way to see Midgeley in his office at the buildings' yard. But I paused for a moment, because I heard voices inside, and promptly recognized Sir Ben's. He was saying, "What does this other fellow do, this Colonel Penny?" And I said to myself, "Oo-er, that doesn't sound too good!"

'So I started looking round for another job.

'Mind you Bruce was very upset to see me depart. He thought it was because I had an aversion to Catholics. But I explained to him that this was really a case of promotion. A better pheasant shoot. And I would be managing a few more thousand acres, with my employer a Duke instead of a Marquess. I didn't like to rub it in that Luptree was by now more or less the property of a mere Knight.'

After Colonel Penny had recovered from his giggles over this last observation, I rose to take my leave.

My best chance of hearing anything about the new regime at Luptree was in my conversation with Mr Gordon Perkins at The Hop and Grape. So I asked him what difference it had made, when Sir Ben Jones took up an active interest in the concern.

He replied, 'A complete difference all round. Under Lord Froome (even after he'd begun to fade into the background), everybody knew that the Wessex Motels were a family concern. We saw our own future in terms of the general well-being of the Tillot family as a whole. But when Sir Ben truly stepped in, we knew from the start that everything was going to change. Nobody seemed to think in terms of the Tillot family any longer. We'd gone national, so to speak, even if national only meant Wessex. (Sir Ben's own financial empire was based on Wessex, you see.)

'They were certainly good days that we'd spent under Lord Froome and I'd always had the greatest respect for him. But I had a great respect for Sir Ben as well. He was an entirely different sort of person altogether. It was bustle, bustle all the time. And, while things were working well, you wouldn't see him at all. But, during the few hours I did pass in his company, I knew that he had me and my capabilities completely in focus. It was a very different kind of organization from the one that we'd all known before. But, after all, the world was changing and we had to keep up with it.'

The Nanny Marks tapes

In a way, it was lucky for Lord Froome that Lady Tillot had surrendered her lease of the house in Jermyn Street. Yet it had changed a lot since he lived there, having been decked out as a night-club and all. He was at a loss, really, to know what he should do with it.

He invited me up to London for Buddy's tenth birthday party. It was down in the cellars which Lady Tillot had used for her night-club. All young people, but very different somehow. You couldn't tell the boys from the girls. The whole lot seemed to be wearing long hair and trousers, including Buddy.

I sat in a corner with Lord Froome for most of the time. And we discussed Sebastian's marriages. We'd just read in the papers that the girl from Granada had given birth to a little boy; while the Pakistani was expecting a child in a couple of months time.

Lord Froome said he'd asked his lawyers about the possibility of excluding any negro children from becoming his heir. But they told him that it was probably too late now to think in terms of disinheriting Sebastian with regard to the marquesate. Yet, as far as those anti-marriages were concerned, they held that all the children would be regarded as illegitimate.

So Lord Froome got them to investigate who his heir might be, if Sebastian never had a legal ceremony with any of his wifelets. And the editor of Debrett's revealed there was a descendant of the second Marquess, who had written to them from Tasmania. He wanted some kind of written proof of his nobility. And it seems that this was the closest male relative they'd been able to find.

Yet Lord Froome wasn't particularly interested in this Mr Tillot. He was working as a dustman in Hobart. To Lord Froome's way of thinking, if his choice of heir lay between a negro and a dustman, he was prepared to wash his hands of the whole business. I remember him putting on that grumpy expression of his to say, 'The Tillot family is dead from the neck upwards. So I'm damned if I'll trouble myself about how their lower halves behave!'

The Sixth Marquess of Froome, interviewed by Mr Simon Manasseh

Q: Did you never make any personal contact with your distant Tillot cousin in Tasmania?

A: What? Write to this dustman fellow? What could I possibly have said to him? 'How do you do, I'm Lord Froome, and I believe we're related.' I could have started the letter like that, I dare say. But I can't think how I'd have continued with it. We simply wouldn't have been interested in the same things. I don't know what *does* interest a Tasmanian dustman, if it comes to that. He probably refers to me as that bleeding Pommy, sitting in his castle, over there in Pommy-land.

No, it was a great pity, as far as I was concerned, that the marquesate couldn't have been transferred to Buddy. She would make an excellent Marquess. Far better than either Bruce or Sebastian. And, seeing that they're allowing women to become Prime Ministers, judges and God knows what nowadays, it's ridiculous when you come to think that they can't allow them to become Marquesses as well.

I went to see my solicitor about it, but he seemed to think I was just making a joke. 'What about the Queen?' I protested. 'Nobody objects to *her* being a woman.' But he just laughed, and moved on to the next subject for discussion.

The Nanny Marks tapes

I found Buddy's birthday party rather sad in many ways. Apart from Buddy, none of Lord Froome's children were present. Nor was Lady Froome for that matter. She seemed to have lost interest in coming to England, now that they'd been turned out from Luptree Court. She was said to be writing her memoirs in Rome.

Not that Lord Froome hadn't his own plans for getting back to work again. He'd decided he was going to re-open Lady Tillot's night-club, but under a different name. It was to be the 1990 Club now.

'The young people don't want to drink,' he said. 'They want to smoke. They're smoking already at Buddy's age. That's what goes on in the school breaks nowadays.' He'd sent her to one of those awful comprehensives, you see.

15

Ready to Depart
1968–71

Sebastian had given up writing to me for a long time now. But, when he finally did, it was to say that he was fed up with England and was returning to Brazil. And he wondered if there was any chance of my coming up to London before he left. Of course, I took the train immediately.

He was looking very different since the time when I'd last seen him. I'm afraid he'd become a hippy. His hair was down to his shoulders and he was wearing an embroidered sarong. There were four girls present. I imagine the fourth must have come from somewhere like Hong Kong. And there were five babies in the flat. I really didn't like to ask if they all belonged to him. But I think he noticed the worry on my face when I was looking at them, because he laughed and said, 'The spit image of their grandfather, don't you think? Except for little Passiflore, and she's quite the spit image of her grandmother!' I didn't have the heart to disagree with him. But they didn't even look English to my eyes.

His wifelets were all very polite to me. But there wasn't very much for us to talk about. In any case, it was Sebastian I had come to see. And, with Brazil being such a long way from England, I couldn't help wondering if I'd ever get the chance to see him again.

He said they were all going out to create some hippy commune on the banks of the Xingu river. 'That's where civilization truly gets left behind,' he explained. (He always did enjoy those Tarzan films.) Yet he had some odd ideas about what living in the jungle was going to be like.

'It means getting rid of all property,' he said. 'In this commune, everything has got to be shared.' I don't know how he thought you can do things like that! I told him that what they'd need was someone to look after the house for them. I might be getting old, but I still wasn't too old to be of use to people. They all thought this was tremendously sporting of me. But Sebastian wouldn't hear of it. He said that there comes a time when people's travelling days are over.

So I asked him if he'd ever be coming home to England again. And he said that he thought he might, once his new society was ready to be launched. Then he would bring them all back to Wessex in time to sweep away the cobwebs, as he called it.

'We haven't got any cobwebs in Wessex,' I told him.

'Oh yes, we have,' he declared, 'and it's going to take some kind of a revolution to get rid of them.'

'What about the monarchy?' I wanted to know. 'Prince Philip will have you beheaded if you carry on like this.'

'The monarchy isn't a problem,' he replied. 'There need to be public attractions for the sake of the tourist industry. London will make as good a use of Buckingham Palace as it will of Whipsnade. They're all very colourful, these things, and I'd hate to see them swept away.'

And then he made some rather cruel remarks about Bruce. Said that he might have measured up to being the prize exhibit in the Wessex Whipsnade, but he'd missed the boat. 'Both the slow boat, and the speedboat, if it comes to that!'

I didn't quite follow what he meant, but I reminded him that it was no proper way for him to talk about his brother. If Bruce didn't want to have Luptree Court, then it was up to Sebastian to take up the banner of the Tillot family, and to fight for what was theirs by right. Yet Sebastian just laughed, and said there were things that required more ambition nowadays than to play Dukes and Duchesses, or even Kings and Queens.

And it wasn't long after this that he did in fact set sail for Brazil. I expect you read about it in the papers. There was a photograph of him and all his wifelets, holding their babies aloft, and leaning over the rail of the ship. And the caption read, LORD SEB COCKS HIS LAST SNOOK. Because he was pulling a long nose at the cameraman.

But Sebastian is right when he says that Britain doesn't mean anything any more. It makes me feel at times that I'm growing old, that I'm ready to depart.

The way I see it, the meanies appear to have taken over in this world. I dare say God helps those who help themselves. But this is no excuse for trying to grab all you can lay your hands on. The people who really know how to get things done seem to be fighting against each other. We've lost the spirit of the Eton boating song. We don't swing together in the fashion that we all used to do – like we did in the war, for example, under the leadership of Mr Churchill.

And people are so unkind to each other nowadays. Even when it's someone like Lord Froome, who'd known nothing but respect since the day when he was born. Who'd have thought they'd have put him on trial? Not that he had anything to do with drugs, I'm sure. It certainly wasn't his fault if cannabis was being sold at the 1990 Club. But then he had terrible luck in coming up before Mr Morgan, my previous employer. If he hadn't been the examining magistrate on that particular day, I'm sure they would have found out some way to reduce the charge.

If you want *my* opinion, it was all a set-up job. The Socialists had always been envious of Lord Froome. They were furious because they couldn't get him *down*, because they couldn't *destroy* him. As soon as they saw he'd managed to build up a successful night-club, they arranged for the police to knock him down again. That's the way they work, you see.

The Sixth Marquess of Froome, interviewed by Mr Simon Manasseh

Q: Would I be right in saying that it was the closeness you felt towards your daughter, Lady Buddleia, which caused you to become involved in the activities of the younger generation?

A: Only in part. I do have an eye upon her future interests, mind you. But she isn't even a teenager yet. It has been far more a question of trying to think up what I should do with a night-club which already existed. I merely changed its name and its character. That's all.

Q: You are here speaking about the 1990 Club. It has been alleged that you oriented it away from sex and towards drugs. Is this a fair assessment?

A: Absolutely not. I did nothing to discourage sex at all. I don't suppose it still took place on the premises, except when I wasn't looking perhaps. But there was some perfectly healthy necking going on whenever I was around.

Q: On the issue of drugs, did you do anything to encourage, or prohibit, their sale and distribution within your club?

A: Now, look here, don't go suggesting for a moment that I might have allowed any of the hard stuff to be sold there. Was that what you were trying to say?

Q: Not necessarily. Did you permit the sale of soft drugs?

A: I don't think I'm allowed to answer that question. I thought this case was *sub judice,* or whatever it's called. Well, it is here in Britain, even if you don't look upon it that way over there in America.

Q: In the event of your being convicted on this drugs charge, what kind of future do you see for yourself?

A: My solicitor tells me that they're quite liable to send me to prison. But I wouldn't have thought there's much of a precedent for sending Marquesses to prison, if you ask me. Unless you go back to the old days. But then it was the Tower of London, or nothing. And I don't think they've got any rooms in the Tower for that sort of thing nowadays. It's all gone over to tourism. Mind you, I could be quite a bit of an attraction in that field, I suppose. I might even enjoy prison life. I'd make friends with the beefeaters, and with the ravens.

Author's narrative

In my conversation with Nadia, the Maharanee of Peshawar, I inquired whether Lord Froome's conviction for permitting the sale of cannabis on the premises of the 1990 Club had come as any surprise to her.

She said, 'Surprise? Well I'd hardly use the word surprise. I mean I did know that he occasionally took little puffs of the stuff. It used to help him relax while we were watching the television after dinner. But I wasn't actually aware that he used to sell any of it to other people.

'I've got an awful feeling that the police may have been making some dreadful mistake. I mean, it does happen sometimes. They get the photographs mixed up, and things like that. But it was a terrible tragedy that Edward had to go to prison. He wasn't really made for that kind of life. He had a weak chest. They ought to have put him in a special wing of the prison, where they could have taken better care of him.'

The Nanny Marks tapes

I felt so sorry for Buddy. And she was so brave too. Sitting there on the steps of the Old Bailey with the editors of *Oz*. They were addressing the television cameras, and waving placards which said something about a new deal for junkies. (She was barely twelve.) And when she came to that part in her speech about waiting outside the prison gates for the full two years, if necessary, I was near to tears, I can tell you. But she wasn't able to carry out her threat, since Lady Froome arranged for her to be flown out to Rome.

One thing that pleased me greatly was the way Lady Tillot sent a letter to the papers in support of Lord Froome. It gave her address as a club in Amsterdam called The Gay Parisian. She always had a flair for choosing lovely names. Not that her letter did much good, I'm afraid. Accusing the police of taking bribes during the years when she'd been running the 1940 Club was all a bit dangerous, I suppose. But, living out there, she may have been safe from their clutches.

I wrote to Bruce at Downside to say that his father would be terribly pleased, I was sure, if he were to receive some manner of letter from him. Just something to take the edge off the bitterness from all those previous events. Lord Froome must have suffered a lot. So it seemed a bit pointless for Bruce to go on harbouring these resentments.

But I don't think he could have received my letter. I'd filled in the sender's name on the back of the envelope. So I imagine that the abbot must have frowned on the idea that Bruce was receiving letters from Miss *Anybody*. I'm told they're very strict about these things in abbeys.

The Sixth Marquess of Froome, interviewed by
Mr Simon Manasseh

Q: What do you see as the future of Luptree Court?
A: Ah, dear me, now that's a difficult question. To tell you the honest truth, I don't like trying to think about it any more. When you've struggled for an entire lifetime to see a family's heritage preserved, and then the family itself falls to pieces, well what have you left? A house. The most lovely house in the entire country. But what use is it now? It stands there as a monument to all that the Tillot family once was. But we're not that any more. And I begin to think that I've outlived my usefulness in this life.

Bruce has made it abundantly clear that he's washed his hands of Luptree Court. The only person who lives there at all nowadays is Sir Ben Jones. But you can bet one thing. It will never come back to life in his hands. He simply doesn't know the place. It's not in his blood, as it was in all of ours. He doesn't give two hoots for what will happen to it. He'd just as soon knock it down, than go without his breakfast to see that the roof got properly repaired.

Between the two of them, I don't know what they'll decide to do with it. Put it up for auction perhaps, and that will be a nice bit of ready cash in their pockets. That's the kind of world that we live in nowadays. Success is measured by the cash in your pocket, not by the titles that distinguish you from the *hoi polloi*.

The Nanny Marks tapes

Camilla doesn't write to me quite as often as she used to. But I got a postcard from her last summer from Greece. She was on a yacht cruising round the Greek islands. Michael had gone to New York for the opening of his new furniture gallery. And before that (around Easter I suppose) I got a card from Mexico, where the two of them were holidaying in Acapulco. They were learning skin-diving from the same instructor who had taught the Duke of Windsor.

Dr Keith came to see me the other day. He's worried about my eyes, you know. The other day I slipped on the stairs, and I bruised myself badly. But my eyesight will come back. I know exactly where to find everything in this house. They don't have to worry about me. And that's what I told him.

I know he means well, but he doesn't really understand how I feel about these things. I don't *want* to be looked after. This cottage is my *home*. And it's where I want to spend the rest of my days.

He says I ought to go to that old people's home in Froome. They call it an old people's home, yet everyone knows it was once the workhouse. Changing the name of things doesn't alter that.

I know that if Lord Froome were still at Luptree Court, he wouldn't allow this kind of thing to happen to me. Nor Bruce for that matter. But it's not *their* fault that they can't take care of me. And Camilla has her family to consider. And of course Sebastian is in Brazil.

But an old people's home is somehow such an *impersonal* place to live in. You lack the dignity of having your own home. And who do you think I might have to share a room with, if I agreed to go there? It might be simply *any* class of person. Certainly not anyone from the kind of company that *I've* been keeping.

I realize that I came from a very humble background, but

I've always felt as if I'd put all that a long way behind me. Now, I can't be sure any longer. It's as if it were all catching up with me again.

I know Dr Keith says that I can always come back to the cottage if my eyesight gets better. But I'm not sure if he really means it. When people go to the workhouse, they usually stay there.

Author's narrative

It has already been stated that Nanny Marks did in fact end her days in the old people's home at Froome. And it was probably during the final preparations for her move there that the hat box containing all the tape cassettes was deposited in the muniments room at Luptree Court. There was a note on the cover to say that the hat box should be handed to Lord Sebastian Tillot, on his return from Brazil, although the family no doubt had discounted the likelihood of such a return, for the tapes had been included in the lot auctioned to me by Sotheby's.

That these tapes have proved invaluable to me is evident from the extensive use I have now made of them. They also had furnished me with much of the factual information that featured within the report on the Tillot family's social standing, which I sent to Mr Ron Tillot in Tasmania. Not entirely unexpectedly, this report did not please Mr Tillot, nor did it encourage him to carry out his intention of returning to the Old Country in pursuit of his heritage. There was even some correspondence in which he rejected my firm's statement of account for the amount in excess of that which he had already paid me by way of an advance, as a result of which I have felt myself at liberty to recuperate my firm's losses by utilizing the material from my research for a publication of my own.

During the process of completing this text, however, word of what I was doing reached the ears of the Duchess of Northumbria: as a result of which I received an abrasive letter from her pen.

Letter from the Duchess of Northumbria, to Mr Neil Fairfield (1979)

Dear Mr Fairfield,

It is reported to me that you are writing a book about my family, compiled from the information we supplied you in interviews. These were given to you on the understanding that you had been commissioned by one of our distant cousins to supply him with detailed information concerning our general family background. At no stage in the proceedings did you reveal to any of us the true nature of your interviews by forewarning us that our words might be quoted in a publication intended to bring profit to yourself. I find such behaviour unethical, to say the least.

It has also been brought to my attention that you may be in possession of certain letters that were written to me by my mother. If this be the case, it is due to an error of judgement by the executors of my father's will. They may have included them inadvertently in a lot that was to be auctioned. I had entrusted this correspondence, which I thought had been terminated, to my father's safe keeping, for storage at Luptree. But there is no question of its ever having been my father's property, to be auctioned as his executors misguidedly saw fit. So I must request the immediate return of all these letters.

On a more personal note, I think I should inform you that I find it most unpleasant that you show yourself to be so eager to intrude upon my family's privacy. We have as much right to privacy as anyone else. You switch on the arc lights, so that we are obliged to accustom ourselves to all this glare of public attention, though it's not as though we either want it or like it. Since we find that it is our lot in life, we have to learn to live with it, which sometimes leads to a bit of exaggerated posturing in the process. But don't think that you wouldn't behave similarly if these arc lights were switched in your own direction. So just be thankful that they are not, and that you are permitted to enjoy some relative anonymity in life.

Indeed, if there has been sufficient public interest in such matters, it is conceivable that I (and my kind) could have taken upon ourselves the task of ferreting out the anecdotes to be found concerning your own relatives. It's not that you and your family didn't behave as ridiculously as mine may have done. It's just that public interest, by no fault of ours, happens to be focused upon us because of our special position in the social spectrum. So you are in a position to hold us up to ridicule, in a manner which, if I attempted to repay the compliment, would only succeed in boring everybody to death.

I have been in touch with our family lawyer, Mr Pike, to see if there is anything I can do to prevent you from publishing an unpleasant book of this kind. I regret to say that his advice is that there is little that I can do at this stage, apart from issuing you what he describes as a solemn warning that, if you get the facts muddled in any way at all, you are liable to find yourself subject to a court prosecution for libel. That is precisely the way that Mr Pike has advised me to phrase it.

Author's narrative

My acquaintance with the law of libel permits me to proceed with the intention to publish, undeterred. The bulk of the evidence which I submit is taken from the lips of the family themselves, or from others at the very centre of their immediate entourage. I make little personal comment upon what they say. The story is told in their own words, by those who know it by heart.

Within a few weeks of receiving the Duchess's warning, I received another letter. This time from her mother.

*Letter from Chloe, Marchioness of Froome
to Mr Neil Fairfield (1979)*

Dear Mr Fairfield,

My daughter has written to me in outrage that you should be writing this book. And she urges me to request the return of those letters I once loaned to you. I dare say you're going to tell me I didn't loan them to you, but gave them. And I dare say you could be right. My recollection of what precisely may have been said during that encounter is less than perfect. But I do seem to remember that you carried a tape recorder dangling round your neck, like an absurd dead albatross (or something else which you had brought along to haunt us). And I have little doubt that this bird of ill omen may speak from the grave to refute my words.

Whether the letters are your property or mine, I appeal to you as a gentleman to return them to me and to expunge their contents from your memory. It distresses me to state, however, that I have little hope of finding that you *will* behave like a gentleman, in which case I must fall back on my second line of defence, which is to ask you to deal kindly with your victims.

When in my cups I may have given you the mistaken impression that I cared little for my children because they had turned their backs on me. If that is the case, then I now wish to correct such an impression. I shall therefore enclose a copy of the letter I recently received from my daughter. I think it will encourage you to perceive her as being generous in spirit; which, over the long run, I have always found her to be.

> Sincerely,
> Chloe Froome

Letter from the Duchess of Northumbria to Chloe, Marchioness of Froome (1979)

Mummy my darling,

I am feeling a bit unhappy about the way we haven't seen each other for quite some time. Michael and I are hoping that you will come and stay with us in the near future, so that we can get our very lovely relationship back on to the terms that it once used to be. But my reason for writing this letter, which I have long intended to write, at this particular moment, is that, as you probably know, there is an unpleasant little man called Mr Fairfield who is planning to write unpleasant (and perhaps libellous) things about us all.

When he came to see me, he told me that he had already visited you in Amsterdam. I realize that it is now too late to request that you do not give him sight of (as he calls it) all the letters we wrote to one another. I am assuming that this damage is already done. Yet there may perhaps be time for you to get your lawyer to write to him, forbidding him to quote any part of those letters which you haven't explicitly approved for publication.

Let's meet again soon, Mummy darling. It is ridiculous that we shouldn't be friends. We got on so well together for most of the time. Let us kiss and forget all those stupidities of the past.

> With all my love,
> Camilla

Author's narrative

My sole encounter with the Duchess had impressed me greatly. To my way of thinking, she is the backbone of this generation of the Tillot family – far more so than either of her brothers. For one thing, she has continued within the same tradition. It is the likes of *her* kind who are today's pillars of the Establishment, whereas Bruce, Lord Tillot, stands more as an example of those who went under in the storm, and Lord Sebastian is a drop-out member of the alternative society.

In the same manner of speaking, I feel that Lady Beatrice Cholmondeley probably was the backbone of the previous generation – far more so than Lord Froome himself, who was more of an eccentric offshoot from the old stock. So I shall now conclude the account of my interview with the formidable Lady Beatrice, in the drawing room of her thatched Dorset vicarage. And she was, it should be remembered, the eldest living representative of the Tillot family.

I asked her if she ever thought nowadays of going back to see what had become of Luptree Court.

She sighed deeply, and then said, 'Never again. In fact I'm told there's nothing much to see there nowadays. They've stripped all the treasures from inside, in any case. It's just one huge hotel, with beastly modern furniture — part of Sir Ben Jones's chain of Wessex Motels. Nobody else had a bid to offer for what was left of the place, after all the trimmings had been removed.

'But there was a time. . . . It was more than five years ago . . . Now let me see, it was my birthday. And Ulrica was here on a visit. She thought it might be a nice idea for her chauffeur to drive us both over to Luptree, for the sake of old memories. So we climbed into her car and off we went.

'We never got further than the lodge gates. Suddenly I told the chauffeur to stop, because I had misgivings. Ulrica and I just sat there in silence for a while, with neither of us saying a word. Then I told her it had been a mistake, driving over there. It had been a delightful drive, but it was none the less a mistake, and we shouldn't go any further. It would be like revisiting some secret flower garden, treasured from the memory of your youth, only to find that someone had filled the place with cabbages and cucumbers. I preferred to remember it the way it was: before Edward ran wild, and before the riff-raff moved in with the roundabouts.

'It was the correct decision. I wouldn't be seen within a mile of Luptree nowadays. It's better that way. I belong to a different era in the house's history.

'But it occurred to me that we still had time to spare. And what could be better than that two old ladies like ourselves should go and pay a call on Nanny Marks? I'd heard how she'd been transferred to the old people's home in Froome recently. So off we went.

'The poor old woman was half blind. But she was delighted that we'd come, and just as talkative as ever. In fact, it was difficult to get a word in edgeways. She was in the geriatric ward with a lot of other people. But she was sat up there in bed, seemingly quite pleased with herself. Framed photographs of all the children were on the bedside table — not that I suppose she could see any of them. But I imagine she used them as a talking point with everyone who came to visit her, though I gathered from the matron that there hadn't been many of these.

'But that didn't seem to be troubling her, I might hasten to add. She was living entirely in the past. Kept talking about the number of celebrities whom she had once upon a time shaken by the hand.

'But, in some ways, she had an absurdly modest sense of her own importance. I remember her sitting up there in her hospital bed and saying that she only *felt* wonderful because she'd had the privilege of bringing up such wonderful children. She seemed to think that this was the general opinion: the criterion by which she was quite happy to be judged. I didn't like to tell her that the majority of my acquaintances would have crossed over to the other side of the street, if that gave them the opportunity to avoid an encounter with any of these wonderful children.

'Her big excitement was that she'd just received a long letter from Sebastian – from Brazil, she insisted. I asked her if she'd like me to read it to her, but she looked offended at that. Mumbled some excuse about being able to see quite all right when she put on her reading glasses, and that Sebastian always liked to think that he was writing to her in private. She kept toying with the envelope. Must have been doing so constantly, since it was already looking dog-eared around the edges.

'The ridiculous thing was that I could see an American stamp there on the envelope, as large as life. But she would have it that he was writing to her from Brazil, and to tell her what a wonderful time they were all having. Well, it wasn't for either of us to correct her. We just sat there for a little while, listening to all her stories. Then we took our departure.

'And that reminds me, young man. . . .' Lady Beatrice fully appreciated that I was of an age that would take such a description as flattery, rather than as belittlement. Reaching for her walking stick, she rose slowly to her feet. 'That reminds me, young man, that I have now been talking to you for far too long. You must give an old lady her privilege to decide when an interview is terminated. And that moment has now arrived. You'll find that I've covered most of the ground. What the rest of the family get up to nowadays is their concern. And the less I know about it, the better. I've given up trying to tell them what they all should do.

'I'll accompany you to the door, but no further. My legs aren't quite as nimble as they used to be.'

After expressing my thanks for her courtesy and cooperation, I took my leave from her at the front door.

It was with a view to tracing this letter from Lord Sebastian to which Lady Beatrice had referred that I paid a visit to the old people's home in Froome. I had the good fortune in finding that the matron, Mrs Gladwyn, was the same as had been there when Miss Marks was an inmate. I inquired if she had left any belongings.

'No doubt she did,' said Mrs Gladwyn. 'But the real question is whether they're still here. We generally keep an inmate's belongings for just a few years after their decease. But, if no one comes to claim them, then you must understand that we have to dispose of them. Still, we should be able to find out in my filing system whether we've still got anything to show you.'

Once again I was in luck. Mrs Gladwyn rang for the porter and asked him to find the suitcase containing Miss Marks's personal belongings, which had been stored somewhere below stairs, since her death in 1971. And, while he was fetching it, I was regaled in her office with some of Mrs Gladwyn's personal reminiscences of Nanny Marks. I noticed that she pursed her lips for a second before saying, 'She upset more than a few people with her remarks. Yet, despite everything, she was a kindly soul. There was no maliciousness about her: which is the main problem I have to deal with in the geriatric ward. They can be just like children at times, you know, only they've learnt a few tricks in their time.'

I inquired if Miss Marks had ever spoken about Lord Sebastian and his activities, since he had left for Brazil.

She said, 'Sebastian? Oh yes, that's the one she used to call her "best little boy". We never heard the end of his exploits: how he'd found a lot of Inca treasure and built his own village out there in the jungle. Married three of the local chieftain's daughters too, as far as I could make out. And I forget how many children there were supposed to be.

'Nanny's great favourite was Passiflore. We never stopped hearing about Passiflore: how she built sand castles on the banks of the Amazon, and brought home mudpies as cakes for her father; how she had an alligator as a pet; and wore real butterflies in her hair. Oh, Passiflore was a great favourite in our geriatric ward.

'I didn't feel that it was my duty to tell everyone that we ought to take her stories with a pinch of salt. I can't see how she could have read that letter, with her eyes being in the state they were. And she wouldn't let any of us lay hands on it. It was a private letter, she used to say. But then entertainers are hard to come by in a geriatric ward. She kept them listening. And she herself was happy. That's the main thing.'

This was the moment when the porter returned, bearing Miss Marks's suitcase.

'Well, I'd better hand this over to you,' said Mrs Gladwyn. 'Nobody else seems to have claimed it. But I find that strange. Seeing how much she used to carry on about Lord Froome and his family, you'd have thought that at least one of them would have turned up at her funeral. Still, it isn't as if she knew anything about that. Some people spend a lifetime giving themselves to the wrong cause. That's something you observe when you're in charge of an old people's home.

'Now, I've my duties to attend to. And here is the suitcase with Miss Marks's belongings. I must ask you for a signature, I'm afraid, just in case someone like a relative turns up, and wants to know what has happened to it. But I don't suppose that's very likely in her case.'

I signed the relevant piece of paper, then departed, with the suitcase in my possession.

*Letter from Lord Sebastian Tillot to Miss Grace Marks
(1971)*

My dearest (and only ever) Nan,

I feel it's time that you all heard from me. But I think
you're the only one who might be interested in receiving such
a letter. Nevertheless, I think I owe the entire family an
explanation of some kind. So, in writing to you, I'll be
explaining myself to all the others as well (just in case they
display any curiosity whatsoever as to what has become of
me); this will put you in your favourite position of being able
to give them all the relevant information concerning what I
have been doing, and even why I have done what I have.

I am also writing because I find myself feeling increasingly
guilty, as the years tick by since last I saw you, that never
once in all my life have I endeavoured to express my thanks
to you. I don't suppose that any of us did for that matter,
because that was the way we were made. And it worries me
now that I could so easily miss the opportunity to say these
words while there is still time, because none of us are here for
ever. In fact, I often feel pretty impermanent myself.

I often wonder how you are getting along, whether people
ple drop in to visit you these days and whom it is that you
discuss now all of our lot have scattered. And I suppose there
are days when you find yourself wondering what became of
me, as well. So I'll give you all there is to tell on that subject,
first.

We went out to Brazil, but didn't ever get to the jungle
proper. Still, we set up a commune of a kind, pretending that
it was far from civilization, although it was still close enough
to buy yesterday's (Brazilian) newspapers at the local store. I
even acquired an additional wifelet: Gloria, who is the
daughter of an American diplomat in Rio. She came to visit
us, and stayed. On the other hand, I lost Bo, who decided she
preferred the way of life back in Rio. So it was a swap, more
or less.

Then Gloria persuaded us to come back to California with
her, because life was really working out to be a bit tough in
Brazil. There was too much of this frontier spirit, and we

were simply in the way. Yet Gloria promised us that things would be very different back home. And her father could fix the visas for us.

She was right, in a way. There are all manner of communes sprouting up around California, each one different in character. In one, you're only welcome if you believe in the same kind of politics. In another, it has to be the same kind of religion. Or there again, there are communes for homosexual men, and others for homosexual women. (But I don't suppose you'd know much about those things!)

The point I'm trying to make is that, here in California, we have every chance to set up *our* sort of family, regardless of what the rest of society may be thinking or doing. It is a tiny little set-up, in the midst of all manner of other marital set-ups. (You name it, and I could find the commune where it's represented.) We're permitted to carry on with our social experiment. After all, we're the guinea pigs, so nobody else need bother. And we don't interfere with the way other people are living their lives either.

I dare say that we all do our share of screaming at the people who run things (up top), accusing them of being Fascist pigs – or whatever. It's all part of the game of letting them see that we (down at the bottom) count for something too. But I've grown to like this free-and-easy, free-for-all, tolerantly liberalized regime, which I scandalize as best I can, by calling it the worst names in my vocabulary.

Naturally I hope that it will change for the better. God knows it's far from perfect. It even stinks. Yet, what regime doesn't stink, if it comes to that? So I think we'll be staying on here, for the foreseeable future: bringing up my seven children to our own way of life, which is permitted to be different from everyone else's.

In a strange sort of way, I was trying to say much the same sort of thing when I stood for Parliament as a Regionalist: that all regions should be permitted to be different from everyone else's, and that the world community at large should furnish the political umbrella of security under which that kind of system could thrive.

It does still strike me that Wessex is the right size for a

regional state to be. And it has the right history to take the lead and show all the other regional states how it should be done. But it's going to be a long struggle before that kind of political framework is hammered into shape.

If the links binding me to Wessex were less easy to sever (if I'd been brought up as the heir perhaps, with the call of Luptree to inspire me, instead of being shunted into the reserves as the second, and traditionally unimportant, son), then I'd be returning to Wessex with a willingness to commit myself to those battles. For it's in Europe, and not here in America, that the idea of world federalism, on a basis of regional states, is first going to take root (with the eastern bloc becoming more individualized, as well as liberalized; and the western bloc becoming more egalitarian and more socially sensitive, as part and parcel of the steps towards an ultimate European union).

Yet it feels as if both Europe and Wessex are very distant from me right now. I'm losing the feeling that it all depended on myself to see that the world started changing fast. Perhaps it's a case of losing my youth rather too rapidly. But I do have to confess that political solutions on a big scale no longer interest me very much. Less ambitiously, I am happy to achieve just *some* aspects of how to live as my individual self within a society which is, after all, far more egalitarian and less snobbish than the one I left back home, despite all the glaring evidence that class consciousness continues even over here – as a plutocracy, rather than an aristocracy. But, in any case, to hell with questions of money – just as much as with questions of birth. I feel as if I've dropped out of both those worlds.

America isn't the territory where the big ideological battles are going to be fought out to the finish. But I am content to pioneer my own small experiment concerning the different ways of living life in a climate that is favourable to it. It isn't an ambitious prospect, but I still feel that I am being useful to humanity in my own way.

I suppose you may be wondering how I can possibly know for sure that all the children I claim as mine were in fact fathered by me. In all honesty, I don't. In each case, the chances are that they are mine. But my wifelets do have their other lovers, on occasions, who dwell outside our commune. You should just accept it as the way of life that suits us best: a polygamous-polyandrous situation, within what is, after all, rapidly emerging as a polymorphous society.

In some ways, the role that I play within our commune is far more akin to that of nanny, than either that of father or mother. Perhaps I take after my old Dad in these matters! (The Dad of more recent years, that is to say.) But the person I would like people to think that I take after is you, Nan.

There have been so many occasions over these last few years, while I sit here playing with my children, when my mind has strayed back to the times when you were playing with all of us. And I ask myself if I am making such a good job of it as you did, whether I have the right talents or the right personality; because you are my highest standard in these matters, even if we all did take you for granted, making our (affectionate) jokes about you and your opinions whenever we were talking amongst ourselves.

It worries me greatly that this letter might not reach you in time, that you might never come to read the way I feel about you now. Of all the people in this world, I can think of no one to whom I owe so much, in terms of what you yourself invested in me, as a measure of self-sacrifice, rather than for personal gain.

Loyalty is a quality that is almost mocked, nowadays, especially when it is unquestioning. But I do admire you for your display of this quality, however best it should be described. Perhaps it lay in your ability to suspend personal criticism towards us, in deference to a trust that we must really be all right: that, once you had decided to love and admire us, then nothing so commonplace as factual evidence was ever going to impair that vision of us which you had created in your heart.

You must forgive me, as one of the objects of that loyalty, for saying that you did manage to scrape up all the wrong reasons for admiring us. Yet, what upsets me now, more than I can clearly say, is that we all took that gift from you for granted – without gratitude, and without reciprocal effort to see that life rewarded you. With the distance that now separates us, I can admit to feeling ashamed about this.

Dear old Nan, I wonder how you're keeping. I wonder if any of us are supporting you properly. I even wonder if you're still with us. But, to me in any case, you're eternal.

There was so little return for you in giving your life to all of us. There were certainly only small material advantages. I don't think I have given you anything of material value in my entire life. Well, a television set perhaps, and a tape recorder. But what else? And what have any of the rest of us done to try and give you comfort (and happiness) in your old age?

Yet here, with all my children (or should I say *these* children?), I do manage to perceive what draws us close to them in spirit. I see that, at some age, like them, I must have been appealing, and that I, in particular, appealed to you (while others only regarded me as a category within the family unit).

If there is any justice in this world, the time will come when they will raise a statue to you. Not to yourself, because you wouldn't really like that. You would only ever accept other people's admiration if it was in some way linked to all of us. But they could erect a statue to all that you stood for, portraying you as the symbol of a life's self-sacrifice to children whom you didn't even bear.

If I was a sculptor, I'd build that memorial myself, and erect it here in my commune. But I'm not a sculptor, dear old Nan. I'm just a person with some odd views on life, who can sometimes manage to express a little of it in letters. So I am sending this to you, as my own (most inadequate) offering of thanks, in the hope that it arrives with you in time, and that you will still be able to read it.

With all the love which you so much deserve, and which I am not worthy of offering,

    from,
        Sebastian
        (or, better still – from all of us)

FICTION

GENERAL

☐	Chains	Justin Adams	£1.25
☐	Secrets	F. Lee Bailey	£1.25
☐	Skyship	John Brosnan	£1.65
☐	The Memoirs of Maria Brown	John Cleland	£1.25
☐	The Last Liberator	John Clive	£1.25
☐	A Forgotten Season	Kathleen Conlon	£1.10
☐	My Father's House	Kathleen Conlon	£1.25
☐	Wyndward Fury	Norman Daniels	£1.50
☐	Ladies in Waiting	Gwen Davis	£1.50
☐	The Money Wolves	Paul Erikson	£1.50
☐	Rich Little Poor Girl	Terence Feely	£1.50
☐	Fever Pitch	Betty Ferm	£1.50
☐	Abingdon's	Michael French	£1.50
☐	Rhythms	Michael French	£1.50
☐	A Sea Change	Lois Gould	80p
☐	Forced Feedings	Maxine Herman	£1.50
☐	Love Among the Mashed Potatoes	Gregory Mcdonald	£1.10
☐	Gossip	Marc Olden	£1.25
☐	The Red Raven	Lilli Palmer	£1.25
☐	Summer Lightning	Judith Richards	£1.25
☐	The Hamptons	Charles Rigdon	£1.35
☐	The Dream Makers	John Sherlock	£1.50
☐	The Affair of Nina B.	Simmel	95p
☐	The Berlin Connection	Simmel	£1.50
☐	The Cain Conspiracy	Simmel	£1.20
☐	Double Agent — Triple Cross	Simmel	£1.35
☐	Celestial Navigation	Anne Tyler	£1.00
☐	Earthly Possessions	Anne Tyler	95p
☐	Searching for Caleb	Anne Tyler	£1.00

WESTERN — BLADE SERIES by Matt Chisholm

☐	No. 1 The Indian Incident	75p
☐	No. 2 The Tucson Conspiracy	75p
☐	No. 3 The Laredo Assignment	75p
☐	No. 4 The Pecos Manhunt	75p
☐	No. 5 The Colorado Virgins	85p
☐	No. 6 The Mexican Proposition	85p
☐	No. 7 The Arizona Climax	85p
☐	No. 8 The Nevada Mustang	85p
☐	No. 9 The Montana Deadlock	85p
☐	No. 10 The Cheyenne Trap	95p
☐	No. 11 The Navaho Trail	95p
☐	No. 12 The Last Act	95p

SCIENCE FICTION

☐	Times Without Number	John Brunner	£1.10
☐	Drinking Sapphire Wine	Tanith Lee	£1.25
☐	Watchtower	Elizabeth A. Lynn	£1.10

WAR

☐	The Anderson Assault	Peter Leslie	£1.25
☐	Killers under a Cruel Sky	Peter Leslie	£1.25
☐	The Serbian Triangle	Peter Saunders	£1.10
☐	Jenny's War	Jack Stoneley	£1.25

NAVAL HISTORICAL

☐	The Mary Celeste	John Maxwell	£1.00
☐	The Baltic Convoy	Showell Styles	95p

FICTION

CRIME/ADVENTURE/SUSPENSE

☐ The Killing In The Market	John Ball with Bevan Smith	£1.00
☐ In the Heat of the Night	John Ball	£1.00
☐ Johnny Get Your Gun	John Ball	£1.00
☐ The Cool Cottontail	John Ball	£1.00
☐ The Megawind Cancellation	Bernard Boucher	£1.25
☐ Slow Burn	Peter Cave	£1.50
☐ Tunnel	Hal Friedman	£1.35
☐ Barracuda	Irving A. Greenfield	£1.25
☐ Tagget	Irving A. Greenfield	£1.25
☐ Don't be no Hero	Leonard Harris	£1.25
☐ The Blunderer	Patricia Highsmith	£1.25
☐ A Game for the Living	Patricia Highsmith	£1.25
☐ Those who Walk Away	Patricia Highsmith	£1.25
☐ The Tremor of Forgery	Patricia Highsmith	£1.25
☐ The Two Faces of January	Patricia Highsmith	£1.25
☐ Labyrinth	Eric Mackenzie-Lamb	£1.25
☐ The Hunted	Elmore Leonard	£1.25
☐ Confess, Fletch	Gregory Mcdonald	90p
☐ Fletch	Gregory Mcdonald	90p
☐ Fletch's Fortune	Gregory Mcdonald	£1.25
☐ Flynn	Gregory Mcdonald	95p
☐ All the Queen's Men	Guiy de Montfort	£1.25
☐ Pandora Man	Kerry Newcomb and Frank Schaefer	£1.25
☐ Sigmet Active	Thomas Page	£1.10
☐ Crash Landing	Mark Regan	£1.25
☐ The Last Prisoner	James Robson	£1.50
☐ The Croesus Conspiracy	Ben Stein	£1.25
☐ Deadline in Jakarta	Ian Stewart	£1.25
☐ An H-Bomb for Alice	Ian Stewart	£1.50
☐ The Peking Payoff	Ian Stewart	90p
☐ The Seizing of Singapore	Ian Stewart	£1.00
☐ Winter Stalk	James L. Stowe	£1.25
☐ Rough Deal	Walter Winward	£1.10

HISTORICAL ROMANCE/ROMANCE/SAGA

☐ Hawksmoor	Aileen Armitage	£1.75
☐ Blaze of Passion	Stephanie Blake	£1.25
☐ Daughter of Destiny	Stephanie Blake	£1.25
☐ Flowers of Fire	Stephanie Blake	£1.50
☐ So Wicked My Desire	Stephanie Blake	£1.50
☐ Wicked is My Flesh	Stephanie Blake	£1.50
☐ Lovers and Dancers	Michael Feeney Callan	£1.50
☐ The Lofty Banners	Brenda Clarke	£1.75
☐ The Enchanted Land	Jude Deveraux	£1.50
☐ My Love, My Land	Judy Gardiner	£1.25
☐ Walburga's Eve	Elizabeth Hann	£1.35
☐ Lily of the Sun	Sandra Heath	95p
☐ Strangers' Forest	Pamela Hill	£1.00
☐ Royal Mistress	Patricia Campbell Horton	£1.50
☐ The Rebel Heart	Anna James	£1.25
☐ Gentlemen Callers	Nancy Lamb	£1.50
☐ Fires of Winter	Johanna Lindsey	£1.50
☐ A Pirate's Love	Johanna Lindsey	£1.25
☐ Trade Imperial	Alan Lloyd	£1.35
☐ Dance Barefoot	Margaret Maddocks	95p
☐ The Open Door	Margaret Maddocks	£1.25
☐ All We Know of Heaven	Dore Mullen	£1.25
☐ The Far Side of Destiny	Dore Mullen	£1.50
☐ New Year's Eve	Jeannie Sakol	£1.50
☐ The Pride	Judith Saxton	£1.50
☐ Heir to Trevayan	Juliet Sefton	£1.25
☐ Never Trust a Handsome Man	Marlene Fanta Shyer	£1.25
☐ Shadow of an Unknown Woman	Daoma Winston	£1.00
☐ Call the Darkness Light	Nancy Zaroulis	£1.95

NON-FICTION

GENERAL
☐ Truly Murderous — John Dunning — 95p
☐ Shocktrauma — Jon Franklin & Alan Doelp — £1.25
☐ The War Machine — James Avery Joyce — £1.50
☐ The Fugu Plan — Tokayer & Swartz — £1.75

BIOGRAPHY/AUTOBIOGRAPHY
☐ Go-Boy — Roger Caron — £1.25
☐ The Queen Mother Herself — Helen Cathcart — £1.25
☐ Clues to the Unknown — Robert Cracknell — £1.50
☐ George Stephenson — Hunter Davies — £1.50
☐ The Borgias — Harry Edgington — £1.50
☐ The Admiral's Daughter — Victoria Fyodorova — £1.50
☐ Rachman — Shirley Green — £1.50
☐ 50 Years with Mountbatten — Charles Smith — £1.25
☐ Kiss — John Swenson — 95p

HEALTH/SELF-HELP
☐ The Hamlyn Family First Aid Book — Dr Robert Andrew — £1.50
☐ Girl! — Brandenburger & Curry — £1.25
☐ The Good Health Guide for Women — Cooke & Dworkin — £2.95
☐ The Babysitter Book — Curry & Cunningham — £1.25
☐ Pulling Your Own Strings — Dr Wayne W. Dyer — 95p
☐ The Pick of Woman's Own Diets — Jo Foley — 95p
☐ Woman X Two — Mary Kenny — £1.10
☐ Cystitis: A Complete Self-help Guide — Angela Kilmartin — £1.00
☐ Fit for Life — Donald Norfolk — £1.35
☐ The Stress Factor — Donald Norfolk — £1.25
☐ Fat is a Feminist Issue — Susie Orbach — 95p
☐ Living With Your New Baby — Rakowitz & Rubin — £1.50
☐ Related to Sex — Claire Rayner — £1.25
☐ The Working Woman's Body Book — Rowen with Winkler — 95p
☐ Natural Sex — Mary Shivanandan — £1.25
☐ Woman's Own Birth Control — Dr Michael Smith — £1.25
☐ Overcoming Depression — Dr Andrew Stanway — £1.50

POCKET HEALTH GUIDES
☐ Migraine — Dr Finlay Campbell — 65p
☐ Pre-menstrual Tension — June Clark — 65p
☐ Back Pain — Dr Paul Dudley — 65p
☐ Allergies — Robert Eagle — 65p
☐ Arthritis & Rheumatism — Dr Luke Fernandes — 65p
☐ Skin Troubles — Deanna Wilson — 65p

TRAVEL
☐ Guide to the Channel Islands — Anderson & Swinglehurst — 90p
☐ The Complete Traveller — Joan Bakewell — £1.95
☐ Time Out London Shopping Guide — Lindsey Bareham — £1.50
☐ A Walk Around the Lakes — Hunter Davies — £1.50
☐ England by Bus — Elizabeth Gundrey — £1.25
☐ Britain at Your Feet — Wickers & Pedersen — £1.75

HUMOUR
☐ Ireland Strikes Back! — Seamus B. Gorrah — 85p
☐ Pun Fun — Paul Jennings — 95p
☐ 1001 Logical Laws — John Peers — 95p
☐ The Devil's Bedside Book — Leonard Rossiter — 85p

FICTION
HORROR/OCCULT/NASTY

☐ Death Walkers	Gary Brandner	£1.00
☐ The Howling	Gary Brandner	£1.00
☐ Return of the Howling	Gary Brandner	95p
☐ The Sanctuary	Glenn Chandler	£1.00
☐ The Tribe	Glenn Chandler	£1.10
☐ Crown of Horn	Louise Cooper	£1.25
☐ Curse	Daniel Farson	95p
☐ Transplant	Daniel Farson	£1.00
☐ Trance	Joy Fielding	90p
☐ The Quick and the Dead	Judy Gardiner	£1.00
☐ The Janissary	Alan Lloyd Gelb	£1.25
☐ Rattlers	Joseph L. Gilmore	95p
☐ Slither	John Halkin	95p
☐ The Wicker Man	Robin Hardy & Anthony Shaffer	£1.25
☐ Devil's Coach-Horse	Richard Lewis	85p
☐ Parasite	Richard Lewis	£1.00
☐ Spiders	Richard Lewis	£1.00
☐ Gate of Fear	Lewis Mallory	£1.00
☐ The Nursery	Lewis Mallory	£1.10
☐ The Summoning	John Pintoro	95p
☐ Bloodthirst	Mark Ronson	£1.00
☐ Ghoul	Mark Ronson	95p
☐ Ogre	Mark Ronson	95p
☐ Return of the Living Dead	John Russo	£1.10
☐ Childmare	Nick Sharman	£1.00
☐ The Scourge	Nick Sharman	£1.00
☐ Deathbell	Guy N. Smith	£1.00
☐ Doomflight	Guy N. Smith	£1.10
☐ Locusts	Guy N. Smith	95p
☐ Manitou Doll	Guy N. Smith	£1.10
☐ Satan's Snowdrop	Guy N. Smith	£1.00
☐ The Specialist	Jasper Smith	£1.00
☐ The Scar	Gerald Suster	£1.25
☐ The Worm Stone	Derek Tyson	£1.10

HAMLYN WHODUNNITS

☐ Some Die Eloquent	Catherine Aird	£1.25
☐ The Case of the Abominable Snowman	Nicholas Blake	£1.10
☐ The Worm of Death	Nicholas Blake	95p
☐ Thou Shell of Death	Nicholas Blake	£1.25
☐ Tour de Force	Christianna Brand	£1.10

NAME ....

ADDRESS ....

....

Write to Hamlyn Paperbacks Cash Sales, PO Box 11, Falmouth, Cornwall TR10 9EN.

Please indicate order and enclose remittance to the value of the cover price plus:

U.K.: Please allow 45p for the first book plus 20p for the second book and 14p for each additional book ordered, to a maximum charge of £1.63.

B.F.P.O. & EIRE: Please allow 45p for the first book plus 20p for the second book and 14p per copy for the next 7 books, thereafter 8p per book.

OVERSEAS: Please allow 75p for the first book and 21p per copy for each additional book.

Whilst every effort is made to keep prices low it is sometimes necessary to increase cover prices and also postage and packing rates at short notice. Hamlyn Paperbacks reserve the right to show new retail prices on covers which may differ from those previously advertised in the text or elsewhere.